THE HOUSE ON VIA GEMITO

ALSO BY

DOMENICO STARNONE

Trick
Ties
Trust

Domenico Starnone

THE HOUSE ON VIA GEMITO

*Translated from the Italian
by Oonagh Stransky*

Europa
editions

Europa Editions
27 Union Square West, Suite 302
New York NY 10003
www.europaeditions.com
info@europaeditions.com

Copyright © 2020 by Giulio Einaudi editore s.p.a., Torino
First publication 2023 by Europa Editions

Translation by Oonagh Stransky
Original title: *Via Gemito*
Translation copyright © 2023 by Europa Editions

*This work has been translated with support from
the Italian Ministry of Culture's Centro per il libro e la lettura.*

CENTRO
PER IL LIBRO
E LA LETTURA

Library of Congress Cataloging in Publication Data is available
ISBN 978-1-60945-923-9

Starnone, Domenico
The House on Via Gemito

Art direction by Emanuele Ragnisco
instagram.com/emanueleragnisco

Cover design by Ginevra Rapisardi

Cover image: Federico Starnone, *Operai che pranzano (I bevitori)*, oil on canvas, 1953.
Council Chambers, Positano. Courtesy of the Positano City Council.
(Photo: Vito Fusco)

Prepress by Grafica Punto Print – Rome

Printed in Canada

CONTENTS

PART I
THE PEACOCK - 13

PART II
THE BOY POURING WATER - 143

PART III
THE DANCER - 343

For Rosa, for Rusinè

THE HOUSE ON VIA GEMITO

PART I
THE PEACOCK

When my father told me he hit my mother only once in twenty-three years of marriage, I didn't even bother replying. A long time had passed since I had challenged any of his stories, with their fabricated events, dates, and details. When I was a boy, I always saw him as a liar and his lies embarrassed me, as if they were my own. Now, as an adult, it didn't even seem to me like he was lying. He truly believed his words could recreate facts according to his desires or regrets.

A few days later, though, his punctilious assertion resurfaced in my thoughts. Initially I felt unease, then growing anger, and finally the desire to pick up the phone and yell into it, "Really? Only once? And all those times I remember seeing you hit her, right up until she started dying, what were they? Love taps?"

Of course I didn't call. Although I had been playing the role of devoted son for decades, I had also managed to hand him a fair number of disappointments. And besides, it was pointless to attack him directly. His jaw would've dropped the way it always did whenever something unexpected happened and, in that mild tone of voice he always used when he disagreed with us children, he'd start to list with great suffering—and via long-distance—all the irrefutable instances of cruelty that he had not inflicted on my mother but she on him. "What difference does it make if he continues to invent things?" I asked myself.

Actually I realized that it changed a lot. To begin with, I changed, and in a way I didn't like. It felt, for example, like I was losing the ability to measure my words, an art that I had proudly mastered as a teenager. Even the question I had considered yelling at him ("And all those times I remember seeing you hit her, right up until she started dying, what were they? Love taps?") was poorly calibrated. When I tried writing it out, I was struck by its crass and impudent style. I seemed to be making exaggerated claims not unlike those of my father. It was as if I wanted to reproach and shout at him for slapping and hitting my mother even as she lay on her death bed, punching her with the expertise of the gifted boxer he said he had been at the age of fifteen, over at the Belfiore gym on Corso Garibaldi.

This was a clear sign that all it took was the slightest hint of my age-old anger and fear to make me lose my poise and erase all the distance I had managed to put between us while growing up. If I actually spoke those impulsive words, it would be like allowing my worst dreams to blend with his lies. It'd be like giving him credence, agreeing to see him the way he chose to represent himself, as someone you don't mess around with, which was what he learned as a kid from European champion Bruno Frattini, who egged him on in the ring, and encouraged him with a smile. "Go on and hit me, Federí! Hit me! Kick me!" What a champ. He had taught him that you dominate fear by striking first and striking hard, a principle he never forgot. And since that time, whenever the occasion arose and without the least preamble, he'd size up his victim and proceed to bash the bones of anyone who tried to boss him around.

To be good enough, he started training on Saturdays and Sundays at the Giulio Luzi sports club. "Giulio Luzi? Not the Belfiore?" I'd ask with a hint of spite. "Giulio Luzi, Belfiore, whatever, they're all the same," he'd reply gruffly. And then he went on: the person responsible for introducing him into the sports club for the first time was none other than Neapolitan featherweight champion Raffaele Sacco, who happened to be walking down the street while he was fighting tooth and nail with a gang from the neighborhood near the railroad station that used to regularly throw rocks at him and his brother Antonio. Sacco, who was eighteen at the time, stepped into the fray. He threw a couple of punches in those sonofabitches' faces and then, after praising Federí for his courage, conducted him to the Giulio Luzi or the Belfiore or whatever the hell you want to call it.

That was where my father started boxing, and not just with Raffaele Sacco and Bruno Frattini but also with the latter's protégé, Michele Palermo, the massive Centobelli, and tiny Rojo, champions one and all. He made swift progress. A kid named Tammaro learned it the hard way when he harassed him as he was walking home from school with his brother Antonio. "You? A boxer? What a joke, Federí!" he taunted him. Without a word, my father knocked him flat with a left hook to the chin. Then he turned to a friend of Tammaro's who stood there paralyzed with terror and said, "When he wakes up, tell the bastard that next time I'm going to kick his ass, not just his face."

His ass. I was frightened by those stories. I was disturbed, too, because I had no idea how to protect my own brother from the kids who threw rocks at us, the way he had done for his brother. I was worried about heading out into the world without knowing how to land a punch. And I felt anxiety, even later on as an adult, when I saw how well my father could do the voices of violence, the posturing, the gestures, kicking and punching the air.

In the meantime, he seemed to derive enormous pleasure from his ferocity, from the way he knew how to deploy it. He used to tell me those stories to incite my admiration. Now and then he succeeded, but for the most part I felt a combination of distress and fear, which stayed with me longer. A case in point: the two shoe-shine boys on Via Milano, in Vasto, at 7 P.M. on a summer evening. My father, seventeen at the time, and his brother Antonio, fifteen, were on their way back from the gym on Corso Garibaldi. Suddenly it started to rain. The two boys—it was Saturday and they were wearing their fascist uniforms, something my father emphasized proudly, even decades later, in the belief that his outfit made him look sharp and terribly manly—ran for cover under the porticoes of the Teatro Apollo, where there was already a cluster of other people, including the two shoe-shine boys. There was clamoring, heavy rain, the smell of wet dust. When the shoe-shine boys caught sight of them, they sneered cruelly. "Those two ugly sonofabitches made it rain," one of them said loudly to the other. Their brutish words offended the boys, their mother, their father, maybe even their ominous black shirts. Without thinking twice, my father reached over and, with his left hand, grabbed the collar of the shoe-shine boy who had spoken those words, even though he was big, tough, and around thirty, and planted an uppercut on that Neanderthal's foul mouth—Neanderthal he called him, to show how primitive he was—knocking out his two front teeth. Thwack. He punched him so hard that one of the man's broken teeth—and at this point in the story, he'd wave his index finger in front of me to show me a scar that I couldn't actually see but to appease him I said yes, Papà, I see it—got wedged into the flesh of his finger. He had to flick his hand hard to make it fall out.

Whenever he told that story, he always flicked his hand hard, as if the fragment of tooth was still stuck in it. I'd stare at him in horrified devotion: lean and lanky, he had a long face, high forehead, and a slender, elegant nose with delicate nostrils, a nose that definitely didn't look as if it belonged to a skilled boxer. He always came home from work furious, as if he had just knocked out Tammaro or the shoe-shine boy; always the victim of some urgent, dramatic situation; always ready, even if faced with a multitude of enemies and it was inevitable that he'd get beaten to a pulp, of courageously chasing back fear. Because he was a man who had been initiated into the world of boxing by none other than a European heavyweight champion. He was a man who wouldn't let anyone kick him around, much less his wife. If anything, he'd be the one to kick her around. Toe kick—that's what I was always afraid he would do to her when he came home—and heel stomp.

One September morning, in order to put my mind at rest, I decided to calmly map out all the times my father had definitely hit my mother.

At first the prospect seemed complex and loaded with details but when I subjected each of the recollected images—a slap, a dish of pasta hurled at the wall, a scream, a glare—to the rigors of prose and articulated them into an organized series of events, memory started to waver and with some alarm I realized that I was left with only two irrefutable episodes.

The first one dated back to 1955, at some point between the fourth and fifteenth of June, the period of time during which my father exhibited twenty-eight of his works of art, including paintings, watercolors, and drawings, at the San Carlo art gallery, located at number 7 in the Galleria Umberto I arcade.

I sought out an image to begin. I envisioned him in bed, their big double bed. I had just brought him coffee and its aroma wafted through the house. He sipped it and read out loud to my mother, brothers, and me from the newspaper reviews that mentioned his name. Now those were the days . . . He always liked recalling those days. Waking up like that, the smell of sleep mixing with that of coffee, the first of an endless number of cigarettes, and the scent of fresh newsprint, anxiously scouring the pages and headlines and columns, and then finding his name—self-taught, no formal training, no art school, no pulling of strings—in print in the city papers or even the provincial ones, followed by a couple hundred of words about his work. See what he had managed to do, him, a man born on Barrettari alley, a man who had been forced by his father, a lathe worker with absolutely no understanding of art, to leave school and get a job. What a waste of youth. By the age of eighteen, in 1935, he was working for the railroad as an electrical repairman. Thanks only to his great intelligence and desire to improve his situation, by 1940 he was already second in charge. Now, as of a few years—it was 1951 at the time—he had become senior station master and train dispatcher for all moving cars on the lines in and around Naples. Now that's satisfaction. An important job. And all because of merit, not thanks to seniority or favors. At the time he had been the youngest station master in all of Italy, word of honor, and much appreciated by his superiors, even if, it's true, he did everything he could to get out of work and stay home and do his real job, the one he had been born to do: paint and draw, or as he said, *pittare*. Sure, a fair number of his colleagues couldn't stand him; they called him a presumptuous shitty artist and accused him of being lazy, arrogant, and a blowhard. It's true, he was lazy. He was arrogant. He was a blowhard. He was all those things, and the first to admit it. He felt he had the right to be lazy, arrogant, and a blowhard—to anyone who busted his balls. He was born to be a painter, not a railroader. But since he was the kind of person who did everything to the hilt, particularly if it offered him the chance to demonstrate that he could do it better than someone else, I believe that he did his job pretty well. Despite all the other ideas that floated around his head, one thing was for certain. When he was on duty—and he was on duty a lot, he had long hours, day shifts and night ones, and I remember because sometimes when I was older I'd stop by his office and watch him direct the traffic of convoy cars, chase them down, smack his ruler, triangle, and pencil on a huge drawing table in a way that was both petulant and extremely lucid—there were never any train wrecks or deaths.

Of course he took full advantage of his role. As senior station master he was authorized—he emphasized the fact that he held authority with great pleasure—to conduct random inspections of the stations in his jurisdiction four times a month. So, between 1954 and 1955, he inspected Cassino, Cancello, Ilva, and the Napoli Smistamento depot. He didn't do it because he enjoyed inspecting: cocky fellow that he was, obsessed only with outshining everyone, the last thing on his mind was the actual inspection. Unless, of course, Federí went on to explain, he encountered an employee who was rude to him and led him to believe that he didn't give a fuck about his role, his opinions, or his artistic endeavors, well then, he could just go straight to hell, and suddenly Federí became extremely meticulous. But otherwise, no. He took advantage of being able to inspect all those stations in order to catch the light and colors of real life in either pastels or tempera.

Because, although he was a railroader, he thought about nothing but the exhibition he was preparing. And indeed, when he was good and ready, he came home, shut himself in, told the station that he had rheumatic fever, gastritis, or any number of other ailments, and spent his time painting line signals, junctions, sidetracks, cattle cars, railyards, depots, and railheads. I remember each and every one of his paintings: my grandmother, brothers, and I slept in the same room where he painted, the dining room, where his monumental easel stood surrounded by his paintbox and canvases. I used to fall asleep staring at those visions, they seemed beautiful to me; I wish I could find them.

Between work and bouts of new illnesses, he completed a further series of paintings devoted to what he saw from the window: the surrounding countryside, but not the one that smelled of mint where I used to play as a kid with my brothers and friends, no; the one of felled trees and severed ancient roots, the flattened one, which by the end of 1954 was rapidly being transformed into a building site. He did studies of wastelands, pile drivers, cement mixers, bulldozers, hoists, storage silos for cement, a detailed rendering of the massacre of a hillside, and a painting crowded with scenes from a construction yard entitled *Cantiere '54*.

Then he went on to still-lifes: he drew bowls we had at home and either a few dried herring or a couple of apples, a hatchet or a bunch of artichokes, a few mussels or some flowers, whatever he found lying around the house. He added two nudes to the group that he had done years earlier when he took classes at the Scuola libera del nudo, one done in sanguine and the other in charcoal. He even included a portrait of my brother when he had nephritis, which came out better, he said, than anything by Battistello Caracciolo. And that was it.

All that work took him eight months. The whole apartment on Via Vincenzo Gemito smelled of paint and turpentine. Every piece of furniture in the room we referred to as the dining room had been shoved up against the wall (how hard my mother had worked to obtain those pieces of furniture, and how carelessly he treated them) and at night there were always canvases drying on our beds. His wife complained, my grandmother grumbled. How could he let his children—meaning me and my three brothers—breathe that poison night and day? Had he forgotten that we slept in there? *Padreterno*, he'd holler, tell me what I've done to deserve a life of ball-busting by these two idiotic women. But then it was over: the task had been completed. I have no idea where he found the money to pay for the exhibition. The fact is that with a little help from Don Luigino Campanile, a shoemaker with a shop in Vomero but also an art-lover, who kindly offered to transport all the artwork in his delivery van, Federí went and hung his paintings on the walls of the San Carlo gallery.

He was thirty-eight years old and it must have felt like a turning point in his life. Even when he was elderly and ill, he'd clearly and proudly rattle off the names of all the important people who came to see the show: Ciardo, Notte, Striccoli and so on, rivers of first and last names, artists—he assured me—of major renown, sounds which have faded over time but which, back then, I heard him mention often, at times with respect but more often than not with bitterness and disdain for all the wrongs they did him, or which he believed they had. All it took was for a fellow painter to be grazed ever so slightly by fame, even at the most local level, and Federí would start spewing insults, both to his face and behind his back. Mostly he had it in for those of his own age or younger. He couldn't stand the fact that they had been luckier than him, and he'd furiously enumerate their artistic shortcomings and petty ways. Now and then he even felt the need to insult and offend people who, underneath it all, he respected, just to let off steam. But on that specific occasion of his exhibit opening, everyone seemed praiseworthy because, even if their intentions might have been cruel, they had come to the event and signed the guest book. Eighty-four signatures, that's not peanuts. And that's not counting the famous people who appeared like the Virgin Mary but considered signing the guest book too much of a commitment: Giovanni Brancaccio, Carlo Verdecchia, and Guido Casciaro. He continued to grumble about that even decades later, deeply pained: what would a signature have cost them? Show a little generosity. Anyway, there was a huge crowd. Visitors and artists stayed on for lively discussions of art, painting, his style of painting until long after the San Carlo closed.

How hard was it for my mother to understand? Even on normal days, she was a pain. After dinner, as soon as he said, "I'm going out for a bit," in order to make the rounds of galleries and discuss art, she'd drop everything and say, "I'll come too." My father would get angry, he didn't know how to explain it to her. Why on earth should she come? What would she say to other artists? And especially on important occasions like that: didn't she realize that she would just be in the way? Every night, after a long, hard day of work at the train depot, he came home exhausted, only to have to go out and do the rounds of the galleries and put in his hours as an artist. It wasn't fun or anything; he had to deal with all those so-called friends, enemies, potential clients, people who wanted to talk prices, people who might be interested in negotiating despite the pit of venomous snakes who tried to distract buyers by suggesting other works, other paintings, more important painters, such as themselves, for example. It wasn't fun; it was war. Cruelty, aggression, insinuations, calumny. Rusinè, please, just stay home.

But my mother didn't want to stay at home, especially on such an occasion. She was thirty-four years old, had four children, and had been married for thirteen years. She grew up fatherless and had worked as a glovemaker ever since she was a child. ("You know how to make gloves? So, make gloves! What do you know about painting?") At the age of five, her job was to pull out the cotton threads that the decorative rivets left inside the fingers of the gloves, and roll them into knots so the stitching didn't come undone, a task that broke her nails and chafed her fingertips. Despite all the talk, things with him hadn't changed that much. But it wasn't all bad. Sure, he had some negative qualities, but there was also something about him that continued to appeal to her. Imaginative, playful, and completely nuts: she had liked him straight away when he had stopped her while she was walking down the street on that warm afternoon in 1938. Pardon me, signorina. He was different from other men, his gestures, his tone of voice. He didn't look like her brother Peppino, her brother's friends, or her mother's sisters' husbands; he didn't look like anyone she knew.

He had seen her while he was chatting with a few of his friends, colleagues from the train depot. One look, that's all it takes. He had seen her from up above, from the bridge that looks down over the switching yard. She was walking down the dusty street, the celestial blue of the Marina reverberating behind her. He couldn't stop himself, he swooped down like a hawk; he, too, compared himself to that bird of prey when nostalgically recalling their encounter. She was beautiful, yes, but it was likely that she was less beautiful than she was now, at the age of thirty-four. She was seventeen at the time. She wore her long black hair loose, had the face of a china doll, and had on a pink, three-quarter length, pleated skirt that fluttered around her well-shaped calves and ankles, a light-colored shirt, and a bolero jacket.

Signorina, pardon me, signorina. He laughed, strutted about, and gesticulated wildly. She didn't say a thing and kept walking, eyes straight ahead, casting only ironic glances at him, sizing this stranger up. He was dressed all in black, his forehead was too big, he had a moustache, and he seemed old. At a certain point, she even tried to discourage his advances by saying as much. "You're too old for me." A little offended, a little peeved, he went on to clarify that he was only twenty-one, that it was the suit that made him look old, maybe the hard work, maybe his moustache.

That's when she realized that she liked him. Who knows why he appealed to her; these things are mysterious and can't be explained. Maybe because he behaved as if he were the son of a king who had dressed up as an electrical repairman for some mysterious reason known only to him. Maybe because he pulled out a piece of paper and pencil and drew her right then and there, her mouth open in surprise. Whatever the reason, she was soon officially engaged to him and pleased to have been so lucky to meet a man who knew how to keep her happy, who talked and talked, and was never silent. And let's not forget that he also had a steady income. Objectively speaking, what more could she hope for?

But here it was, June 1955, and he was set to finally become everything he had promised her fifteen years ago, a well-known artist, and she didn't want to miss her chance of being seen in public, especially as the wife of such a famous artist. And so, while my father continued to swear high and low to all the saints and virgins, she took off the clothes she wore at home and pulled out a selection of dresses from her wardrobe that she had sewn either for some cousin's wedding or for the confirmation of a friend's child or for any number of other occasions. She chose one without hesitation. In a flash, with only a thin layer of Nivea cream (which she pronounced Nivèa) and some lipstick, she turned into a woman of breathtaking beauty.

He cussed even louder. Now, when I think about it, I suspect that he detested his wife's unique beauty; the power that her manner and form had over him (and which he knew so well) made him anxious. There was an indefinable quality about her physique, it was a secret of secrets, the kind that can never be explained and as such is bewitching. Only she knew the secret formula and she used it at her discretion. Rusinè could turn gloomy for months on end and then suddenly dart out again. On that particular occasion, a pair of hair combs, elegantly crafted with decorative swirls and given to her by my father as a gift, added the final touch to her beauty. "Federí, I'm ready," she then announced in dialect. We always spoke in dialect among ourselves.

Ready for what? What's going on? Did someone die, Rusinè? Her husband initially humiliated her by declaring that she was too *impernacchiata*, a word he used to describe my grandmother's nouveau riche relatives when they got decked out in feathered hats, too much rouge, too much gold jewelry: vulgar and gaudy women, I think he meant, women who were about as elegant as the sound of blowing a raspberry. But since she resisted and didn't change her clothes, by way of revenge he wanted my brother and me to come along, too, so that we could enjoy his artistic triumphs. He would've brought along the other two children if one of them hadn't been so vivacious and the other one still an infant. Hell, why not bring them? And grandmother, too. Let's bring everyone, a family outing, so that she wouldn't forget her role as mother of his children and not some chanteuse, which was how she wanted to appear just to make him look like shit in front of all those people who already considered him an intruder and who were trying, night after night, to knock him down. What the hell had he done to deserve a woman like that?

I remember almost nothing from our visit to the exhibition. We probably took the funicular down, crossed Via Toledo, and then walked the rest of the way under the porticoes of Galleria Umberto, my father five steps ahead of my mother, truculent, and us three steps behind.

Rusinè never mentioned the event and Federí, when recalling that era, only talked about all the wrongs he had suffered, the paintings he had nonetheless sold, the reviews of the show, both good and bad. His wife had been neatly expulsed from his memories of those June days. Us kids, too.

But La Padula, the building developer, was there. He strode into the San Carlo elegantly dressed and surrounded by an obsequious and lively entourage, and immediately fell so in love with the painting entitled *Cantiere '54* that he decided to buy it for his son, who would soon graduate with a degree in architecture. And just like that, he wrote out a check for 120,000 lire: two and a half months of a railroad employee's salary. He wrote it out right in front of everyone, including the communist art critic, Paolo Ricci. I never found out if my father exaggerated the amount or if, instead, some backroom deal took place and it was paid for with cash that flowed in rivers thanks to hard labor, money that had been made to the sound of pile-drivers and hoists and silos of cement being poured right outside our windows, and then used to purchase, with great largesse, a painting that would hang like a trophy in an architect's office. Whatever the details, he, the railman-artist or artist-railman or just simply the artist, pocketed the check with the pride of someone who was glad to show that they could make money better and more nobly than those butchers, pastry chefs, salami-makers, and other people who were starting to get rich under his anxious gaze. And yet, there he was making his way over to Engineer Isabella, the building councilman, who was both less powerful than the developer and less sensitive to the cement mixers and concrete molds despite his political role, or maybe precisely because of it. Engineer Isabella was captivated by his painting *Natura morta con pesci* and wanted to buy it and bring it home, but not for its asking price of 50,000 lire (one month of a railroad employee's salary). He wanted it for 40,000 lire (slightly less than one month of a railroad employee's salary). And so the negotiations began. "Fifty," my father said. "Forty," said the engineer. They were just about to come to an agreement, "Fine, forty," when my father turned and saw Rusinè standing in the center of the room.

She was not alone. Nor was she tending to her children, who wandered awkwardly around the gallery. Surrounding her was a dense swarm of second-rate painters, illiterate poets, and incompetent art critics, with one man saying one thing and the other saying something else, while she replied in a bubbly voice or burst into laughter, showing her white teeth and flashing her almond-shaped eyes, which, right in that moment, La Padula the developer seemed to notice and appreciate deeply, as did a middle-aged poet who was busy complimenting her in cadenced phrases, each one almost a perfect hendecasyllable, promising her the gift of a book of his poems with a personalized dedication. "I will come to your house in person tomorrow, and present you with the gift myself, dear lady," he concluded. "Thank you," my mother replied, sighing with pleasure. She was so beautiful that even Engineer Isabella felt obliged to tell my father what an attractive lady she was. But my father didn't have time to reply: walking straight toward them was none other than Chiancone, a painter and professor at the Istituto d'arte, an absolute lunatic, his face ruddy and flustered, keen on adding his two cents to the negotiations. "Chiancone," Engineer Isabella felt obliged to ask, "in your opinion is this *Natura morta con pesci* worth 50,000 lire?" And can you guess what the bastard replied? "Engineer Isabella, taste is a personal matter and a person is entitled to spend his money however he wants on something that he likes, but let me just say that what a person likes is not always a work of art." The man was saying that *Natura morta con pesci* wasn't a work of art. Not a work of art? For fuck's sake. And Chiancone's shitty paintings were works of art? That man needed to have the shit pumped out of him, he was nothing more than a raging sewer full of shit, he needed to puke up all the bile and vomit out all the foul things and get fucked up the ass, both him and Engineer Isabella.

My father, furious, interrupted the negotiations.

Then there's a gap. It all starts up again when I'm at home in bed. My brother and I share a bed head to toe, and he's sleeping, or pretending to sleep. Lying in a bed next to me is my grandmother and the third-born son, who is seven. The youngest one still sleeps with my parents, who aren't sleeping. I hear my father yelling, my mother sobbing her replies, there's the sound of running, things fall and break. I say the prayers that my grandmother taught me when I was young, the Ave Maria, for starters. I say it to myself but really loudly so that the voice in my head drowns out my father's yelling. A futile stratagem. Then it dawns on me that it doesn't matter if I pray or not because the Virgin Mary exists and, if she has any powers at all, she'll do everything she can to stop him from killing my mother. So I whisper softly, in dialect, which is the only language I know well, "Mother Mary, please make him stop." I say it over and over, concentrating as hard as I can, as if repeating it makes the words even more convincing. But the Virgin Mary does nothing. I try to overcome my terror and get up slowly from bed, I walk toward the bedroom door, and open it a crack. I don't know what to do. I'm twelve years old but I'm scared of my father. It's not a physical fear, or rather the physical aspect of my fear is what I notice and remember least. It's another kind of fear. I'm afraid of appearing before him empty-handed, without possessing any logical reasons that he would consider worthy opposition, an echo chamber for all the insults he's screaming, for all his swearing. As a result, I fear that he will force me to admit that he has the sacrosanct right to kill my mother. I fear that I will agree with him. And consequently, my fear is intolerable.

That's when I see him. I also see her. She's crying and is trying to get away from him and moves toward the kitchen. I see bottles and pots and glasses falling to the floor. I understand perfectly what he is yelling at her. "Vain!" he screams, that enigmatic word that will remain forever imprinted in my mind with its injurious sound, a word that's not part of our everyday dialect, his voice strident as he spews other words, obscenities, and insults. No one in our house knows what that word means, not my mother, not even me, and I just completed sixth grade. Only he knows the meaning. He screams it again, Vain! He slaps her repeatedly, both with his open palm and with the back of his hand, ruining her olive skin, her mouth, her hairdo, causing her elegant hair combs to go flying.

I don't know what to do. I add up all the punches that already took place but which I didn't see with the ones that I am seeing; I add up the ones I heard from bed with the ones I am hearing now—I'm still adding them up now as I write—when smacks and words echo endlessly, saying she's no longer allowed to leave the house, never, ever again; because of her my father lost at least 300,000 lire this evening. Engineer Isabella wanted to buy two paintings, they had been negotiating, and what did she do? She started busting his balls with all that smiling, flirting, showing her leg. You don't get it Rusinè, your giggling, your laugh, Rusinè, you don't understand. You have no idea who those people are. They're shit! Poet, my ass. Sculptor, my ass. Engineer, my ass! Right now they're standing around outside the Galleria, laughing, and you know what they're saying? I bet that I bang her before you do, they're saying; that fellow from the railroad only sells his paintings thanks to his wifey, they're saying; without her he'd be zilch, he doesn't even know how to paint; and you, you brought it all on with your vanity, your vanity! You're so vain! And more words followed, all in dialect, all accompanied by the sound of him slapping her, with many colorful, unspeakable offenses.

I was so horrified that I retreated. Or maybe I never actually got up out of bed. Maybe my grandmother stopped me. She was lying there awake and looking at the ceiling, saying things like *ciunkllochemmommò*, black magic incantations that mean stop, freeze, stay in bed, as if you've suddenly been paralyzed, it's all your mamma's fault, she shouldn't talk back to him, I told her a thousand times that she shouldn't talk back to him but she never listens, she's too headstrong, Madonna mia, Madonna mia, *ciunkllochemmommò*, it doesn't concern you, it doesn't concern any of us, it's between husband and wife: tomorrow they'll love each other more than yesterday and less than the day after tomorrow.

She says it in a whisper, but maybe it's enough to stop me. Or maybe what stopped me was the sudden weakness I felt, just like a thousand other times: that absence of energy that my father's angry voice released in me; the horrible way he managed, with one utterance from his throat, to make my body feel both heavy and empty, empty of thoughts and reason, and filled with lead from my head to my toes; a heaviness that always made me cry, though I tried hard not to. And the tears broke me, in the sense that they flattened me and weakened me and humiliated me for what was an indefinite amount of time, maybe my whole life.

The point is that while I see him slapping her, while I see Federí hitting her, and she trying to protect herself, I see her hair combs go flying—and yet somehow even sight is not certain, we see with so many possible eyes, there's no single word or syllable or groan or smack that doesn't get transformed immediately into one image, two, a hundred—while I see all that, I don't see anything else, I only hear him yelling, threatening that if even just one of those dogshit bastards ever comes around, he'll throw them down the stairs, *'st'uommenemmèrd*, those pieces of shit, because they still don't understand what kind of man he is. He's not like Nicola in the fable his grandmother Funzella used to tell him as a child in order to prepare him for life; he's no sheep, he's no *piécoro*, *becco*, *curnuto*, he's not some foolish cuckold like Nicola, all because of that slut of his wife Lillina; no one's going to taunt him with *'a Lillina 'e Don Nicò, fa l'ammore con Totò, 'on Nico, 'on Nico, tu sì piécher'e nuje no*; he'd rather beat his wife to death, strangle her with his hands, oh *padreterno*, what have I done to deserve this? Enough! Give those hair combs to me! You're never going to wear them again! Never, ever again! You're too vain, Rusinè. Such vanity!

Empty. My mother's core is emptied out. Like me, she has no thoughts. She's mere kindling for a fire. When she speaks, her words fan the flames of vanity. Or else she exhales smoke, and it spreads through the house. And then there's that smell. It's the heavy smell of a heat-resistant object releasing a dark, volatile substance and slowly burning in the fireplace grate. My mother wails, my grandmother starts in on a rosary and pleads for revenge, my brother cries in his pretend sleep, and the hair-combs burst into flame—at least, I think they do, that's how I imagine them—on that June night. Their acrid odor makes me nauseous, I feel pain deep in my stomach and in my nose, it's the smell of agony. I will always remember this moment in great detail. It goes on to become indissoluble with my mother's body, as if Federí had not only burned her hair combs in the fire, but her nails or hair or the thick dark eyelashes that shielded her eyes.

This all took place one summer night in long-ago 1955. But whenever I mentioned it later to my father, he referred to it as a passing argument, nothing more. What slapping? What hitting? As for the hair combs, well, he'd gladly share some other, far more important details than those insignificant hair combs. Things related to that era: people, wrongs to which he had been subjected. Cucurra, for example (he changed the names as he wished, like Cucurra for Chiancone), that professor at the Istituto dell'arte, a presumptuous bastard full of vitriol. Had he ever told me how that man had interfered with and ruined the sale of one of his still-lifes? And what about Paolo Ricci, whom everyone called Paolone, the art critic from *L'Unità*: had he ever told me that story? He was a disagreeable man who masked his presumptuousness with his elegant ways: he always wore a red kerchief around his neck and relied on a heavy walking stick, a weapon more than a tool. On June 13, 1955, in a cruel review of Federí's work on show at the San Carlo, that conniving man wrote, "There's still something of a hesitant tone in his art, something superficial, something belabored." What total shit. Hesitant tone? Superficial and belabored tone? With my university degree in literature, I would no doubt agree with him that "a belabored tone" was not even proper grammar! Clearly, comrade Ricci had it in for him, and that was the point. With his own two eyes, comrade Ricci had seen La Padula, the capitalist builder, write out a check for *Cantiere '54* for 120,000 lire. Get it? He took out his jealousies by pretending to defend the proletariat. Proletariat, my ass.

And on he went, freewheeling, first laughing complacently, then bitterly, piling on the details, replacing my own vague reconstructions of the events with his vivid fantasies, while also injecting new venomous thoughts into my memory. But then, all of a sudden, he'd recall how he had beat her and burnt the hair combs and to erase those memories he'd declare in a visibly heartfelt tone his usual phrase: "Oh, how I loved your mother." And then he'd go on to say—as if he wanted to prove it to me— how, out of love for his wife, out of love for his children, he had to give up so many opportunities, chances that you either grab in the moment or lose forever. No, the idea of sacrificing his family for the sake of his art was simply not an option, although he had often thought of going out for a pack of cigarettes and never coming back. Things like that happened; you read about it in the papers. But did he ever do that? No. And why not? Because underneath it all he was a good man, even if he had been wronged and treated unfairly every single step of the way, ever since he was born, beginning with his parents, beginning with his father. Yes, his father. And then he'd start talking about his childhood and youth and himself with such pleasure, reviving memories that had been stored away after each retelling, and enhancing them with a new, energetic cascade of words.

That morning it seemed to me that I had done the right thing.

It was pointless to try and contradict my father and end up in the spiraling gyre of his endless chatter. Better off moving forward with the work I had originally set out to do.

So I concentrated on a different episode. But that turned out to be a mistake; I should've been content and left well enough alone. I ended up spending the whole afternoon trying to remember dates, identify places, and apply structure to fluid images. The results were confounding.

Space and time, for example. The window I recalled seemed to be from the dining room of the apartment on Via Gemito, number 64, in Vomero, where we lived until 1956, and yet the bathroom was definitely the one from the apartment on Corso Arnaldo Lucci, number 149, where we moved in 1957. The first time my mother was hit and slapped was in a building located between Napoli Centrale and the entrance to the Napoli–Pompei highway, the kitchen of which looked out over the freight car depot and its tracks, maybe in 1958. Then I saw her running away from my father—her face puffy and swollen with tears, her bathrobe fluttering open behind her like a cape, her light blue slip with white lace trim torn here and there—and out of the dining room of the house on Via Gemito in 1956. Then I saw her opening a window and trying to throw herself out of it. Someone tried to hold her back (my grandmother, my father, maybe we frightened children? All I see are shadows) but she wriggled out of our grasp with surprising strength and leapt across two years of time, ran down the hall of the apartment on Corso Arnaldo Lucci, reached the bathroom, hurried over to the shelf opposite the mirror, felt around, knocking things over, clawing at objects, and then slit her wrist with a razor blade. Or maybe it was the palm of her hand. Maybe it was with a shard of glass from something she had accidentally broken. First it was a blade, then a piece of glass, they fell into the sink, they fell onto the floor. I saw them both and couldn't make up my mind. She stood still, watching the dripping blood. So did my brothers, so did I. Only my father panicked. He covered his eyes, turned away, and screamed, "Mamma mia bella, mamma mia bella," with all the theatrical horror and alarm he showed any time there was the least bit of blood, at any scrape and scratch, his or ours. My grandmother yelled something at him and shook him. He ran out of the room calling to the *padreterno* for help and came back with an orange tie, grabbed my mother's wrist, cried out to all the saints and virgins, and wrapped that ludicrous thing around it, the blood immediately soaking it red and wetting his hands. My mother, who had since grown calm, gently pushed him away and knotted the tie slightly higher up her arm with the help of her white teeth. "Take me to the hospital," she said.

That's all. Not much. Memories I could've enriched with additional stories my father told about why we moved from Via Gemito to Corso Arnaldo Lucci, about his work as a railroader, and how there was never enough money while my mother's relatives flaunted the money they'd made as shop owners. I could've dipped into that material and sharpened that hazy recollection. Hadn't the process of remembering already been helpful to me in reconstructing the episode of the burnt hair-combs? And without the background details of his job on the railroad, his art, and the exhibition, what was it anyway? Just someone screaming a single word on a summer's night: vain. The anguish of a twelve-year-old kid when he sees his parents fight. The smell of something burning. All the rest—if I got up out of bed or not, if I saw my father hit my mother or not—was just as much the product of childhood nightmares and teenage angst as the ghost of the woman I continued to see, suspended in time and space, running through my mind, even as an adult, running desperately toward death.

Gradually, as time passed, I focused less and less on those two episodes. Irrefutable facts lead nowhere, they're like unimportant country roads that are resistant to maintenance and eventually entirely abandoned. I stopped caring. The problem, I remember thinking, was something else entirely, and it had nothing to do with one particular June night or a woman who tried to cut her wrists. The problem was that for my whole life—even now as I write—I secretly believed that, at some point in time, my father transformed from macebearer into relentless tormenter. Over time, he wore her out and contributed to her death. It didn't matter if he hit her once or a hundred times. What mattered was whether I accused him or let him off the hook before he died. I took note of this with a certain amount of disgust. Let me think about it, I said to myself. There was time: my father had decided he'd die in 2017, at the age of one hundred. He believed he had more important things to do.

Then, with a joyful feeling, I suddenly remembered the peacock. It was an animal that was central to my childhood and a topic I would've gladly discussed with my father, if I had ever been given the chance. It was our secret, his and mine, and it would be easy for him to answer my questions, there was nothing for him to have to wriggle out of, the episode wouldn't trigger any senile regrets. And on a surface level, my mother didn't even have anything to do with it; it would be easy to start there.

But when I decided to go see him and possibly even talk to him about it, I realized that somehow he had shrunk, he had lost something of himself, he was dying before the date he had destined for himself. He cried out in pain at regular intervals. "*Padreterno, padreterno,*" he kept saying and asked for a gun. He'd mime one with his hand, point it at his temple, look up at the ceiling and say, "Bam!" Then he'd flop back down on the pillows and mumble over and over, "Mamma mia, what terrible things I've done."

Later that afternoon, his second wife called me out into the garden. "Would you just listen to him," she sighed, embarrassed and weary. "A friend of ours died from the same illness a few months ago and not once put on such a scene. Why does he always have to exaggerate?"

Whenever I'm in a good mood I feel as though the colorful eyes of a peacock's train are looking down on me, the same peacock that I saw long ago in the house on Via Gemito, when my father yelled, "Cigarettes!" at me in dialect and I ran to get them from his jacket pocket, which was hanging in their bedroom on a chair between their wardrobe and his desk. The house was icy cold and pitch black, the dark glass panes trembled in their casements from the wind. I got up from the dinner table while the embers slowly turned to ash in the grate of the woodburning stove. I always obeyed my father and never objected; I obeyed him for as long as he lived.

One step away from the kitchen door, I turned around to look at him. Or I think I did, anyway. I'm working with the power of suggestion here; I have two or three unstable images, a few yelled words. I definitely see his gaunt back and his thick black hair. He's an unhappy shadow and sits at the head of the table. He's definitely about to shout something, maybe he's already shouted it. He wants to argue, that's for sure, but he also wants to hold back, calm down, and that's why he needs to smoke. I have to hurry. My mother is sitting to his right and holding their third child in her arms, nursing him. The distance between her and her husband is minimal; it would be easy for him to hit her and cause blood to flow from either her nose or mouth.

I'm an anxious child, having already experienced a number of frightening situations, and it's hard for me to leave the warmth of the kitchen. I still don't trust this house, we've only been here for a few months. We used to live on Via Zara with my father's parents in their apartment, but they were evacuated to Savignano with the rest of the family because of the bombings. The apartment was in ruins, nothing more than dust and rubble. A whole wall had crumbled because of a bomb, and the floor led to a dangerous precipice; Federí rigged up a military blanket in its place. My father is relentless, he always thinks ahead. I don't remember anything about those days in the apartment on Via Zara, of course, but he's filled my head with stories, and I know that more than once he managed to save me by grabbing me before I fell into the abyss on the other side of the blanket. *Mannaggiamarròn*, Rusinè! The kid! he'd yell and catch hold of me himself, and I'd start crying and never quit. It's thanks to him that I'm still alive, who knows what the hell my inattentive mother was thinking about. You have to keep a hundred eyes on him at all times, he screams at her, and then he calms down and explains that I'm attracted to the fluttering blanket that's frozen stiff in the winter and thronging with flies in the summer, and she better watch out or the kid's going to fall and die. But she's pregnant for the second time, she's got nausea, a belly, worries: good thing my father has fast reflexes and is there to prevent a disaster from happening.

I imagine growing up like that, surrounded by dust and yelling, for all of 1944 and 1945. The child that still lives inside me somewhere, here inside my skull, must have seen beatings, heard insults, and learned to speak like his father, who sometimes breaks into a fury and wishes that the whole house would collapse and free him of all these hassles, and who, at other times, is cheerful, invents senseless stories in an odd language that is not the language usually spoken on Via Zara, and bounces his first-born on his knee or sings him Neapolitan ditties or throws him into the air and catches him with a whoopla.

It's true, my father can also be great fun and full of surprises. He gave me a sable coat—what is a sable, anyway?—so that I'd be warm. Once he came back from the no-man's lands to which he disappeared each morning with a playful rocking horse painted in bright colors and with a face that seemed almost real. He had a carpenter named Don Peppe build it from a drawing he himself had done. What a special drawing that was . . . Don

Peppe enthusiastically took up his circular saw and cut the rocking horse out of beechwood. Yes, my father can make a person bleed but he can also amaze people with exceptional words and objects. Mimí, you remember all those songs I used to invent, he often asked me over the years so that I wouldn't forget. You remember all those wonderful toys I gave you?

Of course I do. I remember everything about him; he filled my head with his words and thoughts. I have none of my mother's words though, none of my mother's thoughts. And yet the first syllables I spoke must have surely come from her. I wish I could hear her words again, I wish I could feel how I welcomed them in my throat, repeating mutilated versions of them over and over in that room with no walls on Via Zara. But my father, with his usual energy, modified their speed and erased their tone. He injected them with an ambition and will that didn't belong to his wife, but to him. After all, wasn't he the one who brought back to that space—bordered by the bed on one side and the military blanket on the other, by warm milk and the abyss—the desire to be heard, to be the loudest, to stand out? No, my mother's voice, even if it wound its way into every single fiber of my child's body, ultimately gave out, was too fragile. She, who unquestionably played with me, sang to me, and made toys for me, didn't have it in her to leave me with any sounds. She was quickly reduced to the words that her husband screamed at her from the moment he came home from work until late at night: fuck it all, Rusinè, fuck it all.

Suddenly, or so it seemed, in early March 1946, my grandfather came back from Savignano with the whole family. He took back possession of the apartment on Via Zara and threw us all out from one day to the next. "You wanted to marry her, you shithead! Now quit busting my balls!" he yelled at his son. There followed more than the usual amount of shouting, rude offenses, women shrieking. Father and son hurled insults at each other that they had been storing up for some time, almost coming to blows. I must've seen and heard the entire scene, that's what eyes and ears were for after all, and what I saw and heard must have run aground within me somewhere, deep in a gully or gorge of my body, I can feel it in my fingers as I type, as if they know more than what I am actually writing. My grandfather's cussing, for example, and how he wanted his bombed-out apartment back for his numerous family; his enmity for his mendacious son who wasn't content with being a factory worker like himself; their shared obsession for money, the money I gave you, the money you gave me, the money you stole from me. They were surrounded by the war-torn city, where everyday life was risky, its terrors perfectly captured by the chorus of howling women who stood near the two arguing men, the older one yelling and punching at whatever got in his way, the younger one foaming at the mouth with violence but holding back, not saying another word. Phrases like: leave me alone, Papà, don't make me say it, don't make me say it; holy mother of Jesus, help me, don't make me hit my father; you all heard him, my son hitting me, hitting me! *'Stu chiavecchmmèrd, 'stu figliesfaccímm*, that cesspool of shit, that sonofabitch bastard, he wants my neck; in other words, he wants to strangle me; it's a rhetorical device, a part for the whole, he wants to get his hands on his father's body and butcher him, dismember him, in perfect keeping with the landscape littered with butchered bodies left after the recently ended war.

The women scream, but later they'll talk calmly about the ugly encounter. My grandmother said that she saw two males *incarzapellúti*—that's the word she used—two males with hackles up who went at each other's throats like animals. I was in her arms at the time, she said, a three-year-old who stared, agog, at the scene, at how they faced off, hollering at each other for the whole neighborhood to hear. I must've seen and perceived the fierceness necessary to be a part of this world. I was shocked and, from that moment forward, disgusted by my grandfather. Every year on his saint day, August 4, when I had to go to his apartment

on Via Zara, I was filled with angst. I'd wish him a pleasant ono-
mastic and offer up my gift of two packets of Nazionali, but the
scowling and toothless old man barely mumbled a word.

Luckily, the lady upstairs on the sixth floor, Signora Attardi,
a widow of a railroad employee, offered to host Federí, his wife,
their two children, and his mother-in-law in her apartment, in a
space that connected the kitchen to her bedroom. It was a generous show of hospitality and offered free of charge. My father
took advantage of it for more than a year and a half. And so there
we lived, behind more walls of rigged-up military blankets, with
people coming and going and not a shred of privacy. Until one
day, Federí got fed up and, in his usual frenzied rage, went out
one morning and procured the house on Via Gemito for us.

The way it happened—he always enjoyed telling us this
story—was that as soon as the trains started running again more
or less in a normal manner, he went back to working as second
in charge (but now in the ticket office) and started to look for an
apartment right away. He went to the housing office for railroad
employees and applied for lodgings in one of the railway-owned
buildings, both in writing and in person. Come back tomorrow,
come back the day after, they said, but they never had anything
for him, and not because there weren't any apartments available
but because once the war was over, things went back to being
worse than they were before, same old monkey business and
backroom deals. For example—he'd go on to explain to me each
time he told the story—the person in charge of assigning public housing to the railroad workers, a fellow named Lanza, had
worked in that very job, the exact same one, during the fascist
period, and now, even with Mussolini long gone, he continued
to hold the position. So much for a new moral code, so much
for new men. It was all shit, all talk. Whenever my father had a
free moment, he'd go see Lanza. "Any good news for me? Any
apartments open up? Anyone been transferred or retired?" he'd

ask. And Lanza would always answer the same way, no, I'm sorry, and then he'd go back to confabulating with Cannavaccio, head of the railroad police; Lanza and he were like cup and spoon, in cahoots, granting housing only to a select few.

Cannavaccio knew my father well and detested him. Every time he saw Federí stride into the office without knocking, that crazy look in his darting, beady eyes, he'd yell at him, "Hey boss, don't you know you're supposed to knock before you walk in?" as if it was his office and not the housing office for railroad workers and their families. Federí had a hard time holding back. A single uppercut and he'd have broken all his teeth, but he didn't dare; he had to think of his family. And then, one day in September 1947, he walks into the housing building on Via Santa Lucia, already tense from a day of work. He runs up the first flight of stairs, then takes the second; with each step he's getting closer to screaming like a madman. Winter's coming, he has two children, one aged four and the other only two, he can't stay a minute longer in old lady Attardi's place, they have to do something for him.

He walks into Lanza's office and naturally Cannavaccio is there, sitting across from him. Cannavaccio opens his mouth for his usual comment of "Hey boss, don't you know you're supposed to knock before you walk in?" Federí is on fire, ready to unleash all sorts of obscenities and stick his claws into the man's throat when some assistant walks into the room. He extends a bunch of keys to Lanza in his open palm. "Here are the keys from the apartment at 64 Via Gemito, boss. It was vacated an hour ago." My father eyes the keys, Lanza, and Cannavaccio. It's a fraction of a second. "Thanks," my father says and grabs the keys out of the assistant's hand, slips past Cannavaccio, who tries to stop him, and bolts down the stairs two at a time. "Someone catch that piece of shit!" the commissioner orders. Lanza screams at the assistant who let the keys be stolen out of his hand. Cannavaccio chases after my father personally, screaming and threatening him. "Bring the keys back or you're going to be in real trouble!"

But Federí has no intention of returning them. He pauses, turns around, and looks up at Cannavaccio standing at the top of the stairs yelling, "Bring back the keys, we'll shut an eye on the whole affair." Federí gestures for him to go fuck himself, slapping the crook of his arm. As far as gestures go, I make a note to myself, that's not one of his usual ones; while he frequently relies on offensive body language in his stories, it's either that of spitting or pissing in their direction, the latter enacted by standing with his legs spread wide, back arched, fingertips of both hands pointing directly at his pubis, and sneering with contempt. Anyway, off he runs down Via Santa Lucia, a thirty-year-old man, hair flying in the gusty breeze that blows in from the sea that September day. He runs and runs, then stops a taxi, and lets himself be driven to Via Gemito so he can occupy the apartment, with its two large rooms, a modern WC with sink, toilet, and flusher, and a large kitchen: the very same kitchen where he now sits brooding at the table, the dark panes of glass trembling in their casements, the embers slowly turning to ash in the grate of the woodburning stove.

I'm a child when I hear my father tell his stories, and I listen with my mouth wide open. Sometimes I get so mesmerized that my lips go numb and with great embarrassment I realize that I'm drooling worse than my newborn baby brother. For months I'm scared that Cavaliere Lanza and Commissioner Cannavaccio will come and take back the keys to the apartment. But the worry that consumes me doesn't appear to affect my father in the slightest. "Cavaliere Lanza thought he was going to screw me over," he often boasts cheerfully, "and instead, I managed to screw him." He's so proud of his achievement; he risked going to prison for his family but he fought back against the shady dealings that went on in the housing office. When you meet a loudmouth—he instructs me and will continue to instruct me over the years—you have to be even more of a loudmouth, Mimí.

But I already realize that the damp apartment on Via Gemito, wedged between the sports field and the open countryside—which we occupied in a hurry, loading up a donkey cart with all our belongings: five mattresses, their steel bed frames, and a trunk full of linens and military blankets—is a treasure that, as fearful and timid as I am, I'd never be able to defend. If, for example, Commissioner Cannavaccio and Cavaliere Lanza showed up one night, and said, "Give us back the keys," would I be able to help my father kick them out of the house? Would I be able to piss in the face of one and spit in the face of the other, or beat the shit out of both of them? I'm horrified about not having the mettle to do things like that. Lanza and Cannavaccio might kick down the door and reveal that I don't know how to be the loudmouth my father wants me to be. This would be a huge letdown for him, he might yell "Get out!" at me in the same urgent tone that he used only a moment ago for "Cigarettes!" Or he might take the same aggressive tone that I hear him take with my mother as soon as I walk out of the kitchen toward the bedroom. "For fuck's sake, Rusinè, where did all the money go? What did you do with it?" His voice grows louder, more belligerent, to the extent that she detaches my baby brother, Toni, from her breast and hands him to her mother, my grandmother. She does it because she knows exactly what direction this conversation could take and she wants to protect the baby. Once Toni is firmly in my grandmother's arms, she twists around to face him. "What damn money are you talking about?"

I look at my baby brother, his mouth still wet with her milk. This fussy little being was born only two or three months ago, in January 1948. Geppe and I were woken up in the middle of the night by the noise and, when we went out in the hallway, we saw the midwife, Signora D'Eva, holding up sheets soaked with blood. We got scared. But Signora D'Eva explained to us that everything was alright, the stork had come and brought us our brother. But then the stork changed its mind and wanted to take the baby back and my father had to step in and kill the stork and dump its carcass down the toilet and flush it away. That spiraling vortex of water was already of great interest to me and my brother, but from then on it also made us a little sad. We wished we could've played with the stork, at least for a little bit.

Nonna disagrees. Animals with animals, and men with men, if they're real men, that is. But if they're animals, they should be with other animals. Rosy-faced, she either starts chopping parsley near the hearth or sits down in the straight-back chair holding our new little brother and coos: oh-oh, oh-oh, oh-oh, the straw seat creaking as she manages to rock the chair back and forth, first on two legs and then on four, ba-bam, ba-bam, ba-bam, keeping time with the hypnotic rhythm of a nighttime lullaby that my grandmother sings like a dirge.

The song is about animals that kill and animals that get killed. I can only remember a few words and they still sound horrible, ninna nanna ninna nam, the wolf ate up a little lamb. It was the same wolf that prowled around the fields near Via Gemito at dusk. Its dark howls took my breath away in fear; sometimes the sound of the wild beast came from outdoors, sometimes from within.

From within, my grandmother led us to believe, from within. And on that night of the cigarettes, to get our baby brother to fall asleep she had to sing louder than my father was shouting in his ever-growing rage with Rusinè. Uh-oh, the wolf is coming. Uh-oh, the wolf is here. He wants to eat the baby lamb. And now he eats it up. But now the wolf is shouting too, his words getting sharper: "The money I earned from the Teatro Bellini!" My mother insists that she knows nothing about that money; my father says the 100,000 lire, and she replies, what 100,000 lire are you talking about. It's an absurd amount, like all the numbers that come out of Federí's mouth over the course of his lifetime, but a true one in his deceitful mind, so true that he demands that my mother tell him immediately: where's the money from the Teatro Bellini? What did she do with it? How did she spend it? She can't tell him a thing, though, not then and not ever. How could she possibly hand over an imaginary sum of money? That's when all of us—me, on my way to get the cigarettes, my brother Geppe, even Toni, who's now being held by my Nonna, whom we call Nannina but whose official name is Anna Di Lorenzo—know that dinner is over, that soon, because of that money, our father will turn into a dragon and spit forth deathly flames, and that we need to get ready to face the terrified heart of night. He's fidgety, in need of a cigarette, he keeps repeating himself obsessively. "Where's the 100,000 lire from the Teatro Bellini? Where is it?" And Rusinè, instead of being quiet and keeping the peace, just can't help herself and sneers at him, hell if I know.

During that winter of 1948, on the evening I was sent to get his cigarettes, the teatrobellini—all one word, all lower case— was already a vague, fuzzy sign of conjugal discord. Uttered in a tone of voice that grew more and more aggressive as the night went on, it held all sorts of meanings: look at what I managed to do, look at what I could've done, if only you had appreciated me and supported me. The phrase "It's all your fault I had to stop" had not yet made an appearance. It may well have been uttered for the first time that night. The even stronger version, the irrefutable "It was all your mother's fault" only came into usage in the middle of the 1960s, however, when his wife's voice could no longer snicker and contradict him in dialect. "Me? My fault? What did I ever do?"

In any case, before being a bundle of hostile accusations, one of many in the house on Via Gemito, before being an indictment, the first one my father charged at Rusinè, the Teatro Bellini was just a theater. "It was among the most beautiful in Naples," Federí used to say, going on to edify me. "It was built

with Baron Lacapra's money by the architect Carlo Sorgent."
It had six tiers of seats, all gilded, an absolute wonder. At the
young age of twenty-six, he was in charge of set design, choreog-
raphy, everything. He was responsible for recruiting all the staff,
artisans, and dancers. At every opening, he seated Rusinè and
Nonna Nannina in no less than the royal box while I—you, he'd
say—would watch from my mother's lap.

When, three years ago, the first time I tried to write about
the winter of 1948 and the years that led up to it, and ultimately
about the peacock, I remember getting stuck on that "royal box"
for a long time, trying to extricate it from the random arguments
that surrounded it and see it for what it was: spotlights, crown
molding, the sound of the English language, the sound of my
mother's breathing, as well as that of my grandmother. I wanted
that to be the starting point for a wide-angle view of the whole
place as he had experienced it, as we had all experienced it. But
that was a mistake. My efforts were in vain. With each version
of the experience that my father recounted, the theater grew in
his imagination, going from an actual theater to an imaginary
destination, a dazzling stop on his predestined journey, as if all
the horrors of World War II, battle after battle, cadaver after
cadaver, had unfolded from 1939 to 1943 just so that the English
army could requisition the building on Via Conte di Ruvo, so
that Staff Sergeant Leefe of the Naafi-Efi (which is what Federí
called it) could entrust it to him so that he could organize entertainment for soldiers on leave.

The Teatro Bellini was an actual place. It existed just like
so many other real places, each one of which can still be visited today, creating an actual topographical map. Just like the
apartment at 18 Via Zara in the neighborhood of Savignano,
from which he departs one day in August 1943 for Avignon,
France, which was then a German-occupied city (dressed in his
radio operator's uniform, a heinous example of a uniform—he
said—when compared to the beautiful German ones). But, like

all the other places Federí mentioned, it too was a landscape of dreams and nightmares, just one of the many stations on his own way of the cross that he traveled day in and day out, for months on end, plundering hell and then ascending into a paradise where his talents were recognized.

It was pointless to try and seek out the truth. I had to write "royal box" and accept the term "royal box" as he intended it when he decided to educate me about everything, starting with the facts that had befallen him. I couldn't say no thank you, so I just stood there, without moving, hanging onto his every word. I listened and, even though I was always a little scared that he might quiz me to see if I was following carefully, I was especially impressed by his skill at connecting places, seasons, events, and illustrating all the wrongs to which he had been subjected, and principally at the hands of my mother. Listening to him, it always seemed like everything happened just the way he said it did, that the events that unfolded in those years really did take place one after the other with the focus always on his life, the most precious of all materials worth preserving. If there was one design he never complained about, it was that of providence. He couldn't accept that facts fell like rain, casually, without taking him into consideration. No, he was certain that both great and small events had a common thread: the mystery of his destiny. And he constantly tried to prove it to himself, his relatives, his friends, and to us children by weaving a vibrant pattern in which the only events that were true were the ones vitally connected to him. Consequently, all the names of cities and buildings and roads, all of geography, served merely to create a map of his needs, and this was how they were to be remembered.

For example, where had he done his military service? How did Avignon come into the picture? What wartime events had led him to the Bellini? Had he actually done any fighting? Had he really been at the Russian front, marched all the way to Stalingrad?

He believed he had been there. It was a foregone conclusion

that he had been there, maybe he had convinced himself that having fought in Russia and surviving Soviet gunfire and the icy cold were the best proof of his indispensability to the world.

But while he spoke I observed my mother out of the corner of my eye and she didn't let him tell his story in peace. When Federí mentioned his fateful departure for the Russian front and his miraculous return, safe and sound, she shook her head. He noticed her and it made him clench his teeth. "What? Don't you remember?" he'd ask. "Sure, sure," she'd smirk, which he didn't like one bit. Rusinè was an inconvenient witness, she saw the facts as they happened, at random; she didn't understand that the significance of certain events lies in the imagination of the person who experiences them and revisits them, without splitting hairs. So, sometimes, as if to convince her too, he upped the dose of details; other times he carefully wriggled out of things and toward more plausible battlefields.

The result was that his participation in the war always came across as somewhat vague. First he was sent to Russia, then he was about to be sent but the commanding officer sent him to a different front, then he never talked about Russia at all, and his wartime experiences were limited to his stint in Menton as a military radio operator for the German forces, 155th Marconi Company, barracked in the Caravan Palace on the Côte d'Azur.

But then he left Menton and was sent to Pierrefeu-du-Var, where the armored car transceiver was transferred and, between one shift of monitoring and the next, he managed to find time to draw or paint. Then he ended up in Avignon, the city of Popes, a happy place where he had been able to focus less on the transceiver and more on an eighteen-year-old painter with a fragrant name, Rose Fleury, who was born and bred in Nîmes—in the Gard region, a teacher at Les Angles elementary school, and an expert on the Barbizon School—and responsible for both his artistic and sentimental education.

It should be mentioned that the only actual war stories he told with any element of drama in them were those that took place shortly after his first physical exam. Initially, he stood out in a positive way. As one of the tallest men present (with a height of 1.81 m), and also broad-chested (at 90 cm across), he definitely was the best proportioned. In other words, he was well-built, intelligent, and he immediately pointed out that he had a calling as artist. He counted on training to become an officer, even though he hadn't gone to the right school. He hoped to go to officers' school in Fano and felt mentally and physically prepared for it. Instead he was assigned to the depot of the 40th infantry on Corso Emanuele, not far from Mergellina train station. And that's where things started to go downhill.

He blamed his digestion, which got blocked as soon as he walked into the barracks. He blamed the endless forced marches and the heavy food that sat in his belly, weighing him down. He blamed the doctors who didn't listen to him when he reported sick and then only prescribed him Epsom salts which just made him squat over the latrine for hours on end. He blamed the sense of fatigue, exhaustion, solitude, and sadness. He blamed the *salto mortale* test, a death-defying leap without a safety net. He panicked, couldn't breathe, couldn't stop wondering "Will I survive? Will I die?" and ended up with his head so deep in the sand he thought he had broken his neck. He blamed Colonel Uberti, who stood at the podium and screamed, "Cowards! The youth of today is shit!"

Eventually, they had to rush him off to the military hospital. There, the medical lieutenant, a bastard with eyes like the devil, diagnosed him with congenital valvular heart disease and told him he was done for, that he had two months left to live at the most, wiggling his index and middle finger in Federí's face. "Only two months left?" my father asked, incredulous. He, a man who had always known he was destined for great things but hadn't yet had time to accomplish much, had only two months left to live? Bah! He spat in the face of the medical lieutenant—he always had a gob of saliva in his mouth at just the right moment—and then tried to choke him with his bare hands. How dare he diagnose him with imminent death! It took a fair number of nurses to restore calm and the medical visit concluded with him being rejected from the military for serious cardiac issues. This, in turn, led to the loss of his job as an electrical repairman and left him feeling like a poor excuse of a man.

Damn, to be discharged like that. I never really understood his true feelings about it though. I know he wanted to become a soldier, and not even an ordinary soldier, but an officer, something that would impress people. And that's why he always put pressure on me to study when I was a boy. "Mimí, if you have a high school diploma or university degree, you could become an officer." He would've liked it if I had gone on to become a figure of authority. He would've enjoyed seeing soldiers salute me, as if I was the sun and they had to shield their eyes with their hands because I was so bright. He always enjoyed the rituals that set apart people who were respectable from those who were not. Maybe that's why life in the military back then had attracted him, more for its form than its content. Mostly for the "all clear" that life in the service guaranteed. All clear in terms of health, all clear in terms of sexual prowess, all clear to work. It was a green light, it meant you were a man with a backbone, with a sizeable pair of balls, ready for all the major functions of life.

But no. He never admitted that he made a mistake. He did everything to convince me that his relinquishing of arms did not depend on him at all. He attributed it above all to the incompetence and stupidity of people with degrees—doctors, but not only. If those bastards hadn't gotten involved, once he had become an officer and donned his uniform and the appropriate stripes, he would've had all the money and women he wanted, there would've been no more slaving on the railroad, he would've enjoyed a life of pleasure far from home. Instead now, from one day to the next, he found himself with neither uniform nor job, only disoriented. He wandered the streets of Ponti Rossi at night, thinking about how he had been stamped "unfit" for service, how he had a sick heart, how all the girls would laugh at him and say, "Honey, if you're no good for the King, you can't possibly be good for the Queen." Whores. No women for him. Two months left to live. Pretty much dead already. He simply couldn't believe it.

His father didn't believe it either. He quickly reached out to Professor Blasi, a physician from the Ispettorato Sanitario delle Ferrovie dello Stato as well as something of an honorary consul for the railroad militia, to obtain a certificate—for his lazy, *cacacàzz*, pain-in-the-ass son, a *sfacimmemmèrd* who thought he was better than the man who had created him but who was really nothing more than a bum who couldn't even do a *salto mortale* without a safety net—that claimed Federí did not have a congenital heart disease, that he was actually as fit as a fiddle, and that he had to be immediately rehired by the national railroad service and bring home a paycheck which he, his father, desperately needed, as he had a rightfully large family.

And that churlish man didn't stop there. He took his son to see Professor Boeri, an important authority with a beard, who immediately declared, "Dear boy, your heart is perfectly healthy and, God willing, you have years and years ahead of you." Fortified by this diagnosis, his father even wrote to the secretary of the fascist party, Achille Starace, who unfortunately replied, "Kind comrade, I regret to inform you that the judgment pronounced by the military medical commission is unappealable."

Unappealable, that shitty official said. My grandfather, unlike my father, hated the fascists; he was a staunch socialist and would be forever. He forced his dawdling son (who, all things considered, despite being labeled terminally ill and consequently unacceptable to either King or Queen, quite liked the idea of being unemployed and found the prospect of going back to work on the railroad repugnant) to ignore Starace and put in a request to the Ministero delle Comunicazioni to be rehired.

Long story short, after some back and forth, on June 15, 1938 the good news arrived. My grandfather made an announcement to the entire family: even though Federí was a piece-of-shit military reject, even though he only served two weeks in the armed forces, 'o signuríno could finally go back to work.

Things went back to their rightful place, with that dangerous twist in the road serving only to emphasize: Federí, you have a future ahead of you that no one, not even a doctor with the eyes of a devil, can take away. You're tall, strapping, well-proportioned, you learned to box from Sacco, Frattini, Centobelli, and Rojo. It's true that the long marches, the solitude, and especially the *salto mortale* test your nerves, but only because everything that is mortal repulses you. Other people are mortal; let them do the *salto* without a safety net. Let your childhood friends do it: Cannava, Impacciarella, Salzana, and Songes, with his silver medal. They all end up dying in war; that was their destiny. Life sends you other signals. You were born to last. What happened next has a secret meaning that soon becomes clear. Teatro Bellini awaits. Advance fearlessly.

And that's exactly what he did. In 1940, everyone born from 1914 to 1919 who had been rejected was called up, and my father—he said—fearlessly stood before the Commission with his own father putting all his various papers in order, including the letter to Starace. To his great satisfaction, they immediately saw in him a deeply patriotic young man who was competent for battle. Moreover, after being subjected to a highly specialized heart exam, he was declared in perfect health and, on March 18, 1940, was assigned to the 31st Infantry, 2nd machine-gun battalion, A 13 Company. Hear that? A highly specialized heart exam, he said proudly, as recently as two years ago: a perfect bill of health. This was not the usual, speedy checkup they did to everyone; this was for the best soldiers who were being sent to Russia.

And that brings us back to the beginning. Did he ever leave

for Russia or not? Or was the idea merely mentioned? Was he supposed to leave and then got out of it thanks to my grandfather's strategy of mentioning how his son had been scared to do the *salto mortale* and diagnosed with a congenital mitral valve deficiency?

I don't know and I don't really care anymore. I only remember how, when my friends came over to the house, and we're talking about the early 1960s here, he'd say yes, he had been sent to the Russian front. With Giulio Fuiano, he made sure to say, who was only two years younger than him. Poor Fuiano had died, he was a good man. But he hadn't. I'd sit there in a corner nervously fidgeting—I wasn't a kid any more, I felt violence welling up inside me, and his charm no longer had any effect on me. I looked at my classmates' faces and could tell they didn't believe him for a minute, I kept hoping he'd quit talking, what torment it caused me. All those things that had once impressed me as a child—how he spun his stories, one thing always leading to another, nothing left to chance, not even the death of others—I now wished I could tune out entirely.

"So, your father fought on the Russian front?" my friends would later ask me, chuckling. I'd just shrug, change the subject, and sometimes even reply casually, "Just for a week. Then they sent him to Avignon."

He returned to Naples from Avignon to get married in May of 1942. Rusinè's relatives were opposed to the wedding and either shook their heads woefully or gesticulated with dismay. "What if Federí gets shot and dies in war," they said, "what will Rusinè do then? Be a widow for the rest of her life? Maybe even with a child to support?" It would be an awful life, and exactly what had happened to Nonna Nannina. When my grandmother's husband died, she was left with two children: Rusinè, who was two years old, and Peppino, who, at the time, was still in her belly. She had suffered so much and didn't want her daughter to live a similar life. None of the people who cared for Rusinè wanted that, and even if Federí had since been promoted from repairman to a supervisory position, and was consequently a good catch, everyone kept telling her to wait. "What's the big hurry? Wait until the war is over, let's see if Federí lives or dies."

But he was certain he'd survive. The whole thing made him breathe fire. He wanted to get married immediately. And so there was a family meeting, during the course of which, after much debate, it was decided that the two young people could be joined in matrimony but that they should abstain from being united in the flesh. My mother's uncle, Zio Matteo, who was the husband of Nonna Nannina's oldest sister, Zia Assunta, was chosen to relay the news to the future groom. "Federí, swear to me that you'll wait until the war is over to have relations," Zio Matteo said to him in dialect. "What the hell kind of promise is that, Zio Mattè? Do I look like the kind of man who gets married and doesn't have relations?" he snapped angrily. But, realizing that Matteo was blackmailing him, he faked it and solemnly swore as much. Immediately following the wedding, he waved goodbye to them all and whisked his lovely bride off to Florence for a quick honeymoon.

There, the newlyweds were hosted by another one of Nannina's sisters, Zia Nenella, who was married to a policeman whom everyone in the family always called Zio Peppino di Firenze. Federí had never met either of them and traveled there with a fair number of preconceptions. During their engagement period, he explained to me, he had come to believe that Rusinè's family was made up purely of idiots and assholes, and he departed for his honeymoon expecting the duo of Zia Nenella and Zio Peppino di Firenze to be just as much of a pain in the ass. Instead, something happened that rarely took place in his long life. In their cold attic apartment at 18 Via dei Pilastri, Federí actually had a good time. I'm not sure I can say as much for Rusinè, but he, on numerous occasions, told me so. "Mimí, I was really happy there," he said. And it definitely wasn't thanks to Zia Nenella, who was no different from his mother-in-law and her other sisters. It was all because of Zio Peppino di Firenze. When it grew dark, Zia Nenella tried to impose the family's rule. "You, Federí, will sleep with Peppino and I will sleep with Rusinè," she said. But Zio Peppino intervened on their behalf. "They're legally married and they'll sleep here," he said, indicating the double bed. "But Peppí, there's a pact," Zia Nenella tried to object. "Do you want to uphold this pact?" Zio Peppino di Firenze asked the newlyweds. "Screw the pact," Federí said. I'm not sure if Rusinè said anything or not, but I do know that with no further ado Federí was united in flesh with his young bride that night, and that an important friendship with Zio Peppino di Firenze was born.

The same cannot be said for Zia Nenella. Their relationship would be forever tinged with hostility. "I was a recently married man," he often said, "and I was always hungry, I enjoyed being with your mother and it wore me out." But Zia Nenella wasn't sympathetic to his efforts, and at lunch, when he eyed the largest piece of meat and made to spear it with his fork, she'd quickly take it away. "That's for my husband," she'd say. She didn't give a damn that he needed to fortify himself before returning to the front.

Florence soon became a fond memory and he and Rusinè only saw each other again in Saviano, one icy February morning in 1943. Federí was on leave from Menton and had crossed half of Italy to get there, immediately clarifying and listing all the serious risks he had undertaken en route: bombings, machine-gun fire, and so on. Rusinè was pregnant, her nine months were up, her belly stuck out to here, and even so she prepared a basin of hot water for his bath behind a curtain held up with metal wire, and proceeded to scrub him down to get rid of the lice. What else could she do? The situation was what it was, they had been evacuated, she was living with all her relatives in one big room, and they had no privacy. But while he was drying off, his rebellious locks combed forcefully back, Rusinè's pale and gaunt husband made no secret of his displeasure at having to spend his brief period of leave there before returning to the front. He voiced his displeasure at not having been welcomed properly and remarked that not a few things seemed out of place. He complained about the overcrowding and the unfair distribution of beds. "Where are we going to sleep, you and me?" he finally came out and asked.

There were three double beds with large, hay-stuffed mattresses: in one of them slept Nonna Nannina, Nonna Nannina's mother, Nonna Nannina's mother-in-law, and Rusinè; in a second one slept Nonna Nannina's two sisters, Maria and Carmela, with their husbands, Espedito and Attilio (they, too, were brothers) and two young children, one from each couple; Nonna Nannina's third sister, Assunta, slept with her husband Matteo on the third mattress; and Peppino, Rusinè's twenty-year-old brother, slept on the floor on a pure wool mattress. Federí started to complain. "Why do Zio Matteo and Zia Assunta get to sleep on their own in that big comfortable bed? Why does your brother get a whole wool mattress to himself?" It didn't end there. "Do your relatives know that we need some time alone? Do they know that I don't have long and that I might even die in war?"

They knew it perfectly well. One by one, the men—Attilio, a driver and a man of few but courteous words; Espedito, a pastry chef and a pleasant, vivacious man; Matteo, a fruit and vegetable merchant with a kind, virile face; young Peppino, who worked a lathe but acted like a carefree teenager—made their way down to the freezing cold building courtyard. The women followed suit with the same calm discretion. And so, husband and wife were left alone to make love, which calmed Federí and put him in a good mood, and even made Rusinè laugh, after which they fell asleep.

At five o'clock in the afternoon, however, she let out a scream that startled him awake. Her labor pains had begun. My father got up, swearing and calling out for his mother-in-law, who was down in the courtyard. Nonna Nannina went pale and instructed him to run and get the midwife. The midwife, who was an unclean, uncouth, and heavy forty-year-old woman who wore her greasy hair pulled back in a bun, slowly followed Federí, who ran up ahead, out of breath and panicking.

The midwife finally made her entry into the large room, pushed aside all the relatives and friends who were standing around, and plonked down like a stone statue next to the woman giving birth. She didn't move for hours on end, while Rusinè continued to scream from time to time. Standing around them in a circle were: her mother, her two grandmothers, her three aunts, her aunts' three husbands, her aunts and uncles' two children, her brother Peppino, Don Liborio the landlord with his family, Don Ciccillo the goldsmith with his wife and three children, a friend of Rusinè's with her husband, Federí, and the midwife. Twenty-five people. Some of them mumbled softly, some offered advice, some explained the various phases of the process, others just stood around smoking. The only time there was silence was when Rusinè screamed in pain. During those brief pauses, the midwife would raise the blanket, take a peek, and reassure them. "Not to worry, it's all going as planned," she'd say in dialect. And then the chatter would start up again, louder and heavier than before. Minutes and hours passed, it grew dark, night fell. Rusinè's skin was pale and sweaty, her eyes were glazed over, her hair had lost its sheen and stuck to her clammy forehead, she had dark circles under her eyes. She screamed and screamed. "Just another little bit, Signora Rusína, and then it will all be over," the midwife kept saying.

Finally, Federí lost his patience. He started shouting that his wife needed to give birth in peace and quiet, and he chased everyone out. One by one, the relatives left the room, but unwillingly.

It was bitterly cold outside, past curfew, and there was the distant sound of bombs dropping on Naples. What eventually convinced them to leave and face the icy courtyard was unquestionably the fiery dragon glare that Rusinè's husband gave them, which was terrifying. The only one who put up a fight was Don Liborio, the landlord of the apartment and owner of the whole building, courtyard, stables, and surrounding countryside, who wanted to stay and watch. "Get out of here now, Don Libò! The show is over!" Federí screamed at him, his lips purple with rage, threatening him with his life. Don Liborio turned glumly around and followed the others out.

Eventually the only spectators left in the big room were Rusinè's mother, her grandmother, her great-grandmother, the midwife, and Federí. Rusinè herself went on screaming until four o'clock in the morning. For a while, the midwife behaved as if everything was normal. "Push, push, you're almost there," she said in her confident way. But at a certain point, she started to doze off and stopped looking under the blanket or encouraging the birthing woman. Nannina and Federí started to get alarmed: son-in-law looked at mother-in-law and mother-in-law looked at son-in-law in a growing spiral of anxiety. This went on until he saw a pleading look cross his exhausted wife's face, at which point he leapt up and shook the midwife's shoulder. "What the hell is going on here? What the hell kind of midwife are you? Why aren't you doing anything?" he screamed at her. "You'd better go to Nola, it looks like she needs a surgeon," the woman replied.

Federí lost his patience again. He started yelling for a telephone, but there was none. Where could he find one? He ran down to the courtyard to try and get help; all the relatives he had chased out had found refuge at either Don Liborio's house or Don Ciccillo's. "I have to go to Nola! We need a surgeon," he kept screaming over and over. Aware that Don Liborio owned a barouche, Federí rushed over to his house and begged him to lend it to him. "Don Libò, I need a carriage, help me, don't let my wife and child die. Bring me to Nola in your barouche." But Don Libò, who may well have been offended at how he had been thrown out of the apartment some hours earlier, told him that the wheels were rickety and they wouldn't withstand the galloping of the horse. "I'm sorry, Don Federí. But believe me, it's not that I don't want to help, but we'd never make it to Nola," he said.

So he started running up and down the narrow street, swearing and yelling in dialect. "My wife needs a surgeon. I'll pay someone 100 lire to take me to Nola." Nothing. There was curfew, the alleys were empty, no one replied. He ran toward the main road. "Five hundred lire to the person who takes me to Nola, 500 lire!" he hollered at the dark sky. Finally, he heard a voice. "I'll tack up the horse and take you."

A few minutes later, a farmer and cart appeared, he extended a hand to Federí so he could clamber up, and off they galloped down the road that led to Nola. The horse's shoes sent sparks flying as they hit the flint rocks. It was a dangerous night. They could hear Naples being bombed and see the distant glow from the explosions.

Federí found the surgeon right away, thank God, and brought him back in a flash to the room in Saviano. The surgeon was around seventy, calm, and skilled. "Pick up your wife and lay her down on that table," he said as soon as he walked into the room. My father lovingly picked up Rusinè and laid her down on the table, then caressed her sweaty brow. "Look, I brought the surgeon, see? Everything's going to be fine now." And with that, she gave birth and started to laugh so hard that she couldn't stop.

I don't know anything else about the moment Rusinè became my mother beyond her screams and laughter. My father reappropriated the birth and shifted all the physical and emotional trials of labor onto himself, whether it had to do with the midwife, the relatives, Don Liborio, the icy cold night, him sweating heavily and without an overcoat, the barouche, the dangers of war, and the actual amount that I had cost him with my birth: first he said 100, then 500, then 1,000 lire.

By the age of five I knew in precise detail how he had saved my life and that of Rusinè from imminent death, which was caused, I perceived, entirely by my body, that of yours truly, which didn't want to be born the right way. Over the course of time, and with each retelling of the story, I looked at him with a mix of wavering gratitude and a number of questions on the tip of my tongue. Did the doctor need to use forceps? If so, why hadn't they left a mark? Was I born by Cesarean section? Was the surgeon actually necessary, or not? He skipped over these details, considered them unimportant, and preferred to focus on himself. The more he told the story, the more his role as a savior grew. In the 1970s, he even started saying that it was actually my mother's destiny to die during childbirth in 1943. And she surely would've died, he exclaimed, if he hadn't rushed off to get the surgeon, overcoming enormous challenges and facing great dangers on that icy cold night, with no overcoat, bombs raining down from the sky. To my mind it was as if he was saying that all the years that Rusinè had gone on to live, from 1943 to 1965, when her time to die truly came, even though he tried to save her a second time, were all thanks to his largesse, a gift of love that he himself granted her.

His wife owed him so much . . . As an elderly man, he talked about himself as a doting husband. He even passed off the rivers of tears that he forced her to shed shortly after giving birth as the result of his attentive ministrations. In actual fact, before leaving again for Menton, he wrote to his father and asked him to immediately come and get his daughter-in-law and grandson, and take them away from that disgusting large room full of stinking bastards who hadn't lifted a finger to help him in a time of need. He didn't want his son to remain in the care of someone like Don

Liborio or idiots like Peppino, Attilio, Espedito, and Matteo. He decided that it was better if my mother and I stayed with his parents in Savignano. And so, just like that, mid-war, Rusinè was forced to say goodbye to her mother, brother, grandmothers, and the aunts she had grown up with, and go live with people she hardly knew, her parents-in-law and sisters-in-law, with her newborn baby. What immense pain that separation caused. She, Nannina, and the aunts all cried like fountains. Tears of a woman, Federí said. Wielding his newfound power as head of household, he said he did it for my wellbeing and for that of Rusinè. Once that was done, he went back to fighting the war.

He was in Avignon when he received the horrible news that his seventeen-year-old sister, Modesta, had died. Her tragic death—which was how he referred to it in his anecdotes—allowed him to obtain a special leave of absence for fourteen days, including travel, and he set off for Naples.

I know nothing about Modesta. For decades I see her only as a ghost of a girl with fair hair, a sad look in her eyes, and a wan skin tone; sometimes I see her as a half-bust against a dark background, maybe in a watercolor or oil painting done by my father; sometimes I envision her dying in my mother's arms, speaking her final words, "Rosa, stay with me, don't leave me."

As a child, she often appeared to me: suddenly she'd be standing behind the front door of our apartment on Via Gemito, or in the windowless closet at the end of the hall, or in mirrors, or in dark corners around the house. I should point out that it was for this reason, too, that I set out uneasily down the dark, cold hallway to the bedroom for my father's cigarettes in that March of 1948.

Back then I had so many fears I didn't know what to do with them all, so abundant were the memories of recent atrocities. And everything I didn't recall directly, I heard from the lips of others, and they also rattled my nerves. For example, they said my mother cried so hard when her sister-in-law died that her milk dried up. They said that Modesta clung so tightly to Rusinè during her final moments that my mother was caught in the girl's death grip. Because of all those anecdotes, the name "Modesta" came to be an ugly word that meant despair, dying too soon, no time to grow up, a life cut short, discordance, eyes red from crying, a pained moon of a face. That's how my father's mother, Nonna Filomena, talked about it, adding suffering to despair, but never providing any details, never stating the exact cause of death, as if her daughter had been swept away by wind and water, and all she could do was whisper her name while she herself stood on the balcony or at the window. My mother spoke about her that way, too, but she usually communicated in silence, with a feeble smile of regret, or with a sudden change in her expression. Maybe it was their stories, or maybe it was the sound of woodworms munching on dead wood in the heart of the night, that led me to believe I could hear her breathing behind the curtain that separated the dining room from the rest of the house.

My father, meanwhile, referred to his sister—after bestowing upon her, as he did with all the members of his family, an iron constitution, extraordinary good looks, and supreme intelligence—only in terms of the connection that existed between her tragic death and his providential fourteen-day special leave of absence. Indeed, it would seem that the most important consequence of her death was the arrival of the train that carried him—skinny, pale, dressed in a too-large uniform—into Napoli Centrale at dawn on August 27, following a long and dangerous journey.

When he told his stories, he always spoke in the imperfect tense, leaving things unfinished on purpose so that he could go back and retouch them every so often, clarifying connections, and eliminating any incongruencies. On his arrival in Naples, he discovered that the convoy train for Savignano was scheduled to leave in two hours. So he made his way to 18 Via Zara—one of the important addresses of his life and where his father's apartment was located in one of the four railroad-owned buildings, and where he had lived from the age of twelve until the day he left for the front (be it France, Russia, or wherever) and where he potentially could live after the war. Going to Via Zara allowed him to see with his own eyes that an Allied bomb had fallen in July onto the little piazza below and that the explosion had ripped through the stone pavement, damaged his parents' second floor apartment, and knocked out the bedroom wall. Seeing this made it even more important that he head back to the station and take the convoy train to Savignano, where he could weep for Modesta, see his parents, brothers, and sisters, and embrace his twenty-two-year-old wife and six-month-old son. A few days later, however, he decided to take Rusinè and the baby back to Saviano, hoping to make his young wife happy, as she had been deeply affected by Modesta's death and was worried sick about her own mother, brother, and relatives and wanted nothing more than to be with them. And that was why he moved his little family back in to the rank-smelling big room with all those uncles and aunts, his mother-in-law and brother-in-law.

That's how he spoke: in a continuous flow of words, with one sentence leading to the next through a series of consequences. The events that Nonna Filomena mentioned or that my mother communicated through her silences, which they referred to as happening by chance, in my father's telling made it sound like he had seen it coming, something that was frightening. Modesta, Modesta. The two women despaired in different ways about the same thing: what had happened, for heaven's sake, should never have happened. "My daughter, Modesta, should never have died," my grandmother wailed; meanwhile, even late into the 1950s, at certain times during the year, my mother would do some quick math in her head and say, "Today, Modesta would've been thirty-two years old." I, deeply disturbed by their sad sighs, ended up looking at every single thing on earth with a certain amount of perplexity, forcing myself to imagine things weren't really there, or what they'd be like if they were entirely different; nothing under the sun was certain, not even the sun itself. My father, on the other hand, beginning with Modesta's death, started to force connections between things, gradually developing the notion of predetermination, which, although it may not have erased his despair entirely—how horrible the story of Modesta was to him, beginning with the insignificance inherent in her name, he'd say a few words about her and that was it, she was nothing more than a ghostly presence behind a curtain, and that thanks only to my grandmother, the woodworms, and my mother—it managed to communicate a moderate pleasure, an ease, no sadness, and even a certain joy in putting together carefully constructed facts. My young aunt's ghostly figure was responsible for so many things. She died so that her brother (my father) was saved from being deported to Germany. She died—or so I thought as a young boy—out of love for my mother, so that Rusinè could leave that unfamiliar camp to which Federí had deported her, and make her way back to Saviano and her own mother.

When expressed like that, her death released a certain energy. It was not an ending, but a beginning. Even the grief it caused had a secondary purpose: it led to Federí's return home to his family in the nick of time. And just when everything seemed to take a sudden turn for the worse—his period of leave was over, he had to return to the front, he had to say goodbye once again to his dear ones whom he had been able to embrace thanks to Modesta's self-immolation—I knew that I needed only to wait, that his deep voice would soon recreate phrases with words, and use them to stretch out a safety net across the abyss.

His departure from Saviano, for example. There and then, it seemed certain: Federí took out his uniform, put it on, walked over to the Carabinieri command station, showed them his papers, and after many hugs and tears, sorrowfully left for Naples on the Nola–Baiano train. Who knew when he would see his son and Rusinè again. Who knew what disasters war held in store for him. Depressed, he arrived in Naples on September 10 at around four o'clock in the afternoon. There was chaos everywhere. He asked about trains to Rome but there were delays on the Formia line and the Cassino train was only going as far as Capua. He went to ask the station master—a man he knew—for additional information and, in yet another twist of fate, the man warned him about the current situation. "Go home, kid. The Germans are arresting any soldiers they find. Apparently, Badoglio signed the Armistice," he said, and those were his exact words.

Federí glanced around in alarm, but luckily there were no Germans in the station. He asked about a train back to Saviano, but there were none. The next one would leave at six o'clock the following morning. So he set out homeward on foot, walking along the tracks, twenty long and tiring kilometers. At nine in the evening, he stood before Rusinè and his relatives: hungry, tired, and eager to tear off his ugly uniform.

The next day, afraid of being accused of desertion, he went to the officer in charge at the Carabinieri station. "The trains aren't running," he said. "And in Naples they told me that the situation is dangerous. What should I do?" The officer signed an extension of his special leave and sent him home with the same words of caution that the station master had used. "Go home, kid, and don't come out until the Americans arrive."

Federí followed his advice to the letter. He went home—that big, foul-smelling room—and stayed inside until the reconnaissance women received news on September 16 that the Americans had landed in Salerno. Only then did he cautiously stick his nose out. But on September 20 the recon women came back. "Hide, men, hide! The Germans are coming!" they said. And my father shut himself in once again.

I imagine that period of isolation in the room in Saviano as a time of discovery. My mother, for example, probably only then realized what kind of man she had married. Although they were engaged from 1938 to 1940, a fiancé is not at all like a husband. Then, in 1940 he went to war, and their separation, with its limited number of leaves of absence, probably only revealed the melodramatic aspects of the man's character. They were married in 1942, but only had enough time to conceive me in Florence before Federí had to return to the front. All this meant that, except for the brief period my father was conceded for my birth (a tense and hectic time), when had they ever had the chance to get to know each other?

As for me, the obedient child who goes to fetch his father's cigarettes, apparently I only noticed his presence after a certain amount of time, and was deeply bothered by it. I was eight months old when he came to Savignano for Modesta's funeral and then accompanied us back to Saviano because of my mother's desperation. She'd laugh and say that at first I didn't like him, that I used to try and hit him when he walked toward the two of us; if he fussed over me, I'd start crying. Even my father says in his stories that when he put his arm around his wife's shoulders, I'd start whining and try and push him away. Essentially, it was as if I had a hard time accepting that he was my parent. I may have preferred the other men in the family: I adored Rusinè's brother, Peppino, who was kind and fun, the perfect uncle, always ready to play games; or Matteo, Attilio, and Espedito. The anthem of our bloodline, which for my father was both resounding and undeniable, took its time to make itself heard in me. Without a doubt, this contributed in no small part to the impression he had on me back then and, come to think of it, that he still has on me; whenever the least thing happens, the eight-month-old child in me reappears and reaches out to his mother in fear. Why does that chubby baby, who has no real memories to speak of, fuss and cry all the time? Why is he so afraid of that pale stranger with the wide forehead? Who is this anxious and moody young man who wants to sleep in their bed, who insists on demonstrating that this woman is his wife, that this child is his son, and thus has the right to boss the two of them around?

The baby, who was once so easy, is always fussy now. He's only calm when his twenty-two-year-old mother takes him outside, up the hill, in the sunshine, past the public toilets, up an old, ugly, decrepit staircase with black stone steps. Or when she holds his hand and helps him take his first steps in the courtyard, near the entrance to the apartments of Don Ciccillo the goldsmith, and that of Don Liborio, the sinister owner of the whole rundown building. The farther away the child gets from that big room and his father, the calmer he is. Rusinè takes advantage of this fact: cooing and babbling to him, she carries him out the main door and down the alley that leads, in one direction, toward town and, in the other, toward a field of vegetables. But then she thinks she hears her husband shouting for her and so she rushes back.

It takes her time to get used to that voice that screams Rusinè, bring me this, I need that, hurry up. When she finally gets back with the baby in her arms, he's already angry: he doesn't like Peppino, he doesn't like his mother-in-law, he doesn't like her aunts, he doesn't like her aunts' husbands. When they were engaged, he contained himself, but now, as a married man, he lets fly. He spews venom over all the people that she adores.

Everyone who lived in that big room was probably thrilled when my mother and I returned. After my father's displays of rage at my birth eight months earlier, I doubt, however, that they were equally as happy to have him back in their midst. While it was a spacious room and it even had an ample balcony, living together in fourteen made it hard to breathe; cohabitation required a pleasant disposition.

A pleasant disposition he definitely did not have. All his stories, sooner or later, revealed one common element: he hated having to adapt to others, especially when it meant that his true nature and purpose in life were about as useful as withered flowers. It made him caustic and full of regrets. He'd start saying things like, how the hell did I get here? Me? A prisoner in a one-room apartment? Better off fighting at the front. Or on the Côte d'Azur, Mimí. Only a few months earlier, he had been speaking French in Avignon like a local and spending time with his eighteen-year-old painter friend, Rose Fleury. Whenever possible, he'd leave his post at the radio-transmitter and ride his bike down a creek on the Rhône with Rose perched on the handlebars. Now that was the life . . . She boasted about the Barbizon school, he boasted about the school of Posillipo. Together they'd choose a nice spot, set up their things, and paint their impressions of the place. The mood was always festive, the air was filled with the sounds of names of artists they sang out to each other, many of which were new to him because, unfortunately, he was self-taught and only then was beginning to learn who they were. He owed so much to that elegant and well-mannered signorina! It was from her lips that he heard for the first time the names of Rousseau, Millet, Corot, Díaz, Dupré, Troyon, Daubigny. And let's not forget Cézanne, incomprehensible Cézanne, with his ill-conceived landscapes painted from life which my hard-to-please father compared to those of Gigante, Carelli, and Pitloo.

But there in that big malodorous room, what sounds filled the foul air? None. Peppino's farts, if anything. My father disliked my mother's brother intensely. Not just then but for all the years to follow, as if his mere existence wounded him deeply.

If there was something that could always put him in a bad mood, it was the way his mother-in-law constantly boasted about her son. He was so handsome, she used to say. According to her, girls trembled at the sight of him. The mere thought made my father scowl. Good looks? What good looks? In a family of dogs (that included everyone except for Rusinè, who miraculously came out pretty), a halfway-decent dog was considered an Adonis. He couldn't stand exaggeration when other people did it, and was jealous of the attention showered on his brother-in-law, a young man with absolutely nothing exceptional about him: all he did was eat and shit. After returning from the front, my father expected to be welcomed like the important man he was: 1.80 m in height, well-built, with a broad forehead, full lips, and now familiar with the Barbizon school thanks to his recent education by the genteel Rose Fleury. And yet, not a single one of those pigs— except for his wife, and even she was a little distracted—appreciated his great skills and talents, the sketches he did of Rusinè, of Nonna Nannina, of his firstborn, and even of his handsome brother-in-law.

Like pearls before swine. It was pointless to mention that, while searching through the remains of the library at the Caravan Palace in Menton, he had found a book of reproductions of the greatest masterpieces of European art, and that he had copied them. Who in that menagerie gave a hoot about his progress as an artist? Who gave a flying fuck that in Pierrefeu-du-Var, in the haybarn where he and the other radio operators had set up shop, and in Avignon, in the villa where he had been based with five other soldiers, he had copied Gustave Courbet's *Les demoiselles des bordes de la Seine* as well as one of his nudes, Daumier's *Pierrot* and his *Don Quixote*, realizing, for Chrissakes, with a joy that took his breath away, that he was actually very good at copying them: the leaves, the pebbles on the shore, the firm buttocks, the Impressionist colors. But no one in that big room gave a fuck. They treated him like Rusinè's ex-soldier husband, pure and simple. No special treatment. They gave the best food to young Peppino. He, Federí, got cornmeal polenta.

And yet—and this is where he started in on the money— he brought home several thousands of lire from the front. His mother-in-law used it to purchase flour and oil. But even that disappeared quickly, ostensibly pilfered by his piece-of-shit relatives to be consumed in secret, not even with Rusinè and his son, or him. Definitely without him, and he ate less than all the rest of them, seeing that his conscience—he was the only one there to have one—told him to give up part of his ration to Rosa so that she could nurse the baby.

That's right, he wasn't a beast like the rest of them. He brayed such things all day long. Although it was crowded, no one had ever raised their voices there before. They had always lived in peace and harmony. But now he was there. And he was scaring the child. "Hush," Rusinè whispered and glanced at him disapprovingly. But he, who looked for any excuse to pick a fight, started arguing with his wife in a way that soon became a pattern: he mentioned the money, did some quick calculations, and demanded to see the books.

While he was off fighting the war—he'd say to her reproachfully—she had continued to cash his paycheck, month after month. And it wasn't just an ordinary electrical repairman's salary anymore: in 1939, he had taken part in a competitive exam, and in 1940 he was promoted to second in charge of the railroad thanks to his brilliance, with a salary of 1,200 lire each month. So, where the hell was all that money? What had she done with it? Yes, fine, his father regularly screwed him out of 600 lire of it, since he was just a factory worker and had a wife and five children to feed and earned only 450 lire, so obviously he needed some of it. But what about the remaining 600? And what about the 250 that she received as the wife of a soldier? Who the hell had eaten up the 850 lire he received every month, ever since the day they were married, in May 1942, up until and including today, the end of September 1943? Her mother? Her mother's sisters? Her mother's sisters' husbands? Their young children? Handsome Peppino?

He swore at her, scowled at her, hounded her, and pointed at me. "Who's going to feed him?" he yelled. The conclusion was always the same: they would, her relatives would, they had to feed me, seeing that in the past his wife had fed them with his money, and now he couldn't risk going outside to look for food because of the Germans.

But her ungrateful family didn't care. They just gave them crumbs, without the slightest sympathy for the fact that he was in hiding. What was worse, deep down inside they not only considered him a moocher, but someone who expected hefty portions. They had no regard for anything, they looked but they couldn't see. Whether they survived or died, their presence made no difference in the world. He, however, had to survive, he had important things to accomplish. And so he paced back and forth from the window to the door, like a caged beast in a zoo.

The smell of cooking from Don Liborio's apartment wafted upstairs. There was the aroma of bread and baking, of fresh milk and cheese, of fattened animals for steaks and cured meats. "Rusinè, go downstairs and see if Don Liborio's wife needs any help," he said. And so, down she went and helped the woman knead the dough and always came back with one small loaf, which those piece-of-shit relatives of hers were not allowed to touch. Because he was the one who came up with the ideas; he was the one who found a way to survive. What the hell. Even though his wife brought home the bread, it was as if he had gone to work for it himself. And even so, he refused to touch it, not even a small piece, thank you, because he wanted her to eat it all. That's right, all of it. She was the one who needed it, her milk had to be strong enough for yours truly, who was only a few months old. But my mother insisted, "You have some too," and in the end he'd eat a little bit, but only a tiny bit, he was always so fucking starving that it grated on his nerves. Meanwhile, his wife's relatives: they ate, they definitely ate, and how they ate.

I'm standing at the kitchen door in our apartment on Via Gemito, about to open it and walk out into the hall. The argument between my parents has begun. Federí has moved on from accusing her about the money to offending my mother's relatives. I hear his voice rising in tone at my back. I used to think that those arguments with my mother at home were just his way of rehearsing for a more open-ended script, one that was adaptable to other situations in his life. It was a simple and yet well-constructed script, and it inevitably included some worthless person taking away everything that he had worked hard for and deserved, despite destiny having great plans for him. Her aunts, their husbands, all of Rusinè's relatives—Federí has started screaming—had appropriated the fruits of his labors— and here he thumps his chest—he, thank God, always came up with something, yes, he was a railroader with a decent salary but he was also a man who wasn't afraid of working hard for something extra, because he was courageous and creative, an artist, while their thieving ways had both damaged and offended him: most of the great obstacles in his life stemmed from there, and he just couldn't take it anymore. He wanted satisfaction.

"You have to know that when someone has a destiny and it's not fulfilled," he'd repeat in later years, when old age and depression had slowed down his ranting a bit, "it's never the predestined one's fault, but the fault of an evil party, who is also good at clouding the waters and sowing discord, even between father and son." This is why, before he died and starting in 1988, he decided to write down his memories in black on white. *Verba volant.* He wanted to leave behind a jeremiad to remind us kids and our descendants that with a woman like her—meaning my mother—who was fine with fattening up a whole tribe of inept relatives with money that he himself had earned, and ignoring her real family—that with a woman like her—I just heard him yell in the kitchen and it gave me a start; he's yelling now; he's about to yell—What can a man possibly do? What can I do, *pataterno*? Should I continue to slave away just for the hell of it? Who am I, no one? What am I, zero? Nothing?

I open the door and walk out of the kitchen, which is as warm as the ladles hanging near the stove, glinting from both the fiery blaze in the stove and his rage. The icy air in the hallway smacks me in the chest and legs, a bruising draft that batters down walls and leads to nocturnal terrors and bronchitis.

"The door!" my father shouts, immediately after the word zero. "A draft!" he adds, raising the alarm of the risks connected to the wintry currents of air that jab you in the back.

We always leave him sitting in the draft, he says. And then, just to make his life more complicated, we go and sit in the draft. Then comes the cough. Then the mucus. So much of it that we have to call for Corbino, another railroader and neighbor, whose son has a blond mustache like a pansy and is in his second year of medical school, and who comes over when we need someone to open wide and say "Ah."

Because the draft can kill you. It bores down into your chest and between your ribs like sulfuric acid, to the degree that our father, as soon as he feels the draft but before he calls out "A draft!" moans in great pain, as if his throat has been cut with a razor blade, and then mournfully declares, "You want to kill me, that's what you want to do." (His actual words sound like a line out of a play by De Filippo: "ahhh, 'a-currènt! Vuje me vulíte fa' muri a me.") I know I don't want to kill him, not at this point in time, anyway, but I can't say as much for my mother: does she want him to die?

It's hard to say, impossible to know for sure. Unquestionably she is the reason behind most of the drafts, exposing us to cold gusts of air when we're toasty warm, pink-cheeked, and red-eared. According to our father, our high fevers are always the result of her inattention. If she were more careful, we wouldn't get sick. And so, to punish her, on bitterly cold nights he makes her heat up the iron on the stove and pass it repeatedly over pieces of wool which she then has to drape across our chests and backs beneath our undershirts so the phlegm dries up.

I liked the smell of the hot iron on the wool. My mother would then raise my undershirt and lay the warm fabric across my chest. I can see her now, her lively dark eyes and her thick long lashes hovering over me like butterflies on a mobile over a baby's crib. Her eyes were intense, full of carefully protected ideas and thoughts. For years I struggled to believe that she was lacking in intelligence, that her sole purpose had been to give birth to us, and nothing more. "Women," our father said to educate us, "are just broodmares, good only for foaling." And I believed him. I believed him for a very long time, at least up until 1962, at which time I was already an adult.

Broodmares, that's what he said. I never asked him why. I just watched my mother. She'd never get angry, she'd just sigh as if to say, "Each of us has his cross to bear," and I'd smile weakly at my father when he'd wink knowingly at me while trying to slip his hand up her skirt, and when she frowned and swatted him away, he'd gleefully yell out again, "Broodmare!"

I had no idea what that word meant other than it was not part of the dialect we usually spoke. Back in the winter of 1948, I definitely didn't know what it meant but I intuited that there was a connection between it and the word *cazzo*, a word that my father used repeatedly, both with anger and joy. So I pretended to understand—sure, right, broodmare—if only to avoid having to listen to him explain it all to me down to the last detail, with lots of practical and, to his mind, amusing examples. Knowing certain things about my mother made my stomach turn. Better off agreeing with him; it let me get out of it.

Now I'm walking fast down the hall, I don't feel my arms, legs, torso, or head. I wouldn't know what my body looked like if I bumped into it. All I hear is the loud thumping of my irregularly beating heart induced by the explosive shouting that I hear coming from the kitchen.

I know perfectly well that he's not angry with me and that he'd never hurt me. He often says that: even though he could throttle anyone, he'd never throttle his own children. He thinks of us like one of his feet, a leg, an arm. We are identical to him, he says, we have nothing of our mother. For this reason, I believe we are safe. All it would take for him to lump us with her family would be for one of our fingernails to be unlike his; then he'd no longer consider us his children and beat us up constantly.

That's why I do everything I can at this point in time not to upset him and to resemble him in every way. I run down the hallway like water from a broken pipe, drowning in the dark. I fear the thousands of ghosts who grip my heart, including the pale shadow of Modesta, but even so I resist turning on the light switch. Actually, we may not have had electricity on Via Gemito yet, we may still have used the lights that my grandmother made with a piece of wick in a small bowl of oil, which cast horrifying shadows on reddish walls. They might have cut off the electricity after Rusinè let her relatives steal all our money, especially the money from the Teatro Bellini, which made it impossible for us to pay our bill. But mostly I don't turn on the light switch because I'm afraid he'll yell at me. "With all the lights on in this house, you'd think it was the feast of Piedigrotta!" I'm so afraid of hearing him get angry that I keep the lights off even now: I'm writing in the dark. It's Rusinè who wastes money, not me. I do everything I can to seem unlike her and my grandmother, my mother's brother, and even Giuseppe, my maternal grandfather whom I never even met. He was a tram driver. He died either from an illness or on the job, at the age of twenty-four. Worthless folk, dark-skinned Saracens with low foreheads and none of the Norman traits that Federí and his children (us, in other words) have. Yes, that's right, we descend from the princes of the north, my father explains, because Nor means north and Mann means man. He knows all the languages: German, French, English, and Latin. Subsequently we were Swabian, under the control of Frederick II, Duke of Swabia, artists one and all, he says with that sparkle in his eye, as if to say I am who I am. I am me, me, me.

I do everything I can to look and act the right way at the right time. I'm filled with dread that he'll see something in me that reminds him of them, those deceitful people he got to know in the big room in Saviano, those dullards and beasts. I'm so scared that I shiver to think, just as I'm about to walk in their room to get his cigarettes, that my feet might be different from those of my father, that my hands are different, that my thumb, index finger, and middle finger are all wrong. Now I'm afraid that if I catch a glimpse of myself in the mirror that rests on top of the vanity, illuminated only by a devotional candle to the Madonna of Pompei that casts long shadows, I'll discover I no longer look like the son of that man that sits waiting in the kitchen but like the son of a crocodile, for example. Crocodiles disgust me even more than those shiny black cockroaches that scurry across the floor of our home. I don't want to have the body of a beast and the tongue of a reptile. Sssssss.

In his final years, my father talked about life during wartime in Saviano as if the real enemies were Don Liborio the landlord, my mother's brother, and all those other selfish, parasitic family members who took advantage of his wife. Like Zio Matteo.

Federí described Zio Matteo, who was married to Zia Assunta, of course, as a beefy fellow, around forty-five years old, and a man who knew the lay of the land. All you had to do was take one look at him, he said, and it was clear he knew how and where to find food without the least fear of running into Germans. And yet, strangely, he always came home with little, if not empty-handed. This perturbed my father deeply, so he observed him carefully: he was stocky, had a healthy skin tone, and was always in a good mood. My father suspected that before returning to the big room he either devoured an entire roast chicken in an osteria in town or ate everything he managed to purvey so that he wouldn't have to share it with anyone, not even with his own wife. He was a selfish man, in other words. A selfish piece of shit, my father would say, his anger starting to grow.

He obtained hard proof of Matteo's heartless behavior when, one day, while he was alone in the big room with Rusinè ("So, despite the Germans, everyone else was allowed to go outside? Everyone except you?" I always wanted to ask when I was young but kept quiet so he wouldn't get annoyed or embarrassed), he went and rustled through Zio Matteo and Zia Assunta's wardrobe. Casually though, he said, just for something to do. Actually, it wasn't even rustling. What happened was that he had been talking to Rusinè and he accidentally kicked the wardrobe and the door accidentally opened all by itself. Inside, wrapped in a napkin (my father actually said it was hidden under a napkin), was a two-kilo loaf of bread.

When he found it, he exploded in rage. "And this? What's this?" he screamed at his wife. "It's bread," she said. "And who does it belong to?" he asked. "Zio Matteo," she replied. In other words, that piece of shit; what kind of uncle hides bread in his drawer? Your shitty uncle. My father grabbed the loaf and was about to ravenously break it in two pieces. "No, Federí, it's not ours!" Rusinè screamed and ran over to him. She believed deeply in the notion of mine and yours; she sensed that the bread was for Zia Assunta, her mother's sister and the woman who had raised her, to whom she was deeply grateful. It didn't seem right for her husband to sink his teeth into their bread. She tried to tear it out of his hands and that's when he slapped her.

This was the famous slap that he admitted having given her: the only one in twenty-three years of marriage. In addition to telling me about it verbally, he also wrote about it in his notebook memoirs with pathetic solemnity: "It was the first and last slap I gave her." Moreover, it wasn't even a heavy-handed one, he explained: a little cuff across the cheek, just to teach her. Even if I was present, I couldn't possibly remember it, I would've been too young. But he swore to me that he didn't hurt her. He just

smacked her lightly, just to show her once and for all that when
he made up his mind, no one could stand in his way, not even
his wife. And, as a matter of fact, while a welt of his five fingers
appeared on my mother's cheek, he ran to get a knife, stabbed
the bread forcefully, and cut it into three equal parts. He put
one part back into the wardrobe. He took the other two parts,
one for him and one for his wife, and cut them into eight slices,
rubbed them with garlic, poured some olive oil over them, and
began to eat.

Rusinè started crying uncontrollably, the baby in her arms.
"Here, eat," her husband said to her, repeatedly offering her a
slice, but she wouldn't touch it. She just looked at him glumly.
After a bit, Federí not only started to wave the slices under her
nose so that she could smell it, he also started making silly faces
to get her to laugh. Finally, laughing and crying at the same
time, Rusinè accepted some food. Or at least that's what he
said. Then Zio Matteo came home, looked for his bread, and
only found a third of it. "Where's my loaf of bread?" he asked.
Rusinè sat in silence in the corner, her eyes downcast. The hefty
man turned to my father with a quizzical look. "I ate it with
garlic and oil and enjoyed every bite of it," Federí replied forcefully. "Luckily for you, I was full and left you some. Because if
I had still been hungry, I would've left you shit." Those were
his exact words. Zio Matteo shrugged. "What can I say, Federí?
You did good," he mumbled. He was clearly afraid, my father
said. I think so, too.

As a boy I realized with some unease that I would've been
afraid of someone who behaved and spoke the way Federí did.
He must've seemed like a dangerous man. I imagined my other
uncles and aunts sitting there in that big room: they probably
witnessed the whole scene and, realizing how dangerous he was,
they kept their mouths shut to avoid trouble. Or maybe they
just shut an eye on his terrible ways because they were charmed
by other aspects of his personality: the air of superiority he gave

himself, his amusing banter, the talent and speed with which he could sketch people and things with a stub of a pencil.

Nothing about them charmed him, though. With the passing years, the number and intensity of insults he flung at them only grew: go hang on a power line, you worthless bum. The usual cruel and vituperative stuff. I'd sit and listen in silence— I was always silent, each time for a different reason, until he died—without ever daring to confess that I actually loved those relatives, all of them, and I never accepted the fact that they committed the crimes he attributed them with, not a single one. I had loved them ever since I was a child, but always in secret: Zia Assunta, who looked just like my grandmother, sold fruit and vegetables with Zio Matteo throughout the 1960s; Zia Maria, who limped and was slightly hunchback, had a bar where she sold coffee and pastries that Zio Espedito made in the back; Zia Carmela, who always seemed to be in a good mood, gave us bread rolls stuffed with prosciutto or mortadella or salami and talked as much as her husband, Zio Attilio, was quiet; Zio Peppino, my mother's brother, with whom I would've gladly run away from the obscene language and violence in that house if he had asked me to join him. About them, I recall only their great kindness. There were times I wanted to say to my father in a careful and measured tone, "Now be kind, Papà." Other times, I would've liked to say it sarcastically, sharply: "You know there's something called kindness, Papà!" I wanted to yell at him that it was his own relatives who frightened me, ever since I was small, and not just his father, Nonno Mimí, but also Nonna Filomena, and some of his sisters. This was exactly the opposite of what he wanted us kids to feel and think. But nothing doing: my mother's kind character, in my memory, shed warm sunlight evenly across all her relatives, while my father's belligerence cast long shadows even on relatives that I had never seen but had only heard about. This is why, starting in early adolescence, as hard as I tried to accentuate and demonstrate my similarities with him, I tried equally as hard and in total silence to become like my mother's tribe.

Living on the floor below us in the building in Saviano was another evacuated family: Don Ciccillo the goldsmith, a master engraver of gold and silver, his wife, their daughter, who was the same age as Rusinè, their nineteen-year-old son, and their friendly and savvy fourteen-year-old son, who traveled to Naples whenever his father needed to buy or sell something.

Don Ciccillo was someone you could talk to. He wasn't blind or deaf to artistic sentiments like the rest of the people in that building. Every so often, and with great caution, my father would go and pay him a visit. He always found him at his workbench, a magnifying lens in one eye, dexterously handling tiny tools and appliances: miniature hammers and tweezers, scrapers and chisels, blades and hooks. During the course of their conversations, Federí managed to inform the goldsmith that he worked for the railroad purely by chance, but that, in actual fact, he was an artist and master draftsman. Don Ciccillo did not react and just said "Bravo." But then one day, he unexpectedly came to see my father in the big room with two shiny silver spheres at least forty centimeters in diameter. He explained that he had received an order from Naples for two globes; such things were still being commissioned despite the war, it was an urgent job, and they had to be delivered in five days. "If you truly are an artist," he said, handing him the spheres, "would you mind sketching the continents for me on them, the way they were when America was discovered?"

No problem. My father drew him the continents in the blink of an eye, leaving the goldsmith stunned. And he did it solely because he wanted to—I believed him, I still believe him—and not because he was thinking about money. For him, it was more important to use his talent; only afterwards came the thought of money. Even so, Don Ciccillo, who was a generous man, gave him 1,200 lire. My father, seeing that the goldsmith was now more kindly disposed toward him, asked if he could watch while he used the scribe, and the jeweler agreed. Federí watched for a bit and then, seeing how he was one of those people who swiftly understands art and how things work, claimed that he understood and that, if he was given the chance, he'd know how to do it. Don Ciccillo smiled skeptically and handed him the tool. With a steady hand, my father engraved a few caravels and zephyrs with chubby cheeks puffing wind into the sails. Amazing work. From that, my father earned an additional 3,000 lire, even more admiration, and the privilege of learning a secret: the goldsmith told him that people with his talent could make good money in Naples by reproducing and selling fake antiques to the liberators for astronomical prices. He, Don Ciccillo, was already doing it; would Federí like to collaborate with him?

The goldsmith's offer seemed like a turning point and fired up his imagination. In it he saw payback: a chance to prove that, thanks to his talents, they could eat well every single day. Moreover, he'd have the pleasure of using his imagination and working with his eyes and hands. To hell with everyone who refused to acknowledge his potential. They only understood money, damn bastards. Well, here's the cash: 4,200 lire from Don Ciccillo, which Rusinè immediately went and spent on the black market to buy food. For everyone, naturally. How else could he show off his skills if he didn't tie them to his generosity?

And so he got to work, planning and executing all sorts of projects, chiseling away at tons of old junk to sell to the liberators. It didn't take long before he had something to show: strong pieces with imaginative touches. Don Ciccillo's fourteen-year-old son even made a few trips to Naples to get a feel for the market. But unfortunately, the euphoria was short-lived. Just when everything seemed to be going well, the dark cloud of war fell over Saviano and *buonanotte* art.

In 1948 and for some time thereafter, I often pretended to be dead. Dead people had a hold over me even though I hadn't yet seen a real cadaver, excluding (maybe) that of Modesta, in Savignano. I had often heard distant machine-gun fire, that yes, and the whine of howitzer bombs and faraway explosions, but dead people, none. I must have heard people talking about them, though, because as I make my way down the hall from the kitchen, my imagination is filled with cadavers, though none seen firsthand. All the images were spawned by other people's stories and fortified by our games; the cadavers are all young, good looking, and awfully bloody.

When I play with my brother in the hall, at some point I always kill him. First, I slay that poor, dark-haired, and bright-eyed Abel, who never wants to do what I say, and so I shoot him dead. And then I die. The battlefield is vast and littered with lifeless corpses. When I walk down the hall at night, I always see, in addition to young Aunt Modesta's ghost, dead young men, slack-jawed, eyes staring emptily into space.

Tonight there's a crowd of them. To get to my parents' bedroom, I have to walk past the front door, on the other side of which are the stairs that lead down to the street, the sounds of which echo upstairs. Reinforcing the door, and protecting us from all dangers, is an iron shaft that hangs from a ring cemented into the wall and that hooks through a metal eye fixed to the door. This shaft is an important element of our games. We grab it and hang off it, we writhe in pain with our heads lolling forward, we claw at the air, kick out at the emptiness; we do battle with the powers that want to steal us away. All imaginable evil comes to a head in this particular spot, trying with great enmity to overwhelm us. But we resist. We howl and holler and, even as the most monstrous forces try and pry our hands from that shaft, we never give up, we keep on fighting. Only when the game is almost finished do we lose our lives: first Geppe, because he's younger, and then me, because I'm older. We rarely survive. Even when it might look like we're going to make it, we're swallowed up by catastrophe. I made up that rule myself. I'm the oldest. If it was up to Geppe, he'd always survive. But, I say knowingly—and I will continue to say for as long as we are children—lying dead in a pool of our blood is better.

It's all talk, of course. When I rush down the hall, I keep my eyes glued to the ground, I don't want to see the cadavers that our games have scattered across the floor. I especially don't want to see our enemies who are still standing by the door, next to the iron shaft. They're horrible and they hate children most of all.

One afternoon, my father was playing briscola in the big room. He was cussing and slapping down his cards while simultaneously crowing about nearly everything. For example, the Germans. He just couldn't resist: his sympathies for the German forces always came to the surface. He felt closer to them than to the relatives and neighbors with whom he was forced to live and play cards. As for the liberators, assuming that they did actually liberate us, he considered them dirty bastards good only for buying Don Ciccillo's fake antiques.

As a kid, I was well aware of his nuanced admiration for Hitler's soldiers. Maybe he just liked their uniforms better, I told myself uneasily. He definitely appreciated their features, unlike those of Negroes and Levantines, as he called them. He was confident that he was more physically similar to the Germans than to his very own brother-in-law Peppino. "The Germans are a great people," he enjoyed saying; he thought they were kind, polite, and had a rich language, which he avidly started studying when he was a Marconi-radio operator in France. And what's more, he went on, they were big, tall, well-proportioned men, not scrawny pieces of shit. They were strong soldiers: they fought without whining and with great tactical and strategical rigor. He learned this firsthand in Menton, when living shoulder to shoulder with them, and later, when he was in Russia, during that terrible time, what a terrible loss, he said. Sure, it's true, back then they were dangerous for us Italians. But, let's be frank, weren't the so-called liberators just as dangerous?

The so-called liberators—he explained in order to educate me on the realities of the most recent world war—were responsible for bringing the horrors of that global conflict to the small town of Saviano, which had been spared until one day in September between five and six in the evening. He recalled it perfectly, as if it had just happened. They were playing briscola when they heard airplanes flying overhead: Mustangs, he said knowingly. This fact didn't worry him too much. It happened every day. The so-called liberators were probably on their way to bomb Naples. But then the machine-gun fire started up and after a number of rounds there was a deathly silence. Their blood ran cold. There was not a sound, not a single voice. Their generally bustling neighborhood had gone quiet.

Suddenly they heard screaming coming from the main road. All the women in the house—my mother, my grandmother, my grandmother's sisters—started howling without even knowing why, madly, only because they heard the horror in those other, savage screams. "Hurry! The train! They're all dead!" women screamed from down the street and alley. The air was torn apart with the sickening sound of wailing and shouting, shouting and wailing.

Don Ciccillo the goldsmith rushed into the room, as white as chalk. "Those bastard liberators shot everyone on the train that just pulled in to the station," he said. It was the Nola–Baiano train, filled with kids. Those bastards, my father went on to say, had machine-gunned them all. Don Ciccillo started pleading with the *padreterno*—God, oh God, Heavenly God—and praying that his fourteen-year-old boy was not on that train. His son had gone to Naples early that morning dressed in a pair of factory worker's overalls to deliver some fakes that my father had helped create. They sent him because, since he was young, he didn't risk being arrested by the Germans. Other people reasoned the same way: the train was always crowded with youngsters on errands for their families. They thought they would be safe precisely because of their young age. Instead, for Chrissakes, the liberators were hellbent on killing our babies.

My father, who had been so careful about staying in hiding all that time, rushed outside with Don Ciccillo the goldsmith to help look for his son. He ran off ahead, while Don Ciccillo lagged behind. Don Ciccillo's other son and a young man named Alessandro, who was a regular in their card games, came with them. Usually, though, when my father told the story, he made himself out to be the protagonist and sometimes even forgot to include the goldsmith. Consequently, I have no idea where the other men in the family were; the images are confused. For example, I can't help but see young Zio Peppino making his way through the bloody corpses. Or, after the whole neighborhood was bombed, how he ran out of the rubble of the factory where he worked, in Pomigliano d'Arco, all covered in dust, even in his hair and eyelashes. But maybe I'm confusing Nonna Nannina's story, who always made her son out to be the main character, with my father's, in which he was the main actor. To avoid confusing things, I choose to follow my father.

So, there we are on the main road, heading toward Sant'Arpino, and it was complete bedlam, people were running to the train tracks from all directions. When they got to the cemetery, my father and Don Ciccillo encountered a cart full of bodies with two men standing in the middle. One man picked up a cadaver by the arms and the other took its feet; after swinging it from side to side, they heaved it over the cemetery wall. My father and Don Ciccillo went and examined all the bodies on the other side of the wall, but didn't see anyone in GIL factory overalls. In other words, Don Ciccillo's son wasn't among them. Heartened, they rushed on toward the Sirico well, where the train had come to a halt. On the way they encountered four more carts of bodies, but still no trace of Don Ciccillo's son. The only place left to look was on the train, to go through car after car. When they reached it, Don Ciccillo stopped and threw up. My father leapt aboard and made his way quickly through the cars. There were still a lot of youngsters sitting on the wooden benches. It was as if they were sleeping, some of them with chins resting on their chests, others with heads tipped back and mouths wide open. The majority of them were leaning one against the other, as if they had jumped up to escape the bullets and been shot down, one after the other. A girl sat with her head resting against the window, her open eyes looking out at the countryside. There was moaning and chaos. "It's alright, signorina, it's over now," my father said but she didn't move. That's when Don Ciccillo started screaming. He had found his son. He lay face down on the floor of the train between two benches, his overalls soaked with blood. A bullet had been fired into his shoulder and had come out his clavicle. He had just died, bled to death. When his father eventually calmed down, he refused all help and, even though he was a small and scrawny man, he picked up his boy, and carried him in his arms all the way back to the building, where he laid him down on their double bed. That's when the story starts to fade. Liberators?—my father concluded with a certain smugness—what liberators?

The Germans, who had never set foot in Saviano, arrived the day after the train massacre. According to Federí, there was nothing particularly ferocious about them. Sure, they were saboteurs, but young ones, he emphasized. As a boy, I could imagine their youthful faces peeking out from under their helmets, looking through the crosshairs of their assault rifles. And since, with respect to the series of images that the head of household evoked, they came on stage after the train massacre and also not long after the words he spoke to explain away Modesta's death, I came to feel that they—the German soldiers—were not particularly dangerous, but themselves in danger, just like their Italian counterparts who had been killed by the liberators: vulnerable to death the same way that my seventeen-year-old aunt had been before her unfortunate demise.

And so, without realizing it, I adopted my father's sympathies. It was only over time (much later, during my wretched adolescence and especially in 1958, 1959, and 1960) that I started to suspect there was an underlying plan to that contiguity. At times I still think it, especially when I leaf through the pages of his notebook, and notice how he relies less on voice and more on images, how he visualizes that connection, spurring the doubt that it was all calculated. But then I say to myself, no, maybe there was no grand scheme. There was only his sense of all things being related, the need to connect things with a line as demanded by the composition. A visual exercise, nothing more.

And so, here come the Germans. Youthful, beardless, under the command of a man of about forty. They made their way through the town with the goal of looting. Or of exacting justice, at least the little bit that would have satisfied my father, who once again was shut in the big room. There were three of them: him, that Alessandro fellow, and Peppino, his wife's brother.

This time it was Don Liborio, the owner of that stinking room—not to mention the owner of cattle, sacks of flour, salamis, prosciuttos, and cheeses; the man who had made them suffer the darkest days of hunger; the man who had refused to harness his horse to his barouche claiming that the wheels were old and rickety—who came breathlessly rushing in. The Germans, the Germans, he screamed, dragging his son along with him. "You have to help me," he begged my father, Alessandro, and Peppino. The Germans would take all his belongings. The three of them had to take up weapons. They all needed to shoot the Germans. "All of us," he insisted.

My father turned to him coldly. "Us? If you want to shoot them, Don Libò, go right ahead. After all, they're your belongings. *You* have to shoot the Germans, *your son* has to shoot them.

Why should we get involved?" Alessandro also chimed in. "Don Libò, our problem is not to save your stuff. Our problem is to save ourselves. So, please just fuck off." More or less, that's what he said.

Don Libò and his son ran off into the countryside, followed by Peppino, my mother's brother, who went into hiding at the mere sound of the word "Germans," forgetting all about his mother, sister, nephew, friends, and relatives of second or third degree, leaving my father alone to look after all the women and children.

I don't know how he managed to protect us. He never talked much about it. Maybe he hid us under the bed, in the wardrobes, or in the basement. I simply don't know. The fact is that on that occasion, when the young German saboteurs showed up, none of us were around: not my mother, not my grandmother, not me, not a single relative, not even Alessandro. Only he, the man who didn't flee, witnessed what happened next (and he quickly realized that the saboteurs were hunting for provisions and not men). He hid and watched the truck advance slowly down the street, led by the forty-year-old officer.

When they reached Don Liborio's house, the officer made a motion to halt. He was not evil, he was not despotic, he didn't shout commands like a Nazi. Actually, my father made him seem nice and noticed the look of fucking terror on the man's weary face.

The officer tells his young soldiers to go retrieve whatever they can find. The soldiers, six in all, obey. They break down the front door and make their way through Don Liborio's courtyard, grabbing two pigs and a calf, and hoist them up onto the bed of the truck. Then two young rear guards come out of the cellar. My father observes them carefully. They retreat cautiously toward the truck, their Mausers extended, each of them carrying two hocks of prosciutto over their left shoulders. All things that Don Liborio the landlord had kept for himself and his family, without the least bit of humanity. The Germans do good to steal it all from him.

As a child, I listened on the edge of my seat and, honestly, I always hoped that he'd choose to forgive Don Liborio and step out and defend him at the very last minute. I always wanted him to pick up a rifle and start shooting. I wanted him to fight and die, independently of the fact that he was telling the story and so, obviously, was alive. But no, he always managed to bring his stories full circle, and always to his advantage. Apparently, Don Liborio's old wife, who had stayed home and watched in desperation as the Germans had run off with all their belongings, pleaded with my father not to abandon her on her own. Poor old, frightened woman. Of course, Federí took care of her. And in the days to follow, to make sure he didn't leave her alone, she fed him, and abundantly: morning, afternoon, and night. "Eat, eat," she said. "My husband is crazy, he wanted to shoot them, that bastard. Eat up. Better you eat it than the Germans." And when Don Liborio eventually returned home from the countryside, scowling with rage, his hunting rifle slung over his shoulder, and didn't even greet them, his wife continued to give my father food as a way of getting back at her husband. Because of this, my mother regained some color and consequently so did I, thanks to her milk. And things went back—at least temporarily—to going badly for the selfish and well for the truly generous among us. Which is how he saw himself. And he often said as much, explaining to those who refused to understand that if every so often he had taken two steps back it was not out of cowardice but because of his net repulsion for all forms of opportunism; it was all thanks to his artist's dispassionate gaze that could x-ray situations instantly and allow him to say, "Well, would you look at these pieces of shit."

Federí enjoyed saying that he could see more clearly into the future than other people. I think he enjoyed talking about the past not so much out of love for the story itself, but to be able to show that, already halfway through the event, he knew how it would all end. He considered himself a prophet, and believed that he always knew what would happen.

He often spoke about his strong eyesight with enthusiasm. "Twenty-twenty," he said, underscoring his perfect vision. He was so proud of it that when I first started to see poorly and then downright badly—all fuzzy—I hid it from him for a long time; I thought he'd consider it an embarrassing disability, and then there was the cost of the eyeglasses themselves, which would have made him furious. Until I was forced to confess my myopia (at around the age of sixteen, when everything was a complete fog), I discreetly studied all the writing in the shop windows on Via Gemito, large and small, so that every time he wanted to have a competition to see who had better eyesight, I'd rattle them off by heart. "Twenty-twenty," he'd say with deep satisfaction. "You got that from me."

He was pleased not only to see faraway objects with perfect clarity and in all detail, he was also proud of having what he called a good eye for things. "Having a good eye," he said, "is an artist's gift." He went on to explain that all he needed was one look to capture and memorize everything, both what is evident immediately, and that which is hidden behind appearances. "Colors, above all," he said. "I've always seen colors in all their shades, not like people who just see red or blue or black or white." He knew how to look. "Things," he explained, "play hide-and-seek in the general chaos of life." If you look carefully, he said, colors conceal more than reveal. So the artist actually has two jobs: first, to understand with his eye what the real colors of things are, and not be deceived; and secondly, to arrange them on the canvas in just the right way.

Before I turned ten, sometimes he'd call me over and say, "Come here, and I'll teach you the names of colors." I'd go and stand next to him at the easel. On the floor he had an ugly old wooden crate in which he kept his rags and tubes of all sizes. The rags were often stiff with dried paint and thinner, the tubes were rarely full and shiny, usually they had been squeezed out, all the way to their screw-tops. A piece of plywood rested across one corner of the crate on which sat a carafe for his brushes, spatulas, and a jackknife that we were absolutely forbidden to touch. He also used the plywood like a palette, squeezing his colors onto it before beginning to paint. "This," he said, sticking his hand into the crate and pulling them out one at a time, "is yellow ochre. This is carmine. This is burnt sienna. This is Prussian blue. This is emerald green. And this is ultramarine." Each time he picked one up, he'd squeeze a little bit out onto the plywood. Sometimes he got annoyed and would have to use the knife to slice into the tube so he could scrape out the last tiny bit of paint.

I loved the smell of his paints, turpentine, and thinner. Back then I also loved the sound of the names, they were so deeply imaginative: ochre, carmine, burnt sienna, umber, emerald green, Prussian blue, ultramarine. Especially ultramarine: it spoke of vast ocean storms. His impassioned voice made the brief experience feel like a great adventure, all contained in a single smear of blue on the plywood.

But then the lesson was over. Once his palette was ready, which didn't take too long, his speech slowed. He'd start to stare at the canvas, forgetting that he had ever called me over. Maybe he was using his artist's vision. Better not disturb him, I'd think to myself, uncertain about what to do next. I was worried that if I left he'd think I was no longer interested in his lesson and be offended. But if I stayed I was concerned I might bother him. "What're you doing here?" he might ask.

The truth is that when he remembered that I was standing next to him, he was happy. He'd smoke and paint and talk. "Kid, never outline things in black." At that point in time he was certain that anyone who used black didn't know how to paint. Then he changed his mind, something he did often, just out of curiosity. He even started saying positive things about Cézanne, and admitted that when he was young he knew too little about painting to be able to appreciate his work. Back then I believed that everything that came out of his mouth was conclusive. So when he said, "No black paint," I thought, "No black paint."

How could I possibly doubt him? An artist isn't allowed to make mistakes, he used to say. Above all, he can't be duped, in no circumstance, ever. All it takes is one look and an artist can see meaning behind things and the true nature of people. He saw you and painted you the way you were: if you were a piece of shit—and for him most people were—he knew it straight away: this guy's a piece of shit.

When a group of liberators arrived in Saviano in their armored cars, he immediately knew how things would play out.

It started with the church bells ringing festively. The townspeople spilled out into the streets, some of them carrying pitchforks, other carrying hoes or shovels, many wearing red kerchiefs around their necks. The first one to step out of the building was Don Liborio, his rifle slung over his shoulder, and not far behind him were all my mother's relatives, including her brother Peppino, in all likelihood. They hung off the tank turrets like orangutangs, they laughed and threw flowers, hollered and fired their guns into the air.

My father went and watched but remained skeptical. He didn't want to mix with the crowd, he thought of himself as an individualist, and he didn't believe that the Germans would leave quite so easily. So he stood off to one side: tall, with his intelligent forehead, and me in his arms. Next to him stood Rusinè, his mother-in-law, and his mother-in-law's mother (my great-grandmother, who was seventy-two years old at the time).

The liberators marched through Saviano toward Nola. Slowly, the festivities came to an end. My father started walking home, his seven-month-old baby in his arms, his wife in good cheer, his mother-in-law and my great-grandmother chatting away, when suddenly came the furious sound of machine-guns from Nola.

Then, in reply, there was the long sound of something whistling through the air, the curved trajectory of a howitzer projectile that flew past his head, my head, and the head of the three women toward Naples. Then: ka-boom! ka-boom! more explosions and general chaos and people running about. The Allied forces' tanks started retreating, their cannons fired dozens of projectiles that sliced through the air; Peppino ran off and left his mother behind; Espedito, Attilio, and Matteo bolted; their wives, whether agile or limping, hurried after them; Don Liborio fled into a field with his useless weapon; everyone thought only of saving their own skin.

My father, no. He was ready for it. With his fast reflexes, he threw Rusinè and me into a ditch along the side of the road and leapt on top of us to protect us with his body. True, mother-in-law and great-grandmother were left vulnerable. Mary, mother of God, help us! they cried out and begged my father to protect them, too. But he had to shield us first of all, and would only think about them after. And, as a matter of fact, when the first round of fighting stopped, he leapt out, yanked us out of the ditch and rushed toward a nearby refuge, dragging the two matriarchs behind him.

And just in time, too, because soon they started shelling in the direction of Naples again. My father later discovered and recounted smugly that the young German saboteurs who had sacked Don Liborio's house some days earlier were to blame. The courageous young men had chopped down all the plane trees from Saviano to Nola, letting them fall across the road, making it impossible for the so-called liberators to pass. And even more: they fired their Panzerfaust onto the Allied Crusaders that wanted to occupy Nola and forced them to retreat. German soldiers are hard-to-skin cats, he said. He had warned everyone. The next day, to flush them out of hiding, the so-called liberators sent in cannon fodder to Saviano: Indians, Moroccans, and Blacks.

According to my father, Blacks were ugly and looked like horny chimpanzees. His obsession with them began when he first saw them in Saviano. He wouldn't let his wife out of the house unless she was escorted by him or another man from the family. She should never accept anything from those people: no cigarettes, gifts of any kind, or chocolates. He threatened her that there'd be trouble if she had any kind of contact or even exchanged looks with those beasts. They only had one thing on their mind: screwing.

Screwing! he screamed. With no distinction for sex or age. Blacks wanted to screw women, men, and children. That's right, even children. The younger they were, the more they wanted to screw them. Since, at the time, I was less than a year old, I was at risk too, and my mother had to keep me by her side at all times. He told her—especially later on, when we lived on Via Zara—to keep her eyes open, always. He nagged and harassed his brother Antonio and Peppino about it, too. Blacks could break down doors, climb through windows, appear at any moment behind the military blanket that hung in place of the wall that had been razed in July, 1943.

Antonio and Peppino just shrugged. Sometimes they laughed, sometimes they egged him on. "Alright, Federí, so what should we do if Blacks break in? What would you do?" My father, they said—and they often told this story—would start to glower at the mere thought, then begin to swear, and finally he'd get so furious that it was as if Blacks had actually broken in. When I'd start to cry in fear, he'd just get angrier and punch the air around him with his fists. "I'd kill them all," he'd scream.

One day, Antonio and Peppino, who had become fast friends, decided to play a trick on him. My mother begged them not to (Federí's dangerous, he's crazy, she said) but they went ahead just the same. Antonio painted his face with black shoe polish, fashioned a turban out of some rags and basically made himself look like an Indian from the British army. Then they waited for my father to return from the Teatro Bellini. When they saw him coming down the street and heard him in the stairwell, Peppino rushed out of the apartment and yelled, "Federí! Hurry!" He told him that a Black man had broken in and was in the bedroom with Rusinè and the child.

My father's beady eyes grew wide with horror. "Peppino, what the hell are you saying?" he screamed and ran inside, threw open the bedroom door, saw the Indian man in his turban, and jumped on him, intending to choke him. "It's me! Federí, it's me!" Antonio cried. "Let him go! It's just your brother!" my mother called out. Peppino tried to pull his brother-in-law off Antonio. "Let him go. It was just a joke," Peppino said, but my father continued to kick and punch and roar, his eyes blazing like an assassin. Humor was the last thing on his mind.

I could easily imagine his face—that expression of terror, the desire to kill—when Zio Antonio and Zio Peppino told the story. It was horrifying. A vein on his forehead bulged, his black hair was messy, he bared his long teeth, and flared his nostrils. He was intent on choking Antonio because he didn't recognize him; he couldn't possibly recognize him. In those few seconds the truth lay in the color of the shoe polish and not in his brother's features.

When my two uncles told the story, they shook their heads in amazement, even after a number of years had gone by, but as the story went on their mood soured. When my father was present, he'd look at them annoyed and they'd just slap him on the back. "This old bastard. He was about to throttle me," Zio Antonio would say. But when my father wasn't around, the story never actually came to an end. No one wiped their face clean, no one laughed or hugged or said, "What a great joke." That costume foreshadowed another, more serious story, one that wasn't funny in the slightest, and it began when Zio Antonio, I think it was, or maybe Zio Peppino, or possibly both, went out for a walk with my mother.

Rusinè was wearing a pretty, floral dress and I had also been dressed up for the occasion. As usual, she carried me in her arms, teaching me the names of things around us and listening to me repeat them back to her. Apparently, at one point I started fussing, kicking and screaming and yelling, and then laughing, and reaching out toward something or someone behind us. She turned around. Zio Antonio turned around, too. And if Zio Peppino was there, he also turned around.

Walking behind us were a few American soldiers: maybe two, possibly three, maybe white, possibly Black. They were clowning around and making silly faces, sticking their tongues out, and trying to make me laugh. They offered me a small bar of chocolate. "No, no," Zio Antonio said. But apparently, I grabbed it even though my mother scolded me. "Let go, immediately," she ordered me, but I did not. Actually, I kicked and screamed and took a second one. "Tenk u," Zio Antonio said, "Bye bye." And we strode off in one direction and the American soldiers went in another.

Apparently, at this point in the story, my father's brother started to get worried. "Throw them away. Or let's just eat them. Or maybe I should hide them," he recalls having said to my mother. Her reaction, to this day, is incomprehensible to me. "Why?" she asked. She wanted to save a bar. It was as if she was embarrassed to admit to her brother-in-law that it wasn't safe to bring home the chocolate, as if she wasn't used to hiding things from Federí, as if it was disrespectful. Or maybe she just hoped that this time her husband would be less unreasonable than others.

The fact is that when my father came home that evening he found the chocolate bar sitting in plain sight on the table. "What's this?" he asked. My mother told him about the American soldiers on the street. She spoke with the tone of someone who was relaying a pleasant fact or a cheerful event, but then she had to stop.

That's usually where Zio Antonio and even Zio Peppino stopped telling the story, too. They'd shake their heads as if they hadn't been able to do a thing about it, it was pointless to try and reason with my father about certain things. Heaven help them, they just couldn't hold him down. He refused to listen, he wouldn't believe that I had been the one to take the chocolate bar, me, his first-born child, at less than one year old. And so he accused her, he insulted, humiliated, and hit her. "You," he screamed at my mother, "you attracted their attention, you flirted with them." He said she was worse than any of those floozies from Capodichino that all the Blacks chased after. "You have no idea what they do!" he screamed at her. "Those floozies from Capodichino go and make love with Moroccans, and then the Moroccans beat them, they beat them to death." That's what he said. Whores, all of them. They pussy whip them, then pistol whip them.

But all that took place much later, when we lived in Naples. In Saviano, when the Blacks first arrived, he merely said, "You're not allowed to go out, Rusinè." Then he'd go out and practice his English with them. He discovered that he knew it better than the apostles who received the gift of languages from the Holy Spirit. He spoke fluent English, and thanks to that, he was able to enjoy a new phase of life, one with a hint of internationalism. To hell with all those relatives who never believed in him and who now stared at him with mouths open wide while he chatted about this and that with the Black liberators, hoping to trick or swindle them somehow.

To hell with the people in the town and especially Don Liborio, who stood around with his rifle slung over his shoulder like a partisan. A partisan *di questo cazzo*.

A large majority of earthly things, once mentioned by my father, became the undisputed private property *di questo cazzo*, of his cock, this cock, which he not only mentioned eagerly and in various manners, but gestured at energetically, his two hands converging like an arrow sign toward his crotch and genitals.

He used that turn of phrase often. It was one of his favorites. And he's using it now, in dialect, shouting, his voice trembling with rage, in the kitchen in the house on Via Gemito. "Debts *di questo cazzo!*" I recall him yelling those words as if it was a minute ago, although today I have no idea what he might have screamed either before or after. It was just another argument, like so many that had taken place and so many yet to come. It was pointless trying to dig. Years ago, when I started jotting down some notes to help me find clarity on the events related to the peacock, I spent a lot of time thinking about Federí's "debts *di questo cazzo.*" I wanted to understand that five-year-old kid, the origins of his anxiety as he was about to set foot in his parents' bedroom. Both amused and not, I tried to understand how that phrase, when expressed in relation to other everyday words—my uncle, the liberators, partisans, or debts—impacted that child's still-developing brain. But it was pointless, I had to give up. It's absurd to try and go back and experience the very first scratch that words make on us. I opted instead to concentrate on the arrangement of the furniture in the bedroom so that I could at least have a clear picture of where and how the child moved through space.

Sketching a floor plan of a room where I once lived is an act that soothes me, a kind of sedative for the phantasmagories of the past. I got to work. I quickly marked the position of the double bed, the wardrobe, the desk, the vanity, and the window behind it, which must have been open, I realized, but not because I have a clear memory of it being open. Actually, in that precise instant, even though I saw an open window while I was tracing the lines that formed the shape of the room on a piece of paper, I'd never be able to swear that, on that freezing cold night of 1948, the window was really open. A sensation just suddenly came to me, a clear childhood memory of fresh air, a night breeze, not the stale air of cigarettes or bodies or oil paints, but damp air that smelled of leaves, trees, and lowing animals. Howling dogs. Nocturnal animals shrieking in agony. A bird. The crowing of roosters—I was soon carried away by an absurd flow of words—hens, chicks, capons, cockerel, this cock, that cock, cuckoo clock, punch the clock.

Not long after, I wadded up the paper into a ball, shut my dictionaries, gave up on all my objective attempts at recreating a topographical map of the room. In the past few years, such things often happened. I'd go to great lengths to pick up the thread of the story and for a while it even felt like I had found it, and I'd try so very hard not to let it go. But then, if I tugged at it from one direction, my father—either in person or his shadow or what I carry of him inside me—tugged at it from the other. He always had important things to tell me, things to add and clarify. I'd try for days and days to stay on the path. "I was here," I'd clarify to myself, trying to give spatial solidity to the story and thus resist. "I stood here, on the threshold to the bedroom; my grandmother was in the kitchen, sitting near the table, rocking Tonino back and forth in her chair, and singing him a lullaby so he'd fall asleep; my mother and brother, Geppe, were sitting at the table." I tried to see them clearly, I created a space for them where they could tell me what they were doing and feeling. But it was pointless, my father stepped in, overbearing as usual. Maybe by then he had already noisily scraped back his chair from the table. Maybe by then he was already standing and shouting at my mother: "Are you listening to me? Or am I just pissing in the wind?" And so I thought it best just to give up, and give up on myself, too, standing there in the doorway to their bedroom, feeling that gust of cool night air, and so I rested my forehead on my desk for a little bit, as if bowled over by low blood pressure, and surrendered to the sound of his voice.

Because what meaning did I have without him? My experience of that night was significant only if I didn't lose sight of him. I didn't want him to say to me, albeit in a playful way, "Are you listening, Mimí, or am I just pissing in the wind?" He'd say that especially when he started in on the topic of money and I got distracted. "Listen up," he'd say noticing my distracted look, "I always knew how to make money. If I had had a different wife," he'd yell theatrically, "who knows what I might have achieved." And then he'd start complaining how hard he had worked to earn his money, and how Rusinè had squandered it all.

That's where it always started. The spark for arguments was always tied to that subject. His anger grew confusedly: he worried that his wife thought of him as a man with his head in the clouds, lacking in common sense and the audaciousness needed to make money; he'd insist that he knew how to make money, that he had common sense, and that he'd proved it to her on numerous occasions, in particular at the Teatro Bellini; he'd scream that if they didn't have money it was because she had given away everything that he had worked so hard to earn. After a number of broken dishes, threats, and other domestic disturbances, the anger drained out of Federí and he was left face to face with the real reason he constantly wanted to argue: he was unhappy. He was filled with unarticulated and ever-present desperation. Sometimes, when the arguing ended, he'd break down in tears.

By the end of their time in Saviano, he started dealing in meat. He invested 3,000 lire in it, money he may have earned from work done for Don Ciccillo the goldsmith. But to sell his product, he needed to go to Naples, and that wasn't easy. The Napoli–Nola–Baiano line was out of commission. You could get a ride in one of the Bianchi Miles trucks that the local Camorra gang had stolen, charging passengers 2,000 lire each way, which was what a used Fiat Topolino would have cost until not much earlier. And even if you had the cash, you weren't guaranteed a spot. You had to kick, fight, and bribe your way aboard.

Now, it's true, he had been a boxer, he had trained with the European champion Bruno Frattini and, when needed, he'd gladly put up his dukes. But why give those gangsters two of his

3,000 lire? He decided to ask Zio Espedito to loan him the old bicycle that he used for his pastry business. When Zio Espedito didn't want to give it to him, saying that he needed it for work, Federí took it away with force, with no further discussion. The bicycle originally belonged to Rusinè's brother and since he and Rusinè were married, he had more right to use it than Zio Espedito, and that was that.

Butchers butchered animals at night, and in out-of-the-way places, afraid that both policemen and mobsters would show up from one moment to the next and steal everything from them. Policemen and mobsters did this to people who traveled to Naples to sell goods, too. If they found out what you were doing, they'd steal your stuff and crack your skull. My father knew how to handle it. He rode the bike deep into the woods, nightbirds warbling and chirping around him, until he found a butcher. He handed over his 3,000 lire and came home with eight kilos of meat. To trick any potential thieves, he ordered his wife to make waterproof sacks for the meat, which he then tied around his body, under his clothes: two down his back, two on his chest, two on his calves, and two on his thighs. The meat was freezing cold and he thought he was going to die, both from the chill and the disgust, but he mustered up his courage, said farewell to Rusinè and his son, and left for Naples. He pedaled as hard as he could so that thieves wouldn't be able to stop him. He pedaled with such a ferocious expression on his face that both police and gangsters steered clear of him. In fact, no one even said hello.

Once he got to the city, uncertain of whom to contact, he decided to call on an ex-comrade in arms, Vincenzo Mirullo, a man who was full of initiative. The two soldiers had traveled to Italy together in 1942, both on leave to get married, but Mirullo proved to be a shrewd one: after his wedding he managed to stay on in Naples by declaring he had chlamydia, while Federí had to return to his post as radio-operator in Menton.

He found him at home in a *basso* on Corso Garibaldi and

showed him the sacks of meat that he was wearing. Mirullo was thrilled. "Federí, you're so courageous, well done. This is pure gold," Mirullo exclaimed. He proved to be extremely well-organized. He already had a scale that was calibrated at 900 grams for one kilo, which his mother used for selling various goods on the streets of the Borgo Sant'Antonio Abate neighborhood, consistently beating out her competition by charging less but tricking people with the weight. For example, she'd charge 1,600 lire/kilo for meat when local butchers charged 1,800 lire/kilo. Mirullo hollered for his mother, a kind-looking elderly lady. "Ma, how much can we make with eight kilos of meat?" he asked her. "13,500 lire," she replied. Since they were friends, Mirullo took all the meat and gave Federí 9,000 lire plus three kilos of spaghetti. "Bring me more meat tomorrow, Federí," Mirullo said as they shook on the deal.

See? There's your proof—he'd yell at Rusinè during the course of an argument—that he was just as good at the practical side of things as he was at the theoretical side, especially if risks were involved, because risks galvanized him. Sure, once he proved he could do something, he often quit, but it was not due to laziness; he quit because he had to do something else. He couldn't possibly keep pedaling down the regional highway as if he was some kind of Matteo, Attilio, Espedito, or Peppino; he was different, he had a good head on his shoulders. "Why the hell am I carrying beef on my back and strapped to my legs?" he thought as he stood to pedal up each of the hills. "I can't be wasting my time and energy like this." He started complaining and was unhappy. For two or three days he made the trip back and forth, buying and selling, from Saviano to Naples, from Naples to Saviano, twenty kilometers each way. Then he started to lose interest. Between the perspiration and the cold meat on his back, he was scared he'd catch pneumonia. There had to be a better way for him to put food on the table for his family. He thought and thought about it, and then decided to quit. He gave the bicycle back to Zio Espedito, left me and my mother in Saviano, and went to live in Naples, in his father's bombed-out house on Via Zara. He was certain there were endless opportunities in the city. He wanted to find one of those jobs where the people in charge would immediately recognize his talent and say, "For Chrissakes, it's Don Federí: we've been waiting for you, please come in."

Antonio and Peppino went to Naples, too. All three of them went to the employment office in Piazza Carità. His brother and brother-in-law were hired immediately as manual laborers and were sent to work at a building site in Poggioreale, run by Blacks. My father refused to be a manual laborer and work for Blacks. He applied for a job as an interpreter. That line of work seemed well-suited to him. But after waiting in a long line, when it was finally his turn, they said, "No interpreters. Finished."

So no work. No work for days on end. He stubbornly kept going back and applying for the job as interpreter, and the people in charge kept sending him away, always saying no interpreters, finished. In the meantime, Antonio and Peppino slaved away all day but seemed carefree and happy. When they came back at night with potatoes, sticks of Camels, tinned foods, and chocolate bars stuffed into their socks, they were in a good mood, not tired: they joked, teased each other, and roughhoused. He, meanwhile, was depressed. He didn't understand what had happened to his glorious destiny. In the end, he unwillingly agreed to be a day laborer, too, at least until something better came along.

He got to Piazza Carità at five o'clock in the morning. It was cold and there were throngs of desperate people. He got in line to wait his turn, trusting in good fortune. As usual, there was no need for interpreters, but then he heard they were looking for a set designer. His brain lit up: today was the day, he thought, maybe the *padreterno* had something in mind for him. "If you need a set designer, I'm your man," he called out. But when it was his turn, they had already found a set designer. Fine, he said, day laborer.

And so he was lumped together with thirty-one other workers, twenty of which were day laborers, ten were house painters, and then there was that one lucky fellow, the interpreter/ set designer. Where were they sent? Go up Via Toledo to Piazza Dante, turn down Via Conte di Ruvo: their destination was the Teatro Bellini, one of the most beautiful theaters in Naples.

The thirty-two workers gathered in the foyer, its walls a beautiful shade of mother-of-pearl. Soon an English sergeant arrived. "Staff Sergeant Leefe," he said, introducing himself in his lovely English and then going on and on and on. The theater—he explained—had been requisitioned by the Naafi-Efi, who organized entertainment for the troops near the front lines. The first show, *Barrett Family*, would be performed in exactly four days and everything had to be in tip-top shape. The laborers had to clean the place from top to bottom. The painters had to repaint the mother-of-pearl foyer a cinnabar red, cans of which were already off to one side, ready to use. Everyone, including him and his soldiers, had to be ready to receive and unpack the costumes and props that were on their way. Above all, the set designer had to get straight to work on a sketch for a single set that would be built for the show: a middle-class living room. Understand? "Interpreter, translate for them," the sergeant ordered.

The interpreter, whom my father described as a bumptious bumpkin who had, up until that moment, put on all sorts of airs, but whom I honestly imagined as a poor, fat fellow in an undershirt and sweating heavily, turned to the group of men. "O.K., O.K.," he said to the sergeant, and then broke into dialect. "Listen up, guys, I didn't understand a word this man just said. Actually, I have to tell you something: I don't speak Yankee." And in the version that my father told, the man breathlessly proceeded to explain that when he offered himself for the position, he never imagined such an elegant or artsy situation: this theater, with its gilt friezes, and a sergeant who talked so much. He thought he was going to be sent to work with Blacks, who barely speak at all, and who only ask you to do simple tasks, loading and unloading, the most they ever yell is O.K., O.K.

There was total silence. No one (except my father) understood what the sergeant had said, so no one knew what to tell the phony interpreter. No one made a move.

Leefe started to get angry. He looked at the interpreter, then at the workers, then back at the interpreter and, damn, well he was smart—later they learned that in civilian life he was a professional decorator—and he figured out the man was a bogus interpreter. "Get out!" he screamed. "Did anyone here understand what I just said?" he asked the rest of them. My father raised his hand. "May I act as your interpreter, sir?" he asked. "Yes, you can. What is your name?" the sergeant demanded. "My name is Fred," he replied. "Well, Freddy, you start now."

Those were the actual words. I wrote them down just the way my father told them. I have to say that, as a child, I enjoyed this scene immensely. It was moving, and whenever I came across a scene that was even remotely similar, either in a book or at the movies, it felt familiar, and it made me emotional. We had finally arrived at a turning point. His destiny was unfolding; a dramatic series of interconnected events revealed, both in the actual words and between the lines, a deeper significance. "Start now, Freddy," Leefe magnanimously said to my father, immediately promoting him to stage-interpreter, a role invented specifically for the occasion. Freddy's job was to work as an intermediary between the performers and the foreign military; Freddy had to do everything required to bring *Barrett Family* or *Merry Widow* or *Blithe Spirit* to the stage. My father, in other words, was finally about to become the man he was meant—and wanted—to be.

And here we embark on the stories about the Teatro Bellini. Within those walls—he repeated every single time he told me the story—within those walls—and only in a matter of days, even if he had initially been hired as nothing more than a day laborer—within those walls, he ended up wielding more power than Staff Sergeant Leefe himself.

The sergeant immediately recognized his capabilities and gave him carte blanche. "Freddy, you have to make sure that all the renovations get done and that the interiors are in tip-top shape for the two daily shows: the matinee performance and the evening one. I trust that's clear," he said.

My father threw himself into it. He hired close to thirty beautiful Neapolitan girls to sew the costumes. He then took it upon himself to hire their fiancés to do the heavy lifting. Then, to keep people working around the clock, he also organized a canteen, free of charge, with its own cook and two dishwashers, where everyone ate shoulder to shoulder: pretty girls, laborers, and British soldiers. The room was a constant bustle of happy, well-fed people. Fred doled out cash, warmth, good food, pleasure, and the sense of possibility.

And then there was Gutteridge, the fabric warehouse a few steps away from the Bellini, where he purchased the canvas on which the scenery was painted; he discovered they also had endless meters of muslin in the colors of the Italian flag . . . He bought it all, hired two seamstresses, and made uniforms for the girls, who ran around the theater, some in red, some in white, and some in green—all of them beautiful—busily creating costumes. Naturally, he also brought some of the cloth and muslin home to Rusinè so she could make herself some new clothes, as well as some outfits for her mother and all those asshole relatives of hers.

That's right. In those two years at the Teatro Bellini—from the end of 1943 to the middle of 1945, to be specific—he was practically a patron of the arts. You want to eat? Eat. You want new clothes? Here. He draped everyone in gold. And he made lots and lots and lots of money. How? He confessed without a shred of embarrassment. Actually, he said it with a certain amount of pride, obsessively clarifying as he did that he was unlike other people, that he was of a gifted and rare intelligence, ready to seize opportunities when they presented themselves, not some idiot who might say: no, I couldn't possibly, not me.

He made money by skimming off the top, the way a house-keeper does food shopping. So that I'd understand perfectly, he made the gesture of embezzlement: palm downturned and fingers pursed, he quickly slid his thumb over his long, elegant fingertips from pinky to thumb. He used this gesture often in later decades. For example, when he heard about a colleague from work who had managed to buy an apartment or someone who had opened a butcher shop. The gesture was always accompanied by a smirk of spite and scorn, as well as some background details. "That fellow there, even when the fascists were in power, used to steal Westinghouse valves from the brakes on the freight trains—precious stuff, made of bronze, weighing a fair number of kilos. And that man, Mimí, I used to see him taking bribes in exchange for security clearances on freight trains full of rotten cabbages headed to Germany. And that other guy, right after the war ended, used to clear out the freight trains in the switching yard, especially the ones carrying cattle." This was his way of explaining how, behind anything of value, even in minor cabotage, lurked a thief; because, he went on to instruct me, it's impossible to buy a house or open a butcher shop on a normal salary, and if someone does—and here he'd insert the gesture—theft is involved.

While I listened to him, I thought back to the obsessive attention he gave to closing and locking the windows each night in our house on Via Gemito, how he always checked to be sure, before going to bed, that the shaft had been set firmly against the door. He was always worried about thieves breaking in and he managed to pass that fear on to me. I imagined a band of thieves moving stealthily from the railroad station up to Vomero, from Vomero down to Pozzuoli, and from Secondigliano back up to

Vomero. They'd climb up the façades of buildings and even steal sheets hanging out to dry. A little here, a little there, these people managed to put aside enough to open pastry shops, charcuteries, butcher shops, pizzerias, and restaurants that became more famous than Giuseppe il Volante's in Pigna. As a result, I had a hard time getting to sleep at night. I heard creaking and groaning; every single noise made me suspicious. Often, at night, a man in a white smock walked down Via Gemito with a copper-covered platter on his head, hawking his product. The sound of his voice and his call in dialect of "piiiiizzacaaaaalda" scared me because of how he mangled the words, stretching out the syllables into a dolorous lament. I used to imagine the man in his smock swooping through the sky like a bird of prey, cawing, and nosediving toward my house and into the window. Maybe he was the one who stole our sheets that summer night. How angry my father had been in the morning: he swore at everything in sight, ready to go fight the entire mob just to get his sheets back. But that's what I didn't understand: how could he be angry when other people stole things but so proud of himself when he did? It was the circumstances, he explained. The times. The alternative was to be a fucking grunt.

And since he had no intention of being a fucking grunt, he started skimming money off both fixed costs and variable expenses for the canteen he'd set up in the theater. But then he figured out how to palm a little something off everything, and especially foodstuffs. Actually, it was the shopkeepers he patronized who taught him how. "Don Federí," they said, "the English are dumb. Here, take ten kilos of gelatin, go to the theater, put it in a basin to soak and let it swell up so it looks like a hundred. I'll give you a receipt for twenty-five kilos, pay me for fifteen, and the ten difference is yours. Got it?"

Got it. That's just how things worked. Even Sergeant Leefe fleeced the system. Everyone fleeced it, including Don Peppe the carpenter, the man who built me a rocking horse and had contacts on the black market around Cavone. People skimmed off everything. Condoms, for example. At the end of every theater performance, everyone—Brits, Yanks, Blacks, Whites, all clapping and hollering in a sweaty, cheering mass—inflated condoms and tossed them off the upper circle and boxes into the crowd. Oblong balloons floated down onto the stage, occasionally popping like pistols under people's shoes or in their hands. The following day, following Fred's orders, the crew of girls gathered up the condoms that hadn't popped, re-rolled them carefully and slipped them back into the wrappers they picked up off the floor. In this way, my father got two hundred, or two hundred and fifty, condoms from each performance, which he would then stack up and bring to Don Peppe, who sold them on the black market.

That's how he earned the Teatro Bellini money that Rusinè eventually frittered away. There was your proof that he was no coward or dreamy artist with his head in the clouds. He knew how to keep his feet firmly on the ground when needed. And if he had wanted, he too could've started a business with that money, and quit working for the Ferrovie dello Stato. He could've made more money than his wife's relatives. The difference was, he'd mutter, the difference was that he spat on money, pffft, he pissed on it, pssshh. He, with his brand of genius, found the pettiness of making money with money repugnant. There was no feeling in it whatsoever. It was enough for him to prove that he could do whatever he put his mind to, whether good or bad. Not for himself, obviously. For me, for his firstborn son. For Rusinè, whom he had married with love in his heart, and whom he still loved deeply. To show that he was more determined than Matteo, Attilio, Espedito, or Peppino, or any of those Camorra thugs from the Sanità neighborhood.

Once he received carte blanche from Sergeant Leefe, Federí and the scenographer made their way up to a large room under the roof of the theater with a giant skylight, which became the atelier where they built the scenery. Everything was already there: tins of colored paints, paintbrushes of various sizes tied to long poles, an abandoned set on the wood floor, and a Fragonard-style sketch off to one side.

"Time to get to work," my father said, managing to inform the scenographer as they climbed the stairs that, although he worked for the railroad, he was actually a talented painter who had discovered as a young child that he saw and experienced the world like a true artist. When they reached the atelier, the scenographer, whose name was Mario Cito, a portly man under fifty, turned to Federí with a sad look in his eyes. "Don Federí, I'm sorry," he said. "But I'm an air force captain, not a scenographer. Unfortunately, I'm going to let you down the same way the interpreter did. I just can't explain it, not even to myself. Maybe it was because I was hungry, maybe the *Padreterno* wanted it to be this way, but the fact is that when the man at the employment office asked me if I was a set designer, I couldn't resist and said yes. Now what do we do?"

Not to worry. My father reassured Mario Cito, an educated man with an easy-going temperament, who, more importantly than anything else, was willing to venerate my father as if he were the son of God on earth, and together they got to work. In a short amount of time, they painted a background and sets that depicted the Barrett living room, with curtains, standing lamps, knickknacks, and a large window.

Cito, my father admitted, was a hard worker. He was an up-standing man, solid, and well-mannered, which helped a great deal in public relations. But with regards to the sets, he, Federí, prepared the colors, he knew how to apply them, he gave the bourgeois sitting room that looked out onto a square its realistic touch. When Leefe saw the set he said, "Damn, you're good, Freddy," and my father would feel that shiver of pleasure that ran through his body whenever someone acknowledged his talent, ever since he was a child. It was a kind of contraction of all his energy followed by a slow dilation of his entire being. It made him feel at one with the pure rays of sun that shone through the skylight, with the smell of wood shavings, glue, and paint, with the taste of iron and grime from the nails he held between his lips as he hammered one thing to another.

From that day on, he never stopped. He was everywhere. He walked out of the ruins of the house on Via Zara early every morning, made his way to the theater, and stayed there until late at night. If the actors were rehearsing, he'd help them with their prompts, not just because he enjoyed perfecting his English through the scripts of *Barrett Family*, *Blithe Spirit*, and *Merry Widow*, but for the pleasure of being in their midst, of being surrounded by people from other countries, who spoke different languages, and yet who shared his artistic spirit. If they needed gorgeous showgirls who'd kick up their heels under the shower of condoms, he'd find them. He even managed, in July 1944, to organize an Italian-language performance with Italian actors for a public comprised not only of foreign troops but paying Neapolitans. It was a huge success. To arrange it, he traveled to Caserta to meet Nino Taranto, the great actor, who had been evacuated there with his family; they discussed his creative needs and Federí convinced him to appear on their stage. And so it came to pass that he, Nino Taranto, Carlo Taranto, Dolores Palumbo, Enzo Turco, the three beautiful Nava sisters, Nazarro, the imaginative writer, and Angelini, the famous orchestra director, put on a show for the Brits, Canadians, Blacks, and Neapolitans that brought down the house, boxes, stalls, and peanut gallery.

There were whoops of joy and laughter and hooting and hollering every night. It was a different world: a fictional one, of course, but artfully created. It was as if the war in Italy and across the world had ended. It was as if people in that city weren't killing each other for a fistful of dollars. It was as if those alleys and dark streets and the no-man's land known as the Spanish quarter weren't places where both foreign soldiers and fearless citizens got stabbed in the back or had their throats slit. It was as if every horrible detail of those frightening days was just a part of the happy composition that my father devoted himself to creating far from Via Zara and within the now cinnabar-colored foyer of the theater behind the scenes so skillfully painted with Mario Cito, in the workshop of Don Peppe the carpenter with his shady dealings on the black market, and in the set designers' atelier, where sunlight rained down laden with motes of dust.

There, in that spacious room with its wood floors, into which swallows and doves and gulls sometimes flew, Federí found a way to paint and draw once again. Leefe, who had become a fervent admirer, procured colors, brushes, and canvases for him. Federí himself had managed to obtain a massive easel from a shop-owner friend and accomplice. And so, whenever possible, he felt like Courbet in his artist's studio. While downstairs Sergeant Leefe commanded like a sergeant and the day laborers labored and the painters painted with their female assistants and the pretty Neapolitan girls rouged their cheeks with rouge belonging to the English soubrettes and twelve pretty legs high-kicked to the sound of the cancan, Federí felt for the first time in his life that he was playing the right part in the right way and with all the right tools, and so he drew and painted, and then he drew some more.

He drew beautiful, bright things, depicted with care and in lively colors. He gave many of his paintings from that period away—he said—to Sergeant Leefe, who paid him all sorts of compliments. Views of Piazza Bellini or sketches of the theater world, which the sergeant later took back to England. Exceptionally well done, he repeated over and over. But now and then, after emphasizing how much the sergeant admired his work, he'd become morose. "I drew and painted but what did I really know about art created in the past hundred years?" he said, deeply pained. "Nothing. I had only seen the crap done by other railroaders and exhibited at the collective art shows."

But then he'd catch himself; it only lasted a moment. And soon he'd be bragging about his experiences as an apprentice during wartime—with eighteen-year-old Rose Fleury, the painter—and he'd go back to laughing, always telling new versions of his life on the Côte d'Azur while working as a military radio operator. Before leaving Menton for good, he said, before bidding adieu to Avignon and Les Angles and Rose Fleury, he took a few short trips to Paris to see art at the Louvre, to train his eye, and study the works of the masters. And let's not forget his sweet little teacher-artist had been a fine instructor of the most important aspects of painting. Yes, they had argued about modern art, and especially about Cézanne—he'd assert something and she'd assert something else and he'd agree and she'd disagree and in the end it was never clear who was pro-Cézanne and who was not— asking themselves, how the hell had he gone from being a dilettante to such an expert, having admired Delacroix and Courbet so intensely when he was young?

Ultimately, his talk about that distant period forged an image in my head of all his art work hanging on the walls of the theater atelier: the studies of nudes done in gouache; his version of a number of important details from Velázquez's *Los Borrachos*, all done from memory; his sketches of Via Bellini, a view of Piazza Dante, an old scrap merchant sitting and reading at his stand in Piazza San Gregorio Armeno, all done from real life. Just like a real nineteenth-century master ("What did I know about the twentieth century?" he'd suddenly angrily demand of himself again), with his brushes and paints and palette like some Giacinto Gigante or Consalvo Carelli: he carried the entire school of Posillipo within.

In the meantime, it was as if distances were shortening, oceans were shrinking, skies that had been too remote and foreign and even hostile now peered with kind interest into the skylight of the Teatro Bellini. When did the famous actor Ben Lyon and his company come to the theater? What about Douglas Fairbanks Jr.? I had no idea who those people were but I sat there gaping. Not only had my father earned heaps of money in his shady dealings with shopkeepers and Don Peppe the carpenter, but he also spent time with cinema divas who had exotic names: not Nino or Carlo or Enzo, but Douglas and Ben, people who had left Hollywood and crossed the skies and oceans to appear on the stage of the Teatro Bellini, to stand in front of sets painted with his hands and those of Mario Cito, the air force officer. "Fred," Ben called him. "Fred," Douglas called him. Even Bebe Daniels, an actress who had appeared alongside Rudolph Valentino in old films that my father had seen and admired as a boy, called him "Fred."

Bebe really and truly liked him. And he felt the same way about her. That delicate-looking woman was as beautiful as he recalled she was in her old films, he said. On stage she looked like a young woman and her presence drove the troops wild. She just needed to be lit in the right way. "Fred," she always said to him, "when I'm on stage I want you to handle the lights. You're the best there is when it comes to lighting. You don't just illuminate me, you paint me with light." All in English, of course, in her ringing voice. Only when my father impersonated her did I deduce that, not only was he the interpreter, set designer, acting coach, and impresario for the Teatro Bellini, he was also in charge of lighting, of directing the spots. No surprise there: Fred was everywhere and ingenious and a man of great talents. If I listened carefully to his stories, I'd surely learn even more about his involvement. He may well have been a soundman, singer, or musician too. His rendition of "Io te vurría vasà" was brilliant, especially when he was in a good mood and a little drunk. And sometimes, when he wasn't angry, he played the mandolin for us at night. And sometimes, if we urged him, even a dusty old violin—a real Stradivarius, he said, and he showed me a label inside the sound chamber that really did say Stradivarius—which we had inherited from Zio Peppino di Firenze, and which is probably still among his things.

My father had been everything, but never a dancer; dancers were fags. So were tailors. And a few degenerate, talentless artists. And that group of young men who once even managed to trick Sergeant Leefe and performed a wild cancan exceptionally well (women in practically all other respects, and gorgeous); they were so happy dancing that they didn't even stop when the sirens went off and the Germans started bombing. They continued to kick their legs up high, the musicians kept right on playing, and the troops—who could hold them back!—were flabbergasted, in total rapture, they forgot about the horrors outside and kept their eyes and thoughts glued to those twelve trumped-up women, inflating condoms and batting them toward the stage.

That period lasted nearly two years. But Rusinè was unhappy and didn't understand. Despite all the dangers that existed in Naples during the day, and even more at night, she wanted to be with him, to walk with him down Via Zara, Via Colonnello Lahalle, Via Alessio Mazzocchi, Piazza Carlo III, Via Foria, Via Constantinopoli, Via Conte di Ruvo, and back again. She wanted to be present at every performance, even the most outré (one night a dancer's tits fell out of her brassiere and the comments heard from the upper circle, the boxes, and the stalls were unmentionable), she wanted to be present at every "opening night," sit in the royal box like a princess with her child-infante and matriarch Nannina, all well-dressed thanks to her sewing skills, looking like the queen in I Tre Moschettieri, waiting for D'Artagnan to bring her the jewels.

My father bristled at the thought. The audience was full of horny soldiers, Blacks, the scum of Naples, whores, fags, and man-ladies with their wigs and rouge and fake moles calling out ué-ué belluguaglió vieniaccà. There was everything imaginable. And he, with all the important tasks he had to do, couldn't stay and protect her, he had to go places and see people. His wife didn't want to reason, but he did. He knew perfectly well that things could change drastically from one minute to the next, and that he had to take full advantage of the moment when it presented itself, or never again. But she held him back, she tried to hinder his movements. "Look Rusinè," he said, "one day soon, the trains will start running again, and I'll have to choose. What will I do then? Leave the theater? Go back to grunt work?" Of course you will, she said, basta theater. Basta atelier with its skylight. Basta getting home late at night, keeping her up, worrying her to death. Basta with this obsession of being an artist, forgetting about his wife, his one-and-a-half-year-old child, a second one on the way. Or else he could do both, grunt work and art. But he definitely couldn't leave his job on the railroad. How would they manage without his steady income?

In fact, when the first trains started running again and he received his summons, he went back to his old job. He knew exactly what kind of shit he'd have to deal with every day. He knew exactly what kind of *chiavica all'aria aperta* the so-called new Italy was going to be: an open-air cloaca, a raw sewage dump. He realized it after his first day of work at the Bellini.

He left the theater late at night, tired but satisfied. Leefe had just named him interpreter and set designer. He was happy about the turn his life was taking. When all of a sudden, that shithead Gigino Campo, fellow railroader and comrade from the militia ski team, the 10th Legion of the Ferrovie dello Stato, came up to him, greeted him warmly, and showed him a piece of paper. "Here, sign it, Federí," he said smoothly.

My father took the piece of paper, read it, and saw that it was some kind of self-declaration that attested that the undersigned (Gigino Campo as commanding officer, then him, and then who knows how many other people would go on to sign it) had fought hard to defend the Ponte della Sanità against the German army during the course of the Quattro Giornate uprising in Naples. "The Ponte della Sanità . . ." my father mumbled.

"Yup," Gigino said. "And you were commanding officer of the partisan army . . ." my father continued to mumble. "Yup," Gigino said. "And I was a partisan fighter . . ." my father said just to make sure he understood. "Yup, that's right," Gigino said. My father looked Gigino squarely in the eyes. "Gigí, you know what? I really don't remember fighting to defend the Ponte della Sanità . . ." And then, his eyes bulging like a madman straight out of the psychiatric hospital in Aversa, he started screaming at Gigino: "Go fuck yourself, you steaming piece of shit! What do you take me for? A clown like you?" By refusing to sign, he waived the possibility of being recognized as a partisan, which would have made his life easier later on, but—and this he said proudly—being the man that he was, he'd never, ever, act like that piece-of-shit idiot clown. *Buonanotte*, Gigí.

Gigino was offended. My father didn't give a flying fuck. Sometimes he wondered out loud, but only to hear someone say that he did the right thing, whether he should have signed that document. Maybe having defended the Ponte della Sanità during the Quattro Giornate uprising would've helped boost his artistic career and stay out of hot water, like the time they tried to kill him a little over a year after that encounter, only a few days after the birth of his second son, on either April 28, 1945 or on May 1, 1945.

If I could talk to the child who'd been asked to retrieve his father's cigarettes in 1948 about the significance of those two dates that I just wrote down, I'd learn that he has no chronological understanding of things. He doesn't know the relevance of dates, but his father does. He doesn't know how to distinguish today from yesterday from tomorrow. He doesn't even know that he is living in March, 1948. For him "April 28, 1945" or "May 1, 1945" are meaningless sounds. Since he also has a hard time with basic numbers, I fear he might not even be able to count from one to ten. He merely knows that when his father is at work, he can run around the apartment freely, whether the one on Via Zara or that on Via Gemito. Even the sound of his mother or grandmother's voice calling him to attention is part of a series of playful activities that unfold without the slightest shadow of pain. But if his father is home, the child doesn't even try and play. And not because his father stops him (if anyone, his mother does, with phrases like "hush, your father's still sleeping"), but because his presence, whether awake or asleep, erases all notion of play, discourages it.

How can he let go and lose himself in his happy alternate world when his father comes home lugging his own burden? No, the child does not play when his father is home. He's silent, he waits, he tries not to disturb him. All passing of time is marked in one way only: the sound of the door slamming when his father leaves and the sound of the door slamming when he comes home. If I were to press the child about that evening in 1945, he'd reply vaguely. "My father went out one morning and came home so late that I hoped he'd never return."

That evening Federí was working in the ticket office at Napoli Centrale, where he had been asked to be temporarily stationed. He kept one foot there and the rest of his mind and body at the Teatro Bellini, a position he absolutely did not want to leave. From the Bellini, he could see all the way to New York and the rest of America, he could see the future, and he spent all his time chronicling ways he might escape before it was too late. In the meantime, each week he gave a stick of Senior Services cigarettes to the office manager, an ex-captain of the railroad militia, so that he'd mark him present while he was actually following Sergeant Leefe's orders every day of the week. He only worked in the ticket office on Sundays, from 9 A.M. to 6 P.M., managing the office while the real office manager stayed unwillingly at home.

Why unwillingly? Because in those days it was a true privilege to work in the ticket office. There were few daily trains, few seats, and the seats for sale were inversely proportionate to the distance. In other words, the farther you went, the harder it was to get a ticket; there might be ten spots for Naples–Rome, twenty for Naples–Latina, and fifty for Naples–Aversa.

People lined up at the window ready to fight for the right to travel. And it wasn't easy: a portion of tickets had already been doled out to the railroad police, who had their own personal clients; a portion had been sold to scalpers in cahoots with the ticket office; and a portion was sold fair and square to the public by the person at the ticket booth. However, the person at the booth was only allowed to issue tickets to people who had a valid ID card. Since people had been busy thinking about other things during wartime than renewing their ID cards, the only way to purchase a ticket was by bribing the ticket vendor. Their ID cards would then be immediately renewed. Considering that the majority of people who traveled back then were contrabanders, the police, scalpers, and ticket vendors all made a pretty penny without any remorse. This was why working in the ticket office was a popular job, and also why my father didn't have to worry about relinquishing his post during the week so he could spend time at the Teatro Bellini. Everyone was happy. No one complained. Least of all, him. He was raking in both money and glory at the Teatro.

Lots of money. So much so that he was able to permit himself some new threads. Up until then, his wardrobe had been limited to a pair of military trousers and a British bomber jacket without the insignia, but it didn't correspond to the managerial role he had taken on at the Teatro. So he had a tailor make him an elegant beige carded wool suit with fabric that had been recently woven in Salerno. It cost him 30,000 lire and it fit him perfectly. On the morning of April 28, 1945 (or if you prefer May 1, 1945) my father was wearing that suit to impress his colleagues at the ticket booth. "Watch out for your suit, Federí, don't get it dirty, you look so good in it," Rusinè said in dialect as she walked him to the door that morning.

Elegantly dressed, with his princely swagger (when he walked, he swung his arms in an ungainly way and lumbered forward chest first, a gait that I inherited and have spent my whole life trying to modify and normalize), he crossed Piazza Garibaldi, his thoughts on the future. Deep in his fantasy of great artist, he barely noticed a group of hotheads shouting slogans and cheering hip-hip-hurrah for the Allied forces. The crowds changed with each version, and I had a hard time identifying them clearly: sometimes they wore red kerchiefs around their necks, other times they wore olive drab shirts and helmets from the Great War. The point is that he strode right by them and took up his shift as office manager, which gave him time to sketch, in ink or pencil, on the back of the forms that lay in a stack on his desk, while the faces of hopeful travelers peered into the ticket booth and at the ticket vendor, a fellow named Cisa, who scrutinized their documents, looking for ways to fleece them.

The day passed slowly. Around four o'clock in the afternoon, Cisa, who at the time was busy selling the Naples–Rome tickets, came to inform him that the train leaving at 8 P.M. was full. Soon he'd close up the window and tally the numbers, and then start selling tickets for the same train on the following day.

Fine, fine. My father went back to his drawing. Suddenly, though, a machinist named Barradoro, the union rep for all locomotive engineers, conductors, and train-service crew members, came barging into his office. "The name's Barradoro, comrade. Issue me a ticket for the eight o'clock train for Rome," he said haughtily. "My dear Bardarono," my father calmly replied, "I'm sorry but there are no more tickets for Rome, not even for union reps and other celestial figures. If you really want me to write up a ticket for you, go to the head conductor and bring me a written order." Barradoro was offended. "Maybe you don't know who I am," he said testily. "You're nothing more than a *strunzemmèrd*!" my father replied. "Watch your mouth when you speak to me," Barradoro said, shocked. "You watch yours, you pile of stinking shit," my father said, going on to add, "Now do me a favor and get the hell out of this office right now. If you want to complain, take it to Loffredo, the leader of the union, and quit busting my balls!"

Barradoro walked out, threatening fire and brimstone, but Federí ignored him and went back to drawing. The peace and quiet was over and done. Not five minutes passed after Barradoro had left, Cisa walked into his office. "Don Federí, you've got to come out front," he said nervously. Apparently, as soon as he opened the booth to sell tickets for the Naples–Rome train for the following day, a fellow surrounded by mean-looking mobsters started yelling and screaming at him "Go get your fucking boss!" Cisa tried but couldn't quiet him down.

My father slowly got to his feet and went to see what was going on. The five brutes had stirred up chaos in the crowd of people waiting for tickets for the following day, and now stood menacingly at the front of the line, on the other side of the tinted glass that separated the ticket booth from the main hall, wearing expressions that said "Would you look at how these people are wasting our time." He didn't back down, not even for a minute. He slid open the ticket window and found himself face to face with the ringleader. "How can I help you?" he asked. "Look, boss, we have to get to Rome tonight for urgent political reasons and need tickets for the eight o'clock train," the man explained. "I'm sorry but the eight o'clock train is full," my father objected politely. "Not for us it isn't," the delinquent said and went on: "There have to be tickets. Give them to us now. What the hell did we fight to save Italy for if we can't get five tickets from Naples to Rome?" Then he took a few steps back and unbuttoned his shirt to show him a few recent scars that proved he had saved Italy. "Look at this! And this one, too! You fascist bastard, all dressed in your fancy clothes! We should've lined you up against the wall, all of you: your mother, sister, father, grandfather, and your kids, if you have any! See my scar? See it? Hand over five tickets, now!" He was beside himself with rage. My father kept trying to explain that it simply wasn't possible. "Now!" the man kept screaming, "Now!" Soon their voices sounded like some kind of call and response tune. "But—" "Now!" "If—" "Now!" And it would've gone on for who knows how long if that jerk hadn't decided to fire off his last round of ammo. "I'm fed up! I'm going tell Cacciapuoti, we're family."

Silence. My father just sneered. Cacciapuoti? Then, articulating his words very clearly and speaking in proper Italian in order to intimidate him, he replied. "Ah, you're family, are you? Well, please give him my sincerest regards. If he's an upstanding fellow, he'll understand perfectly that as a man following orders, I can't, of my own initiative—" and while he was ending his sentence he started to slide the ticket booth shut on Cacciapuoti's relative. But the mobster realized what was happening and leaned into the still-open window and, patooey, spat in his face.

He spat in my father's face. This was mind-boggling. A truly anomalous situation. Usually it was he who spat in the faces of his adversaries. On that particular occasion, however, Cacciapuoti's relative got him first. And since, apparently, given the situation— the glass booth and so on—it was hard to react in his normal manner—i.e. by pissing in his face—my father, with admirable precision, swiftly reached his right arm through the booth, which couldn't have been more than 15 cm across, and reverse punched him so hard that he split his face wide open.

There was blood everywhere. People started screaming. "I'm going to kill you," Cacciapuoti's relative yelled, rushing toward the staff entrance with his henchmen and shouting, "Death to the fascist!"

Cisa, the ticket salesman, shut and locked the door. But those hotheads didn't give up and started to kick and ram it with their shoulders. So my father and his subordinates pushed all the furniture against the door and picked up the clubs and sticks they kept on hand in case of fighting in the ticket line. The clubs were heavy and gnarled. Eventually, the five mobsters quieted down, the door stopped shaking, and the shouting faded. Cisa carefully peered out and glanced around the crowded hall. Certain that the worst had passed, he decided to go back to the booth and continue to pocket the money coming from the renewal of expired ID cards. Everything slowly went back to normal.

But my father remained on guard. He was worried that Cacciapuoti's relative and his crew were plotting something behind the scenes, so he telephoned Commissioner Cannavaccio from the railroad police. "Calm down, boss," the official said to him. "I don't have any men free at the moment. Easy does it, boss, quit screaming, don't be rude, not with me. Today was a rough day. Your situation is minor compared to everything else I've had to deal with. You can handle it on your own, I know you can."

By then it was almost six o'clock in the evening, the shift was almost over, and soon their replacements would arrive. My father peeked out the glass booth: it looked like everything had gone back to normal, there was still a long line of hopeful travelers in the hall. To be certain, he beckoned for the porter-scalper who ambled through the crowds looking for potential clients, and asked him to scope out the situation. The man reassured him. "No danger, boss." Should he trust him or not? Should he go out or not?

He was wondering what to do when the telephone rang. "Hello?" he said. It was Salentini, a station manager and a real loudmouth. "You want to tell me what's going on down there? Issue a ticket to union rep Barradoro right away; he has to get on the eight o'clock train to Rome," Salentini commanded. "You're a station manager," my father retaliated, "you can issue tickets to anyone you want, whenever you want. You issue the tickets to Barradoro. Or, if you absolutely insist that I do it, then I'll need special authorization from you in writing that shows you assume all responsibility." The station manager was irate. "Is that so? Well, fine! Come on over here with your block of tickets so I can fill them out! Barradoro has already waited too long!" What could my father do? He took his block of tickets and cautiously walked out of the office.

Here's the layout of Napoli Centrale in 1945, my father would say, pausing for a moment to both accentuate the element of suspense and get a piece of paper and pen, with which he capably and firmly drew an actual, and awfully boring, topographical map. This, he explained, was the façade, this was the ticket office, and over here were the two side buildings where the offices were located. Before the war, a heavy glass and iron roof extended out from the façade all the way to the side buildings and the train tracks, providing shelter over the hallways, staircases, and two narrow walkways that crossed Piazza Garibaldi to the metro station. But in 1941, my father went on to explain in great detail, this roof was dismantled and used for war materials, and since that time, the area had remained exposed to the elements. This lack of roof explained how, on the evening of April 28, 1945 or May 1, 1945, he, Federí, was seen from above as he walked out of the ticket office at a brisk pace, turned down a hallway to the right, and got ready to cross the closest of the two bridges that crossed the tracks of Piazza Garibaldi, the block of tickets in his left hand.

Waiting for him on the other side of the bridge were station manager Salentini and machinist-union rep, Barradoro. But they actually took less notice of him than the crowd of violent men who started to scream and point at him. "There he is! The fascist! Let's get him! Kill him!"

They could taste blood. It was hard to say exactly how many of them there were, but it was a sizeable crowd. They rushed across the bridge shouting and screaming. My father understood they were coming for him. He also understood that those goons had been egged on by Cacciapuoti's relative, even though neither he nor any of his underlings were among the crowd. He did recognize, however, their leader: Carnaciaro Fulgenti, who later

became well known—he explained—as the leader of the popu-
list "Uomo Qualunque" movement, but who, on that particular
occasion, was intent on screaming "Kill the fascist."

What terrifying chaos: union rep Barradoro, the goons who
considered Cacciapuoti's relative their leader, and Carnaciaro
Fulgenti's foot soldiers. But holy moly, it was exciting to listen
to him. I was all ears. I wanted to hear about the trap they laid,
and how they got their revenge. It was an endless nightmare, a
free-for-all of kicking and punching. In a matter of seconds, they
attacked my father on the bridge, under which lay cobblestones,
train tracks, the metro. He threw himself into the fray with his
usual audacity, which he had learnt from European champion
Bruno Frattini, but there were simply too many of them. He got
kicked and punched in the face, he never took so many punches
in his life as he did that day. Or maybe that wasn't true: once,
at the end of the 1970s in some gallery, an artist, whose work
Federí had lambasted, as usual, knocked him to the ground and
jumped up and down on his chest with all his weight; he had
so many broken bones, he had to stay in bed for a month and
could barely even breathe. But there, on that pedestrian walk-
way at the station, things were different. They really did want
to kill him—one body more, one body less, back then no one
would really notice. He saw the expressions on their faces, the
knife blades. He thought his luck had run out, that his life was
over. He surrendered and curled up in a fetal position, arms and
hands protecting his face, without realizing that he was still gripping the book of tickets.

And then he heard a voice. It was Barradoro. "Pardon me,"
he said, "excuse me a minute, I just need to get the ticket book,
sorry." He shoved the men aside, creating a path, halting and
confusing the vigilantes. Barradoro came up to my father and
yanked the ticket book out of his hands, thanked him, and then
started back the way he came. That tiny, almost imperceptible
pause before receiving his final, mortal blows proved to be

decisive. With a sudden spurt of energy and great agility, my father leapt to his feet and ran off, taking advantage of the path that Barradoro had cut through the crowd.

Now I hear the wan echo of my mother's voice. Yes, she confirmed, it was horrible. When she opened the rickety front door of the apartment on Via Zara to her husband, it was as if he was wearing a mask of blood. His beautiful beige carded wool suit was ruined.

She had never seen him in such a bad way. It was entirely unlike anything he had ever done to her, and right away he started in with his rant: "See what I have to do in order to survive? See what happens when I go to work at the railroad? And you expect me to find the time to paint?"

Sometimes it even seemed like he blamed her for what Carnaciaro Fulgenti's gang did to him on the bridge that day. Actually, he ran into Fulgenti at the station bar sometime later; the shithead was now a flunky for the monarchists, smooth-talking, and unctuous. "Forgive me, Don Federí. Cacciapuoti's relative said you were a fascist. I didn't know that you fought at the Russian front, forgive me," he said when he recognized my father. "What should I forgive you for, Carnacià?" my father replied, calling out warmly and generously to the barman, "A coffee for Signor Carnaciaro Fulgenti!" When the coffee arrived, Federí turned quickly to Fulgenti. "Don't let it go cold now," he said and, without a moment's hesitation, threw the scalding drink in the man's face, together with the cup and saucer.

My father never let anyone get away with anything, and I knew that nothing would ever stop him. I knew it from the sound of his step on the stairs, how it brought all the fun my brothers and I ever had to an end. Even if he was badly beaten up, he'd call out "Rusinè!" and have her prepare him an elixir to soothe his nerves, and then he'd start to plot how to get back at his enemies as if he was the Grim Reaper with a scythe. Now even more obstinately than before. When his work at the Teatro Bellini came to an end, he became even more bitter and argued with absolutely everyone, whether he was right or wrong, on the giving or receiving end.

All he had left was his paycheck, his wife, three sons, a mother-in-law, and a brother-in-law. Fuck each and every single one of you, he screamed. "Where's all the money I made at the Teatro Bellini? Where is it?" he'd yell over and over, after dinner in the kitchen. "I want it all, and right now! I need it!" He really did want every single lira from her. Or to know who had taken it. Had Rusinè given the money to her mother's sisters and their husbands? Had they gone and used his hard-earned cash to open a pastry shop that was even more successful than Pintauro's? Had they used it to start their highly profitable *salumeria*, or their fruit and vegetable store? If they did, fine, but they had to pay him back the money that they'd screwed him out of. "Go ask them for a loan, right now," he'd order her. She'd say no. Yes. No. And since they really were feeling the pinch, Rusinè caved in and, in great embarrassment, went to ask her relatives for money, which held them over until his paycheck arrived. "Federí, we have a ton of debts we need to pay off," she'd then remind him. To which he'd invariably reply: "Debts *di questo cazzo*."

This was not just a passing comment uttered in vexation. This was a precise strategy. He had worked it out—he informed me authoritatively—when we moved up to Vomero, to 64 Via Gemito, stairwell C, apartment 10. At the time, he and my mother didn't own a single piece of furniture. They used to hang things off wires they strung across the room, the same way they had done on Via Zara. The problem was that Rusinè hassled him about it. "Federí, we need furniture," she used to say. "You want furniture? Fine, go borrow 100,000 lire from your aunts and uncles, seeing how they're now rich shop owners," he'd reply. "No, we can't, we already owe them money," she'd say. "Who gives a fuck, now we'll owe them more," he'd perfunctorily reply.

Finally, they went together to ask for a loan that amounted to five months of a railroad employee's salary in 1947. His plan was the following: "I'll get them to give me 100,000 lire and will never pay those damn bastards back." That was how he thought. And he thought that way, I believe, not just because the amount of money he had earned from the Teatro Bellini was an unknowable, unimaginable amount, and not just because his in-laws had dipped into it with my mother's consent and therefore he believed he had every right to borrow whatever amount he wanted from his in-laws for as long as he lived, but also because, as an artist forced to temporarily live a miserable life all because of his wife, he felt he deserved benefactors, and since there was no one else to fill the role, Attilio, Matteo, Espedito, Carmela, Assunta and Maria could do it. So he went over there and sweet-talked them and teased them, then he got angry, then he went back to laughing and making them laugh, until he finally came out and asked for it. "100,000 lire. I have to buy furniture." But apparently they were fed up and, in their polite way, they banded together and said, "Federí, we're just merchants, all we do is keep the money moving. Try and see it from our perspective. We're sorry but we can't."

How dare they! My father tried to explain just how much of an offense that was. And since he detected that I was on my mother's relatives' side (not verbally, of course, because who'd risk contradicting him? but sentimentally), there was never a time in my life either as a child or an adult when he didn't angrily describe them as 'sti chiavechemmèrd, those stinking pieces of shit. He had fed them when they were hungry, he screamed, when they didn't have a pot to piss in, and they still wouldn't give him the money. Or rather, those ingrates made it clear that if they did lend him the money, they'd want interest. Interest! Loan sharks! Strozzini! He'd laugh with derision and then add, who gives a fuck. He'd never given a fuck about anyone. They'd buy furniture with money earned from his talent; he'd paint in the dining room, next to the window.

And that's exactly what he did. "And that's exactly what I did, Mimí," he said again for emphasis. He wanted me to pay close attention to him when he talked, he wouldn't stand for any kind of distraction. He managed to purchase the furniture that Rusinè desired so that she could beautify the rooms of the apartment on Via Gemito by agreeing to complete in record time (for a certain Caporali, whose nickname was 'o zannuto, or "Fangs," who had a degree in business, a straight-up fellow) fifteen portraits of American soldiers who wanted to send their happy, young, freckled mugs back to their families across the ocean. All the other painters were doing it, too, nothing to be ashamed of. Maestro Emilio Notte did it, Rubens Capaldo did it, and he may well have been the best of them, Federí excluded of course. They sketched out the soldiers' features from their photos, projected the images onto canvas, doweled them, prepared the colors, and filled them in. "I worked night and day," he used to say. The furniture was purchased with his hard-earned cash on December 12, 1947, just before Christmas, to please my mother, who was pregnant for the third time and who wouldn't stop complaining. "How can we live without furniture? How can we live?"

While he went on and on, I thought back to each one of those pieces of furniture in detail. I remembered the three-door wardrobe: the middle door was paneled with a mirror, and when the door creaked open, it reflected the ghost of Modesta, as pale and blonde as Ophelia, hiding in a corner of the bedroom. I remembered the desk, on top of which rested my father's Perseo watch from the railroad, how it ticked away the seconds in the deep shadows. I remembered the vanity. I even remembered the dining table where we ate our special holiday meals.

It was brand new and smelled of varnish. That first year, we ate our Christmas lunch at that table, straight out of the woodshop. Then, at the end of the meal, Nonna brought out a bowl of dried fruit and nuts: figs, almonds, hazelnuts, walnuts. If only she hadn't. My father picked up a walnut and since he was in a good mood, chatting and laughing and not really thinking straight, he put it down on a corner of the table, steadied it with his left thumb and index finger and smacked it hard and fast with the heel of his right hand.

My mother cried out only a fraction of a second before he hit it. "The table!" And when Federí peered under the tablecloth to see if there was any damage, he realized that the brand new, perfectly planed surface was now ruined. There was a dent in the wood and a long, white crack ran through the shiny surface, like a fault line.

How Rusinè cried. My father looked at her insensitively. For fuck's sake, he muttered, what on earth did I do? It's nothing serious. Women cry about such idiotic things. Just be quiet. Could you shut up? Or do you want a gusher? He was both upset and disturbed, and didn't know how to get out of it without punching her, without giving her a gusher, a romper, a knuckle sandwich. His usual way of dealing with things, in other words. Fortunately, I was able to tune out his stories. Fortunately, as the years passed, I developed a strategy for blocking out his words. Using this technique, which I perfected as a teenager, the angrier he grew when telling the stories of his life and the reasons for his actions, the thicker the fog grew inside my head, allowing me to think about other things. It helped establish a distance between us. It helped curb the desire to kill him.

Even when I was young, I didn't always pay careful attention to him, of this I am certain. Even when I was most entranced or frightened, my mind somehow emptied out, and my thoughts traveled elsewhere. It's hard to say exactly why it happened. Maybe his talkative manner and invasive presence bothered me. Maybe I suspected that there'd eventually be a flaw in the fabric of his stories and soon enough they'd all fall apart, humiliating both him and me. Maybe I confusedly perceived that, behind my enthusiasm for how carefully connected the events of his life were, even at their most critical junctures, there lurked the bitterness of a person who had been betrayed, who had grown cruel because they had refused to accept the betrayal, and who consequently was always only a short distance away from exacting the worst kind of revenge.

I stood on the threshold to the bedroom, a few steps away from his cigarettes, and that's exactly how I felt: empty, void of both sounds and images. The only scent I could smell was the distant countryside, that hint of fresh air, as if the window was open. Anxiety was suffocating me, I felt the pressure to be whatever my father wanted, whether he was ecstatic or enraged.

Every day I learned something from him. I spied on him, observed his gestures, copied them. I tried in all ways possible to show him how much I hung onto his words, each breath. I was horrified by the idea that he might think differently. He constantly needed affirmation. He wanted others to concentrate on him and recognize his superiority the same way he concentrated on them to show them how worthless they were. "See what your Papà did?" he'd ask me now and again, without warning, leaning back in his chair in front of the easel. "You like it?" he'd say and hold up a piece of paper or plyboard with a portrait on it of Zio Peppino or my grandmother chopping vegetables or my mother sitting and reading a magazine like "Annabella" or my brother with his lost gaze, or even me, which although he had done once before, he was dissatisfied with, and so decided to do it again better, in pencil, charcoal, tempera, watercolor. He was so hungry for recognition that he sought out the enthusiasm of a child. He needed even that. His sudden queries of "You like it?" always caught me off guard, troubled me, and led me to exaggerate my affirmative reply. And, even so, I was never entirely sure if I had exaggerated enough.

All this excessive nodding and stammering combined with the simultaneous feeling of everything emptying out of me caused me to lose a sense of myself. I was uncertain of what I even looked like. That was the way I felt when I walked into my parents' room where they slept together every night; I slammed the brakes on my heart as if my heart might slide across the tiled floor, as if I could stop it by stepping on it with my feet or ungulated hoofs or webbed feet or whatever they were, anything to stop myself from seeing myself in the mirror on the vanity, my mother's dressing table. Since December 12 of the preceding year, the day the new furniture arrived, that spot had been where she was supposed to sit like a movie diva, putting mascara on her already dark eyelashes, contouring her naturally contoured eyes, painting her lips that were already blood-red. But she was never allowed to sit there. Her husband didn't like it. And besides, he said, the room was too small, the headboard from the bed practically touched the vanity mirror, it was hard to reach the window. And so the tufted ottoman, which would've been the perfect spot to sit and brush her coal-black hair in her nightie (if only she had a brush and that luxurious lifestyle and a patient man, the kind you see in the movies) remained at the vanity table for only the briefest amount of time. Soon my father moved it to a spot between the wardrobe and the desk; he put a straight-backed chair in its place, on which he could hang his jacket. He preferred to use the ottoman as a stool, climbing onto it in his shoes when he needed to get something off the top of the wardrobe. Or else we kids would jump on it like a trampoline, trying to reach whatever was up there, and then flopping back onto our parents' bed.

I played that jumping game most of all. In the early months of 1948, my two brothers were still too young to play it. Afterward I'd lie on my belly on their bed, raise my head a tiny bit and peer at myself in the mirror. I'd examine myself carefully, maybe waiting for someone to confirm that, yes, "That is you." But meanwhile, other things were happening at home, my parents were yelling at each other, there was no time for anyone to talk to me. So I'd stare at the geometric pattern of the tiles beyond the end of the bed and lose myself, as if I had just eaten a big breakfast of bread and warm milk, my full belly absorbing the energy, and I felt myself slipping away. How horrible it would be, I thought, if I really was the son of a crocodile.

While I already had serious doubts about my actual body structure, I especially did on that night in March. I walked into the room cautiously, less afraid of seeing the ghost of Modesta in the mirror than a reflection that would reveal my true nature.

But that didn't happen. Illuminated by the feeble light of the electric prayer candle on the desk, I saw no crocodiles or hippopotamuses or other dangerous animals, no screaming ancestors or relatives had snuck into the room and were visible in the silvered glass, under the master bed, or on top of the wardrobe with its stacks of boxes and rolls of drawings and painted canvases. Instead, standing in my parents' bedroom, between the vanity and the window, its thin panes of glass trembling in the wind (was it open or closed?), was a peacock.

It was enormous. Its crest reached all the way to the ceiling; I could hear it softly brushing up against it as it bobbed its head. Its puffed-out chest was purplish-azure, like the sea just after sunset. It fanned its majestic train, the eyes painting the room as many colors as my father left on his palette in the dining room, in a thick and shiny paste, expertly blended along the edges.

I want to write about the child who saw the peacock. He stands there without moving, dazzled, flashes of pleasure flicking on and off with a surprising energy. He then formulates two thoughts which I jealously preserve somewhere in the shape they had then: two silent, clean steel spheres.

First, the child thinks to himself: he'll like it. Then, right after: he won't like it. He means his father. Will he or won't he like that animal whose radiance is so strong that it makes your heart stop while continuing to beat, that makes you notice its quivering outline while its sudden creative impulse also takes your breath away? Will he let it stay in the room? Will he discuss the colors of its feathers with great passion and at length, talk about its patterns and shades, comment on how such marvels are possible, and name the techniques needed to successfully reproduce them on canvas (the child knew no other parent who understood or talked so well about colors)? Or would he run toward the window, screaming wildly, and chase the animal out, hitting, kicking, and spitting at it, pissing in its face, telling it to go back to the countryside from which it came? Or would he kill it and chop it into pieces the way he had done with the stork that had recently brought him his third son, the same stork—I later remember— he drew so well for us? Or would he grab it by the neck as he had done two months earlier when, in order to provide his wife with a fortifying broth so she could regain her strength after giving birth, he went and bought a live chicken and tried to kill it with a knife, but the thrashing beast, frenzy in its eyes, red crest fluttering, yellow talons extended, fluttered so hard to get free that he, the head of household intent on performing a sacrifice, turned as pale as a cadaver but nonetheless managed to hack part-way through its neck, draining its black blood into the stone sink, and then dropped the knife in disgust, as if the whole thing had been a mistake, and the chicken got free, blood spurting from its neck, running and flapping and fluttering up and down the house (with everyone in pursuit: his father, his three-year-old second-born, Nonna Nannina, and his first-born, who was now five years old), first down the hall, then into the bedroom where it climbed onto Rusinè's weary body, the newborn by her side, and then back down the hall, and finally into the dining room, where it sprayed blood on the new table, the freshly-painted canvases that were sitting there to dry, the palette with all its colors, and the window sill, before finally leaping out the third floor window, wings spread wide, and making its way off to die, its head hanging on by a thread, in the bushes of the fields across the street?

The yelling that came from the kitchen was not promising. Recalling it now, it's hard to tell if the glass windows trembled because of the wind or because of my father's excessively loud voice.

He had just finished dissecting the question of money. He had just finished insulting each and every one of Rusinè's relatives. He had moved on to accusing his wife of her greatest crime: that she enchained him, took advantage of his love, burdened him with children, made him as weak as Samson. Oh, what a fool he'd been. He should've upped and crossed the ocean, gone to America, back when he still worked at the Bellini. Douglas Fairbanks Jr. had offered him a job as an assistant set designer more than once. Bebe, the silent film star, had urged him to leave. "Fred, your talents are wasted here," she said. "You have a better eye than anyone. You see things that no one else sees. You have the gaze of the *Padreterno* and you exist to show us its beauty through your painting. Listen to me: leave this shitty country. Come meet me in Hollywood. All doors will be open to you. Your destiny is there." But what had he done? Had he crossed the ocean? Had he gone to Hollywood where he could've become a painter and set designer and artist and earned the fame he deserved? No. One reason he did not was because he hadn't landed the right wife, the kind to encourage him, urge him on, follow him. Not to mention the children: how could he leave us behind in Naples and go to Hollywood? And so, gradually, everything at the Teatro Bellini came to an end. Ben left, Douglas left, Bebe left. Even Sergeant Leefe left. They left him behind like one of those floozies from Capodichino. Left behind to toil like a poor beast. No, he hadn't gone to America, but those shitty portraits he had copied from photographs had, and now they hung who knew where, in some ranch in Texas or Arizona. He was left behind to watch his merchant relatives *di questo cazzo* make as much gold as some second-rate gilder. The railroad had swallowed him up yet again.

Now and then the fury in his voice broke with genuine suffering. But then his tone would rise again, punctuated by the sound of things breaking, my mother's sobbing, the rhythmic hammering of my grandmother's chair, where she rocked the third-born by singing him that frightening lullaby: "Ninna nanna, ninna nam, the wolf will eat the baby lamb." Why oh why had she chosen him over her own mother, brother, aunts, and uncles? Why hadn't she had the generosity to say, "Go to Hollywood with the money you earned, I'll join you there." Why wasn't she even the slightest bit grateful that he hadn't left her, her and the children, without giving a fuck, the way so many cruel men do, out of the blue, disappearing into nothingness?

He just couldn't get his mind around it. He felt his gut knotting up, he was beside himself with torment. "Mimí! For fuck's sake! The cigarettes! Now!" To find a little peace, he needed his cigarettes.

In a panic, I started to riffle through the pockets of my father's jacket. In so doing, my elbow rubbed up against the peacock's brilliant feathers. I felt all the energy of the extremely beautiful bird and for a moment it felt like its colors turned to liquid and rained down on me from the ceiling of the room: emerald green, ultramarine, brown, golden yellow or lilac, gentle tears from the hundreds of eyes on its staggeringly beautiful train.

I grabbed the packet of cigarettes and stepped back. I knew I had to hurry and bring them to my father, back to that din, to the devastated landscape of the kitchen, but I just couldn't leave that small room or the unmeasurable joy that had come over me. So I hesitated another little bit and looked into the eyes at the top of those elegant feathers that rustled in the air with their long, purplish lashes. I knew those eyes saw me.

They weren't eyes like, I don't know, a potato has eyes. They saw me, redrew me, repositioned me. How well they knew the art of blending colors: they sprinkled their blue-green over me, added a bright dab of coppery yellow, mixed in some purplish substance that was rich in golden flake. They gave the room an entirely new tone, and even brought new life to the reproduction of Domenico Morelli's *Assunzione* that was reflected in the wardrobe mirror.

"They'll understand each other," I thought to myself. The harlequin peacock and my father would understand each other perfectly. They'd look at each other and recognize each other, forge an alliance. But while this idea initially consoled me (the peacock would not get massacred like the stork, it wouldn't run around the house with its head dangling off, spraying blood everywhere), directly afterward I felt something like loss, emptiness. That stunning creature would become just another one of my father's stories. He would bend it to his needs and after his initial enthusiasm, he'd start to list its flaws (what ugly feet it had, for starters: peacocks do have ugly feet) and he'd show the cruelty and jealousy he reserved for his rival painters to the extent that he'd soon reduce the creature to a measly cockerel. He'd soon flutter around it himself, with his own wings, resentful and chatty: a vanessa butterfly, his vainglorious ego.

I really didn't know what to do. I saw that bird with its wheel of colors and kept my joy to myself for as long as I possibly could. The kitchen, the apartment, Via Gemito: all soundless, erased. I didn't even hear my father walking down the hall. He stepped into the room and switched on the lights (so there was electricity in the apartment on Via Gemito, all it took was my father's will to make it come pouring out of the fixture). "What's going on here?" he said, but in a controlled way, his forehead pale, his eyes fiery with anger and dissatisfaction.

I handed him the packet of cigarettes. But then I turned back toward the peacock, which, under the electric light, was more splendid than before, an iridescent wave of colors. "Papà, look,"

I said, pointing it out to him. He was already nervously lighting a cigarette. He looked up from the flickering match and turned in the direction of the vanity table. "What am I supposed to look at, Mimí?" he said in a distracted way, restraining himself, as if gently warning me not to bother him any further. Then he rushed out of the room, exhaling the smoke, following the thread of his anger. "I made a huge mistake. What a fool I was. Rusinè, I should have said 'Goodbye, farewell, arrivederci, and quit busting my balls!' to all of you."

I watched him walk back down the hall. I was stunned. He hadn't noticed the peacock. And even though their argument was starting up even more ferociously than before, I felt cheerful. It wasn't the utter joy of a few minutes earlier, nor was it a sense of being completely carefree. I was in a good mood: there was a harmony of syllables, colors, and musical notes that I still feel now when I'm working on something I love and the weather is fine.

Back then I understood the reasons for these feelings in a confused way. I was amused and felt like laughing. In the mirror I saw a child grinning with his mouth closed, the smile nonetheless lighting up his eyes. He didn't smile widely out of respect for his father, the man who—each time I said it to myself my happiness grew—had looked at the peacock with his extraordinary eyes but hadn't been able to see a thing.

The peacock returned to my mind only once, when I was around fourteen—yes, it must have been 1957—when a cousin, older than me by four or five years, put me on the spot. "And when he beats her, what do you do? Stand around watching?"

That question stayed with me for a long time. In the end I was forced to say to myself with self-disgust: yes, I do nothing, I stand around watching. And then I'd wonder, what could I do?

I was not growing up well. I forced myself to do difficult and pointless exercises. I had long arms and when I walked they swung wildly back and forth, as if they were about to fly off my shoulders and torso. I tried to hold them back so my manner of walking wouldn't resemble that of my father. I spoke in monosyllables in order not to be as loquacious as he. I tried to behave meekly and declined all forms of competition to avoid his boastful ways. I stole furtive glances at myself in the mirror to reassure myself that we had little in common and if I saw any similar traits I would deform myself in order to camouflage them. I detested anyone who tried to compliment me by saying that I was "identical" to my father. I waited.

I didn't know how to do anything except wait. "As soon as they start to fight," my cousin suggested, "get between them, scream, and start to cry." It was pointless. I couldn't. It didn't feel like my role. I think that was when I recalled the peacock. It occurred to me that I should talk to my mother and tell her that her husband was a liar: he didn't have the eyes of an artist the way he said he did; she had let herself be duped. But I gave up on that, too. I was scared that, for whatever obscure reason, she was his accomplice, and would tell him everything. And if that happened, what would I do then? There'd be nothing left for me to do but kill him.

Those were ugly years; my hands throbbed with violence. I was certain that I could count the number of people who deserved to be alive on my fingers. I had gotten hold of a knife, nothing more than a pocketknife really, and I carried it around with the blade open in my pocket, ready to use. I was eager to stick it into someone's gut. Sometimes I asked myself who I wanted to kill. When I answered my own question, I realized with disgust that the categories of people I wanted to eliminate were the exact same ones that my father ranted about in his stories. I was repulsed by all that hatred inside of me. I would've gladly cut off my own head and replaced it with someone else's, like that of Zio Peppino or Zio Attilio or Zio Espedito.

In 1960—it was a Sunday morning, springtime, I think—I

got up early and went into the kitchen. My mother was standing there, alone and dazed. One of her eyes was swollen, purple striated with red veins. "I'm going to kill him," I said with as much conviction as I could muster up. "You're dumber than your father," she said with a lopsided grin.

PART II
THE BOY POURING WATER

A year after my father died, I became obsessed with finding one of his old paintings, *I Bevitori (The Drinkers)*. All that remained of the artwork was a black and white reproduction in an old catalog. Over time I had forgotten its original colors and even though I imagined a painting as big as a wall, I wasn't sure if I was exaggerating or if it really had been that large. It occurred to me that I wanted to give it back its former luminosity and shadows, and know its actual length and width.

So, one morning in September I called general information and got the number for the municipality of Positano, whose offices, my father used to say, had purchased the painting in 1953 for 100,000 lire. He always made sure to mention that the painting hung in the council chambers, above the mayor's seat, so when I phoned I told the staff member as much. "I'm calling for information. Would you be able to tell me if a large painting hangs in the city council chambers? I am not sure of its length or its width for that matter but it's an extremely large painting. If it's there, you will have seen it."

The woman was helpful and wanted to know the subject of the painting. I described it to her briefly. "It's of a construction site and it's called *The Drinkers*. It shows four workers eating and drinking, a Neapolitan mastiff, and a boy pouring water from a demijohn." The employee said no, she had never seen a large painting of construction workers, at least not there in the municipal hall. However, to be certain, she decided to transfer me to a colleague who was more proficient in such matters.

The woman's colleague wanted more details. I told her about my father and said that the painting was important to me for personal reasons. She tried hard to be helpful. She put me on hold and went, I think, to have a look. When I was reconnected to her, she said, "It's definitely not here. However, your father's painting might have hung in the old town hall; when we moved they might have put it somewhere else." She went on to explain to me that at one point in time the municipal hall was at a different location. "Have you ever been to Positano?" she asked in an aside. Now, however, their offices were situated in a beautiful villa. "Really? You've never been to Positano?" she asked again and then said, "Call back Monday." In the meantime, she would talk to her uncle who was a painter, maybe he'd recall my father's painting.

I said alright, thank you, I'll call Monday.

There's a story behind *The Drinkers* that I've never told anyone. It has to do with my father's artistic vocation, my mother's illness, an artless flow of water, and an arm that was at first too short and later too long. Even now as I begin to write about it, I feel unease come over me.

Almost up until the day he died, my father used to talk about that painting as if it were a major achievement, the memory of which brought him both pleasure and sadness. "Mimí," he'd confide in me, "when I was painting it, I truly felt like I was in a state of grace." And then he'd peer at me closely to see if I knew what a state of grace was. Whenever he thought I didn't know—basically, always—he went on to explain it. A state of grace, he said, is feeling like an arrow headed directly toward its target. You travel straight and determined through the air, no one can stop you from getting where you have decided you'll go. "Not even the biggest piece of shit in the world," he'd say angrily, "not even someone who tries to humiliate you as hard as they can, purely out of spite and jealousy and disrespect."

While he was talking, he'd move his index finger back and forth from left to right, illustrating the path of the arrow. Maybe it was the light in his eyes, but he made the line seem luminous. Then, as usual, he forgot all about the painting and started talking about all the obstacles he had to face. Back then—he said—between the end of the 1940s and beginning of the 1950s, after a long and tiring day of work on the railroad, he periodically went to gallery openings so that he could get a foot in the door of the art world and to exchange opinions with painters in galleries up in Vomero or on Via Chiaia or Via dei Mille.

He met lots of brilliant people that way: art critics from all the newspapers in the city, like Barbieri, Ricci, Schettini, Girace; artists such as Ciardo, Notte, Striccoli, Verdecchia, and Casciaro, who taught at the Accademia and at other art schools; there were young and pretty women painters like Tullia Matania, who was beautiful, elegant, and deeply enthusiastic about his art ever since they showed their work together at the Galleria Romanella in Vomero. In short, it was a lively and open setting. People talked, debated, Emilio Notte said one thing, Vincenzo Ciardo said another, the critic Carlo Barbieri told stories about the days when Via Cesare Rosaroll was something of a Latin quarter, how lots of artists used to live there and work there and all the late nights they had.

My father also had late nights but they were joyless ones because he was always skittish, on edge. He could never relax completely, he couldn't revel in that life of pure aesthetics. Firstly, because he was dead tired after having worked on the railroad all day; secondly, because he was depressed by the thought that he'd have to go back and waste more time there the following day, and so on for the rest of his life; and thirdly, because it was hard for him to stay quiet: he wanted to be at the center of attention and hold court and never have to stop.

If he didn't talk, if he restrained himself from speaking, he who rambled on and on so willingly, it was out of fear that something would happen the way it did one night at the Medea gallery (which was owned by Dr. Mario Mele), when the sculptor Giovanni Tizzano, an ex-policeman in the Guardia di Finanza, turned to him and asked, in front of everyone and out of pure spite, "Excuse me, Federí, but can you tell me if there's a train for Rome between midday and one o'clock?"

People started to snicker and look over at him. "Can you imagine how deeply offensive that was?" he asked me, his eyes blazing as if it had happened only an hour earlier. Tizzano, behaving like some famous artist who needed to travel to the capital to see other important artists, had addressed him in public not as a talented painter but as an employee of the railroad; his question about the train schedule was like a slap in the face. And, to make things worse, it happened while he was sitting in a corner discussing art with Tullia Matania, who had been listening to him with her mouth open and staring at him with her beautiful eyes.

"Can you believe it?" Federí insisted. Could I believe, in other words, the extent to which he had been wronged? Tizzano had the advantage of being elderly. With his white hair, my father couldn't lay a finger on him. He could only smile and reply, "Don Giuvà, if you need to go to Rome to ask about backpay from your policeman's pension fund, wouldn't it be better if you left in the morning?" A few people had laughed at that, including Tullia Matania. But Tizzano didn't back down and drove his knife in even further. "Why are you all laughing? Didn't you know that Federí is a hard-working railroad employee?"

In his early years he had to put up with things like that and far worse, my father would go on to say in a dark tone of voice. Rivalries, conspiracies, betrayals. His dream was to find a way to leave his job on the railroad and become a nationally and internationally renowned painter, to hell with all those Neapolitan detractors. He always hoped to meet an art dealer who'd say, "Federí, give me ten paintings a month and I'll pay you so well that you and your family will be able to live on easy street. Agreed?" Agreed. Leave his job on the railroad. Get paid to paint day and night. Know that each brushstroke was money in the bank. That was his dream, his hope. Mornings when he didn't have to rush off to work, he'd lie in bed smoking, staring at the ceiling and fantasizing for hours. He thought about the future. He looked silently at the shadows and imagined works of art that would make everyone sit up and say, "You truly are a great artist, Federí."

I can see him now, his large head leaning back against the head-board. I hear him clearing his throat and spitting his smoker's phlegm onto a piece of newspaper lying on the floor by the bed for that precise purpose. The room smells like sleep and night, even if it is midday. He calls out to Rusinè to bring him a coffee. His wife, who's been pumping the treadle of her sewing machine since dawn (she used to make blouses for a Slavic woman with a keen business sense), stops what she's doing, brings him a cup of coffee, and then goes back to her Singer. He sips his coffee and muses, muses and sips. "If an Istrian refugee, who doesn't even know our Neapolitans customs and ways, can make money by sewing blouses, why can't I do the same with my paintings?" he thinks. After all, art is nobler than blouses. And, in the best possible circumstances, art sells better. His wife's relatives, those stinking pieces of shit, managed to buy themselves apartments and cars by selling mortadella and cream puffs. Why can't he get rich with his art? In the past, princes and bankers used to take care of artists. Who would take care of him?

In order not to have to sigh in frustration all on his own, he called out to his wife to bring him more coffee. He could drink a whole Neapolitan moka by himself, coffee and cigarettes, cigarettes and coffee. He has an iron constitution and a strong heart. Rusinè comes in, sits down on the side of the bed, they confabulate for a bit and have a few laughs. He fantasizes about money, wants to hit the road with a portfolio of drawings under his arm, reiterates his desire to meet a dealer who'll let him paint in peace and buy houses and cars.

After their tête-à-tête, he gets up in a better mood. He's wearing a wool undershirt and large white briefs. His wife opens the window to let in some fresh air and picks up the phlegm-flecked piece of newspaper with a look of disgust. He puts on his trousers, singing to himself. Maybe he already envisions a better life for himself: going to galleries every single night if he wants, chatting with Tullia Matania without the danger of Tizzano interrupting and slinging mud on him by saying, "He's not a painter, he's a railroader."

His good mood lasts for a while. Sometimes he even sits in the kitchen and plays his mandolin. But then something sets him off; no day passes without something bad happening. Troubles on the railroad or with his colleagues. Other artists conspiring against him. Money runs out too fast. And then, Attilio and Carmela, who own the salumeria, manage to buy an apartment in a new building on Via Carelli, next to the Cinema Stadio, just a few streets away from Via Gemito. It's offensive. They already own a home and now they're buying a second one. Flaunting their wealth in front of his eyes, the eyes of a great artist. This is yet another reason why he decides, in 1953, to stun everyone—critics, painters, and quite possibly, if he manages to sell it well or win an important prize, even his relatives—and conceives of a painting that he believes will be better than Manet's *Déjeuner sur l'herbe*. A painting reminiscent of the great masters of the past, a sweeping and large-scale work—he says—the length and width of *Los Borrachos* by Velázquez. You know what I mean, Mimí? *Los Borrachos* by Velázquez at the Prado in Madrid?

When he talked about those days, he'd grip my arm tightly. "You know it, don't you?" he'd ask.

The weekend passed, Monday came, but I didn't call Positano. I decided to go in person but not right away, I had other things to do first. I thought about the painting as if it were a precious object, a treasure chest full of secrets. When, in October, my brother Geppe came to visit me in Rome, the first thing I said to him was, "Do you remember *The Drinkers*?" We talked about it at length and compared our memories. We talked and talked, and I ended up going back to Naples with him when the time came for him to leave.

My goal was to spend one night at his house and leave for Positano the next day. But the morning after, I woke up wanting to revisit a number of places in the city that were important to my father. It was hot, but even so I felt like taking a long walk. While I was walking down from Capodimonte along Santa Teresa degli Scalzi at an early hour, breathing in the already heavy air, I realized that my father and I never actually went for a walk together through Naples. There was no single place in the city where I could say this is where we stopped, this is where we said this or that to each other.

I often went out with my mother though, even as an adult. Until she fell ill. If I wanted to, I could rely on her figure as a kind of bookmark to indicate important areas and sections of roads, even. For example, at the end of the 1950s, we often walked up that exact street, Santa Teresa degli Scalzi, to see my father in a clinic not far from Ponte della Sanità. He had been operated on—I'm embarrassed to say—for hemorrhoids and was in great pain, and yet he still found the strength to tell everyone about the operation. He said the doctors had strung him upside down and, with him hanging there like that, they had worked on him, in an area that was exceedingly delicate, of course, using a scalpel and ice. He was extremely proud of how courageous he was, embellishing the experience and narrating the events in his usual manner. I just wanted him to be quiet. I couldn't understand how my mother put up with all his talking. I was embarrassed that my father had been operated on for hemorrhoids. To my friends I either said nothing, or if I absolutely had to, I told them that he had undergone a complex procedure on his stomach, a part of the body that my Zio Attilio had been operated on some years earlier with far more dignity. In short, I wished he would've been more discreet. I preferred how Rusinè handled things; she never complained about her physical or mental ailments and always bounced back, even from miscarriages and childbirth, with surprising speed and without fanfare. Federí, on the other hand, saw the slightest malady as a straight path to death, and he had to talk and talk and talk about it to exorcise his fear that, if he died, he wouldn't be able to complete the masterful works he had in mind. As I walked down Santa Teresa degli Scalzi, recognizing various corners along the way, I felt my mother's presence through her silence and heard my father's voice in the rising clamor of the city.

Once past the Museo—it was now decidedly hot—I was struck with sudden trepidation and slowed down. I could've turned onto Via Correra and headed up towards Cavone, where my father said he bought and sold things on the black market with Don Peppe the carpenter. Or else I could seek refuge in the Museo, cool down, and imagine how Federí admired Euridice's arm reaching out to Orpheus or the feet of drunken Silenus or sleeping Bacchus's bloated belly or Atlas holding up the globe and constellations. But I decided not to go in and went back to strolling at a normal pace. I walked along Via Pessina toward Piazza Dante and turned left on Via Conte di Ruvo.

That was the street my father had turned down together with the other day laborers after being assigned a job in Piazza Carità but before meeting Sergeant Leefe, before becoming the interpreter, set designer, and all the rest. There was the Teatro Bellini. That was where he had unloaded tools, pails, and cartons, constantly ranting about the bad luck he had, never any good luck.

When I was young, I always carefully avoided that street and tried not to look at the theater. As an adult, if I happened to read something that critiqued it—a grim place, reminiscent of a gilded funeral carriage, the kind that was all the rage in the late nineteenth century—I only found proof of my father's tendency to exaggerate. On that particular day, however, I perceived the importance that he had attributed to the place. I tried to imagine him turning the corner, one of a horde of desperate souls. But I realized that I conserved few memories of his features that were not from period photographs: his wide forehead, his slightly oblique and small eyes, his mouth always slightly open. These features were enough to give me an impression of him, but not enough to see him on the streets of the city.

I stopped on the corner of Via Bellini with all its bars and restaurants, now cordoned off to traffic by several large stone vases. I stood there and took in the grey stone façade of the theater with its five entrances, the white globe lights hanging from black iron brackets, the narrow balcony and second floor railing, and finally the winged lions, cherubim with lyres, and a series of theatrical masks and musical instruments up top, all crowned with the writing: TEATRO BELLINI.

I crossed over and examined the photographs hanging in the display cases out front. There was a matinee performance of *La Morte di Carnevale* by Viviani, interpreted and directed by Renato Carpentieri. After some hesitation, I made my way into the foyer: it was painted pearl-white and lush green palm fronds reached up to the ceiling. "You can't be here," a girl told me straight away. "You have to leave, or else I'll get in trouble." I asked her to let me have a quick look inside, but nothing doing. She sent me around to the artists' entrance, where there was a custodian.

I found him, an elderly man, and told him that I just wanted to have a quick look at the theater. I told him I was especially interested in the spaces upstairs, if there was a skylight, how light came in. "You need the owner's permission," he said. I tried to be charming and asked him about the theater in the years between 1944 and 45, if he recalled any of the performances put on by the English soldiers. "I'm not Methuselah or anything" he said, interrupting me. "All I need is a quick look," I said, trying one last time. "I'm sorry, but you need permission," he said, shaking his head. I thanked him and left.

I ended up spending quite a bit of time on Via Bellini, first at a bar where I had some mineral water, and then wandering around in front of the Accademia di Belle Arti, a roughly hewn stone building with two black lions at the entrance, where all the students were dressed like artists.

My father had always wished he could've spent his youth within those walls. He also would've liked it if, later on, when he was older, thanks to his reputation, they had asked him to teach art there: outsider art, insider art, whatever kind. But nothing of the sort ever happened. I looked at the yellowish façade and noticed the scant distance that separated the Bellini from the Accademia. Yes, it really was too bad that the only words I had to describe Federí were skinny, beady-eyed, wide forehead, open-mouthed. I wish I could've seen him as a young man, lively and anxious, with a fair number of years ahead of him and endless dreams.

After the Teatro Bellini, after forever closing the door on the atelier with its skylight, where, for the first time in his life, he had felt—or so he said—like a truly brilliant painter, his desire to be an artist grew even more pronounced, which led to a perennial restlessness. Over the years, his sense of disquiet grew into a never-ending torrent of nervous energy, which, by 1953, mutated into a desire to accomplish great things and the expectation that he would be acknowledged for them.

In order to tackle *The Drinkers* and all the challenges that particular painting presented, he turned our entire house, as well as the sentiments of everyone living inside it, upside down. The minor incident that caused the major earthquake was a short walk (although sometimes he said it was a meeting) with Armando De

Stefano, the painter. My father nurtured a sincere admiration for this artist, who was a few years younger than he. His respect for him was constant, it lasted through thick and thin, and when De Stefano gave him a gift of one of his paintings, my father always kept it hanging next to his own; whenever they moved house, he'd always bring the painting with him and never chucked it into a corner in disgust, the way he did with other people's work. Every chance he got, even after emitting a long series of insults, he'd always say, "Armando is the real thing, a true painter, and one of the best to come out of Naples in the post-war period."

Today I can't say where that meeting took place. Maybe on Via Caracciolo at winter's end, when you can stroll down the street with your overcoat draped over a shoulder, certain that warm days are on the way. Perhaps it took place on Via dei Mille, after having a coffee together. Unquestionably, they talked about paintings and exhibitions they'd seen—the big show in Rome at the Palazzo delle Esposizioni, for example—and they shared their displeasure, what a let-down it was, and for my father in particular. At one point, De Stefano interrupted their conversation. "Federí, we should do a show, just you and me. And not just of older paintings, but new, large-scale work." My father's jaw dropped. He immediately and enthusiastically agreed.

He came home in a great mood that day. It meant a lot to him that a young painter, someone connected to the Accademia as well as a professor at the Liceo artistico, had extended such an invitation to him. De Stefano, he said, wasn't a shithead like those other painters, even if they were locally, nationally, or internationally famous; he was a reputable man and mentally free. With De Stefano he didn't have to worry about his job, that he worked for the railroad and wasn't a full-time artist. He didn't feel the slightest bit awkward for not having studied at the art academy or gone to special schools. It didn't matter if he could never be a teacher of drawing at the art school. De Stefano had asked him because he admired him, pure and simple. "Federí, let's do a show together of new, large-scale work." Of course he had replied without thinking twice. "What a fantastic idea, Armà. I'll get straight to work."

That evening I went back to the theater and saw *La morte di Carnevale*. In the intermission between the first and second act, I left my seat and snuck upstairs to the top floor. The theater was clean and had been renovated with care. I looked out over the stage: the ceiling, painted with clouds and cherubim, seemed within touch, winged horses with frenzied looks on their faces galloped from one side to the other, their haunches illuminated.

I tried to imagine Rusinè sitting in the royal box, as my father said she had when Bebe and Douglas Fairbanks Jr. were performing. But it was pointless. My mother existed more in my memories than she did in those of her husband. Even in the memoir he later wrote, he always nullified her with one of two short phrases: that's how Rusinè was, or, she just couldn't control herself. So I walked back down to the orchestra pit. The lights had dimmed and the stage had the warm glow of a fireplace in a dark, shadowy room. If Federí, there or anyplace else, had ever acted the part of a young man with an artist's sensitivity, his wife—I imagined—had simply tried to seem like an acceptable life companion. Nothing more. But he wouldn't have any of it. His wife, he said, embarrassed him. Afterward, late at night, he fought with her and let out all his anger. "You're not coming with me to the theater ever again. You're just not good enough for it."

In his eyes, my mother was never good enough for anything, the theater or any other public place. And yet she tried. She liked women who knew how to stand up for themselves, who spoke frankly and were at ease with men, whose casual manners were both striking and scandalous. She was interested, for example, in the women artists who stayed at the galleries until late at night. She was attracted to people like Tullia Matania, who knew about art, had their own ideas, spoke their minds, and didn't worry about showing a little leg. On the rare public occasions that Federí allowed her to go with him, she always tried to copy Tullia. But that only made him angry, as he wanted her to be herself.

And what was that exactly? I will never know. When she got dressed to go out with my father, she had the staggering beauty of a movie star. Then, it was Federí who didn't seem good enough. An angry glower came over his face, everyone bothered him, he was far less entertaining than she was, and maybe he even realized it. I watched the two of them with apprehension: they were an unsteady couple—sometimes allies and sometimes rivals according to their own agendas that I knew little about. Now, in the dark theater, they seemed like flickering flames, like actors performing the death of Carnevale. Eventually, I let myself relax and enjoy the show, laughing along with the audience. What pleasures exist for those who make art. Federí knew them all: how to be at the center of attention, how to make someone laugh, how to make them cry, how to make their heart race.

With regards to *The Drinkers*, I especially recall the consistency of the bare canvas. I must've touched it several times before it was painted because I can still feel its texture in my fingertips. When my father talked about the project in that grandiloquent way of his, he used to spread his arms open wide to show me just how big it was. He had needed, he said, one whole double bedsheet for the painting, and we owned only one that was in good condition: it was a rough cloth, somewhat yellowed with age, made of hemp, coarse to sleep on. According to him, Rusinè was slow to comprehend the needs of an artist and initially she refused to give it to him. "Over my dead body," she said. He exploded with rage and she gave in.

I really can't imagine how my mother might have felt. I imagine her standing in the doorway, her ugly bathrobe wrapped tightly around her, a grimace of impotent unhappiness on her peaked face. The image I conserve of her is so worn out and yet so mobile in my memory that she seems transparent. She looks feeble, as if she has stopped believing in her own power of reasoning, as if she has resigned herself to giving him everything he demands: the bedsheet, her energy, the ironic twinkle in her eyes.

But then, my father used to say, she started to help him, laughing nervously as she did. That's just how she was: first she reared up and then she worked with him. She helped him by soaking the sheet in a copper basin and then wringing it out, but not too much, as he instructed her. Water splashing across the floor, they laid the sheet over the stretcher, she pulled it ably from one side, he tugged on it unhappily from the other. Maybe there was laughter in the air, it's possible: for me, bedsheets always meant playtime. When Rusinè and my grandmother folded them, standing at a fair distance from one another and pulling them taut in opposite directions, my brother Geppe and I leapt in the middle, got in the way, waited for them to flap the sheet over us, reveling in the gusts of air and the smell of clean laundry. But it's also possible that on that particular occasion anxiety dominated the room. We kids were called on to run to the closet to get various things: the hammer, the nails, not those nails, "the little nails; they have to be there, Mimí," my father would holler. "I bought them less than a month ago, now where the hell did you put them?" In other words, it was not fun. There was commotion, a flurry of emotions, the sheet continued to drip water. Never wrung out enough, never taut enough. My parents laid it over the stretcher, took it down, laid it out again, the house was a fen. The frame (was it constructed at home, too? Yes, no, maybe), with its four vertical wooden beams and a fifth horizontal one, took up most of the tiled floor, which had been liberated of all the furniture.

That much I remember for sure: all the furniture had been moved out. I clearly recall the ruckus of shifting everything out so that the frame and canvas for *The Drinkers* could be brought in. There goes my father down the hall with one green armchair stacked on top of the other, the floral upholstery already in bad condition. Once he puts them down in a corner of their already crowded bedroom under my mother's watchful eye, he joyfully heads back to the dining room, now intent on relocating the table. And he does it without preamble, in a dismissive frenzy. And while Rusinè and my grandmother assist, one of them picking up a hobnail glass vase of a greenish hue and the other a pair of majolica ashtrays they considered precious, he, uncombed, unshaven, in an old pair of pants caked with dry paint from crotch to knee that he wears for painting, grunts and shoves the table up against a wall, wedging it between a vitrine that we call our silver cabinet even if we don't own any silver, and a settee that, less than six years earlier, was brand new but which is now ruined beyond repair thanks to me, my two brothers, and the wet paintings he sets there to dry.

What a racket. "The feet," my mother complains and even if she didn't actually do it then, she definitely did on another occasion. By "feet" she means the legs of the table. She says it more with an anguished sigh of surrender than as an exclamation of concern. Now, when she complains about something, she does it to point out her husband's bombastic manner; she has already lost, in a matter of years, all the love she had for those mistreated pieces of furniture, mere encumbrances in their small home, which he treats as if it was a room in the Royal Alcazar made available to the great painter, Velázquez.

Such foolish fantasies: the actual facts of their domestic life are completely different. The table, the rare times we use it for eating all together, wobbles and emits a loud groan. It's been moved around too many times, the cheap wood softens like butter, sawdust spills out of each juncture and piles up in a mound on the floor in a depressing sign of disintegration. A pane of glass in the silver cabinet is broken. The settee is rickety and stained.

The upholstered chairs are torn and losing their stuffing. It's a mess.

Does Federí care? Not in the slightest. He regularly shows aristocratic disdain for their household belongings. And on occasions like that, he struts around with a superciliousness that declares that no terrestrial belongings will ever come between him and his needs as an artist. What are the table, the hobnail glass vase, or the majolica ashtrays to him? What purpose do the armchairs, the settee, the silver cabinet, or the chairs have? None, when compared with his urgent need for space around his easel and crate of colors. The more my mother protests, the more he vaunts his disdain for material objects, as if trying to show her just how unimportant they are. And then, possibly to prove just how deeply the creative urge runs through him, how it takes over his body, he shuts down all pathways of communication with her, and if she tries to talk to him, he doesn't respond, he merely looks off absently into the distance like someone who doesn't know their own name or address. This goes on until my mother has to grab his arm and shake him to get him to speak again. "Huh?" he says.

My days in Naples flew by. At night I scribbled down a mess of notes and kept saying to myself, tomorrow I'll go look for *The Drinkers*. But then the following morning I'd wake up and change my mind: today I want to go back to Via Gemito, to see that railroad-owned building where we lived, and the window that my father looked out of while he painted.

The metro station was less than a hundred meters from my brother's house. It was easy: all I had to do was descend into the abyss, with its pleasant grey walls and yellow handrails, its red bricks and the smooth black rubber pavement that smelled new, like everything down there, get on the first train, and get off at Piazza Medaglie d'Oro. From there, one morning, I strolled idly to Piazza Antignano, and observed the dilapidated old buildings, loitered around the market, no different after all these years, and slowly made my way to Via Gemito.

I stopped to look at the number plate on the building. It was the same one and there were the same two digits on it. But Via Gemito itself, in that precise spot across from the sports field, had been given the name of Piazza Quattro Giornate. And in the center of the piazza, surrounded by a metal enclosure, was some scaffolding with the word METROSUD on it, a sign of work in progress for a new metro station. There was no trace of the countryside or that wide open space between our building and sports field where, when the weather was good, neighborhood children played football, rode their bikes, or formed armies and threw rocks at each other. Luckily, the urban landscape changes, just like everything else; it becomes a shadow that provides a background for other shadows. Heavy traffic, cars and motorbikes, careened around the Metrosud enclosure.

I glanced up at the building. The color didn't look the same. Now it was white and grey, but I remembered it as being painted in warmer, brighter colors, though I can't say which exactly. Nobody appeared on the balconies. The ground floor windows had thick bars on them. The cornice that ran all the way around the building, just above the basement windows, which we kids used to climb on to look into our friends' houses and call them out to play, had been removed, maybe for security.

I walked through the gate and asked the young porter if I could have a look at the courtyard. I was hunting for changes but found few. The garden with its elegant stone border was still there. The only notable difference as far as I could see was a fountain with a statue of a woman set amid four thriving palm trees, and the pale green of the hortensia, which I recall as being somewhat lusher. In the summer, Don Ciro the caretaker used to water them every day with a hose. I'd stand by his side watching the spray—I spent a lot of time between the ages of six and eight doing that—in the hopes that he'd either say, "Here, you water them," or playfully turn the hose on me. But Don Ciro never let me spray the flowers, nor did he ever spray me. Like so many other figures in my memory, he was always in a position to do good but never did.

I counted the floors and windows on the façade. When the door to Staircase C opened suddenly and a middle-aged man came out, I gestured to him to leave it open, and walked in. I had lived on the third floor of that building from the age of four to fourteen. I take a deep breath. There's now an elevator in the stairwell, but the wooden handrail, the one I used to climb onto when I was small and slide down fast from one floor to the next, pretending not to be afraid, seemed to be the same.

I walked up the stairs slowly. The apartment where my friends once lived was now a radiology lab. The staircase was cool and dark, there were no sounds of voices or traffic outside, it was as if the apartments were empty. We, all those years ago, had been a terribly noisy family. Sometimes my parents' arguments used to break through the barrier of our apartment door and make their way out onto the landing. This happened whenever Federí threatened to leave us forever and he'd rush down the staircase yelling and swearing. On one occasion, Nannina, who never did such things, decided to take our family drama beyond our four walls. While my father was busy screaming and ranting about something pointless, she went into the bathroom or bedroom and came out wearing the dark dress that she saved for holidays and gripping her old handbag. She walked down the hall, eyes straight ahead, opened the front door, turned to her daughter, and said, "Rusinè, I'm going to live with Peppino." Something had offended her in an irremediable way. Maybe my father had said something ugly about her son. Rusinè stopped arguing with her husband and ran after her mother in tears. We grandchildren suddenly grew scared, too, and ran out onto the landing. Nonna, Nonna, we called. She walked down the steps without looking back. Her daughter hurried after her, grabbed her arm, and sobbed, "He didn't mean it, Mamma. You know how Federico is, it's all talk." We kids rushed ahead and tried to form a barrier so she couldn't get by and would have to come back upstairs. Even my father seemed a little worried. "Mother-in-law!" he started hollering from the front door of the apartment. "Can you tell me what the fuck I said that was so awful? Tell me!" And seeing that his mother-in-law didn't answer him and continued on her way in silence, making every effort to push aside her grandchildren, he went on to issue a few sarcastic remarks, got even angrier, and started cussing at the heavens above. "Since when can't I say what I want in my own home? Who the fuck runs the show here, you or me? Leave, if you want to! Leave! What the fuck do I care if you go?"

Eventually, my grandmother calmed down and decided to stay. The stairwell grew quiet again and the front door was closed. The very same door in front of which I now stood for no apparent reason. Our nameplate used to be blue with our last name painted in red by Federí. Now it was shiny brass.

Back out on the street, I stopped to lean against the back of a bench, and looked up at the main door and the gate. Each and every day, my father had rushed out that portal on his way to work at the railroad. And because he was always late and in a rush, he never entirely managed to remove the smell of paint from his skin and clothes.

He left the house swearing, carrying *The Drinkers* with him in his head. He painted the canvas as he walked down the road, rode the tram, and at work, the colors unfurling like fog down Via Gemito all the way to Piazza Garibaldi. He'd sit quietly on the tram or do his job well only if nothing or no one interfered with his thought process. If they did, he grew argumentative, deriving pleasure from the altercation, using it as a release.

Every morning he'd disappear down Via Luca Giordano and would reappear there each evening. Sometimes, mainly in the spring and summer, my mother would do her makeup, dress the three of us boys decently—me, my brother Geppe, and my brother Toni—and after the sun went down, the four of us would go wait for Federí at the tram stop opposite San Gennaro in Antignano, with its sculpture of the saint on the architrave flanked by two kneeling angels, which I liked a lot. When his tram arrived, he'd jump off the running board like a warrior home from battle. He was happy to see us all and would kiss my mother and us, too. But along the way home, he'd start to disappear; it was as if he hadn't entirely returned. "I've got too many worries, Rusinè," he'd say defensively when my mother said something like, "We should have stayed at home." Too many worries, indeed. Worries about the painting. All the interruptions. The room he was forced to paint in. It was impossible to get any work done in there, there wasn't enough light, not enough room. My father was embarrassed to have his painter friends come over to the house—he said it clearly, as if it was our fault. Did Velázquez have to work in such conditions? Did Courbet have to work in such conditions? Did any of those dabbling assholes who filled the art galleries of Naples until late at night have to work in those conditions? No, they all had a room, an attic, a space of their own. "I, on the other hand," he said even as recently as last year, "was forced to paint in a corner between the window and the dining-room table." Could I imagine what life was like for him? Did I remember the apartment on Via Gemito? As soon as it got dark, we kids had to go to bed, we slept in there, he had to put a cork in his inspiration and keep everything in his head, in his chest, until he could start up again. How could he possibly get anything done?

When he thought back to the past, my father would turn sullen. Not only was he not allowed to live the carefree life of an artist, he didn't have a proper space to work in. When old Vincenzo Ciardo talked about how well he had painted while living on Via Cesare Rosaroll, the Latin Quarter of Naples, or when Alfredo

Schettini, who was now an art critic but had been a painter when he was younger and also lived on Via Rosaroll, said the same, my father doubled over in envy and exploded with anger. "How did I get stuck painting here, in a building on Via Gemito, owned by the railroad?"

He wanted to walk away from all of it, he wanted new horizons, fresh artistic experiences. Sometimes he climbed aboard a train and went to see exhibitions in Rome, Florence, or Milan, taking advantage of the fact that railroad employees traveled for free. He used to tell the story about how once, in 1948, he had even gone to the Biennale di Venezia, to hell with his job at the Ferrovie dello Stato. He wanted to see and learn. If he didn't see or learn, how would he ever be able put chaos in order on his canvases and be the god that brings structure to the general shitshow of natural events? Rusinè didn't want him to go. "Oh shut up, it's important," he said, and off he went to Venice with his gang of critics and artists.

At first, he talked about that trip with great enthusiasm. He had gone with Striccoli and Verdecchia, the painters, and Barbieri and Ricci, the critics (he didn't bother mentioning any of the others because they weren't important to him). In terms of artistic growth, he said, the trip was worth less than zero: room after room he either saw things that he'd been doing since forever or so ugly that he'd never, ever be caught dead doing them. But he did manage to have a bit of fun with Striccoli at the expense of Carlo Barbieri in the rooms dedicated to Juan Miró.

The art critic, he told me, lowering his voice in a confidential manner, stopped dead in front of a triptych by the Spanish artist that portrayed a grey bull on a light background, first with a flaccid cock in flat red cadmium, then with a long and erect cock, and finally with the cock shooting sperm everywhere. Clearly, Barbieri's attention to the painting had nothing to do with art criticism. "Mimí," my father explained, leaning in toward me, "despite having a vast culture and artistic sensitivity, Carlo

Barbieri was a fag. That's why he spent so much time looking at the Miró."

When I was a boy, this kind of information disturbed me but I hid it; when I was older, it made me angry, and I still hid it. In the past few years, though, each time this story comes up, I get angry at myself. "Why am I still listening to this stupidity?" I ask myself. "Why does he find it so funny? What the hell am I doing here with him? I don't even know if he really went to the Biennale di Venezia, or if there really was a room dedicated to Miró. Maybe he invented the whole thing." So I acted bored by it. "Yeah, and so?" I would say sometimes. But it was pointless, he kept talking and, as usual, he ignored me, just like he did with all his interlocutors. All he wanted to do was talk. In fact, after having a hearty laugh, he continued with the story. So, we snuck up on the critic from behind and yelled, "Caught you with your pants down, Don Carlè!" But the man didn't blink. He just sighed and said, "My dear friends, have you seen this Miró? Such a huge talent!" There followed much elbowing, joking, and guffawing. Barbieri tried to defend his aesthetic point of view, waving them away. "Leave me alone, would you? Let me admire the Miró." When he finally realized that my father and Striccoli wouldn't stop teasing him, he snapped. "The truth is that you're both mediocre in comparison. That's why you can't appreciate Miró. You feel ashamed of your own mediocrity," he said.

I think that's when the fun and games at the Biennale came to an end. "Now that's enough, Don Carlè. Miró is only at the apex because you critics put him there. He wouldn't have gotten anywhere on his own," Striccoli commented in so many words, deeply offended. "Don't you dare touch my Miró! He's a rare one," Barbieri replied. "He sure is. Like some kind of stamp." And so on it went, thrust and parry.

My father said nothing. But each time he told the story, from that point forward he grew taciturn, and the tone of the narrative changed. He couldn't accept that someone had called him mediocre. Was old Barbieri offended because neither he nor Striccoli appreciated the childish cartoons that Miró, that shithead, had done? What did they have worth appreciating? Was it possible that those images possessed truth and beauty and that he couldn't see it?

Slowly, he distanced himself from Striccoli and Barbieri, who continued to argue. Walking through the hall with his hands in his pockets, a supercilious look on his face but feeling full of doubts, he forced himself to observe Miró's works more carefully. Was his own work really mediocre? Wasn't the work he did brilliant, the way he felt it was? Should he change? For a bit he toyed with the idea of creating colorful, infantile drawings like the ones in that room. Or else, the kinds of paintings that were easy to create: dab a blob of paint on a canvas and spread it with a spatula and it's done, ready to be signed. Or else, splatter different colored paints onto a canvas, as if pissing on piss, dribbles of color: do you know what I mean, Mimí? He considered all the options for a long time. I can still see him looking around the room, frowning with worry, frowning with anger, always frowning. However, caring about others and their artwork was not his forte. Soon he had forgotten the Mirós on the wall and was lost in his own projects again.

I remember how all expression faded suddenly from his face. It looked like he had some kind of inward-facing retina that saw images only he could envision, and nothing of the people or things in the world around him. During his, shall we say, irrepressibly furious and creative phase that led to the realization of *The Drinkers*, he always wore that expression. He ignored the house, his job at the railroad, his wife, all of us. He even snubbed food. He worked for hours and hours on the painting and thought of nothing else.

It wasn't that he didn't eat, but that Rusinè had a hard time getting him to come and sit down at the table. "Federí! Dinner's ready," she'd yell and then send me to tell him to come. "Papà, it's dinner time, come on, it's getting cold," I'd say in dialect. Yes, yes, he'd say and continue to dab at the canvas. I'd wait a minute or two and then tiptoe out. "He said he's coming," I'd tell my mother so she wouldn't yell again and risk getting him upset. Then I'd go sit back down at the kitchen table and we'd all continue to toy with the food on our plates: me, my brother Geppe, my brother Toni, my mother, and my grandmother.

Finally he'd arrive: the scent of his paint thinner mixing with the smell of the sauces. He'd sit down and start in on how we had waited for him and shouldn't have. Of course he was lying: if we had started without him, he would've been furious. In the meantime, his expression had changed to disgust. He said that he couldn't taste anything, that he only needed food for nutrition, that he had other things to think about. And to prove that it wasn't just an artist's pose, he ate in silence and with excruciating lassitude.

One course lasted an eternity. He'd stop with his spoon suspended in mid-air, his mouth half-open, and sit there with his eyes glazed over, staring off into space. He only snapped out of it when my mother addressed him. "Eat up," she'd say kindly but impatiently, "we're waiting for you." Startled, it was as if her words had disturbed his innermost thoughts and he reacted caustically, like someone who thought that normal people could never understand him. Actually, if he was in a good mood, he'd start to devour his food as fast as he could. "Eat up, eat up, we're waiting for you," he'd say in a monstrously cruel voice, just to irritate Rusinè. And he'd proceed to eat everything in sight, then get up from the kitchen table, go back to the dining room, and sit down at his easel to paint, correct, fix, alter, and even sing. That's right. Sometimes he even sang while he painted.

I turned right and then right again down the road known as Andrea da Salerno. I wanted to see the façade of the apartment building where I had lived from a distance, and especially our three windows. They were still there, of course, and yet somehow they were different. The window frames were now made of metal whereas before they had been made of wood and not well caulked, with cold air always managing to get in. The two small windows that had once been those of the kitchen and bathroom, next door to each other but divided by a light wall, now looked, from the outside, like one single big window of a large room, not two. Maybe it had been renovated. If so, this meant that a child would never again be able to undergo the test of courage I invented with my brother: risking our lives, we challenged each other to crawl out the bathroom window, along the sill, and in through the kitchen. At least there was that.

I stopped and tried to remember the view from up there: the countryside with its smell of mint; later, the work site that flattened it; then the building with the porticoes that grew in its place, the same one beneath which I now stood, looking up. Back then it had seemed like an elegant building, and I thought the people who lived in it were lucky. One day, some kids my age moved into an apartment on the fifth floor. We talked about building a rope and pulley system to transport things from our window to their balcony, comic books and so on. We never did, though. It was too complicated. Not even my brother Geppe, who had that kind of intelligence, managed to figure out how to do it.

Those years had a certain kind of instability to them. As quickly as faces came into focus, they lost whatever made them unique; there was always something else going on. Friends came and went. The pulley kids disappeared in a matter of months. A little girl moved into an apartment on the second floor of the new building. She played under a loggia that we envied. Our balcony was always in the shade, while hers looked cheerful and always bright white with sun. Then summer came and the little girl went to the beach, where somehow she drowned and died. It was an ugly surprise. First there was life and then it was gone. An actual person suddenly became a daydream. Even the loggia: what was it really? Empty, shuttered. I took a few steps forward and then turned around to look up at it: just another squalid balcony. The whole building had lost all traces of innovation. It stood vulnerable and fragile, the metal security gates on the shops below pulled shut and covered with graffiti. I went back to looking up at our old windows.

I hesitated on the third from the left, next to a balcony that was not ours. Behind that window—closed in the winter and open wide in the summer—my father sat at his easel and painted, year in and year out. Looking and painting. Painting and looking. I wished I could conjure him up, just for a moment, behind that metal frame, behind the glass. Instead, the kitchen window suddenly opens and my mother leans out. "Come inside, dinner's ready," she calls out in dialect. She always had that ability. After she died, for a long time I saw her everywhere. Once I even saw her walking along a rooftop cornice in her green housecoat, grimacing with pain. I squeezed my eyes shut, opened them, and turned down Via Paisiello.

I'm now going to ponder the mystery that is Rusinè. "I don't know anything about her and yet she's everywhere," I find myself thinking. I must've followed her with my eyes wherever she went when I was small, and somehow I stole her away from herself and glued her to the streets without even realizing it. At each junction, she left her image on things, the way a printer releases ink onto the blank page, forming letters and words of a text. Like the day I saw her in the park in Piazza degli Artisti, around Antignano, on Via Annella di Massimo. She wore the same hairstyle and manner of dress as always, and in the background I even saw the craftsmen's workshops and their old-fashioned tools: the shoemaker, the haberdasher, and the old *chianca* with his butcher block and green laurel wreathes adorning vats of red *soffritto*, the hanging quarters of beef and bladders of lard, followed by the *friggitoria,* where they sold hot *graffe* sprinkled with sugar.

After leaving her standing at the kitchen window of the apartment on Via Gemito, I now see her in the shop window on Via Carelli, the one run by the Slavic lady, for whom she cut and sewed blouses. It was a kind of haberdasher's, and it was situated next door to the Cinema Stadio, where my grandmother brought us children every single afternoon to get us out of the too-small house so we wouldn't bother my father while he painted or my mother while she sewed. It was there, in the mid-1950s that Rusinè and the Slavic woman tried to open a boutique. The lady put up the shop, my mother her ability as a seamstress. They were imaginative and encouraged each other. Moreover, they were both beautiful, or at least I thought so, and they were quite a vision in that hole in the wall. "This is going to be a ladies' paradise," they claimed. "We'll create outfits for special occasions. It'll be the start of a major fashion house."

Then, obviously, my father had to stick his nose in the middle of it. I don't recall him being entirely convinced at the outset, he was too worried about cheats and cons. But he let himself be enticed by the thought that his wife could make money in the fashion business and his imagination was especially fired up by what his role might be. To begin with, he suggested rebaptizing the Slavic woman's shop to "Lady's Fashion" (originally it was called "Tip Top") because—he said to the two women—we have to think big, sophisticated, international. In the meantime, he did drawings and watercolors of women modeling clothes for Rusinè so that, in case the drawings got picked up by some major fashion magazines, the experts would notice his work. "Sure, the clothes are pretty," they might say, "But who drew these elegant figures? Who's the talented artist?" And then he'd step out of the shadows and say, "Me! I am!"

It was possible; life is full of opportunities. For a while, Federí even believed in it. He hoped that his wife's sewing would be a conduit for both money and fame, that it would lead him to meet an art dealer capable of influencing the critics (shitheads, one and all, each with their own price tag) and thereby transform him into a renowned artist. And to that end—this may have all taken place the same year that he started in on *The Drinkers*—he went to great lengths. He decorated the entire shop with images of fish and jellyfish and other underwater creatures without sparing himself, indefatigable as usual when it had to do with art.

Bar Stadio on Via Carelli was gone, and so was Cinema Stadio. There was no more "Tip Top" shop, which never became "Lady's Fashion" because the law at the time made it costly to use a foreign name, and the shop never amounted to much anyway. When Federí realized that things weren't progressing as he had imagined they would, he started to hassle Rusinè about all the time she was wasting there when she ought to have been with her family. And then there was the fact, he discovered, that to keep the commercial activity alive, his wife had to do business not just with women but with men of every kind—representatives, wholesalers, traffickers, and everyone knew they just wanted to screw around—and this did not please him in the slightest. She was beautiful and a little vain; he was worried that friends and acquaintances would end up singing vulgar ditties behind his back like the one that goes, "'on Nicò, 'on Nicò, tu sí piécher'e nuje no." (Don Nico, Don Nico, you have to hit her but we, no.) As a result, he stopped supporting her and hounded her until she gave up on it, too, and came home and shut herself in.

The failure of their business was also due, and in no small part, to objective facts. For example, as the days went by, their clientele didn't increase but decreased; people didn't want couture but preferred ready-to-wear clothes, which were more comfortable and often nicer. But more significantly, neither of my parents ever managed to accept business for what it was; they weren't happy accumulating wealth lira by lira, unlike my much-detested relatives. They both tended to dignify their work with the desire to stand out, and in this they were perfectly aligned. My mother sat in the shop with its subaquatic décor painted by her husband, with its seagrass and marine creatures and fish, like an undine emerging from the ocean depths. She's still there. Not him, though. I see her waving to me the same way she did when I stopped by the shop on my way home after school.

Suddenly, Rusinè lost her youthful blitheness. I associate *The Drinkers*, and all the upset it brought into our home, with this first, slow yielding of her body.

She always looked alarmed, as if life was disintegrating beneath her feet. And there were other things. To my mind, I think she started to quietly ask herself what that man wanted from her. On the one hand she felt love for him, he continued to amaze her, and she admired him. On the other hand, she was scared that one day Federí would lose his mind running after art the way he did, and in the throes of some creative frenzy, without even realizing it, might kill all of us, the whole family—her, Nonna Nannina, us kids—and then run off, as he so often threatened to do, and play the part of the misunderstood genius, just not on Via Gemito, but somewhere in the South Seas.

And so she came to look at him with the same regard she had for Vesuvius, majestic and stunning but deadly, capable of creating earthquakes and spreading lava and ash, with no logic except his own thoughts on life and destiny. He needed a bedsheet? He wanted to build a stretcher as big as the room? He required four dining chairs, which would quickly get splattered with paint, to hold up that mausoleum? But had he taken into account the cost of paint? At times she was amused by it all and spoke to him ironically, in a tone of mock consent that I keep tucked away somewhere; more often than not, however, she smiled just to keep the peace.

Like now, for example. She watches him skeptically as he stirs a dense liquid in an old tin can. It's an extremely sticky, greyish mixture of his own invention that he carefully spreads onto the canvas to prepare it for the color. The stuff stinks like a henhouse, like something feral, like something rotting, and when he mixes all the ingredients together and cooks them on the stove, the stench sticks to the walls for days on end. With this, my father explains to us chattily as he smears the gluey paste across the canvas, the hemp sheet will contract and the brush will glide better than an expert skier, and the color won't fade but will remain brilliant in perpetuity.

He wants us to think of him as some kind of scientist, or expert in all sorts of techniques, like the nobleman and wizard-inventor Raimondo di Sangro, whom he often mentions. He began his study of the tools of the trade casually when the war ended and now every occasion is good for showing off how well he knows the world of brushes and pigments. He goes through periods when he toys with the idea of making everything himself in order to save money. Brushes, for example. What would it take to tie together a handful of boar bristles or ox hair, wrap some strips of aluminum around them, and then attach them to a wooden stick? As for colors, he throws around even more complex words: poisonous oxides and sulfurs and chlorides and antimonies, which he blends with his colorful, everyday language.

When he was an elderly man, he said that he had invented everything, that he was always ahead of his times. Resins and pigments really pissed him off; he was already using them with success long before that shithead Yves Klein (whom he swore he met in Nice in 1943, just like he swore he met so many other extremely famous painters) had the silly idea of covering his whores in Klein blue and rolling them around on his canvases. Then there were the tools and instruments: he knew how to use them all, from A to Z, from acquaforte to xylography and serigraphy. "Mimí," he instructed me, "this is what you need to say to yourself: if some jackass can do it, you—if you want—can definitely do it better." And that's why he, himself, in first person, got straight down to it: chiseling, engraving, fiddling with zinc plates and nitric acid. "You remember the movie projectors? You remember the movie camera I bought in instalments in 1955?"

I remembered. But we're still in 1953. April, I think it was. And right now he's spreading a paste made of rabbit skin and fermented gesso and minced muck and ammonia and I don't know what else onto the now-dry hemp sheet which they had stretched taut on the frame, continuing to talk and talk, issuing commands and orders for us to execute instantaneously.

He needs so many things urgently and never gets up to get them himself. The rare times that he does, he stumbles around the room, adding chaos to the general disorder. "It's impossible to find anything in this house," he grumbles, and since he needs whatever he's looking for immediately, it practically requires a straightjacket to calm him down. Until my mother steps in. She leads him by the hand to the object he's looking for, speaking to him in the way you would a crazy person. "Here it is, here where you left it, where it always was. No one ever touched it."

I know next to nothing about how or when he started working on *The Drinkers*. He might have started the large-scale painting with the mastiff, but I wouldn't swear on it. I definitely recall him walking around the room, rustling through his papers, examining sketches of figures or landscapes, touching old objects, always disgruntled. Then suddenly that dog appears, with its vigilant eyes, alert and threatening. But I can't exclude the fact that I'm now giving that image more importance than it's due merely because it had a powerful impression on me and my imagination.

Federí used to talk about how hard he worked on the mastiff. He traveled all around the countryside near Vomero, did endless preparatory sketches, even risked getting bitten by a few angry dogs. I remember the drawings, some of them still exist.

But for me, the dog in the painting had a different source. It was made of marble and there was a photograph of it in a book with a bright blue cover that my father generally kept in a crate next to his easel. The book had once belonged to Zio Peppino di Firenze, whose house my parents stayed at during their honeymoon. When he died, that book and several other objects—as well as his ghost, the second most important ghost of my life after Modesta—ended up at our house. Federí was deeply attached to those heirlooms. He leafed endlessly through the old book, looking at the illustrations. He used some of the silver bowls, chinoiserie, statuettes, and the violin as part of the compositions for his still-lifes, or simply for inspiration. To him, they weren't just objects, they were imbued with an aura of affection. They had been bequeathed to him, a man who argued with absolutely everyone, by someone with whom he had gotten along miraculously well.

I went to Zio Peppino's house in Florence on Via dei Pilastri, building number 18 once, too. I must have been seven or eight years old and was amazed at how cluttered it was with both large and small antiques. I remember seeing a jade Buddha, a delicate fan painted with Japanese ladies, an enormous shell that held the sound of a stormy sea, and paper lanterns on which ugly and malevolent faces were painted.

I was not the only one to be enchanted by those objects; my father was, too. It must have seemed to him that Zio Peppino di Firenze shared a particular sensitivity. The point is this: he always spoke well of the man. He was an amazing person, he'd say, a heavyweight, sure, tall and fat, but always playful and cheerful, a friend to friends and enemies alike. During the fascist period, he had been a member of the political police; after the war, he seamlessly became part of the normal police. Federí interpreted this as a sign that Zio Peppino di Firenze had always done the right thing and never hurt anyone, that he'd even been willing, when needed, to hide fellow policemen, anti-fascists, and Jews alike, whom he was supposed to have been locking up. He worked as a marshal of public safety until the day he died but never carried a gun; he wanted to avoid saving his own life by taking another's. When he found himself in danger, he'd intimidate the bad guys by yelling at them in his blend of Tuscan and Neapolitan, deck them with formidable punches, and slap a pair of cuffs on them.

In spite of his scant policeman's pay, Zio Peppino di Firenze managed to make a little money by teaming up with a junkyard dealer-friend who worked throughout the war and who, after the Liberation, discovered he was rich. The scrap-metal dealer used to pass Zio Peppino time-consuming jobs which he did after his public marshaling, like extracting as much iron that could possibly be extracted from old electrical meters. He paid him by letting him keep the copper wire bobbins and the remaining bit of silver or platinum in the meters. The money Zio Peppino made from that allowed him to start a small antiques business and build up his own collection, which was on show in his home. He had some extraordinary things. There were no less than one thousand antique objects in that apartment, including statuettes, old books, postcards, photographs from the early nineteen hundreds, a wooden cylinder that you peered into and turned a crank and saw vistas of Florence, and paintings by Fattori, Giacino Gigante, and Pitloo.

All this brought Federí great pleasure and he went to Florence whenever he could. Zio Peppino recognized his acquired nephew's genius, and the acquired nephew recognized that his uncle may indeed have had the developing taste of an artist. Together they shared many a laugh. Zio Peppino, for example, loved to break wind as he walked down the street, in the stairwells of buildings, everywhere. And he liked to do it loudly. My father liked to indulge his humor and constantly encouraged him to fart, especially when they came home late at night. "Zio Peppí, announce your arrival," he egged him on. And, on command, Zio Peppino would disturb his sleeping neighbors by tooting loudly as they climbed the staircase, pressing his broad derriere up against the doors of each and every apartment and releasing a phenomenal fusillade. What laughs they had. Jokes of all kinds.

To be entirely honest, I didn't feel entirely comfortable sharing in their revelry. Despite the great sympathy that my father felt for him, or perhaps precisely because of it, I remember, on the rare occasions we went to stay with Zio Peppino and his wife Nenella in their house in Florence, being scared of him. I didn't like his florid skin. I didn't like how he was always sweaty. I was scared by the fact that he was a policeman. And I found it both amusing and disgusting that, at his age, he could fart the way we kids could.

Even his house made me feel uneasy. I didn't like those dark and shadowy corners, I didn't like the musty smell in the air, I was bothered by the fact that it was there, in Zio Peppino and Zia Nenella's bed, that my father had to go to such efforts with my mother so that I would one day be born, which he told absolutely everyone. At the same time, I was also attracted by all the lovely things in the house. That book with the bright blue cover, for example; I looked at the pictures over and over. All the statuettes. And the two Flobert rifles that my uncle kept in a glass case near the front door. My brother Geppe and I admired them all day long. When Zio Peppino went out in the morning to do his policing, we always accompanied him to the door and politely said goodbye, and he always said, "What well brought-up children, they really do adore me." In truth, we couldn't wait until he was out of the house. To get us to behave, Zia Nenella would open the glass case for us and let us have the experience of touching the rifles.

And yet, I was never entirely at ease. I was always scared that Zio Peppino di Firenze would suddenly come back, get angry, and toss us behind bars. As a matter of fact, he expressly forbade us to touch those rifles. Only he was allowed to do so. When he got home from work in the evening (always a little tipsy given that he either stopped at a bar and then in an osteria, my father

said, and couldn't say no to a little drink, or he visited his lover, a
widow with a generous body with whom he drank, cavorted, and
farted in complete freedom, and all before dinner), he'd pick out
one of the rifles and call my father and us kids out onto the ter-
race. "Let's scare the Jews a little," he'd say and start shooting at
the dome of the synagogue, which echoed loudly when he hit it.
And then he'd laugh and shower us all with his good cheer and
abundant physical presence. Don't worry, he said, he was friends
with all the Jews and especially the custodian of the synagogue,
who got scared but never angry.

I stood there and listened. I watched as my uncle reloaded
and fired again. I saw how happy my father was in his company.
But the long, sorrowful tolling of the dome made me apprehensive and that fact wasn't lost on Zio Peppino. "The kid doesn't
know how to have fun," he said to my father, as if it were his
fault. So, to avoid being scolded by my father, I pretended that I
enjoyed it a great deal.

I always felt awkward around him. Once, I couldn't have
been more than seven years old, I recall getting so anxious about
being in his house and exposed to so many strange novelties that
I suddenly had to pee very badly but didn't manage to get to the
john in time, and so I wet my pants. I tried hiding it by telling
my mother that water had splashed on me while I was drinking
from the tap and she fell for it. But not Zio Peppino di Firenze.
"Water? Water splashed on you? From the tap?" he hooted and
hollered. His laughter was so contagious that soon everyone was
laughing: my brother, my mother, my father, Zia Nenella, and in
the end, even me.

When we got back to Naples, I decided to exact my revenge
by writing him a letter. I used to write all kinds of letters and
notes when I was young, and then I'd stick them in the mailbox in secret. Mailboxes always fascinated me, the old kinds, but
even the kinds they have today. And so I wrote him a letter and
drew some pictures with the intention of secretly putting it in

the mailbox, and maybe even drawing a stamp on the envelope. I wrote about how disgustingly fat Zio Peppino di Firenze was and how much his farts stunk. But then my father found the piece of paper and scolded me. "Mimí, never joke about people's physical defects," he said. This coming from a man who constantly joked about people's physical defects.

Evidently their relationship meant a lot to him and he didn't want to ruin it. When my father was in Naples, he was obsessed with all those shitheads and their conspiracies against him, but in that house on Via dei Pilastri he managed to relax. When we went to Florence at the end of the 1940s for a few days as their guests, while Zia Nenella and Rusinè prattled among themselves, first laughing and then crying, he and Zio Peppino spent all their time poring over his antiques, especially the paintings on wood by Gigante, Palizzi, and Pitloo. My father finally felt like he had met someone who appreciated him, without drama or artifice. "Zi' Peppí," he confessed, "in Naples no one understands me. Your wife's relatives are all pieces of shit, other painters are jealous, and the critics don't understand a thing." And then, unable to contain himself, he showed the police marshal the clippings from the newspaper where his name was mentioned. "See how well known I am?" he said, going on to relay his various successes. "They even gave me a prize at the first regional competition in Campania." He flaunted how much collectors spent to buy his paintings. "I'm pretty bankable now." Every so often he called over to his wife. "Isn't that right, Rusinè, that I won a prize?" Whether true or not, my mother always said yes, as if by tacit agreement.

Zio Peppino read the reviews and listened carefully as Federí told him about the awards and prices of his paintings. "Damn!" he exclaimed now and then, rediscovering his Neapolitan accent that life in Florence had caused to fade somewhat. He genuinely admired Federí. What an intelligent man, Federí would recollect fondly: he understood straightaway that his acquired

nephew was a superior being and that he deserved all manners of respect. Never in his life had my father felt so at ease,
so loved. Sometimes, the two men wandered around Florence
with Zio Peppino's paint box—he, too, had a propensity for
the brushes—and they painted side by side. They chatted and
painted, painted and chatted. Even though Zio Peppino wasn't
a true artist, something my father didn't hesitate to point out to
him every chance he got and which Zio Peppino accepted without offense, he could still paint small countryside landscapes that
resembled those done in the late 1800s. What wonderful times
they spent together. Uncle and nephew agreed on all sorts of
topics, from politics—which they saw as pure shit—to art, the
only exciting thing in life besides fucking. Now and then they'd
stop to compare their work: Zio Peppino was enthusiastic about
everything his nephew did, while my father consistently offered
his uncle some minor corrections.

"Nineteenth-century art," Federí explained to his uncle,
"is complex stuff. You need to know how it is done." He then
showed him the right brushstroke, the magic touch. Once, to
show him, he reproduced Lega's *La scellerata* on an antique plate
with excellent results. Zio Peppino was amazed and showed the
plate to an art expert named Nocentini who took it for an authen-
tic Lega. The expert adored the piece and handed Zio Peppino
the beauty of 100,000 lire for it. He, in turn, gave my father fifty
percent. You understand what kind of man he was?

I listened to that happy story and others but never felt entirely happy myself. Everything having to do with Zio Peppino
di Firenze filled me with an uneasy mix of joy and fear. That
feeling only grew in intensity when my father had to rush off one
morning because the news had reached us that Zio had died during the night from a heart attack. He was only forty-eight years
old. He had woken up suddenly at four o'clock in the morning.
Initially, the deadly contractions made him laugh nervously, but
then he got so angry that he threw one of his heavy punches at

the wall. Luckily (or unluckily, according to Federí), he didn't hit his wife by mistake and kill her.

My father came home with a fair number of objects from Via dei Pilastri that we had often admired (definitely the blue cloth-covered book with its many reproductions, including the mastiff; definitely the Stradivarius violin; and definitely a statuette of a drunkard), further cluttering the tight space in our apartment. "That's all we need: more junk," Rusinè protested. And that's when, to my mind, the shade of Zio Peppino came to live with us in the apartment on Via Gemito. For a long time I considered him a secret protector of all the knickknacks and dusty books, as well as a dangerous phantasm. From that point on, whenever something frightening happened or appeared in the house, I felt it came directly from his meaty hands, bringing with it both a bit of warm joy and a graveyard chill.

Even the mastiff had something of that ambiguous nature. When it started to peek out from the hemp canvas of *The Drinkers*, I immediately recognized it. What a long, tiring journey it had made from Via dei Pilastri to Via Gemito. Then it got mixed up with the dogs that my father sketched while walking around the countryside and later, thanks to art, it started to become the mastiff in *The Drinkers*.

I shut my eyes and envision the painting: it was so tall that it barely fit through the door and so long that it filled three quarters of the room. It diminished the space available to us in such a way that, to prepare the beds that we slept on each night and to put away the plants on their iron stands and the side tables, my grandmother had to double over and move with great agility. She'd mutter to herself angrily in dialect. Sometimes, when her son-in-law was out at his job on the railroad, she'd call Rusinè over. "Would you look at this mess," she'd complain in frustration. I know, I know, my mother would listlessly say. "You know how he is, Mamma; when he's got to paint, he's got to paint."

I have often reflected on those words. Today is an ugly autumn day and I just wrote them out reluctantly, as if they should be read with a tone of resignation. But maybe tomorrow, when I re-read them, I'll change my mind and instead, in her words, I'll see a desire to defend her husband, an attempt to explain to her mother that her son-in-law had serious motivations which ought to be respected. But right now I'm certain that Rusinè had already begun to give up, on both her rebellion against those preposterous living conditions and her hope of changing the man she'd been allotted. Or worse: maybe all she thought about was smoothing over friction and avoiding troubles that would make her life, or our own, any stormier than it already was.

That was probably the direction her anxious thoughts took each time she set foot in the dining room and saw her bedsheet ready to be covered with colors. She was afraid of the living situation getting worse than it was. "If no one buys it, where are we going to put such a huge painting?" she probably thought to herself. But she never expressed her anguish in actual words or sentences. She'd just lean against the doorway and peep in, check how the painting was coming along, and either frown or look sad. To me it was clear what was going through her head because I was thinking the same thing. I wondered what would happen if we had to keep the painting, what problems it would create at home: my father wouldn't be able to paint anything else for lack of space, my grandmother would never be able to clean properly and give the apartment a semblance of order, we would forever have to sleep in a corner of the room, head to toe, me, my brother Geppe, my brother Toni, and Nonna Nannina. And that's why I always had a hard time getting to sleep at night.

A beam of light from the kitchen, where my mother worked until late on her Singer, shone into the room through the slightly open door. The noise of the sewing machine sounded like metal marbles rolling across the floor. If my father wasn't on a night shift at the station, every so often there'd be the sound of him clearing his throat, which burned from all his smoking. From ten o'clock on, his sleepy children took over the studio and he smoked to calm his nerves, frustrated at not being able to paint through the night. He wandered around the house, spat loudly into the sink, tried to encourage sleep by reading and learning about any number of topics: ancient and modern languages, science, literature, art. He wanted to accumulate as many notions and ideas as he could to prove that he knew more than the painters who didn't know shit, even though they taught in schools. But sleep never came, he could only think about his painting, his head was crowded with all sorts of possible compositions, an infinite number of variations. Something would come to him, he'd discard it, then go back to it. He'd start to sketch, quickly scribbling, then ask my mother something (for a coffee, for example). She'd stop the clatter of the Singer and get up to serve him. Federí would say a few words, but never thank you. Rusinè would reply, he'd snap back, and soon they'd be squabbling.

From the end of the bed where I lay, the painting was a dark theater set. The soft glow from the kitchen fell on the large muzzle of the Neapolitan mastiff that he had started to draw. It felt like it was looking in my direction. I shut my eyes so as not to see the mastiff's ugly mug, the apoplectic stare of Zio Peppino's ghost. But then I reopened them. The unfinished outline of that dog, with one alert ear, one alarmed eye, a well-developed neck and chest but no legs, seemed to mirror the fragments of words I heard coming from the kitchen: syllables, partial signs, things spoken and unspoken. Meanings that struggled to emerge, shapes left hanging.

My mother's words were especially this way. By then she had stopped confronting him directly, the way she had in earlier years, and even though she was more cautious, she still managed to insinuate herself into the conversation by latching onto his words and expressing her criticism of his boastful and blusterous ways. In one particular instance, she was taking him to task for his behavior in public, and I didn't quite understand why. She told him—I think—that she didn't like the way he talked to Armando De Stefano and other painters and critics like Paolo Ricci, Barbieri, and Piero Girace. "Oh really? And how exactly do I talk?" he said to her, annoyed. "Too softly," she replied quickly, pointing out how Armando often interrupted him and said, pardon me, Federí, I didn't quite hear you. How was it that when he talked to Armando De Stefano he whispered as if at confession, while he always yelled at other people? And with her comment she meant, although she didn't come out and say it but I understood it anyway, that he always raised his voice with people who didn't matter to him. With her, for example, or her mother and brother and all her relatives. Meanwhile, with people like Armando De Stefano, it was almost as if he was afraid of being heard. "You should speak up, say what you think," she said in a slightly mocking way, whispering because she was afraid of making a mistake. After all, Armando was a professor, a figure of authority, and if he told Federí to make a large-scale painting, he'd do it, and without thinking of the consequences, taking away her one good bedsheet, making life intolerable for everyone, wouldn't he?

Late-night questions, sounds that fell in the dark somewhere between me and the mastiff. My father grew enraged and yelled loudly at her. "I speak softly because people with manners speak softly!" Rusinè didn't have manners and that was why she always screamed. He, however, had manners and spoke in a soft voice with polite people and yelled at fucking idiots. Was that clear? Why should he listen to what she had to say about how he spoke with Armando De Stefano? What did she want from him? Did she even realize how far he had come, in just a matter of years? Did she remember what things were like for him when he started out? Did she realize that he used to be a nobody? And now Armando De Stefano came up to him and said, "Let's do an exhibit together of large-scale works"? For Chrissakes, Rusinè, you're always busting my balls. As if he hadn't learned from experience how he should speak and how he shouldn't. He'd raise his voice when and where he felt like it, depending on the situation, depending on how the fuck he felt, depending on the need.

It took nothing for him to fly into a rage. Those late-night conversations quickly grew into arguments that would end only when it seemed to him that Rusinè had eaten her words. He simply couldn't tolerate her sticking her nose into his business, not even indirectly. Even more importantly, he couldn't accept the hypothesis subtly put forth by his wife through her comment about his timid voice, that he suffered from an inferiority complex. He had never felt inferior to anyone in his whole life, not even when people did everything they could to make him feel it. And to prove it to her, he told the story about the early days of his artistic career, before he had even shown a single one of his works, when he still was chomping at the bit. "My time will come!" he used to say.

And his time indeed came one day in the spring of 1945, when he read in the *Risorgimento* that Galleria Forti, on Via dei Mille across from the Cinema Corona, was organizing the first postwar group art show, and that it was open to all young Neapolitan artists of the new Italy, regardless of education or political party or union affiliation. Perfect. "I'm a young Neapolitan artist, aren't I?" he asked himself. Yes, he replied emphatically, and ran straight away to see Don Peppe the carpenter, so that he'd cut him some simple but elegant strips of wood that he would use to frame his stunning *Piazza Dante* (as he had seen in Les Anges, at the house of his teacher, Rose Fleury), a painting which had been greatly admired by both Sergeant Leefe and Bebe Daniels, as well as his portrait of a junk dealer, *Vecchio Rigattiere*, painted from real life on Via San Gregorio Armeno. Once framed, he admired his work at length; they looked exceptional and he brought them in person to Galleria Forti.

For days on end he reveled in his debut as if it were a major triumph. Ever since he was young, he knew it could be no other way. He even imagined that he'd be awarded first prize. Instead he got something of a punch in the face. He learned that *Piazza Dante* and the *Rigattiere* had been turned down by the jury. Thrown out, essentially. He took it badly and almost started to cry. "Who do they think I am? Some fucking loser?" Rusinè didn't know how to calm him down, and he felt a pain growing inside that grew sharper with every passing minute.

The night of the opening he went to the gallery spitting venom. "Federí, don't act crazy," his wife pleaded. He didn't reply. He had reacquired much of his energy and wanted to see the paintings that had been chosen, to compare them with his, to see if they really were better. He walked into the gallery, looked around, examined the paintings one by one, and concluded that the whole thing was a *chiavica*, a steaming pile of shit. He started complaining about it loudly, how offended he was, the angry feeling in his chest was coming back. He started talking to one fellow, argued with another, and finally figured out what was really going on. Not coincidentally, he told me, a member of the jury was related to two of the artists whose work was on show. Not coincidentally, the exhibition had purportedly been organized to show the work of the art-school students, whose professors had held their posts under the fascist dictatorship and who, while wanting to exhibit the bravura of their students, also wanted to prove their own, and were eager to carry on as if nothing had happened. In an effort to calm him down, one fellow told him that a number of artworks had been turned down simply because the gallery didn't have space to show them all. Oh, is that so? Turned down for that? And who the hell decided that the space ought to be filled with those revolting pieces of shit, and not his *Piazza Dante* or his *Rigattiere*?

He stormed out of the gallery cussing and swearing and headed straight toward Via Medina, where the offices of the communist newspaper *La Voce del Mezzogiorno* were located. Naturally, he grew up believing that communists were *chiavicóni maísti*, enormous pools of shit, as well as rotten, dangerous people. Over the course of his life he often used that term to describe them to me, especially at the end of the 1960s and throughout the 1970s. Communists, socialists, no difference at all, he said. All *chiavicóni*. His father, Don Mimí, had always considered himself a socialist and that explains a lot about Socialism, Federí said. In any case, with regards to the situation in which my father found himself, he urgently needed to find someone who'd listen to him, he wanted the entire left-wing press to know what he had discovered, that the country was turning to shit, yet again. But when he turned down Via Medina, he hesitated. Should I or shouldn't I? Should I go upstairs to their offices or not? He did. He climbed the stairs resolutely.

Once he got to the newsroom, they sent him to talk to Paolo Ricci, also known as Paolone, a painter and art critic. In all my father's stories, whatever the season and whatever the occasion, Paolone always wore a red silk kerchief and carried a dangerous looking walking stick. And that is exactly how he found him on that occasion. Ricci listened to him carefully while twiddling his walking stick. "You're right, Federí," he eventually said. "There has been no changeover whatsoever in the art schools. The teachers are still the same sissy *scurnacchiati* eunuchs who ruined the young artists of Italy with all their empty rhetoric about fascist art." Then, after discussing one of the goals of democracy—to free young and promising painters of preconceived notions of painting and drawing, and to give them a broader critical vision—he gave him some advice. "Federí, write a letter for our editorial page and denounce this horrible thing that happened to you."

My father agreed enthusiastically, but the meeting didn't end there. Ricci took his arm and asked him if he had ever heard about the Salon des Refusés. My father nodded uncertainly because he wasn't sure if he had heard about it or not. Even with me, when he told me this story, he was ambiguous. His version changed depending on his mood. "Rose Fleury mentioned it but, at the time, I was so smitten with her that I didn't pay too much attention," he sometimes said. "Whatever I knew about the Salon des Refusés was little or nothing," he said on other occasions. In any case, Ricci started explaining how, about eighty years earlier, the Salon de Paris had turned away some extremely talented painters—people who went on to become famous, like the great Edouard Manet, with his scandalouse *Le Déjeuner sur l'herbe*—simply because they considered them unworthy. Those artists, however, didn't give up and went on to organize a counter-salon. "And that was the Salon des Refusés, Federí. An exhibition of cast-offs," he concluded, tapping Federí meaningfully on his broad forehead with his walking stick.

My father walked out of the newsroom, his thoughts blazing like a match on fire. I imagined him flying through the night, a blindingly bright rebel angel windmilling light down Via Medina, already planning a Neapolitan counter-salon in opposition to the filth on show at Galleria Forti. He got home, climbed into bed, and woke up my mother to tell her the news. "Tomorrow morning, with the support of *La Voce del Mezzogiorno* and Paolo Ricci, the communist art critic, I'm going to organize an exhibition of everyone who was rejected to protest those assholes at Galleria Forti." The show would be identical, he went on to explain to her, to the exhibition organized by a number of important French painters who had been turned away by the Salon de Paris some eighty years earlier. He wanted to keep going and tell her the whole story because he couldn't fall asleep. But Rusinè was exhausted after a long, tense, and tiring day. "Calm down, Federí, now sleep a little."

To hell with sleep. He wanted to stay awake and catch up on all the time he had wasted, and continued to waste, at his job on the railroad. It became clear to him that since he was born in

Naples, and since the city of Naples had become his geographical destiny, then Naples could become what Paris was for those people rejected by the Salon. Yes. Destiny was definitely paving certain roads for him.

One road in particular, Via Bisignano, seemed to have a particularly strong impression on him, because he never, ever forgot its name and, in particular, building number 20. It was located only a few steps away from Via dei Mille. If you walked out of the enemy gallery, where they were busy awarding the Premio Forti, all you had to do was walk down Via Filangieri and into Piazza Rodinò, and there, on the right, was Via Bisignano; it led straight to the back entrance of the municipal hall and Via Caracciolo. On that road was a small shop owned by a certain Signor Improta, a true gentleman, who embraced my father's cause and wanted to help him and the other rejected painters. In fact, Improta shared Federí's belief that art, just like everything else, had remained in the hands of fascists. "Don Federí, I am on your side. Take my shop and use it for your counter-salon."

And so it was that there in that venue, thanks to a true gentleman, and with no strings attached (No strings! he often repeated, for it was rare that someone did him a favor without expecting anything in return: he never took it for granted and was forever grateful, especially as the relationship with the man was too brief for him to suffer any wrongs by him), there in that shop space, as I was saying, he swiftly set up a Paris-style counter-exhibition of the cast-offs baptized the "Mostra degli scartati."

It was a deeply gratifying event. When an article came out in *La Voce del Mezzogiorno* by Paolo Ricci that discussed the protest behind that initiative, Federí felt that he was, to all intents and purposes, an artist. And from then on, he began to collect clippings from newspapers as if they were the only true witnesses of his presence in that world, sacred reliquaries of his existence. I remember them well: some were even minuscule. As a child first, and later as a boy, I felt the same sense of pride and satisfaction for those pieces of printed paper with his first and last name on them as he did. The words that spoke of him were not valuable for what they said (whether good or bad), but for the dignity that they, to his eyes and consequently to mine, brought him. When he said, "Look, Mimí, look what they wrote about your father," in that proud tone, I deduced that if a person wanted to live a memorable life, their name needed to appear in the newspaper. The painters in that counter-salon enjoyed that glory. But not all of them. Thanks to Ricci, those with talent saw their names mentioned in black and white—"Look, Mimí!"—for all perpetuity, including: Salvatore Esposito, also known as Cocco Bagnoli, who was an Ilva steelworker, student of architecture, and expert draftsman, and who later disappeared and did nothing further in the world of art; Mario Colucci, who went on to become a tenured professor at the Liceo artistico (an elegant man, he later suggested my father read the correspondence between Vincent Van Gogh and his brother Theo, launching him into the world of art theory); and my father, there was his name, who for now had painted only a vivid landscape of Piazza Dante but who surely had a strong future ahead of him with large-scale works that promised to be even better than those of Delacriox and Courbet, better than *Los Borrachos* by Velázquez, and even better than anything by the scurrilous Manet.

He came home jumpier than ever, but jumpy from happiness. He showed my mother, his brother-in-law, his brother, and probably even me, who could still barely speak, and maybe even my grandmother, who had forgotten how to read, what Ricci had written about him. Few but important words. His first name and last name came right after those of Salvatore Esposito and Mario Colucci. Paolo Ricci had named him third. Third place among the rejects, whom—I imagined, whenever I heard that heroic word—must have all been just like him: unhappy, anxious, their hair slicked back to seem receptive and consequently more aggressive. So aggressive that when I lay in bed and couldn't fall asleep, back when we still lived on Via Gemito, I would imagine all the rejects running down the street in a gang like a screaming pack of animals all the way to Via dei Mille and on to the Galleria Forti, where they'd make obscene gestures and yell epithets at their rivals, spitting or pissing on them or throwing *cazzimbocchi*, the phallus-shaped paving stones, and then run off into the empty night, shouting and swearing.

When he was less in the mood for fibbing and more inclined towards self-soothing fantasies, Federí said that in the seven-year period between 1945 and 1952 he took part in more than forty shows nationally and that his work had been exhibited in Paris, France and later in Miami, Florida thanks to Rose Fleury initially and Douglas Fairbanks Jr. and Bebe after. When he got a little depressed, though, he forgot all about his international expositions and the forty (a randomly invented number) shows and spoke in a warmer, somewhat more tender voice to complain about the many obstacles that he had to overcome. This included the enormous fatigue it had cost him and particularly at the beginning. It was a physical fatigue, he emphasized: his muscles were tired, his heart worked overtime, his bones ached, he was always on his feet, running here and there, his nerves wore against each other like stone and flint, or were as tautly strung as Ulysses' bow when he shot the first arrow that led to the massacre of all those shitheads who wanted to take his place in Ithaca.

To begin with, after having the opportunity of showing with the other rejects and thanks to Paolo Ricci's willingness, he discovered the communists. So, in addition to holding down his job on the railroad, after work he started going to the offices of both *L'Unità* and *La Voce del Mezzogiorno*, where he'd say good evening comrades, and go on to show that he knew how to draw well, with both good taste and a sense of humor.

Now that I'm working on his stories, I can see him making his rounds of the smoky newsrooms, walking between the desks of click-clacking typewriters, stopping to chew the ear off first one fellow and then another, always yammering about himself in a setting he knew nothing about, not least what kind of language to use to avoid saying the wrong thing.

How nerve-wracking. This is how—he told me on various occasions and at different periods in his life, adding and subtracting elements at will—he spent his days: first off, he had to put in his hours at the station, which guaranteed him a salary of 48,000 lire a month; after that he had to hurry to *L'Unità* and *La Voce del Mezzogiorno*, where he earned a monthly stipend of 8,000 lire for his drawings and vignettes. Political vignettes, of course, he pointed out with the usual cockiness, and illustrations. He came home briefly between the two, just to give his wife and children a kiss hello; sometimes he found the time to wash, change, and eat a bite (but just a bite: he had little interest in food, as I already mentioned); then he'd rush back out, slamming the door behind him, to go—and here he never skipped a detail—to Angiporto, a gallery in Piazzetta Matilde Serao, the same square where the newsroom was located.

I imagined him with his mussed-up hair, wide forehead and lanky body, hurrying from Via Gemito to Via Luca Giordano, leaping onto the running board of a tram, and off he went. He'd walk into the newsroom and immediately out again in the company of Aldo De Jaco, the journalist, to go and visit various factories where he'd sketch portraits of the workers while De Jaco would gather information for his articles. The two were inseparable. Federí illustrated the world inside the factories and Aldo described the workers' lives, and the stories the pair published together were phenomenal.

As a boy, I listened to him enrapt. I didn't know how to be cruelly skeptical, the way I would eventually become. I imagined my father driving off in a Topolino with De Jaco or in a motorcycle sidecar or truck, in the rain or icy wind that blew off the sea, all the way to—let's say—the Ilva steelworks, through

lightning and fires and reddish smoke, sketching in pencil
while De Jaco scribbled his notes in pen. Sketching and scribbling, what a partnership. Although I can still see him today,
I don't believe him the way I used to, unfortunately. Had *The
Drinkers*, with its depiction of workers on their lunch break,
grown out of his experiences as militant-painter, as a member
of the PCI? And when exactly did he become a card-carrying
member? When was it that he started working at *L'Unità* and
La Voce del Mezzogiorno?

He replied to questions like that without skipping a beat, as
usual. "Of course I painted workers because I was a communist.
I enrolled in the party in August of 1944 and was hired with
a steady salary by *L'Unità* and *La Voce del Mezzogiorno* at the
end of March, 1948." Month and year, always. Had I asked, he
would've probably told me the exact date and time of day. So did
that mean, I wondered, that he was already a communist when
he worked with the English at the Teatro Bellini? Did that mean
that he was already a communist—I asked him once, but cautiously—when Cacciapuoti's relative stood in front of him at the
ticket booth at Napoli Centrale and showed him his chest full of
scars like a true patriot and called him a fascist? Was he already
a communist when, according to the story he often told us and
especially over meals, while taking part in a strike, he found himself surrounded by members of the mob screaming, "Barricade
the city, comrades, and burn everything!" so he jumped up onto
a tram that had been knocked over onto its side, the electrical
cable darting about this way and that, and had shouted, "Idiots,
fellow comrades *di questo cazzo*, how the hell are we going to get
to work tomorrow if you burn the trams?"

I headed up Via Carelli and then turned right on Via Luca
Giordano. I was in no hurry and didn't glance at my watch once.
I walked past my old elementary school, stopping for a couple of
minutes in front of D'Avino's flower shop. To celebrate Rusinè's

saint day, my father always sent me out early in the morning to buy her flowers. It was one kindness he enjoyed doing and never hesitated to spend lavishly, even if it was the last bit of money in his wallet. We kids gave her yellow roses, he nothing less than an orchid. He put on a grand show as her cavalier servente, took her in his arms, and kissed her like a movie star would. It was fun to watch. "Oh, Federí, you always exaggerate," my mother would say, cooing artificially while she removed the orchid from its box. Then she'd devote herself to the roses we held out to her and put them in water in the green hobnail vase.

It occurred to me that maybe I should dedicate more space to his attribute of affectionate husband who doesn't skimp on things out of love. But it's hard for me to do so: it happened rarely and never lasted long. He went straight from being kind, almost playful, to aggressive. For example, the story of Via Pitloo. When I turned down that street, I recalled how Rusinè used to pronounce it "Via Pitlòn." It's pronounced "Via Pitlò," Federí would correct her with amusement. She'd laugh shyly and blush with confusion, but went right back to saying "Pitlòn." And then, all of a sudden, he'd get fed up. "It's Pitlò. Is it too hard for you to say Pitlò? You always make me look like shit."

She was a little slow, he'd say, and he told her as much. Once he instructed her how she should vote; he was worried she'd choose the wrong symbol. He was irascibly pedantic with both her and my grandmother, even quizzing them on the spot. Rusinè would always try to get out of it and say she understood, that she wasn't some idiot, but he insisted just to be sure. And then he'd indicate me, I was small at the time, and say, "How much do you want to bet that Mimí understood, but not you?"

On another occasion, she came back from Mass and told him in a normal voice that, in his homily, the priest at St. Gennaro church in Antignano had said that communists and socialists would all end up in hell, and in the confessional, he had instructed her to "Tell God everything you do with your husband." Now, it could be that my mother underestimated her husband's eventual reaction, but I highly doubt that. It's more probable that, as always, she didn't want to hide something serious from him, which would only make him angrier. The result was that all hell broke loose. First, my father blew up at her, as if she was in cahoots with the priest. Then he yelled that he'd go straight over there and beat that stinking piece of shit to a pulp. "I want to bust open his face," he shouted, finding the threat of hell for communists and socialists less intolerable than the intimacies the priest demanded Rusinè entrust to God. I remember him running to the front door and yanking it open. He wanted to rush out in his pants and undershirt, with no shirt on, not even a jacket. He would've done it, too, I think, if my mother hadn't stood in his way. "No, Federí, don't do it!" she screamed in fear.

He often saw her as being in cahoots with all the people who did everything they could to get him angry. Once he came home furious because, as he explained it to us, although he had been ("unanimously") elected district secretary of the railroad union, the head of the Communist party federation had asked him to step down so that the seats could be fairly divvied up and the position given to Antonio Santoro, a socialist. That's when my mother made a mistake. "Better that way! All we need now is the union," she said, or something to that effect. Federí lashed out at her so hard, it was as if she were the head of the Communist party federation or even Santoro himself. An artist, he screamed furiously, needs experience, Rusinè: connections, people, politics, the union, everything. If not, no one ever finds out who he is or what he's worth, no one will ever say: Let's get Federí to do the poster for the CGIL railroad workers union or the commemorative painting about the Quattro Giornate.

I returned to Via Gemito the long way, stopping next to the sports field, in front of the small building that houses the police station. On its façade I noticed the stone plaque that had

had a strong impact on me as a kid. I took out a notebook and copied down the words that were engraved on it. "This building was used as a fort by young patriots during their final brutal struggle for freedom, holding off the vile and ferocious German forces . . ."

My father never explained to me why the stone plaque was there, what it had to do with the vile and ferocious German forces, why there had been a brutal struggle, and what the young patriots were seeking. And yet, since 1947, it had been affixed to the exterior of that building that sat directly opposite the one where we lived, 50 meters away, at most. I read it on my own and by chance one day, somewhere between the ages of eight and nine, while I was playing, I think: running, playing chase, tumbling around the ticket turnstiles. I used to read everything back then, even though I didn't understand it all. I remember being struck by the word fort, a word we often used back then in our games of cowboys and Indians, as well as by some capital letters—HERE 7 SOLDIERS FELL, DIED UNKNOWN—words that evoked images of men who got so hurt they couldn't even bring themselves to say my name is so-and-so.

I stood there writing it down when an elegantly dressed, distinguished-looking gentleman with white hair walked by. He noticed that I was transcribing the words on the plaque and stopped. He stood off to one side and glanced at me, my notebook, and the plaque. Then, certain that a person who copies down the words on a plaque must be connected to the municipality, he said, "Someone should tell the mayor that they should call the new station 'Quattro Giornate' and not 'Cilea.' That way, people would say, 'I got off the metro at Quattro Giornate,' or, 'I got on at Quattro Giornate,' and then people would remember it." I nodded in agreement and he kept talking. "They buried the dead not far away from here, on Via Rossini. But when they built the swimming pool they had to disinter them. Who knows where they put them afterward," he said. "Probably the cemetery," I

said. "Or else they just dumped them," he commented skeptically. "Don't forget," he said when we said goodbye, "If you get
the chance, tell the mayor to call the station 'Quattro Giornate.'"
Alright, I said to him, if I get the chance.

I went back to strolling around. I walked down Via Cile to
Belvedere, and on to Via Aniello Falcone, then turned around
and came back. I kind of wish my father had been like that man.
Measured and calm, not someone who always exaggerated. Or
maybe not. Whenever Federí mentioned the uprising of Naples
against the Nazi-fascist forces, it was always as if he was annoyed
by it; he didn't believe that the city of Naples had insurrected.
For him "the city" or "the people" were abstractions of propaganda. In actual fact—he would point out even as late as the
1970s, when every opportunity was good for revealing just how
antithetical our outlooks were—the so-called insurrection took
place thanks to the efforts of a very few pure of heart, an expression he often used, and a ton of Camorra thugs who couldn't
stomach the German steely discipline because it interfered with
their usual criminal trafficking.

"You don't believe me?" he'd ask me in dialect when he realized I was skeptical about his theory. "All of a sudden, when
it was all over, there were thousands of patriots." Sometimes
he even mentioned Gigino Campo, and how he had given him
the chance to sign that document full of lies that said they had
fought side by side to defend the Ponte della Sanità. Other times
he just got angry. "The pure of heart end up dead, and the stinking pieces of shit end up with careers."

The career he aspired to was that of artist. All of his tirades
leaned in that direction. If someone had commissioned a painting from him about the Quattro Giornate uprising, I believe he
would've immediately re-evaluated his stance. But since that
never happened, he said the Quattro Giornate had been invented so his rival painters could do ugly, commemorative drawings and paintings, which the communist press went on to call

masterpieces. "Four heroic days," the people in the party used to say. Heroes *di questo cazzo.* "Back then, Mimí," he'd whine, "the communists would've gladly executed followers of Trotsky or Bordiga, or even just decent folk who risked their lives on the street every single day."

My mother always listened to her husband's political harangues without saying a word. Had they both been communists, him and her? When did they stop? What were their politics? I don't think she ever really knew for sure. She had so many other problems, and politics were the least of her worries. He, meanwhile, did nothing but confuse the matter. Even when he showed her which symbol to tick on the ballot, he expressed his displeasure with the party and griped about its leaders. It wasn't that he complained about domestic or international policies; he never even mentioned those topics. He complained about trifling matters that he considered extremely important. For example, he often used to tell the story of how he, Aldo De Jaco, Luisella Viviani, and the Hon. Mario Palermo went to Salerno for an assembly. (For some strange reason, in his political-party anecdotes, he was always in the company of well-known journalists, bureaucrats, and members of Parliament). After the speeches, the singing of *Bandiera Rossa,* and the applause, a delegation of factory workers accompanied the four of them to the station with great fanfare. Hon. Palermo reached out of his first-class train compartment window and shook hands with each and every member of his devoted electorate. Then, however, as soon as the train pulled out of the station, he ran to the john to wash his hands of all traces of the working class. My father couldn't stand that he did that. "Can you believe it? Do you realize what that means?" he inquired, staring straight at either my mother or me depending on the occasion, to make sure that we truly understood the implication.

I always nodded my head, as usual. My mother, however,

seemed more skeptical. "And what was Palermo supposed to do? Never wash his hands again?" she may have asked. Come to think of it, it must have been in 1966, right when I was about to become a card-carrying communist myself, one evening, after him telling that story, that I decided to put her exact question to him. "What was Palermo supposed to do? Never wash his hands again?" I asked, essentially in homage to Rusinè, who had recently died.

Federí got upset. "It's no laughing matter," he said brusquely and then started mumbling. "Never mind, kid, maybe I wasn't clear. But don't forget that I started working on the railroad as an electrical repairman back when I was eighteen." He knew what the working class was all about. Even in his art, workers were always the subject of his paintings, like in *The Drinkers*. Don't you get it? How could Mario Palermo have possibly gone and washed his hands? Communists took advantage of the working class and then showed disgust for them; they didn't understand them, they didn't comprehend their language or morals, etcetera.

Sometimes he'd start to denigrate them and it seemed like he'd never stop. He'd begin with Palermo's squeaky clean hands and go on until he was talking about their sexual proclivities, a subject that piqued my mother's interest. "Really!" she'd exclaim, suddenly attentive. It wasn't a shocked "Really?" but more of an amazed "Really!" However, my father thought her question stemmed from curiosity or awe, and this made him nervous and consequently angrier, which led him to become even more vulgar and reveal all sorts of details. For example, he talked about how, over at the party headquarters, in the newsroom, or in the union offices, this fellow's wife was screwing another woman's husband, how everyone was screwing someone, and so on and so on, naming names; basically it was a jungle of cheating wives and *curnuti*, cuckolds, who knew what was going on and *curnuti* who didn't know what was going on and ball-less *scurnacchiati* of all kinds, with their so-called special friendships and intimacies and all sorts of other bogus crap that he divulged to Rusinè in order to reach his conclusion: "See what kind of place it is? Don't you ever think about setting foot in there."

He continued to tell me this story up until a few years ago. "That's why I never let your mother come with me." Sure, she would've liked to, no doubt about it. She wished she could've always been by his side and seen the world. She wanted to learn more about the women who were involved in politics, the ones who debated issues openly with men, how they dressed, gesticulated, spoke, laughed, and even crossed their legs. "But I never wanted her to," he said to me over and over. It was hard enough for him to spend time with those people. It was absurd—he said suddenly, shifting the focus of his complaints—how the communists fucked wildly among themselves in secret, but would rap your knuckles in public if you used foul language or made vulgar comments.

For example, once, he lowered his voice in a confidential manner, he had said to comrade D'Avenio, who was comrade De Jaco's wife, that comrade Tina De Angelis, who was comrade Obici's partner, had beautiful legs. "That's all I said," he emphasized, "beautiful legs." Harmless words said in a friendly tone, just to make conversation. But what did comrade D'Avenio do? Did she smile? Did she giggle and give him a playful shove and say, "Federí, how dare you!" No. She scolded him acrimoniously. She curtly took him to task. She said that his way of talking was both indecent and offensive. He just stood there speechless and stunned. Eventually, with some embarrassment, he said that he had only wanted to pay her a compliment. He then went on to say allusively to me that, actually, he had often admired Tina's legs, at length, back when they had been setting up the *Festival dell'Unità* in Castellamare together, and he often wished that he could sketch or paint her, that his was just a compliment coming from an artist and fellow member of the working class. That D'Avenio woman, meanwhile, walked off, nose in the air, like someone who thinks, "Would you look at the degenerate people you meet in the newsroom."

I then headed up Vico Acitillo which, if I'm not mistaken, used to be a simple country road back when I was a boy, a place young couples went to make out. Now it was a busy thoroughfare that ran parallel to Via Gemito, and evidently a place favored by dogs, judging by the mounds of feces that littered the sidewalk. I had to make my way cautiously down the street, being careful where I stepped. It occurred to me that maybe my father was angry with the communists less for political reasons and more because they barely even took notice of him, despite the fact that he dedicated a great deal of time to representing the life of the working class between the end of the 1940s and the early 1950s. Deep down, he seethed, they preferred Juan Miró; they thought an employee of the railroad could only ever be an employee of the railroad, and never a great artist, even though they preached proletarian art. "Kid," he said, squinting his eyes at me, "Never, ever did the commies truly believe in equality. Actually, they wanted me to genuflect when they walked by." Take Mario Alicata, for example. He'd walk into the newsroom haughtily, without greeting anyone, no good morning or good afternoon, as if he descended straight from Abraham's nuts. When people saw him come in, they'd jump to their feet and bow their heads ever so slightly, but it was still a bow. My father, no. "Your father," he exclaimed, "never got to his feet and never bowed his head." Who the hell did that bastard think he was.

One day, Alicata came in and, instead of heading straight to his own desk, stopped in front of Federí's. "You're not in the habit of greeting people, are you, Federí?" he asked. "Comrade Alicata, who should I greet if I already greeted everyone when I came in? You're the one who just got here; you should be the one to greet us, not me. Me, I choose to follow the example of Giorgione, who used to greet his assistants when he walked in his studio so as not to appear superior to them in any way. And that's exactly what you should do, too." More or less, that's what he said. "I was born an artist, not a sheep," he used to say. "I hate herds."

When I was a kid, I'd sit and listen to him and then repeat back exactly the same things to my buddies. I was scared I wouldn't distinguish myself the way he had. Maybe that's another reason I was struck by the plaque on Via Gemito that said HERE 7 SOLDIERS FELL, DIED UNKNOWN. I was worried about dying unknown. My father, it occurred to me, would never die unknown. Whenever something happened, he did everything possible to make sure people knew and remembered exactly who he was. If there was no way of getting them to remember him, he'd get angry, and say that the events simply weren't important enough. He hated all situations where he was not a main actor, all the occasions where either for one reason or another he did not manage to shine. When he couldn't create an important role for himself, he defended himself by spitting on it. The Quattro Giornate uprising? Patooey. The Resistance? Patooey. Communist press? Patooey. The union? Patooey. I grew up surrounded by spit and phlegm. As soon as he'd start talking about some important event, I hoped he'd had an important role in it just to avoid those bitter tirades.

Even Rusinè didn't like his tendency to constantly denigrate people. She grew dejected as she listened to him. "He makes people hate him," she said. She, meanwhile, liked being on good terms with everyone. She greeted acquaintances warmly. Everyone liked her, especially other women, and particularly Signora Pagnano, who was nothing less than the wife of a general and whose daughter, Signorina Pagnano, came to Rusinè to have her dresses made for balls and parties. Rusinè was also treated with great respect by men, including: Luigi, the roving fruit and vegetable vendor, who was extremely shy and always polite with her; Don Ciro the porter, who considered her a princess; and even by all the painters who came to our house over the years. She wished she had married a man who hadn't made her congeniality shrivel up inside, a man who had allowed her to share it with the rest of the world. But no. He kept the world to himself or would wave it like a fan in front of her with his stories. But the minute she said, "Let me come with you," he'd quickly snap that fan shut.

They argued about this often, but never overtly. While I stood by the entrance to the swimming pool on Via Rossini, I remembered how once she said to him, "You're always so crabby." She wanted him to understand that his bitterness made him less likeable and this upset her.

Federí immediately tensed up. "Me? I'm not crabby. I look at the facts and act accordingly," he replied. "No, actually you just get angry; you're always so testy," she said. What she meant was that his unpleasant character not only led him to spend his life arguing and complaining, but forced her to live hers without any great expressions of joy. The only thing my father heard was that she accused him of being too aggressive—he never really listened to her, or anyone, for more than thirty seconds—and so he started to crow about how sincere and frank he was and how his thoughts were not subjected to any form of conditioning, but really and truly free, the spontaneous efflorescence of his intellect.

Federí had the mind-boggling certainty that he needed nothing more than his intelligence to pass judgement. He didn't read the papers or listen to the radio; he overheard names and events and used those to form and express his opinion. "It's just how you are," his wife said to him that time. "Oh, just shut up," he screamed at her. He knew everything he could possibly need to know, he said. He knew it via his own sources. Either he had met people directly at certain junctures of his life, whether they were politicians, cultural figures, scientists, or artists, and could thereby pronounce directly on their deficiencies; or he was in contact with people he trusted who told him how things actually stood; or he reduced the information he overheard to other information that he knew a little something about, like something that had happened to him or to his relatives, which clarified the events that were being discussed in the newspaper or on the radio or, in later years, on TV. That's how my father was. And so Rusinè shut up that day. And gradually she gave up trying to say anything at all.

"Luckily, you didn't turn out like him," my grandmother used to say to me. And once, although I can't remember exactly when, my mother agreed with her and said, "No, you're not like him at all." However, in other circumstances, she used to lovingly say the exact opposite: "You're dumber than your father."

I still didn't even know exactly who "I" was. Let's just say I tended to be quiet rather than talkative, even on my own. I warded off any and all similarities with Federí through detachment. As a teenager I started consciously detesting every single word he said. I would've gladly traded him with a father who had died fighting the Nazis; or one who'd been tortured to death rather than speak; or one who'd fought and spilled blood on street after street to protect Naples from the vile and ferocious Germans. Until I was almost twenty years old, I hid my thoughts from him and tried to shield myself from his. And even later, in the second half of the 1960s, our disputes were always contained and never personal. We discussed—though surely that's an exaggerated term to describe it—politics. At the time, I had accumulated a lot of information; at first, trying not to hurt him too much, I agreed with him (in particular about the Stalinist communists; I admired Trotsky and so it was easy to agree with him on Stalin's crimes), but then I started systematically disagreeing with him. At a certain point, he'd get angry and say that all the books I was reading were pointless. "Who gives a fuck about all that shit," he'd exclaim. Then he went on to explain that the important books were not about politics, history, or economics, but about art, literature, and even science. "All the rest is propaganda, Mimí," he'd conclude. "Forget about politics: real history is made by artists. Think about art and literature. Think about the things that really matter."

In time, I calmed down, but he never did. Up until three years ago, he continued to grumble about the same things over the phone. "Everything passes, kid. The value of the lira changes and soon it won't even be called 'lira' any more. No one remembers the symbols of the old political parties. As for all the politicians' names, those *scurnacchiati*, they're nobodies. If you remember them, it's because of the wrongs they did you. So let's think about ourselves. At the very least, let's try and keep our name alive."

I kept my reply to myself: "Papà, a name is nothing more than the sound of someone clearing their throat, a smear of ink." But he never gave up. He wanted me to agree with him and say, it's true, everything passes, but you will last, the paintings you created will last forever, your signature there at the bottom right, in red, it will last. But because I didn't say that, he'd flare up into a rage and force me to engage in endless long-distance phone calls. "Do you remember *The Drinkers*, Mimí?" he'd ask. And then he'd start in complaining about the terrible conditions in which he had to work, about all the wrongs he had been done by his relatives and others, even by people he didn't know, all the obstacles that had been set in his path. I'd listen and soon enough, with a growing sense of unease, I became a child again. I heard the drama and urgency in his voice. At a certain point I stopped hearing his voice and only saw him: he was standing on the tram that had been tipped over at whatever protest it was in whichever piazza, the electric cable darting this way and that, a crowd of protesters around him, while he yelled, "Hey idiots, comrades *di questo cazzo*, how the hell are we going to get to work tomorrow if we burn the trams?" I could even see both his real and imaginary enemies in the crowd, even Mario Alicata, tall and hunchbacked, who stared at him in amazement, shook his head, and walked off.

Whether real or imagined, one of my father's principal enemies was the painter, Raffaele Lippi. He didn't like Raffaele Lippi at all. He thought his art was overpraised by the communist party federation. Lippi also worked at *La Voce del Mezzogiorno* but since he wasn't capable of drawing from life in the factories in tandem with a journalist, he focused on political vignettes and, Federí said with growing enmity, he'd walk into the newsroom and show off his lousy, two-bit drawings. He'd come prancing in and wave them under everyone's noses as if those ugly stains, those fouled pieces of paper were true works of art. He'd show them to Giorgio Amendola, Mario Alicata, Abdon Alinovi, Aldo De Jaco, and Nino Sansone and say, "Get it? Good one, right? You like it? Go on, tell the truth."

The truth, in my father's opinion, was the following: master Raffaele Lippi, while gifted with determination, barely had basic drawing skills. He had dedicated himself to painting in a social realist style, but it had been a rash decision, and the results were terrible, because to draw in a social realistic style you needed basic skills. While an artist like Vespignani had made a fortune embracing the style, and while it had allowed a visionary the likes of Guttuso to set out on his deeply personal path, it had also ruined a painter like Pizzinato. You can well imagine what it did to someone like Lippi, who cried out, "I'm a social realist!" from the rooftops.

"Lippi?" my father would ask. "Forget about him." The only thing Lippi knew how to do was show his vignettes to people and say, "Get it? Good one, right? You like it? Go on, tell the truth." Or else calumny other people and spread rumors around the newsroom in a whisper. "What's Federico doing here? I know him: he's a fascist."

Back at my brother's house, even though I was exhausted from my day of roaming around, I had a hard time falling asleep. I tossed and turned, switched the light on and off, got up and lay down. Fascist was a bad word, and particularly in a communist milieu. If Lippi had spoken about my father like that, it meant that he considered him an occasional visitor, someone who stopped in now and then whom people didn't know well, not a real party member, not a salaried employee of *La Voce del Mezzogiorno*.

There were discrepancies in Federí's stories. One day something was true, another it was a lie. Communist, fascist. My father definitely didn't feel like a fascist. He felt like a person who cared only about making art, he was a person with a phenomenal brain: free, bold, full of important ideas. In other words, he frequently said with audacity, he didn't give a flying fuck about fascism or communism, about monarchists or Christian democrats. When he engaged with those kind of people, it was only to see if they were truly capable of appreciating his art. The fact that he was five years old when the March on Rome took place and twenty-five when the Fascist Grand Council voted to remove the Duce from office was a minor detail, background information, like the shadow cast by a tree on the façade of a building. He had spent his childhood, adolescence, and youth standing next to that tree, in its shade, and what of it? He was himself and himself alone, he declaimed arrogantly. His words were his own, his beliefs were his own, the ideas that came to him were his own, his painting skills were his own. He refused to accept that fascism may have left its slag within him. He had never been—he screamed—one of those goose-stepping, fasces-toting lictors who had dodged a bullet by taking part in the Lictorial games and were now back in positions of power as if nothing had ever happened, even within the Communist Federation, and even at *L'Unità*. He wasn't like Raffaele Lippi. Now that Lippi, he was a fascist. Ten years ago he would've done anything to paint Mussolini's portrait; now he was doing whatever he could to paint Stalin's.

He found out about it one day when he went to the newsroom.

He found Lippi in the hallway standing next to a slender crate, the kind used for shipping paintings. On it were the words, COMRADE JOSEPH STALIN, MOSCOW USSR. "What's in there, Rafè? Are you exporting paintings?" he asked without hesitating. "Inside that crate is a portrait of Stalin," Lippi replied. "Did you do it?" my father asked. "Yes, for the head of the Soviet Union's 70th birthday," Lippi said. "Who commissioned it, Rafè?" my father asked. "The Federation," Lippi said. "All hush-hush?" my father asked. "Actually, in the bright light of day," Lippi said. "I'm sure Stalin will be thrilled," my father said. "Actually, he has already said that he's going to hang it in the Pushkin Museum," Lippi said. "Damn! The Pushkin Museum?" my father asked. "Yes, Guttuso and I are the only Italian artists who have the honor of being exhibited in the Pushkin Museum," Lippi said.

From that day on, whenever Lippi brought his vignettes to the newsroom, not only did he turn to this or that person and say "Get it? Good one, right? You like it? Go on, tell the truth," he also added, "And don't forget: I'm the second artist after Guttuso to have the honor of being exhibited in the Pushkin Museum." My father had such a hard time holding back and not screaming out what the newspaper factotum had confided in him. "Poor Joseph Stalin," the man had said, "You have no idea how ugly Comrade Lippi painted him! All the comrades are worried that when Stalin sees how Lippi depicted him, he'll blow a fuse. Mamma mia, what a terrible impression we Neapolitan communists are going to make with that painting! The Federation ought to have assigned you the job of doing a portrait of Comrade Stalin, Federí."

That's exactly what my father thought, too, and he secretly tormented himself with the belief that, "Yes, there's no doubt: if the Federation had commissioned me, my painting would've been much better."

He also believed he was a far better satirical cartoonist than Lippi. He captured politicians just the way they were with only a few slightly exaggerated traits. I remember him drawing some right in front of my mother and me, just like that, while we were sitting and waiting in a fabric shop in Antignano: an image of De Gasperi with a crown on his head and one of Scelba with a helmet. The shopkeeper insisted on saving the piece of paper as a keepsake. "How talented you are, Don Federí," the man had said.

No doubt about it. He could've become famous, if it hadn't been for Lippi. Because Lippi did whatever he could to set obstacles in his path and scowled when my father discreetly offered to do the cartoons. This went on until November 1951, when there was a major natural disaster and a state of emergency was declared. It had rained so hard that the Po River burst its banks and flooded the entire surrounding plains, all the way to Polesine. An appropriate cartoon was needed but Lippi had already handed his in for the day, and naturally it had nothing to do with the recent catastrophe. What should we do? Where's Raffaèle? "Call Lippi, find him, get him to draw something about the evacuees," people were shouting in the newsroom. But no one could find Lippi; he was nowhere to be found. My father, who was there at the time, and as high-strung as ever, started yelling, "*Padreterno*, there are other people who know how to draw besides Lippi!" Time was ticking, they needed to find a solution. "Here's our solution," Nino Sansone suddenly said to De Jaco, pointing at my father.

There was a long pause. "Fine, but how do we tell Lippi?" De Jaco said, furrowing his brow. "Screw Lippi," Sansone replied. "We tried looking for him, didn't we? Enough is enough. We can't waste any more time. Federí, get to work."

His heart leapt, he heard his blood pumping in his eardrums, his brain was on fire. He imagined the dark sky and heavy clouds overhead, he saw the rising gray waters of the Po, he felt the rain beating down on him the way it had fallen on the people in the area for days on end; he then envisioned Amintore Fanfani saying to them in a steady voice, "We will do whatever it takes to help the flood victims, at whatever the cost." And then he began to draw.

In a matter of seconds, he drew a likeness of Fanfani standing on the street outside Palazzo Montecitorio and confabulating with an umbrella vendor. "I'll take them all," he wrote for a caption. Then he added some finishing touches and rushed it over to Sansone. "Perfect," Sansone said. "Perfect," Aldo De Jaco said.

But just then, Raffaele Lippi came running in with Rubens Capaldo. "What's going on?" Lippi asked in alarm and out of breath, but the vignette was already safe in the hands of Giorgio Amendola, who approved of it, with Mario Alicata also giving it a thumb's up.

"Ciao, Rafè," De Jaco said and pulled Lippi aside to explain the situation to him: "You weren't around, so . . ." In the meantime, the vignette, which my father was eyeing nervously, his heart beating fast, had been passed to the messenger who would take it to be electrotyped. Lippi was arguing with De Jaco. "Well, you could have waited . . ." he said. "I have to go, it's already late," the messenger said, starting to leave, when Rubens Capaldo stopped him in his tracks so he could see the cartoon. "My what a fine drawing, what a likeness!" he said, looking at Alicata. "Well done, Federí," he continued, and then called Lippi over. "Rafè, come see how good the cartoon is that Federico did."

Annoyed, Lippi was flustered, then left De Jaco's side and went to examine the drawing. "You actually like this?" he said in a disgusted voice to Rubens Capaldo, waving it around. "Did you even look at it? Don't tell me, Rubbè, that you actually like this."

My father's heart was beating so hard it felt like it was going to explode out of his chest and into Lippi's face. Capaldo took the piece of paper out of his friend's hands and handed it to the messenger. "Hurry up, kid," he said, "Calm down, Rafè. It's great." As the messenger ran off, my father heaved a sigh of relief and then turned to Lippi with some advice. "Maybe you need glasses."

The following day—he went on to tell me but without much enthusiasm, as if the story contained more bad omens than good ones—*La Voce del Mezzogiorno* flew off the newsstands: his vignette was plastered to every wall of every piazza in Italy. Lippi never forgot it and, from that moment on, he spent all his energy slandering Federí, saying he was evil, a member of the Camorra, out to get his job, dangerous. One day, Lippi even said to his face, "Thank Polesine and your lucky stars that I wasn't around. What are you trying to do? Compete with me? Remember that I'm one of only two Italian artists, together with Guttuso, whose work hangs in the Pushkin Museum."

This only made my father's blood boil and frayed his nerves even more. He was so on edge that whenever Rusinè decided to surprise him with a visit to the newsroom—fixing herself up so prettily that she looked like Jennifer Jones, cleaning up me and my brother Geppe, fighting the anxiety that he'd make a scene, and making her way down from Vomero all the way to Piazzetta Matilde Serao where the newsroom was located—he always said that he was happy, but we knew that he wasn't, and that actually he had to bite his tongue in order not to scream at her to get out and go home.

Did his wife have the slightest inkling of what she did to him? All of a sudden, there she was with their two sons, embarrassing him in front of all those scumbags, distracting him while he tried to get work done in a situation of extreme tension, leaving him angry and bothered when he sent her home, making him worry they made it back safely, and that nothing happened to them on the way.

For Chrissakes, it was awful. He hadn't signed up for that. "Mimí," he solemnly concluded, "I became a member of the communist party firstly to contribute to the cause of the working class, having been a worker myself since 1935, and secondly because I wanted a quiet life, to live under a governing force that I thought espoused order and discipline." A governing force that would recognize his talents, despite being an employee of the railroad, and take advantage of them. "And instead," he exclaimed bluntly, "see how shittily they treated me?"

The next morning, seeing that I was in Naples, I decided to go to the Biblioteca Nazionale and look for that satirical drawing of Amintore Fanfani. I left the house feeling rather chipper. I hoped that a flash of truth would soon cast its light on all my father's fantasies, and all the falsities he had invented would be meaningless, unimportant. "I'll go to Positano tomorrow," I said to myself, "in the right frame of mind and clear-headed."

But my mood quickly soured. It was hot and sticky outside, and my feet and ankles hurt from all the walking I had done. Crossing the heavily trafficked streets seemed harder than usual, and I felt a growing sense of unease and instability. What's worse, the main entrance to the library was closed and I had to walk all the way around Teatro San Carlo and down Piazza Trieste e Trento. I stumbled around a pretty but dry and dirty park that was filled with disheveled students until I found the entrance. I left my belongings in a locker in the lobby and headed up a staircase. I had lost all desire to sift through newspapers and scroll through microfiches.

The library was apparently under construction and it looked like it had been hit by an earthquake. Although I had spent a lot of afternoons there as a kid, I suddenly realized that the time I remembered most clearly had to do with Rusinè, even if she never actually set foot inside. I went there one day in July 1965 to read about her illness. By then she'd already been in the hospital for a month, and she went on to die only a few months later, in October. I remember asking for the book that I needed, then waiting, and finally choosing a table where I could peruse it.

Of that morning in 1965, I have several clear memories: the
beautiful light shining off the sea and through the window,
the gilded ceiling, a fire extinguisher in one corner, the wooden
bookshelves. I sat and read for a long time, learning everything
I could about my mother's illness and its three phases. The most
painful aspect was learning the duration of the first phase: anywhere from three to twelve years. Exhuming her old aches and
pains, I did the math and realized instantly that the illness started
back in 1953. I tried to remember what made that year different.
I recalled *The Drinkers*. While my mother may have been getting
sick, that painting had taken over our life and seemed like the
most important thing in the world.

My suspicion stayed with me for years and spread like mil-
dew over my recollection of the painting. Later it occurred to
me that perhaps I was exaggerating. Why choose the maximum
incubation period of twelve years? The pathogen, the book said,
could have first appeared in the spleen via her blood in 1953,
1954, 1955, 1956, 1957, all the way to 1962. For a long time I
chose 1953. Over time, however, I realized that telling the story
of a body that falls ill is the hardest one to tell, and so I gave
up. But back in 1965, while Rusinè was living the last months
of her life, I felt as though I finally possessed the truth. I read
about the symptoms: weakness, physical debilitation, sluggish-
ness, anorexia, vomiting, nosebleeds. I recalled how my mother
often had nosebleeds. I came to believe that her anxious gid-
diness, lack of appetite, palpitations, shortness of breath while
climbing the stairs, ashen skin tone, purplish gums, and above all
her sudden bouts of nausea (twice or three times while walking
down the road she'd grip my arm, struck by violent nausea, and
say, "Please, I need to stop, everything is turning yellow, maybe
a lemonade will help") may well have been symptoms that we
hadn't taken seriously enough. I felt, for the first time, more than
a sense of guilt, a need to confess my crimes.

I walked out of the reading room feeling like I had witnessed a heinous act and not intervened. At the same time, I said to myself, how could I have known? Rusinè was beautiful, she looked youthful, and it always seemed like she could tolerate all sorts of pain. One day she wasn't well and the next she was invulnerable. Sure, every so often she said to her husband, "Maybe we should call the doctor." But she always said it half-heartedly, she knew her husband didn't like hearing things like that. They made him lose his patience. Federí always hated doctors, he never wanted to talk about illness. Even more, he hated the thought of his wife undressing in front of a man who would use the excuse of examining her to touch her all over. This was yet another reason why he minimized any symptoms she might have felt. He considered the ailments she complained about as female things, and he encouraged his sons to think the same. Just look at her, he said expertly. One minute our mother was crying and said she felt sick and had to vomit, and the next, she felt great. This was the proof that there was nothing wrong with her. He screamed at her to calm her down and to calm himself down. When she started in with, "I feel something heavy inside me here," he'd look up from where he was sitting in front of the easel with his brush in the air and an expression of alarm mixed with disgust on his face. Then he'd grumble and mumble and get back to work. "You're obsessed, you're fine, now quit busting my balls," he'd yell. His words made Rusinè feel significatively better and off she went, back to the kitchen.

"Call the doctor, don't listen to your husband," her mother, Nannina, said to her. Her aunts (Zia Carmela, Zia Maria, Zia Assunta, Zia Nenella) all said, "Call the doctor, and the sooner the better." Back when they still used to spend time together, even the Slavic woman said, "Rosa, get it checked out." But she put up with it (she was embarrassed to go to the doctor), and when she stopped complaining, we stopped noticing. It seemed impossible that she'd actually get sick. Besides, we had our own things to worry about.

In any case, at some point between 1954 and 1955, my father got annoyed with all her complaining and talked about it with Dr. Papa, the general practitioner we called when one of us had a high fever and none of the usual remedies worked. He did it principally so that his wife would stop her complaining and quit ruining his life. Dr. Papa wanted to hear all her symptoms, then he smiled, and issued an advanced diagnosis for the times. "It's a nervous breakdown," he said. In other words, it's your nerves—my father explained to Rusinè with the air of someone who says, See? I told you there's nothing to worry about—they're all tense because of everything you have going on, because of those recent miscarriages, because of the responsibility of raising four children, and now they're sending you signals, that's why you can't stop sobbing and crying.

My mother let out a sigh of relief and went back to working on her Singer, to being tormented by her husband, to putting up with us four boys. When the sick feeling came back, she learned how to pretend it was nothing. But then, in 1957, when she fainted out on the street and Dr. Papa was called back in, he just smiled and shrugged. "Don Federí," he said, "It's time to get to work. There's just one thing your wife needs, and that's another baby."

The following year, my sister Nuccia was born. Rusinè was thrilled to finally have a baby girl. Not long after giving birth—I remember it well—my mother fixed herself up and braided her hair prettily. She was thirty-seven-years-old but looked twenty-seven. It really is true—my father, who was also happy, said—women are broodmares. It's part of their nature. They're only happy when they're foaling.

While climbing the stairs of the library, I shook my head to chase away those words and the image of a happy woman with a secretly ill body. The desire to hunt down my father's political cartoon about the flooding of the Po River had vanished.

I went to the main card catalog and looked up *La Voce del Mezzogiorno* and saw that the call number had been struck through in red. At the bottom of the card someone had written the words *passata a giornale*.

I cautiously approached a young librarian who was studying for some kind of exam. "What does this mean? Do I have to go to the periodicals room?" I asked her. The girl stopped highlighting her book in pencil and explained that "*passata a giornale*" actually meant that *La Voce del Mezzogiorno* had been put away in boxes. What kind of boxes? I asked. Storage boxes? Were they accessible? The librarian looked at me skeptically and merely repeated the word: boxes. "Go to the periodicals room, maybe you'll find it there. You never know."

I headed toward the periodicals room. I walked down hallways under renovation, through dusty rooms where furniture sat under clear plastic drop cloths, past areas that were blocked off by thick wires and cables that tumbled out of holes in the ceiling and dropped down to floors below. At a certain point, I even had to walk out onto a long balcony, down it some distance, and re-enter the building through another door. Finally, I reached my destination.

"No, I'm sorry, we don't have *La Voce del Mezzogiorno*," a considerate librarian told me. "If they told you it's been boxed up, that means it's in boxes. What we can do is find out if another library in Naples has copies." She thumbed through a dog-eared volume and then announced her findings with some regret. "Unfortunately, it looks like we're the only ones to have them. If you really need to see them, you'll have to go look in some other city. Let's go put the question to the computer; come with me."

She went over to a colleague who immediately typed the query into the search engine. I sat down in a dusty chair next to the window and looked outside and waited. As the computer was taking its time to reply, I pulled out my notebook and started making some notes. My handwriting was uncontrolled, messy, anxious. An old obsession was coming back: identify symptoms of the encroaching illness behind the appearance of youth and gaiety; imagine the poisons circulating through her system, making her body weaker day by day. I was already calculating the weight of my mother's spleen. How much did she weigh in 1953? And in 1955? And in 1958? After she died, I thought a lot about things like that, and now all those ideas were coming back to me. Rusinè's body—while she wore herself out dipping and dunking that bedsheet for *The Drinkers* into the copper basin of water, while she wasted precious energy wringing it out and stretching over the frame according to each and every peevish order issued by that other body known as Federí—was busy circulating toxins through her splenic vein that would go on to cause liver damage. "All he had to do," I thought to myself, the same way I thought it in 1965, "was pay more attention to her and less to *The Drinkers*." If only, I scribbled down in my notes, he had spent less time talking about Mario Palermo's handwashing, Mario Alicata's rude manners, Tina De Angelis's legs, and Raffaele Lippi. The medical volume that I read as a boy said, "A removal of the spleen leads to complete recovery." The key thing was to get it out quickly.

Just then I heard the voice of the librarian at the computer. "Excuse me, sir," he said. When he saw that he had my attention, he went on. "Apparently a lot of people are online: you're better off trying later on."

I thanked him and left.

I looked for a bench in the shade. I found one that looked out at Molosiglio harbor, which was teeming with masts: I needed to calm down. A little bit of green, the boats, the red and grey buildings, a lot of police, the park with its palm trees, the pale blue sky. On my right was the sea, glaring in the sunlight, and a ship that seemed as though it was flying. The distant shadow of the Amalfi coast. Beyond Monte Faito and the Monti Lattari, Positano.

I daydreamed. "How lovely it would be to have a place here, on Via Acton, or in one of the grand buildings on the waterfront." With blue tiles and waves of sunlight in the morning. To be born into a life of ease, to be well off. No need to prove yourself, everything already proven for you. "Maybe," I said to myself, "if my father had grown up in a world more in keeping with his own dreams, everything would've turned out differently: Rusinè wouldn't have died so soon and even we kids would have become different people." Or maybe not: maybe everything would've been exactly the way it was, because a person's existence is not made up of things, but of flesh and bones and blood; a great view from a balcony doesn't erase a person's obsession with themselves. "But," I thought, "it gives you sharper pearly whites." It's a lenitive. It's the ease of painting a large-scale work in a big, bright room without a care in the world. It's a cease-fire in an endless war against the world.

Lippi, for example. I don't think that my father was still angry with him when he told all those stories. He had encountered him on his path and turned him into an icon of bitterness. Nothing more. His problem was a different one: how to get beyond the confines within which he felt unjustly imprisoned.

Soon it wasn't enough that one of his paintings hung on the wall of an art gallery or that he be written up in the local newspapers by the critics. For example, when he took part in a group show in 1952 at the Galleria Medea, Alfredo Schettini wrote in the *Corriere di Napoli* that Federí's work redefined themes present in the late works of Léger. Federí showed me the clipping as proof. Nice comment, he said, thanks a lot. But did Schettini have any idea, he started to rant, what kinds of conditions he had to work in while redefining those themes present in the late works of Léger? Did Vespignani ever have to work in conditions like the ones he faced? Did Guttuso have to work the way he did on Via Gemito?

At this point he'd bring up my mother's relatives. In the early 1950s, he considered them a constant affront to his most urgent needs, especially when they showed up at our house bearing gifts of all kinds. They arrived all at once: Zio Matteo and Zia Assunta, Zio Espedito and Zia Maria, Zio Attilio and Zia Carmela. Out of love for their niece (and definitely not her husband), Zio Espedito the baker brought baba, cassata, *sfogliatelle ricce*, *sfogliatelle frolle*, and cannoli. At Christmas, he'd bring *raffiuoli*, *roccocò*, and *mustacciuoli*. Zio Attilio showed up with trays of sliced mortadella, salami, prosciutto, or an Auricchio provolone, fresh mozzarella, and a bladder of lard. Zio Matteo the greengrocer crowded our kitchen table with pumpkins, gourds, squash of all kinds, tomatoes, peppers, and everything colorful the season had to offer.

It was the end of Lent, carnival. My mother looked rejuvenated, her cheeks were flushed pink, her eyes were bright with affection. Even my father, when he saw that bounty, lightened up, he joked and laughed, his puns were a source of great entertainment, his sexual allusions and bawdy jokes made my aunts turn beet red and laugh hysterically. He became almost excessively sociable.

On one particular festivity (it may have been my mother's saint day), the kitchen was so packed with live chickens, freshly butchered meat, charcuterie of all kinds, desserts, and wines that the table looked like a still-life from the 1600s or the stock room of a top-notch restaurant. The eating and drinking went on for hours. At one point, my father grew rowdy and started to shout, "Hey, Espedì, is your wife a cigar-smoker?" He kept repeating the question in various ways ("So, Marì, d'you like to smoke the old cigar? You know what I mean, a good cigar, once in a while? Tell us!") making everyone double over with laughter, even Zio Espedito, who threw a glass of water in his face in the name of fun. This amused my father so much that he poured an entire bottle of seltzer water on Zio Espedito. Not long after, to the delight and fear of all the children present, that mass of people, stuffed with food and swollen with wine, started running up and down the house, from the kitchen to the dining room and back, laughing and splashing each other with liquids, whether it was from a glass, pitcher, soup tureen, straw-covered fiasco, or pail. It was a war: the floor was slippery and wet, it was family against family, tensions were released, and feuds were ended once and for all.

As soon as the party was over, after the uncles and aunts had left, my father started to grumble and complain. To his mind, the gifts brought by their relatives were not really tokens of generosity. Actually, he said to my mother, wounding her feelings deeply, your uncles and aunts are using them to trick us. Those gifts aren't really gifts; we've already paid for them handsomely without even realizing it. How? He explained to her how. Don't we do all our shopping in their stores? Don't they deliver us our food each month? Don't we have to pay for every single purchase, whether it's pasta or sauce or anything else? And how is it that all those foodstuffs never lasted a whole month, but were finished within two weeks? Did Rusinè ever check to see if what she paid actually corresponded to the amount that her stinking pieces-of-shit aunts and uncles said they delivered?

My mother turned ashen; such insinuations were anathema to her. She replied that the provisions finished quickly not because her relatives tricked them with the weights but because we, meaning him and us boys, ate like wolves and it was difficult to budget and control us and that's why we always needed more things, more money. When she talked about such things, her lower lip trembled as if she was about to cry, but Federí didn't care and insisted with his theory. There was a hostile rally of insults: "Don't say things like that, you're lying!" she said. "Me? Tell lies? I only tell the truth!" he replied. "Your version of the truth!" she answered him back. It ended with shouting, crying, and the sound of her being slapped.

Following that episode, my father, in addition to having to work for the railroad, make humiliating portraits for the Americans, and conceive of his own works of art, was forced to keep a watchful eye ("like the KGB of home economics," he said) on the sugar, coffee, pasta, beans, rice, chick peas, basically every single article those stinking pieces of shit delivered to his wife, their cost and weight and quality and brand, and so forth and so on.

His inspection lasted only long enough to see that his wife was right, that they weren't being ripped-off or cheated, but that there were hungry mouths to feed and a constant need for money, money, money. And so he stepped back with the excuse that he had far more important things to think about. "You want to get screwed out of money?" he yelled at Rusinè, "Fine, get screwed, it's your loss. I'm not going to give you a single lira more than necessary: you'll have make do!"

And that's what my mother did. She hunched over her Singer day and night, except when she had to rest due to illness or a miscarriage. Even so, she had a hard time making ends meet. And when she had no other choice, she'd sigh, and drag us boys over to my father. For the most part, Federí could be found sitting at his easel. She wouldn't bother with any overtures, she'd jump right in and say, "Look at these kids' shoes." Geppe and Toni and I would lift up our feet and show him the worn bottoms of our shoes. "What's wrong with them?" he'd mumble distractedly. "There's nothing left to them," she'd say. "Get them re-soled," he'd say. "The shoemaker said there's nothing left to be re-soled," she said. "The shoemaker is a fucking idiot," he'd say. "The shoemaker makes shoes and he knows what he's talking about," she'd say. "Oh really? Well, as soon as I have a little free time, I'll fix their shoes, and we'll see if the shoemaker knows what he's talking about." Then, in conclusion, he'd turn to us and say, "Don't worry, kids. Papà will make you each a new pair of shoes."

But my mother didn't back down. Our shoes were so ruined that even if she wanted to, she couldn't. She was as perseverant as a dripping tap. She bothered him so frequently that, in order to continue painting in peace, he'd chase us out of the room, dig through his secret hiding places, and then walk into the kitchen with hauteur and munificently hand her some money. "Here, take it, Rusinè," he'd say. "And quit busting my balls."

Then he'd go back to the easel. Fuck food, money, clothes, shoes: the only true pleasure in life was painting.

Painting. This was Federí's absolute passion and it tortured him his entire life. He always thought that if he had had more money, a better space, or more light, he would've been able to fulfill his destiny as an artist faster and more efficiently. Because— he explained to me, with regards to *The Drinkers*—while it's true that a person can feel as though they were born to be a painter, there are also practical aspects to consider; you need a Neapolitan mastiff, you need construction workers who don't look alike, each one has to be different, with their own character- istics. In other words, he exclaimed, you need reality. But it can't seem too real because real life is actually always changing and unstable, and it can't be too artificial either, or else what purpose will it serve?

The fragments of reality that, over the course of the spring of 1953, would go on to become that enormous painting appeared in our house not all at once, but in bits and pieces. One after- noon someone knocked on the door and I went to open it. It was Luigi, the street fruit and vegetable vendor, *'o verdummàro*.

A swarthy and stocky man, every day he made his way down Via Gemito with his donkey and cart, pulling the animal along by its halter. "*Puparuóli-friariéll!*" he'd holler and the women would lean out their windows, yell down their orders, and lower their baskets. Luigi would weigh out the merchandise on a scale that he handled with great ability, wrap the goods in a piece of newspaper, and place them in the basket so his clients could pull them up. After serving everyone, he'd grab the donkey by the halter and shuffle off, calling out his wares as he went.

Until that day, I had only ever seen Luigi from the window. His savage appearance and strange call struck me almost as much as the knife-sharpener's ugly mug and cry, or the ghostly white pizza vendor who bellowed under our window at dinner-time. I often watched Luigi from upstairs and was actually doing so on the day the donkey bit off his thumb: he was filling an order of a kilo of potatoes for my mother and reached around to the halter with his right hand in his usual manner when the animal chomped down on his thumb and didn't let go until it had chewed it off entirely. For as long as the donkey's teeth were firmly clenched down, Luigi leapt this way and that, following the movements of the donkey's head and neck, screaming, "Argh, let go! Aaargh!" When his thumb was finally severed, the fruit and vegetable vendor fell to the ground, covered in blood.

And now there he was standing in front of me, with his dark hair and thick eyebrows and stubbly cheeks. Even before he spoke, I glanced down at his right hand to see if the donkey really had eaten off his thumb: it had. Then, to my great surprise, I heard him ask not for my mother about an issue related to vegetables or money but for Don Federí. It all happened very quickly. He hadn't even finished saying his name when my father came out of the dining room and greeted him warmly. "Come in, Luigi, come in."

My mother and grandmother looked in both to say hello to the vendor and to try and understand what exactly he was doing in their home. Even my brothers and I were curious. It soon became clear that Luigi had come to sit for my father. I stared at his mutilated hand some more: it seemed to me to be an atrocious omen. I wondered why my father had chosen to use him for inspiration. The construction site across the street and the ones that were popping up like mushrooms in the countryside around Vomero were filled with real builders. Theoretically, all he had to do was say to one of them, "Come and pose for me." Instead he had chosen Luigi and he was already instructing him on where he should sit, and how, in what position.

The vendor looked uncertain about it all. He smiled with embarrassment, he wasn't entirely sure if he should. My father, annoyed, turned to his mother-in-law and wife who were standing in the doorway. "What's the matter? Don't you have anything to do around the house?" he yelled, and the women retreated. He then politely explained to Luigi that he needed him to take off his shirt: he wanted him sitting on the ground, bare-chested. "You have to do me the favor of staying still," my father explained. He then lifted up Luigi's mutilated hand. "You have to keep your hand like this," he said, wanting it in full view. But Luigi pulled his hand back in embarrassment. At that point, my father sent us kids out, too, and he closed the door behind him.

We stood there in the hallway: Geppe, Toni, and me. Toni wanted to play, but Geppe and I were older and knew better. "Be quiet," we said. If we disturbed him, he'd get angry. He needed total concentration. There were no fathers like him in any of the other apartments on Via Gemito. He was the only one to have rolls of drawing paper, canvases, paints, charcoal, and that special colored pencil that made blood-red markings. He was probably already hard at work, intent on capturing that stump of a hand, maybe even the donkey with its yellow chompers, and the way it brayed ferociously when it bit through its owner's finger. I was daydreaming. Daydreaming that my father knew how to draw the sound of Luigi screaming, people standing on their balconies and at their windows watching, blood shooting out of the animal's mouth and onto the cobblestones. I imagined that my father was capable of reproducing not only that specific individual, the man who had brought barnyard smells and street sounds into our house, but everything about him that existed in my head, all my memories of that incident, the ascetic distance with which I had seen it unfold, as if a nightmare. I stood outside the door waiting to see the miracle on the canvas.

When the door reopened, and while my father accompanied Luigi to the door and said, "I'll let you know when I need you again," I snuck into the dining room. The vast canvas was still grey. Scattered across the floor, torn rapidly from a pad of drawing paper, were my father's charcoal sketches of a man sitting on the floor, as seen from the back, with no shirt. There was only a hint of his arms, and they ended at the wrists. It was nothing like I expected.

I went into the kitchen, where Federí was already arguing with his wife. He wanted to know why she had come and stuck her nose into his business. Had she wanted to see Luigi's bare chest? "You're crazy," Rusinè replied indignantly. What did she care about seeing Luigi's bare chest? Don't say such stupid things, of course not. It took a while for them both to quiet down because he needed to be convinced that she was entirely indifferent to that man's hairy chest. When that was accomplished, he started complaining about the street vendor's qualities as a model. "That idiot can't even sit still for a minute." It was exasperating, he was a terrible model, he kept looking around, got easily distracted, kept turning this way and that. "What a shithead," my father said, getting angry at the mere thought. "What does it take to sit still for sixty seconds?"

Even worse was the fact that he refused to let Federí paint his mutilated hand, and that was the main reason Federí had asked him there. He had wanted to study the stump, that was his goal; he wanted to reproduce it exactly as it was, scar and all. But Luigi had asked him, begged him, almost as a kind of favor, to paint his hand intact, with all his fingers, the way it was before the donkey bit off his thumb. My father was in a quandary. What could he possibly say? "Alright," he had agreed unwillingly. "Fine." This was a perfect example of how hard it was to do his work well. This was a perfect example of how things were different in Caravaggio's time, when an artist could use a whore for a Madonna. He, meanwhile, couldn't even paint a builder whose hand truly was mutilated. And to make things worse, the bastard couldn't even sit still for a minute.

As a child I was always scared that one day my father would say, "Sit down, I want to do your portrait." The anxiety I experienced while sitting for him is a wound that has never entirely healed. Federí was dissatisfied with everyone—relative, friend, or acquaintance—who modeled for him. "He kept fidgeting, it didn't come out well," he'd say afterward. "What are you talking about, Federí? It looks just like him," my mother would say in reply. "No, he kept moving," he'd insist with a disgusted look.

He wanted her to understand that the results he was capable of obtaining, despite the thousands of other obstacles he had to deal with, would've been far greater if the people who posed for him had been more aware of their actual role. But they didn't even know their right hand from their left, he said, and as fast as he tried to work, if he glanced down to refinish a few details, when he looked up it was inevitable: the model had moved.

The more time passed, and we're talking seconds, not minutes, the more the figure he had started to draw differed from the person sitting opposite him. It was impossible; he'd never get anything done that way. "I told him he had to sit still, and even so, that idiot moved," he'd gripe. "Look how badly this ear turned out," he might say, or, "I got the nose all wrong."

All of us thought his ears and noses were excellent, but not him. When he was a student at the Scuola libera del nudo, he used to say, things like this would never happen. Models there had self-discipline, especially the women. They sat there completely nude, even when it was cold, which was often, but they never moved. You could take all the time you wanted to study one of their feet, their ass, one of their tits, a single varicose vein, or the hair on their cootch. No one ever complained. You put them in a position and there they stayed. Without moving. If you needed to, you could even go and touch them, and feel their ankles, feet, shoulders, to understand the musculature better, to study it.

But none of his friends or relatives, not even Rusinè and his mother-in-law, had self-discipline. First they'd beg him to do their portrait and then they wouldn't sit still, not even for one single minute. They all thought he was like some kind of photographer: click. Done. They didn't understand how art was fatigue, sweat, suffering. An artist who works from real life suffers, and likewise, real life suffers under the eyes of the artist. If a person doesn't understand that, it's pointless for them to model for him.

He shook his big head with visible discontent. You want an example of someone who didn't understand at all? He could give me hundreds of them. But the worst was Peppino, his brother-in-law. Draw me, Federí, he said. Do a portrait of me, Federí, I'll sit still, I'll be good. Fine, Peppì, take a seat. The man couldn't even hold a position for a single minute. He yawned, laughed, turned around, and looked at his watch. He apologized and tried to find the position again, but the idiot couldn't remember it any more. And there he was, wasting his time. No one ever did it right.

He got frustrated with everyone, even with members of his own family: his brothers Antonio and Vincenzo. He'd sit them down, close the door, and for a while there'd be silence. We'd be sitting in the kitchen, relaxing, busy with our own things. Then, inevitably, the screaming would start. "Viciè, for fuck's sake! Can't you sit still? Not even for a second?" We'd all look at each other with concern: mother, grandmother, children. When he screamed like that, it felt like I was being whipped.

I stopped in a café on Via Partenope to admire the imposing palazzi of the grand hotels and munched on a plain croissant, the kind with a crunchy knob at one end. All of a sudden an old, beat-up Ford careened down Via Santa Lucia, nearly swiping a taxi and cutting off an oncoming Renault Clio, the driver of which slammed on the brakes to avoid an accident. Then the driver of the Clio, a middle-aged man, leaned out his window and started screaming insults at the car. The old Ford swerved to the left, stopped, and two young men jumped out, shouting insults at him in reply. The middle-aged man drove quickly off up Via Partenope. The two young men chased after the car for a hundred meters or so on foot, hurling bloody threats at him and waving their arms around like swords: demons of intimidation in the heart of a city where people knew their place. They then rushed back to their car, jumped in, did a quick U-turn, their tires screeching, and zipped past me, I could see their profiles pointed with rage, bodies craning toward the windshield, intent on pursuing the Clio.

That scene completely ruined my enjoyment of the pastry. My father got angry in exactly the same way, hurling ancient invectives passed down from generation to generation. If you tried to reproach him for something he did wrong, he'd become irate. He was never wrong, never guilty, he always had good reasons for doing everything he did. It wasn't about him, it was about art. So what if the people who posed for him got tired? The shitheads should've been stronger. They agreed to sit for him; they should've been willing to drop dead without complaining. What were they made of? He asked this question in a disparaging tone, and often, when I was a kid, it just increased my level of anxiety. They were flesh, bone, nerves, live organs, a pulsating vein on their forehead or hand, nothing more. They were living matter, there for him to look at. So, let him do his work, let him transform them into laborers, fishermen, construction workers, and other permanent symbols of the human condition. That's why artists exist, after all. That's why Federí didn't hesitate to call on those stinking pieces of shit that were his wife's relatives; he needed them. Anyway, in his hands, even shit turned to gold.

That's why, during *The Drinkers* period, even Zio Matteo was forced to sit and pose for him. After mulling it over at length, Federí realized that his stocky build, crude features, and aura of calm resignation would make him, despite the fact that he was selfish through and through, a good *fravecatòre,* a profession that was once considered truly noble, he said, back when the people who built houses didn't just put one stone on top of another, but were engineers, architects, artists, and not just lousy, stupid, vulgar builders.

And so Zio Matteo started coming regularly to our house to pose for my father. His job was to sit on a wooden crate, a glass in his right hand, a benevolent smile on his face, and stare off in the exact same direction as the Neapolitan mastiff.

By then already older and heavier, but still good-looking and always wearing a kind expression, he usually arrived at our house with a basket full of fruit and vegetables from his shop, a gift from him and Zia Assunta.

He'd walk into the kitchen somewhat out of breath and set the basket full of aromatic goodies down on the table. The scent I liked best was that of the basket itself, which was woven out of tender chestnut branches, pliable shoots that still revealed their clean, white pulp.

We'd gather around him, clambering to see what delicious things he had brought us. My grandmother treated him with kind respect, my mother fêted him with childish joy, happy to receive the gifts. He sat down and mumbled phrases of appreciation for the warm welcome. After a bit, my father would arrive and invite him into the other room. Zio Matteo would follow him out in his easygoing manner.

It was always that way, with his models. They'd arrive happy and leave angry. Initially they thought that somehow they'd benefit from being painted, that it would make them look good. But they were always disillusioned. It was tiring to stay still for so long and it was pointless, really: being in a great artist's painting wasn't so appealing after all. This was not only because they didn't understand a single thing about art, my father said, but because they didn't understand anything about anything. Zio Matteo, for example, had driven a cart most of his life, travelling through the countryside of the province. That's how he had spent his time. When he eventually made enough money and got his license and bought an automobile, the first time he went for a drive was a terribly exciting moment. Unfortunately, when the automobile started going excessively fast, he got scared, and, instead of hitting the brakes, he pulled on the steering wheel as if it was reins and shouted, "Whoah." He crashed into an electrical pole and destroyed the new car. A complete disaster. I loved that story, it was both funny and heart-warming. But Federí told it to make his point: "How could my likeness of his hand possibly turn out well, how could my likeness of his drinker's face possibly turn out well, when I was forced to work with such an idiot for a model?"

Meanwhile, the image started to extend across the canvas. One side of it grew carefully and steadily; the other side looked overrun, as if the smell of the oil paints had gone to his head, dazed him. It was fascinating to see how what was in his head transformed into color. The Neapolitan mastiff looked tensely off to the left: paws, muzzle, all of it. A builder's muscular back was visible in a play of light and shadows: that was Luigi. Zio Matteo sat on a wooden crate with a glass of wine in his right hand, but the figure wasn't Zio Matteo any more, he was an expert mason with a trowel. Heavy rain clouds suffocated other figures and the construction site background, or pressed down heavily on the right side of the canvas as reminders of chaos.

Sometimes my father stood up and walked back to the door and tried to get a look at the work as a whole. He was not pleased with it. He complained that some areas were unfinished or, to his mind, unsuccessful. "Look at your uncle," he said to Rusinè, if by chance she came into the room. "He said he had to leave, that he was in a hurry. Now what on earth could that insignificant man have to do that was so important?"

One day, suddenly, I was called to sit for him. I had just gotten back from school. With my satchel still across my chest, I went to greet my father, who expected a kiss from us when we left the house and when we came home, when we went to bed and when we woke up. It was an important ritual of affection for him, and he got annoyed if we skipped it even once. He kissed us and he let himself be kissed as if every farewell kiss might be the last and every hello kiss celebrated our safe return from journeys taken either wide-eyed or asleep. He was the only one who kissed us and expected to be kissed. My mother never showed the same obsessive rituality. Neither did my grandmother. Only him.

He was standing at the easel that day, absent-mindedly smoking. He looked sullen. I could tell that something was wrong. Maybe he didn't like the painting any more. I kissed his cheek, the thick dark beard of a disheveled man who shaved unwillingly. He kissed me swiftly in return, more the air than me. Then, without any preamble, he told me to take off my shoes.

I took them off with some hesitation. Normally he didn't want us to walk around the house barefoot, worried that the cold of tile floors coming into contact with the bottom of our feet would climb up into our bronchial passages and lungs and cause us to become ill. But this time he ordered me. "Mimí, take off your shoes," he said in dialect. Then he pushed me into the center of the room, made me get down on my right knee, wedged a straw-covered demijohn with a dark green glass neck under my left arm, and tipped it forward as if pouring out a liquid. "Stay just like that," he ordered me.

I stayed in that exact position while he went back to the easel and peered at me carefully from there. "Look down at the ground," he said.

I looked down at the ground but not too much, just enough so that I could still perceive his movements, his mood. He scoffed with dissatisfaction and came back over to me, took my head between his hands (he was holding his cigarette between his index and middle finger, the smell of paint mixed with tobacco always made me a little nervous), rotated my head a tiny bit toward the demijohn, and, pressing on it lightly, forced me to look farther down. "Don't move," he said firmly and went back to the easel to look at me again from afar.

In that new position, I could no longer see him. I could only see the neck of the bottle and the hexagonal-shaped floor tiles. And yet I felt his presence and perceived the tension. I don't think he was entirely pleased with me. Maybe I didn't live up to whatever he was imagining. In fact, he came over to me again, placed his fingers under my chin and raised it ever so slightly, less than a centimeter. "Listen to me carefully: stay just like that," he said, then came over to my left side, grabbed my ankle and slowly dragged it toward him until my knee was in a deep bend and only the big toe of my left foot rested on the ground.

He kept his cigarette firmly between his lips, squinting one eye almost shut to shield it from the spiral of smoke. I heard him breathing, the sound of a phlegmatic man with blackened lungs. He straightened up and was about to head back to the easel but then he thought of something else and bent down to position the demijohn better under my arm, assuring himself that my right hand held it firmly, that the vessel rested with the appropriate heaviness in my left hand and that the back of my left hand was pressed deeply into my thigh. "You are the boy pouring the water," he explained. And then he added, pointing to a space slightly beneath the neck of the demijohn: "The glass is here. That's where you have to look."

I looked at the spot intently. I hoped that my father was pleased and that he'd step back soon because the smoke from the cigarette, which he had since removed from between his lips and now held in his fingers, was getting in my eyes, and making them smart and tear.

With relief, I heard him make his way back to the easel. He

picked up his roll of sketching paper and started to unfurl it. "When you get tired, tell me," he instructed me. I didn't move a muscle, nor even nod in understanding. I already knew that I'd never confess "I can't do this anymore."

I returned to my brother's house around dinner time. At the table we discussed how we'd travel to Positano. The best way, Geppe said, is by car. But he knew I hated driving, all those vehicles on the road, the traffic jams, the aggressive honking. And the insults, I added, the rage, the angry pursuits, everything I had seen on Via Partenope and Via Santa Lucia. "I'm not courageous enough to get behind the wheel," I said firmly.

The boyfriend of one of my nieces took it upon himself to offer to be our driver. With a daily rate of a hundred thousand, he said playfully. "A little over budget, but I'll think about it," I promised, and there and then I liked the idea of a trip down the coast without any worries, going from Portici to Sorrento and Sant'Agata sui Due Golfi, with Vesuvius behind us, as if floating on the horizon. Then, surprising even myself, I announced, "I'm going to stay another day or two." There were other streets and places in Naples I wanted to see. And I like your house, I added, it's relaxing.

After dinner, pleasantly exhausted, I observed my brother's children without him noticing. I was looking for traits passed down from Federico and Rusinè. I found several similarities here and there: eyebrows, eyes, fingers, even a whole hand; their way of moving; they were like apparitions present in their living bodies; phantasmatic details that appeared and then disappeared in beings that were entirely unlike them, that had different builds, different histories. I noticed an ironic look that seemed familiar, a warm greeting, a cocky gaze from an excess of self-esteem. It occurred to me that I should spy on all my siblings, on their children and my own, on relatives both close and distant, and on myself, rather than wander around the city, go to dusty libraries, look through old photos and films, decipher calligraphy, and do some of my own writing, create lasting impressions of people and facts.

When I went back into my bedroom, before turning off the light and falling asleep, I studied my father's framed drawings on the wall. There was my grandmother, with her head bowed, knitting, wearing a dark dress and apron. There was my mother, sitting with her face in the shadows, reading a magazine, *Annabella* perhaps, her hair done in an unrecognizable style. There was my father, around fifty years old, the skin on his face hanging from his cheekbones like a stretched-out sweater, looking at me obliquely, the way an artist looks when he does a self-portrait in a mirror.

Pieces of art, traces. He had a strong hand, he definitely had talent. And yet it seemed like there was actually nothing of those once-living and breathing human beings on the paper, under the glass. While my memories of them may have been dull, they were still more intense than what the reliable seismograph of art had been able to register. What point was there to holding a pose? What point was there to moving around in front of a camera lens? What point is there, now, imagining them while they talk, yell, and laugh? What point is there, now, trying to preserve, through mere combinations of the letters of the alphabet, the residue of their lives conserved in mine? Much more sensitive tools and sophisticated techniques are needed to capture that cluster of voices, gestures, pulsations, instances of illness and health, hiccups, belly laughs, and groans of pain that we conventionally refer to as individual. Layer on top of layer, messily added. The remote past that lives within him. Other people who invade his space, dissipating him; him, spilling over into others, dissipating himself. Federí, Rusinè. The deception of graphic signs.

I yawned, my eyes started to close. Earlier that evening, my other brother, Toni, told me that recently he went to Pompei for work and in the office of some council member he saw one of our father's paintings hanging on the wall. He spoke about it with pride. The sense of the conversation was: "Papà didn't just tell lies; his art really does hang in important places." I promised him that I would go to Pompei to see the painting. "If you want, you can even see some at Palazzo San Giacomo," my brother Geppe added. In Naples, in the municipal offices, in other words. "When we come back from Positano, I'll go see those, too," I replied, but without much feeling. Each in their own way, my brothers were trying to tell me something different. They were encouraging me to look at our father with less bitterness. They expressed themselves with restrained pride. They mentioned paintings that hung in grand rooms of imposing palazzi, in the offices of powerful people. It was as if they were hinting, "After all is said and done, we should be happy."

I hadn't been able to explain to them that it wasn't our father's talent that was up for discussion. For many reasons, I loved his paintings at least as much as they did, but I was confusedly searching for something else. I was trying to understand how life decays when we're overpowered by an obsession for results. That's why I wanted to find *The Drinkers*; I recalled it as being full of decay. But I wasn't illuding myself. The dregs of all that torment and unhappiness and violence and disdain and arrogance and desperation and even love really only existed in my body and theirs, in the bodies of their children, in the teeming images that crowd your mind before you fall asleep and which then turn into either dreams or nightmares. When faced with that electrical storm of nerves, all art falls short. Living and thinking matter—I seemed to comprehend while falling asleep—is the only set design worth loving.

I'm standing in the center of the room, I hold a demijohn under my arm, and the event I have always feared is now happening: my father needed me and now I am posing for him.

I feel a great responsibility but my sentiments are confused. I want to offer him my complete assistance and am even willing to die under his gaze just to help him become the artist he wants. But my objectives do not follow a straight line, my thoughts pile up, it's difficult to put them in order according to the tenets of filial devotion alone. I am also looking for an exchange, for affirmation. I have decided to hold the pose so well and with such rigor that my father can't possibly complain. I want to see if he'll calm down, if he'll finally stop unloading all his blame on us for getting in the way of his art.

A few months earlier we lived through a major turning point, first joy and then disillusion. Initially my father received heaps of praise and then was deeply wronged. He suffered and he made us suffer. Why he mistreated us merely because he was mistreated still confuses me, and I wish I understood it better. But I only think about it in spurts, sporadically and not in complete thoughts. The recent insults came from Rome, but the whole story started in Naples and that's where he unleashed his rage, shouting and threatening people. Everything begins at the Scuola libera del nudo, where he learns to draw the human figure thanks to those oft-praised models, whom I am now seeking to imitate. The Scuola is part of the Accademia di Belle Arti and Federí first signed up for classes in 1951. His instructor is Emilio Notte, an older painter who admires the speed with which he sketches and the deftness and precision of his line. Federí attends classes after his job on the railroad, and when he comes home, his satchel is full to bursting with female or male nudes done in charcoal or sanguine. He shows them to my mother and doesn't stop us kids from looking at them; we're boys after all. I examine the drawings carefully. "So this is what my father studies when he goes to school," I think with embarrassment. His math and science are tits and asses. I imagine Federí walking into a classroom just like mine at Vanvitelli elementary school, sitting down at a desk, opening his satchel, and taking out pencils and pastels. His teacher, Emilio Notte, doesn't bring books or a geographical map into the room, but a fully dressed woman who looks like my mother when she gets dressed up for special occasions. "Listen, today I am going to explain this lady to you," the teacher says. And he explains her by taking off layer after layer of clothing, even her brassiere and underwear. Sometimes, as Federí enjoys telling us, he has to massage her body with his hands so he can understand her musculature better. As he shows us the drawings, I imagine every single gesture, and all that imagining causes a pleasant warm tingling inside which comes to a sudden halt when I think, "Wait, what if my father wants to draw us naked? Or my grandmother?" What if he draws my mother naked? This potential situation makes me deeply anxious, and I truly hope he does not. It's so hard to hold a pose, and he's never happy. He only smiles and seems happy when he comes home from class and says that Notte praised his work. Notte or anyone else. In his second year, 1952, they get a new teacher, a man named Bresciani. Raffaele Lippi is a fellow student. My father doesn't give a damn about him and continues to study with great zeal; he knows he's the best one there.

One day, Lippi, just to put him in a foul mood, turns to him and says, "Guess what, Federí? I've been invited to take part in the 'Mostra dell'arte nella vita del Mezzogiorno d'Italia' show that'll be held in Rome at the Palazzo delle Esposizioni next year." Then he adds that other great Neapolitan artists like Armando De Stefano and Mario Colucci have also been invited. "Were you invited?" he asks roguishly.

My father feels like he's been stabbed with a flaming sword. He blinks quickly, opens his mouth to speak and is forced to admit that not only was he not invited, but he hasn't even heard about the exhibition, the goal of which is to bring together works by contemporary artists from all parts of southern Italy. To prevent Federí from starting to rant about how things are always organized in secret in order to exclude dangerous competition like himself, Lippi informs him that the exhibition participation guidelines are posted in the foyer of the Accademia, that he should go look for himself.

My father stomps over there, chewing gall. That's just how he is, always on the verge of losing self-control. According to him, he's always calm, sees the big picture, in control of the situation. But over the years, I have learned to decipher the secret signals in his voice, and I can tell he's not at all pleased about it. He can shut an eye on the fact that the organizers in Rome invited Armando De Stefano to take part—Armando is young, only twenty-six years old (nine less than him), he's cultured, well-educated, talented, and he has good connections with people who count. But the others? Why Raffaele Lippi and not him? Why Mario Colucci and not him? Who the hell are those two? What do they have that he does not?

He studies the guidelines and learns them by heart. He discovers that a number of prizes will be awarded according to rules that have yet to be written. He discovers that although the exhibition is by invitation only, artists can also be granted entry by sending three pieces of art to Rome, where a jury will examine them and make their final decision. He discovers that it's easy to take part: fill out a form, submit a description of the works by December 20, and send the actual pieces by January 10. And that's exactly what he does, immediately.

He is then overcome by the usual frenzy that we, at home, know well. First, he pretends to be sick so he doesn't have to go to work. He then stops doing portraits for the Americans, even if the amount they pay combined with his meager salary as second-class station manager allow us to survive (his work for the communist press is nonexistent, he no longer talks about it, who knows if it ever really existed in the first place). With the money he has squirreled away in the pages of his books and among the boxes and knickknacks he inherited from Zio Peppino di Firenze, he buys canvases and paints. To hell with the bastards who hate him and continue to plot against him: he'll create three paintings that will leave the Roman jury stunned, paintings that will rip both Lippi and Colucci new assholes, as well as anyone else who tries, either overtly or covertly, to rip him one.

This is the ferocious language of revenge. And watch out, never contradict him or make objections. Never say, "But the electric bill needs to be paid; they might cut us off." At times such as these, he doesn't care about the house, us, or anything. If he doesn't have enough money for cigarettes, he gathers up old butts, extracts any leftover tobacco, and rolls it up in either regular paper or cigarette papers and angrily blackens his already tarry lungs, and keeps on painting.

First he arranged a still-life on one of the military blankets that we use to stay warm at night: a globe, some books, an iron, and a Neapolitan coffeemaker. While I spied on him painting that with his steady hand, it occurred to me that those objects lay as still as the dead, they didn't get tired, they didn't have bodies that trembled or blood that ran through their veins. They let themselves be studied and painted, and the canvas filled up quickly and easily, without fuss or frustration.

But as soon as my father moved on to his next idea for two paintings, one of a happy fisherman and one of a sad fisherman, I felt his impatience growing. Models came and went: Zio Peppino, Zio Antonio, Zio Vincenzo. He sighed, groaned, and huffed in anger. He tried to get something out of each of them, and did endless drawings. He went through at least ten good sanguine sticks before moving on to painting on canvas. A thousand or so sketches were shredded in rage, a terrifying sight to see.

When he wasn't home, I went into the room and studied the paintings in progress. I didn't see them for what they actually were but only perceived his discontent. I begged the Virgin Mary and saints and even the *Padreterno* to help him concentrate and succeed at what he set out do, and overcome all of Zio Peppino, Zio Antonio, and Zio Vincenzo's shortcomings. Just like in the prayers they taught us at school, I asked that we be able to live in peace, without the burden of his dissatisfaction, or his cussing and obscenities. I wanted this joyless period to come to an end, I wanted him to be in such a good mood that he'd want to take his mandolin out of the closet and play it like he did on the rare occasions when he truly was happy.

I imagined he did precisely that when the paintings were finished. Because I remember them as stunning, among his most beautiful. He left them to dry, played the mandolin, and praised them over and over, saying, "You can forget about social realism, forget about Guttuso, Pizzinato, Paolo Ricci, and Lippi. Here you see the true influence of Caravaggio and his school." And when they were dry, he took the paintings to Rome personally.

The jury was made up of several important artists: Giovanni Brancaccio, Pippo Rizzo, Giovanni Consolazione, Marino Mazzacurati, and Alessandro Monteleone. My father dropped off the paintings and asked for a receipt. He said he was confident even though he actually was not, he said he was calm even though a storm was brewing in his chest and his eyes were popping out of his head. And then he waited and waited, and didn't want to do a thing.

Those were awful days, but I can't say that he was particularly argumentative. He was like a heavy, dark sky that never seems to break into lightning or dissolve into a thunderstorm. Not only was he disgusted more than usual by his job on the railroad, he didn't even have the energy to think about painting. He lived in expectation, and weeks and months went by.

That November, at the age of thirty-one, my mother gave birth to her fourth son, Walter. Federí, being distracted and under pressure from his mother-in-law and all of Rusinè's relatives, called for three midwives, and in the end had to pay all three, swearing high and low as he did. Four sons, a wife, his mother-in-law: they all depended on him. He felt defeated. Then, in March of 1953, two days before the opening of the exhibition in Rome, by which time he had forgotten about it altogether, he received the news that his paintings had been accepted.

Here I could say that he rejoiced, but that would be too easy. First he celebrated: he told anyone he encountered in the street, "The jury in Rome accepted all three of my paintings!" and then he grew even more arrogant, garrulous, and presumptuous. Then, just like that, he went back to his anxious self, exultation blending with a state of alarm. I can't just sit here, he said, firing off a volley of announcements: I have to go to Rome, I have to make my move, I have to take advantage of the opportunity.

My mother rooted through her closet to find the prettiest dress that she could adapt for the exhibition opening. When he was euphoric, he let her do whatever she wanted. Then, when his mood grew more complex, he asked her where the hell did she think she was going, she'd just given birth, she looked jaundiced, and the baby needed to be nursed. But Rusinè persisted and tried as hard as she could to go with him. Federí screamed no at her, she asked why, he screamed back because I said so.

In fact, there was little for him to explain. He didn't have a single good reason why she shouldn't come with him. He just wanted to feel free to move about and see beautiful people and make strong connections and even make a fool of himself or be subjected to humiliation if he wanted, all without his wife sitting there and eyeing him, judging him all the time. And so he left her behind with us in Naples, and set off with Armando De Stefano, and went and mingled with that outfit of artists, critics, intellectuals, and art-lovers that filled the rooms of the Palazzo delle Esposizioni.

There was a crowd, and he felt lost. Now, as I write, it pains me to think of him there. He arrives, thinking he will be met by applause, that important people will come up to him and say bravo. Instead, it's a melee: he learns that the total number of works of art on display, both invited and jury-approved, is 807.

Eight hundred and seven. The walls of the gallery were covered with art, painting above painting, one next to the other as if it was the Sistine Chapel, Mimí, like ex-votos in a church. Never seen so many pieces of crap all at once.

It didn't take my father long to understand that, thanks to the usual shady dealings, they'd included everyone in the show, *oves et boves*, every ragtag and bobtail, without distinction. All his enthusiasm and hope vanished, with malicious rancor taking its place. The only consolation was that his paintings hung in room number 50 alongside those of Paolo Ricci, Armando De Stefano, Pippo Giuffrida, Nino Suppressa, and Giovanni Savarese. Lippi's work, luckily, was in a different room, number 51. At least there was that.

He stayed in Rome for a total of two days. He couldn't stay any longer. He and De Stefano shared a hotel room, the two men exchanged numerous opinions on art, they ate at restaurants together, and became even closer friends than they already were. But then Federí, who had a job and a family, had to go back to Naples, back to work at the railroad. De Stefano stayed on in Rome to keep an eye on the situation.

It was an unusual time. At work he was calm, at home his behavior was quietly forlorn. He talked about how everyone was up there in Rome, at the Palazzo delle Esposizioni, taking care of business, and that he was the only poor bastard tied down with a family and job on the railroad. But he didn't yell or scream, he didn't kick and shout. He just kept repeating in a feeble voice how much he regretted not being able to be there to keep an eye on exhibition room 50 and watch the people come in and admire his work. Other than that, he slept a lot, didn't paint at all, and ate little, always with a distant look in his eyes.

Then, suddenly, he came roaring back to life. One morning at around seven o'clock, on his way home from a night shift at the railroad, he bumped into Carlo Montarsolo at Napoli Centrale. Carlo was an air force captain and painter, whose work, my father said, had been admitted by the jury in Rome thanks only to some pulling of strings by his brother, a famous baritone. Montarsolo told him that he was rushing off to Rome because they had finally published a catalog for the exhibition and he wanted to buy a copy as a keepsake. There was a catalog? my father enquired dejectedly. "Yes," Montarsolo replied, "and you'd better hurry up if you want one because they're selling out quickly. It would be a shame if you didn't get one as they even included a picture of one of your fishermen in it."

My father lit up with pleasure, his mood suddenly changed. His work had been included in the catalog. He knew in a flash that fame and recognition were about to rain down on him. "Are you certain?" he asked Montarsolo with great excitement. Completely certain. He was the only painter whose work had been accepted by the jury to have been included in the catalog. Basically, the baritone's brother explained to him with great admiration as he boarded his train to Rome, that meant that Federí's paintings had been highly appreciated and he stood a good chance of winning the Mancini prize, with its purse of 500,000 lire generously offered by the Cassa del Mezzogiorno. The award was to be given to a painter from the south (he was from the south), under the age of forty (he was under forty), whose work was in the show at the Palazzo delle Esposizioni not by invitation but thanks to the jury. *Buona fortuna*, Federí.

He came home beside himself with joy. He announced the good news to his wife, saying he had to go to Rome right away to buy the catalog, even though it cost 1,000 lire, which was a pretty penny indeed. He started hunting around the house, in every nook and cranny, but he couldn't find any money. He started swearing. He asked Rusinè to go knock on her relatives' door and ask for the money. It was important, his destiny was on the line. She let him scream and yell but didn't give in. They owed the relatives so much money already that she was embarrassed to go and say, "I need 1,000 lire so that Federí can purchase a catalog from the exhibition." He shouted at her and threatened her, maybe he even hit her, but she was firm. My father gave up and ran to his parents' house on Via Zara. He managed to get 1,000 lire from his mother, Donna Filomena, without his father, Don Mimí, finding out; had his father known about the existence of that money, he would've spent it on a game of cards or at the horse or dog races. Thanks to his mother, Federí was able to jump on the first train to Rome and that was that.

Once he arrived in the capital, he went straight to the Palazzo delle Esposizioni and bought one of the last available copies of the catalog, a slender book with a red cover, published by De Luca Editore, with Table CLVIII a reproduction of his unhappy fisherman staring absent-mindedly at his empty vat, a crust of bread in his hand.

He leafed through the rest of the book, examining the other images and comparing them with his own in order to have the proof that his was the best. Bolstered by what he found, he approached the gallery receptionist, Signora Dompré, with all the charm he could muster, and started chatting with her to find out how things were going.

The receptionist greeted him politely. "There's great interest in your work, Maestro; everyone is talking about it," she said. Federí's mind went blank. "Ah," was all he could say. "And what about the Mancini prize, the half a million lire award?" he asked point blank. The secretary looked at him complicitly and smiled. "What are you trying to do? Get me to talk?"

Her words were enigmatic, but my father knew—and he told us about it for the rest of his life, every chance he got, with both sadness and longing—that the wind was blowing in his favor. He went back to Naples and proudly waved the catalog under Rusinè's nose and made her admire Table CLVIII at least a dozen times, then he showed it to mother-in-law Nannina, then to Don Ciro the building porter, then to all the neighbors, and finally to his stinking piece-of-shit relatives. He especially enjoyed show-ing it to the three of us kids, but not to his youngest son because he was only four months old.

While I can't speak for Geppe or Toni, I personally derived great pleasure from the catalog. Whenever possible, I went and secretly admired the image of the fisherman. The book felt like it was imbued with good magic, as though it had the power to transform my father into a man free of all discontent. He would finally make peace with fidgety models, with everyone, with real-ity. He'd go from being a gaunt man with a crazed look in his eye to a calm, reflective one, like the other fathers on Via Gemito. What a relief. I had already started seeing signs of his transfor-mation. I saw him whisper into my mother's ear and saw how she giggled. "Rusinè, I'm clearly going to win the prize of a half a million lire," he'd say, and she'd laugh some more.

Was there a reason for that good cheer? I'm not entirely sure. As the days and weeks went by, it seemed to him that there was. Words of praise grew and multiplied. They arrived on a daily ba-sis, and when none came, my father immediately grew anxious. "Why no compliments today? What's going on?" he wondered.

One day he had to rush up to Rome because Signora Dompré called for him. He went to work on his shift from eight o'clock in the morning until two in the afternoon and then jumped on the first train for Rome. When he got to the Palazzo, Signora Dompré gave him some wonderful news. "Maestro, all three of your artworks have been sold." Unfortunately, I can't say now to whom; my father often changed his mind about who purchased them and mentioned several names, and yet they were always famous people. In his notebooks, there in black on white, he says that the happy fisherman was bought by Senator Paolo Rossi, the sad fisherman was bought by film director Roberto Rossellini, and the still life with the iron was bought by Spanish actor Juan de Landa. Total earnings: 270,000 lire.

A tidy sum. Everyone wanted to celebrate so my father took

them all to the bar across the street from the Palazzo delle Esposizioni and offered pastries. Marcello Gallian, the art critic for *Turismo-Svago* ate a whole mountain of them, and while he used the photograph of the sad fisherman to illustrate something or other in his review, he forgot to include the artist's name. Piece of shit. But what did it matter? Unbelievably, nothing could make Federí angry.

He came back to Naples loaded with money and good cheer. The first thing he did was buy Rusinè a diamond ring. Then he got everyone a new wardrobe (in a manner of speaking, since we had no actual wardrobe to speak of and always wore the same thing). The next thing he did was let those stinking pieces-of-shit relatives taste the sweetness of his success. And finally, he handed out confirmation gifts to the children of friends and relatives, thus acquiring a whole host of godsons and goddaughters for his wife and himself. In a short amount of time, even though he tried to hide some of the money so he could spend it on his own in Rome as needed, he frittered it all away with active assistance from Rusinè. Somehow the sun always comes out from behind the clouds.

As a matter of fact, on a splendid late-March day, as he was walking out of Bar 2000 in Piazza Carità, he heard someone call his name. It was his old teacher, Maestro Emilio Notte, and he was yelling his name from the newspaper kiosk across the street. "Federí, come here, I have to tell you something important!"

Federí crossed the street to see what the elderly painter had to say to him. He was in the company of his student Bruno Starita, who would in turn go on to become a professor of etching at the Accademia. "Bravo, you troublemaker! We were just talking about you. How much money did you make in Rome?" he asked. "270,000 lire," my father proudly divulged. "No, my friend, you earned much, much more than that. You earned 770,000 lire," he said. "I don't understand, Maestro . . ." my father said.

"Federí, I am part of the commission in Rome that decides who gets the awards. Even though I, personally, don't care much for your work as it's not in line with social realism, we've decided to award you the Mancini prize of 500,000 lire because your work is strong. Now let's go celebrate!" he said, insisting they go to Bar Motta, which was nearby. "And now," he went on to suggest, "you should hurry up to Rome and get a copy of the official announcement; don't wait for it to come by mail. Stay well, Federí."

My father let himself be warmed by his good fortune. He told Rusinè about the good news and went back to Rome. He ran to see Signora Dompré to verify that it was true—that he had indeed won the Mancini prize—and he tried to get his hands on the money right there and then, or at least an advance. But he had to wait, as dictated by the rules, until the official letter arrived by mail. "In the meantime, enjoy the good news," Signora Dompré said.

And that is exactly what Federí did. With eyes on fire and skin stretched taut across his cheekbones from the tension and enthusiasm, he went and told everyone he saw there at the Palazzo delle Esposizioni, that he had won half a million lire from the Cassa del Mezzogiorno; he, who, at the age of thirty-five, had been admitted to the exhibition not by invitation but via a jury. He happily flitted from person to person. No one could stop him. His heart was filled with joy, pure joy pumped through his veins, infinite joy.

"That's just how things work," he said when he was elderly, "one good thing leads to another." Sometimes he even added philosophically, "Success stays with the successful, bad luck with the unlucky." He spoke in clichés just for the love of hearing himself talk. When he was going strong, there was no stopping him, his stories flowed with great creativity; he was always at the center of a surprising dance full of joyful moves.

This afternoon I'd like to get those tones down on paper, the scenes from the life of an artist the way I still hear them in my head, stories about days that were complaint-free, stories that occasionally were over the top, and sometimes didn't quite add up. Federí accumulated experiences left and right, he doesn't know how to simply be happy, it's hard for him. He spends a lot of time at the bar at the Palazzo delle Esposizioni, sitting there and reflecting on art and his future as an artist. Suddenly, Guttuso walks in with Vespignani, Monachesi, Pizzinato, the whole gang; he walks up to the bar and starts talking about Courbet. My father listens without saying a word, off to one side. He'd like to add a few things but he doesn't want to draw attention to himself, not in front of Guttuso, who's famous. Even though he has three works on show in the exhibition, even though he sold them to famous people like Roberto Rossellini, and even though he won the Mancini prize, he doesn't want to stand out, he's scared that someone in the group will try and embarrass him as usual, ask him what time the next train to Naples is. His story could well end there: the bar, Guttuso, his sense of malaise, but I know—ever since I was small I've known—that he can't stop himself, not even if I were to ask him to do so explicitly. He keeps going. He talks at length about his composure while also describing the sycophantic manners of the lackeys that hang around the famous painters. This goes on until Guttuso, who clearly had asked Signora Dompré about him and his exceptional work, and consequently knows who he is, turns to him in a friendly manner. "Federí, what're you doing there all on your own? Come and join us." He, grateful for the warm invitation, immediately joins the group and shares his thoughts on Courbet. Everyone is impressed: Guttuso, as well as Vespignani, Pizzinato, and Monachesi. Before he says goodbye, he feels compelled to buy them all a coffee.

He romanticizes. He roams around the city through the month of March and possibly April, too. Piazza di Spagna is full of springtime flowers and gaiety. He stays on in Rome so he can closely follow the events related to the prize but, in his spare time, he sits with his back to Via Condotti, not far from the La Barcaccia gallery, and sketches the Trinità dei Monti.

I listen carefully. I'm ten, so Rome feels light years away and my father seems like a man who has been kissed by a thousand marvels: there's a piazza filled with flowers, sunlight, rich women stroll down the street, elegant gentlemen pass by and praise his work, saying things like, "Well, would you look at how well this artist draws." It occurs to me that maybe the warm spring light and breeze will be good for him, and his adventures, too.

And then, suddenly, a young Egyptian appears before him: he's a relative of King Faruk and his name is Fuadí. The prince wants to immediately purchase all his drawings for 30,000 lire. Federí hands them over. Here you go, Prince, 30,000 is fine. It's a good deal. Fuadí then wants to chat about art and the kinds of colors that were used in the pharaohs' tombs. Federí talks to him in English, thinking with delight at how easy life is for an artist in Rome: you draw a few lines on a sketch pad, a foreign prince appears, you chat about the funerary art of ancient Egypt, and have an international conversation. If only he were always on his own, with no family obligations. If only he could move here.

Then Nino Ruyu, the official mail carrier between Naples and Rome, walks by. "Federí, I'm on my way to Renato's studio. Do you want to come along?" he asks. My father says sure, and Prince Fuadí joins them. They walk from Piazza di Spagna to Via del Babuino and down Via Margutta. "Me and Guttuso," Ruyu says over and over, "we're good buddies. If you ever need anything, Federí, I can put in a word for you with him." My father shakes his head. "I don't need anything, Ruyu. I was born a painter. All I need is my talent. Did you hear that I won the Mancini prize? 500,000 lire," Federí says proudly. "Oh, really? I had no idea," Ruyu says ironically and congratulates him but then goes back to talking about his close friendship with Guttuso to the degree that my father can't get a word in edgewise and continue boasting, as he wishes he could, about the Mancini prize, about its purse of half a million lire.

Springtime in Rome. I envision the three of them walking down the street. I especially like the prince, who wears a red turban and carries a precious dagger tucked into his purple silk belt. Fuadí tells them about Egypt, the pyramids, camels, odalisques; Federí talks about the Mancini prize; Ruyu talks about Guttuso and other things. At a certain point Ruyu speaks up. "Federí, if you say they awarded you the Mancini prize, I'm happy for you, really. But watch out, because you know how things are here in Italy: you never get something for nothing," he says ominously. "What do you mean?" Federí asks, feeling suddenly nervous. Ruyu explains that he was just speaking in general, that bribery is everywhere, in Russia as well as in the USA. Then he turns to Fuadí and laughs. "Even in Egypt, isn't that right, Prince?" Ruyu asks. Yes, Fuadí replies.

In the meantime they reach Guttuso's studio. Ruyu looks at his watch in surprise. "Hell's bells," he says, "it's lunch time. Maybe I should go up on my own, Renato might be having lunch. I'm sorry, I'll be right back."

Ruyu runs upstairs, leaving my father and the prince waiting in the street. Not a minute passes and he's already back. "He has guests," he says, "and I don't want to disturb them. Let's go to the Pincio gallery in Piazza del Popolo instead. Carlo Levi is having a solo show there. I'd like to say hello."

My father shrugs and turns to Prince Fuadí. "What do you think, Prince? To be completely honest, I don't give a fuck about Carlo Levi but if you want to go . . ." The prince wants to go so they all walk over to the Pincio gallery. I see Ruyu in his postman's uniform, my father in his artist's clothes, and Fuadí dressed like a prince in his turban.

At the Pincio gallery they see Carlo Levi. His skin is blotchy with rosacea and he's wearing a fur coat even though it's relatively warm outside. He also has on a fur hat that's pulled down tight around his ears, and curly ringlets poke out from underneath it, damp with sweat. Ruyu goes and greets him politely, but Levi just looks at him suspiciously and doesn't say a word. The mail carrier is about to try again when all of a sudden Renato Guttuso and his entourage appear in the doorway.

The air is tense. Federí doesn't want to be the first to say hello so he pretends to be keenly interested in a painting. In the meantime, Guttuso goes and pays his respects to Levi, at which point Ruyu calls out a "Greetings, Maestro," and throws himself into the melee. Guttuso looks at him squarely. "I'm sorry, but do we know each other?" he asks. "My name is Ruyu, I'm the mail carrier, and a pupil of Vincenzo Ciardo, with whom I study landscape painting. We were introduced by Paolo Ricci, if you recall," Ruyu says, bowing deeply. "Ah, I see, do give my regards to Ciardo and Ricci," Guttuso says, waving him away dismissively. He then turns toward Carlo Levi but catches sight of my father's striking figure and calls out to him warmly. "Federí, what are you doing here? Come say hello."

My father makes his way forward. All of them—Pizzinato and Penelope and Salvatore and Sarra and Monachesi, as well as all the other lackeys in the entourage—treat him like an old friend. Even Levi says hello and praises his work. "Your fishermen are beautiful, Federí." This makes Ruyu green with envy. Prince Fuadí, meanwhile, is delighted and reverentially calls my father Maestro.

Later it occurs to Federí that Ruyu, with that allusion to bribery, might have been giving him a sign, letting him know he was plotting something behind his back. In fact, not long after, the villains got the upper hand and everything changed course. First off, he received an unpleasant surprise tied to the Cinema Ideal, on Via Scarlatti, in Vomero. My father was walking by when he bumped into his friend Salvatore Affuso, who had just walked out of the cinema, where they were showing *Orfeu Negro*. Affuso embraced him warmly, congratulated him, and said bravo, well done. Seeing that my father didn't understand what he was referring to, Affuso explained. "What? Don't you know? Before the feature film they showed a color documentary about art. It's called *Il sole sorge nel Sud* and you're in it. Or rather, your paintings are in it, the ones on show in Rome."

My father went into the cinema, his heart beating wildly in his chest, watched the film, and saw his paintings on the big screen, in color. He also saw Armando De Stefano's painting, *Antonio*, and Domenico Purificato's *Ricordi della Ciociaria*, but he had the impression that the camera rested a little longer on his works. Deeply excited, he rushed home to tell Rusinè. The following day, he told her to dress us up as if it was a holiday, and took her, my brother Geppe, and me to the Ideal. I saw everything with my own eyes but I can't say exactly what it was. That's right, I have to admit it. I just don't know what I saw. My experience of it is worth nothing. My father told me the story about the Cinema Ideal so many times that, now that I am trying to write about it, I can't distinguish between what I saw and what he led me to see with his words. But since it's his words that matter here, I will say that I saw his three paintings, and especially the unhappy fisherman, and that my jaw dropped. My father's art was on the big screen. It truly was incredible.

The following day he rushed over to Via Zara and dragged his mother and father out of the house to see the film. They wanted to invite a few of their special friends. Fine, he agreed with pleasure. He accompanied them all to Vomero, paid for everybody's ticket, and had them sit in good seats.

The documentary started. It showed De Stefano's paintings, it showed Purificato's paintings, each still frame, one after the other, but not his. Fuck. They were gone.

His father (my grandfather) flew off the handle at what a waste of time it had been, his son had to stop inventing things for once and for all. "You're full of shit," he shouted at my father, you've been a liar since day one, you made him look stupid in front of his friends, with all that famous painter bullshit. Painter *di questo cazzo*.

Federí left him standing in the cinema foyer and ran upstairs to the projectionist's booth. "Where are my paintings?" he screamed. "What paintings?" the projectionist asked. "The ones that were in the documentary *Il Sole sorge nel Sud*," my father replied. "The film got burnt," the man said. "You're saying it burnt right at the point where my paintings appear?" my father asked. "Yes," the man said and then continued in a whisper, "Let it go, Maestro. Don't fool around with these commies. They came in and told me to cut that part out, they're jealous. Go see your paintings in a movie theater in Caserta or Rome. People are too envious of you here in Naples."

After that, things went back to being the way they always were. My father went back to being nasty and lashing out at my mother, believing it was all a plot by Lippi or Paolo Ricci, or all of them put together, whatever their political affiliation—pinkos, blackshirts, the white whale—they were all against him. He rushed to Rome in a state of alarm to find out if the official letter announcing the conferment of the Mancini prize had finally been sent. Signora Dompré, with somewhat less warmth than on other occasions, told him that the delay was due to bureaucracy: 500,000 lire was a large amount of money, they needed approval from the Cassa del Mezziogiorno before they could send out the official letter. "Go back to Naples," she ended, "and be patient. No one can take away what you rightfully deserve."

Of course they can. One morning, Francesco Caiazzo, another painter who had a couple of paintings in the show in Rome, showed up at our house on Via Gemito. "I'm sorry, Federí," he said in a singsong voice, "but it looks like they took the Mancini prize away from you. Apparently, someone told them that you work for the railroad and the rules clearly state that the money has to go to someone who makes his living from painting. However a part of the jury is on your side and resigned in protest. Even Emilio Notte resigned." Moreover, he continued, while Federí grew paler and paler by the second and felt like he was dying of unhappiness, the person named as the recipient is twenty-four-year-old Claudio Lezoche, a war orphan, backed by both Segni and Scelba.

My father waited until Caiazzo left the house before starting to rail against the corruption that permeated Italy and how it had worked—and always would work—against him. Then he started in on God, the Virgin Mary, the saints, communists, Christian democrats, Segni, Scelba, Caiazzo, Lezoche, and my mother, who told him to calm down.

Later, he went to see Emilio Notte. "Don Emí, is it true what they say about this whole story?" It was true. What could be done? Not a single thing.

Still beside himself with rage, he hunted down the communist critic and painter Paolo Ricci and faced him squarely. "Do you know what they did to me?" he said. "They took away the Mancini prize. Segni and Scelba want to give it to Lezoche. Maybe we should inform Amendola, maybe the party ought to know . . ." But Paolo Ricci replied firmly, "The party has nothing to do with your personal interests, Federí. The party is not at your beck and call." That's exactly what he said.

What could he do next? My father, yellow with nausea, his lips livid, made his way back to Rome and stood in front of Signora Dompré's desk, hurling vulgar obscenities and swearing that he'd kill Lezoche the first chance he got if they gave him the prize. It was pointless. Discordant rumors abounded. First, maybe to calm him down, they said that the prize would be divided between five painters, a hundred thousand each: him, Lezoche, Giuseppe Ruggiero, Agata Pistone, and even Mario Caiazzo. Then everything went silent, there was no more talk about the Mancini prize at all, it was as if the Cassa del Mezzogiorno had backed out and said, "Screw them all, easier just to cancel the Mancini from the list of prizes." Finally, rumor had it that the entire sum of half a million lire was given to Claudio Lezoche but in the form of a scholarship.

My father was well into painting *The Drinkers* the day the bad news arrived. By then he'd already gotten it out of his system. "Those stinking pieces of shit," was all he muttered, frowning and painting with renewed spite and rancor. I was left with a feeling of mistrust, like when I was small and I'd bring him a toy to fix and he'd repair it, and then it would break again as soon as I started playing with it.

Now Federí is sitting at the easel and I'm seated across from him in this uncomfortable pose that he's forcing me to hold. He's starting to draw. I feel him casting glances at me, not his normal looks but those of an artist, the ones that feel like ropes with huge hooks or barbs or spears attached to the ends. They pierce me at regular intervals, and are accompanied by rapid, tense gasps; they tear off parts of me that he will use to build his builder's apprentice, so that I will pour water into the foreman's glass. The charcoal stick scratches the piece of paper with a nerve-wracking sound, capturing his dark mood and dissatisfaction. I feel my blood pulsing through me but try to avoid letting even the smallest of vibrations resonate through the neck of the demijohn.

After some time, my brothers come to the door and peer in. They see me kneeling in that pose, they're surprised, they snicker and run off. Then I detect other sounds in the distance, exclamations and laughter from the kitchen. A few minutes later I hear my grandmother shuffling down the hall in her slippers. She also stops at the entrance. "Are you tired, Mimí?" she asks me in dialect, as if her son-in-law doesn't exist. My father, peevish as ever, replies for me. "We haven't even started yet; could you please let us work in peace?" And when Nonna Nannina turns and heads back to the kitchen, he starts to sing nervously, first in a deep voice and then in an unusually high-pitched one, and only stops when certain parts of me, the most difficult ones, require all his artistic attention.

He didn't sing for long. At one point, he threw all the sketches on the floor and went to get more paper. Then he started drawing again, but not in silence; this time around he talked to me. I can't remember exactly what he said, initially it was just nervous chatter. But I imagine that he said the usual things about art, showing off his skills, in the same way ancient warriors roared before going into battle, both to diminish their adversaries' courage and to boost their own. It's highly probable, actually, that he went back to talking about the exhibition in Rome, as it had been deeply gratifying nonetheless. He liked talking about the standing he had acquired in the capital and how, even if he had initially been at a disadvantage, and despite all the usual shady deals, his work was considered even better than Armando De Stefano's—and he was a good painter. He counted up every single line from every positive review that had been written about him and compared them to the scant number that other artists had received. Basically, he enjoyed giving numeric proof of the great leap he had made and backed up his case with trivial figures (all of which he wrote down in a notebook in 1992, providing me with my source): the indisputable mathematics of how much his work was liked.

"The jury," he'd begin, "had to choose from a grand total of 807 paintings, 162 sculptures, 148 black and white photographs, and 47 works of craftmanship. If you do the math, that means that only 289 of us artists were selected to take part in that important exhibition in Rome, with an average of 1.83 works per artist."

Here he stopped to see if I was following him. Since, at all ages, young and old, whether I was ten, thirty, or fifty, my eyes glaze over with repulsion at the mere mention of numbers, he'd sigh with disappointment and get to the crux of the matter.

"In actual fact," he went on to explain, "the statistic of averages doesn't reveal the full truth. Even though each artist submitted three works of art, not all three of them were accepted. 126 artists had only 1 piece of work accepted, 60 had 2 pieces accepted, and only 27 artists had 3 works accepted. Your father, Mimí, was one of those 27." I listened and said nothing. Just like in the Teatro Bellini story when he was offered the chance to move to Hollywood, here too, at some point, he'd start in on his wife, how attached he was to our mother, how he didn't want to move far away from the family, and so on and so on. That was the only reason—he complained obsessively—he hadn't been able to take advantage of his enormous triumph in Rome and continued to be an employee of the railroad in Naples. He really ought to have said to hell with it all—Via Gemito, those *scurnacchiati* sissy painters from Vomero and Via dei Mille, the tram that took him to the station each day and brought him home exhausted, the Americans with their big teeth who sought him out, family, all of it, even us kids (he didn't actually say us, he never would've said that)—and finally break free; he'd find an attic on Via Margutta, join the group that rallied around his friend Renato Guttuso, who wasn't some bastard like the others, that man knew straight off the bat who had talent and who did not.

That's what he said in 1953 and on subsequent occasions. And although I wouldn't bet on it, maybe he made comments like that when he started to sketch me. At some point, my mother would come into the room and say, "Time to stop, come and eat," but I only heard her voice, I never saw her—my eyes only saw the green neck of the demijohn and the hexagonal floor tiles—and I thought he'd yell at her for interrupting him. But the sound of the charcoal stick scratching the paper kept going. "Do you want to eat, Mimí?" my father would ask. I would answer him with the reply that the forcefulness of his question commanded, "No," but in an almost imperceptible whisper so that my breath, uttering the word, wouldn't disrupt my posture at all.

My mother hesitates in the doorway. Clearly, she's not happy that he's forcing me to stand there like a pillar of salt and she's upset. But even though my temples are throbbing and my knee on the ground hurts and my arm holding the demijohn is falling asleep, I hope she leaves me alone and goes away. I'm frightened that if she dares say one more word, he'll throw the paper and charcoal sticks down, turn the room upside down, destroy the large canvas, and start screaming and sobbing that, in this manner, he'll never be able to accomplish everything he wants. Ever since I can recall, I'd been terrified by scenes like that, as I've already mentioned. And even when my mother forces us to band together with her, "Let's go talk to your father," so that we can, all together, voice our needs as children and tell him how our shoes are falling apart or how we desperately need haircuts or pens or notebooks or have to pay our school taxes or even my teacher, Bonanni, who insists that I take private lessons in light of upcoming middle school examinations, I always hold back and beg her in a whisper, "No, no, I don't want to go talk to him, let's leave him alone, I don't want to go in there." I try every single way I can to avoid creating the kind of disturbance that she wants to provoke at all costs. But now I feel something else, something new. The repugnant admiration that I feel for my father, that blend of devotion and disgust that, ever since I was a child, I've always felt for his art—how exposed and fragile and vilified it is, and yet so absurdly central to our lives—now rests on my shoulders, and it is almost too heavy a burden for me to bear.

I observe Rusinè's tired and blasé disregard for the hours of ecstasy that he spends in front of the easel, her mistrust in the hierarchy of important things that he presumes to impose on her, her feeble disobedience of his implicit and explicit rules, and wonder what I should do. The thought of emulating her behavior frightens me, so I retreat from it, I tell myself she's making a mistake. My mother does everything possible so that he'll end up blaming her if the paintings don't come out the way that nature intended them to, absolutely perfect, in other words. That really doesn't seem helpful to me. I would prefer, especially now that I have suddenly been forced into holding this pose, to help him the best way possible, so that he can draw and paint to the best of his abilities. I don't want to give him any reasons for blaming me the way that he blamed his other models. I want him to be entirely satisfied with my participation. I wish that everyone, absolutely everyone, would behave the way I am, and my mother most of all.

I feel great relief when she walks out of the room without a word, leaving me there to feel as though the tiled floor is slowly opening its jaws and devouring my knee, cutting into it. I want my father to obtain everything he desires so that even if De Stefano becomes more famous than he, even if Lippi is chosen to do another portrait of Stalin, even if Lezoche wins the Mancini prize and he does not, he has no reason to blame me, and I can legitimately wonder, as I may have been wanting to do ever since I saw the peacock in the bedroom with its entire train, if the time hasn't come, *cazzo*, for him to assume his responsibilities.

"*Cazzo*" sits there in the fictional world of the page of writing as if to emphasize my first unsteadying jolt of intolerance. But back then, those words were unutterable, unthinkable even. When I woke up after a sleepless night and decided to go see the places where my father had been raised, I remembered how he completely forbade us from using obscenities. That memory put me in an altogether surprisingly good mood and, walking down street after street, I kept repeating vulgarities to myself. As I wandered down the wide and dirty Via Casanova, one clothing shop after the next, I enjoyed whispering expressions like *ocazzochecacàto*, *mannaggiacchitemuòrt*, *figliesfaccímm*. I walked through Porta Nolana and wound up in Piazza Santa Maria La Scala, stepping over garbage that had been tossed here and there on the disconnected black paving stones—past long, narrow alleys of shuttered shops, old warehouses that looked like grottoes, a Phone Center in the middle of it all, then squalor and more squalor all the way to Piazza Mercato with its abundance of merchandise for sale—but my good mood held up, and even if the city was so quiet it seemed empty, I continued to hear the music of foul language, whether offensive descriptions or insults, *sfaccimmúso*, *peretasanguégna*, *stupplecèss*. This was the rosary of my youth.

As a child I used to know tons of vivid expressions such as those. Although they were often on the tip of my tongue, I always had to stop myself from using them and keep them tucked away inside, secret. My brothers and I never used bad words, Nannina forbade us. She herself would never have said "*vafanculo*" to someone simply because of the presence of the word "*culo*" in it, which sounded to her like an offensive word. She preferred using imprecations without obscenities, such as "*vafammoccam-mammeta*" which she used frequently throughout the day and which meant something like "go take a hike" or "buzz off" or ominous expressions that she'd hurl in our direction, words like "*puozzesculà*" which had nothing to do with *culo* but *scolare*, referring to the process used to bleed or drain corpses of fluids before being buried.

Nannina was contrary to obscenities because she wanted to stop us from growing up like our father who, she said with great disgust, was born in Lavinaio, a section of the city known for its uncouthness, and that's why he didn't know how to speak without dirtying his mouth. "Alright then, let's hear how people in Lavinaio talk," I said to myself as I walked around that neighborhood of Naples, which I knew well. I made my way around Piazza Mercato, headed toward Piazza del Carmine, climbed confidently up Via del Lavinaio—shady dealings taking place on every corner—past Vico Molino, Vico Zite, Vico Grazie a Soprammuro, always looking for the source of the linguistic tones that Federí used when he said things like *strunzemmérd*. But I didn't hear anything that I didn't already know. Words were as clear as crystal, like dewdrops in a garden, some of which I loved, some of which amused me; they were the sounds and smirks and gestures that form the humor of the school of hard-knocks. There was nothing vulgar about them, nothing at all.

Sometimes my mother also pointed out her husband's roots, especially when her eyes were red and puffy. She'd say he was born *rintolavenàro*, in the heart of Lavinaio, which when she uttered it sounded like a revolting place, a place of decay of both body and soul, a geographical term that meant you'd grown up rotten. We shouldn't be like him—she urged us—but, instead, like Zio Peppino or her or our grandmother, her relatives. They were better brought up. They came from somewhere (I'm not sure where: I know the road where Federí was born but I never bothered finding out where Nannina grew up or where my mother was born) that was far less coarse than our father and consequently they took it upon themselves to raise us well.

Naturally we resisted their efforts. We knew all the bad words, inside and out, even the most colorful ones, and we could have easily used them out of earshot. But we never did, and I, not even as an adult. The reason for this was not because my grandmother and mother were against them; it would have been easy to break their rules because their threats carried no weight. It was because my father didn't want us to.

"Don't use bad language, Mimí," he advised me. He wanted me to grow up saying complex words, words full of knowledge. Not that bad words, he stressed, didn't have their own kind of beauty, especially those in Neapolitan dialect, which were truly phenomenal. Actually, he often not only explained them to me but invented etymologies for them, on two feet and with great imagination. Because, even though he tended to speak with a Tuscan air, like Zio Peppino di Firenze, in order to impress people, he adored using the obscenities of dialect and the dialect

itself: it was his true language. All the same, he'd add, it was better if we kids grew up speaking properly, as if we were the children of an artist who had grown up on Vomero, on Via Gemito.
He wanted us to mature well so that we'd have a less difficult
time accomplishing all the important things in life.

At that point, he'd start in on his childhood, which, he said,
was definitely not one of the best, and a frequent source of his
unhappiness. To make up for that, he talked about it. He talked
about his early years especially when something in his painting went wrong. As things stand now (but I reserve the right to
change my mind), I can say with almost complete certainty that
he talked about his childhood a great deal when I was posing for
him. I actually believe that his anecdotes filled all the hours and
days that I sat for him. I deduce this by the fact that every time
I think about his childhood, the image of *The Drinkers* comes
to mind, as does my mother walking out of the room, my father
sitting down at his easel and saying about her, "What a goddamn
cacacàzz, that one." And yet, he never blamed any shortcomings
or limitations he might have had on his childhood or the slums
where he grew up, he never said anything like, "The reason De
Stefano became such a successful artist so quickly and not me
was because I was born in Lavinaio." Rarely did I hear him make
claims like, "Mimí, if I had been born in a richer, more educated family, I could have achieved much more." If anything, I
could've been the one to suggest things along those lines, but
he'd never rely on arguments like that. He didn't like sociolo-
gisms, they were the stuff of communists. He was convinced,
and he said it over and over, that if the *Padreterno* gives you a
special kind of brain and a certain kind of genius, you will, no
matter what the circumstances, become a man of intelligence, a
genius, not a shithead. He talked about what kind of child he
had been only to clarify the details about the state of poverty
he grew up in, and to highlight how he had been chosen out of
the billions of creatures that crawl across the face of the earth.

"Chosen," he underlined with virulent stubbornness. Lavinaio or non-Lavinaio. And anyway—he'd rear up proudly—what was so bad about being a *Lavenaro*? "Nowadays it sounds like a terrible place," he said, enlightening me with imagination as the charcoal moved swiftly across paper, "but actually the word is quite beautiful. It has the fiery 'lava' inside it as well as the Latin word '*lavare*,' the cleansing waters of rain that wash over the earth, the way the Fiumara river used to run down Vomero all the way out to sea . . ." He could turn the tables on anything, just to get his revenge. He erased the decay, ugliness, and obscenity and artfully dabbed water and fire around him and the place of his birth.

Donna Filomena—he said—gave birth to him on January 17, 1917 in the Za Rella *fondaco* on Vico dei Barrettari, right behind Piazza del Mercato, while the bonfires burned wildly that night in honor of St. Anthony the Abbot. The *fondaco* was so huge that there was room for at least two bonfires, he clarified as if recalling it personally, and the flames had accompanied both Filomena's labor pains and the actual birth, which took place at ten o'clock at night. The blaze threw sparks into the sky and was accompanied by much dancing and singing. He went on and on about the lively neighborhood, its bustle, the shops, Piazza del Carmine, and the Marina. It was as if the colorful streets had influenced his vision immediately, even as a newborn baby.

Then, gradually, he'd shift away from the urban setting and go on to talk about his mother, Donna Filomena, praising her beauty, sensitivity, and intelligence, all qualities that she had passed on to him. As I listened, it occurred to me that, yes, they did have the same nose and mouth, it was true, but I just couldn't imagine Nonna Filomena as a young woman, or pretty, or even intelligent, since on several other occasions he had called her crazy. As he talked about her, I imagined her giving birth on the bed, already the scary old woman with grey hair that I remember coming over to our house on Via Gemito when I was eight years old, pulling me aside to tell me a story about St. Anthony the Abbot, as a matter of fact. She practically whispered the story in my ear, as if it were a secret. One evening, she said, a young, dark-haired woman went up to the saint; after much brushing up against him and moaning in a seductive voice and giving him flirtatious looks, she showed him her ample bosom and said, "Oh, St. Anthony, won't you please touch my titties!"

I looked up at my paternal grandmother—whose eyes, come to think of it, were exactly like those of her son—hoping that my maternal grandmother, Nannina, hadn't heard her. Nannina would never tell me a story like that and if she had heard Nonna Filomena say "Touch my titties, St. Anthony!" she would've said, like mother, like son. Same low-class, foulmouthed Lavinaio talk. But in the meantime, Nonna Filomena's story went on. St. Anthony refused to touch her tits. Since the young woman was actually the devil, to punish him she transformed into tall flames of fire that went all the way up to the ceiling: tits, coal-black hair, everything.

I remember being deeply impressed by the story. Every time my father talked about his birth, I saw that bonfire of a woman-devil blazing in the Za Rella *fondaco*, with his coming into this world seeming even more grandiose because of it. What extraordinary things happened in Lavinaio. There was Nonna Filomena, lying on the bed in her black housedress just like the one she always wore as an elderly lady, surrounded by saints and candles and holy cards. She sweated and suffered and swore through her way through labor, her cheeks red from St. Anthony's bonfire that devoured everything in sight in the *fondaco* on that cold, winter's night. And then, suddenly, my father appeared: a radiant newborn baby. He was immediately placed on a light blue cushion with golden tassels. Meanwhile, the beautiful demon girl burst into flames like dry grass. Even if it was dark and the middle of the night, the light she gave off was more blinding than the sun.

His father—my grandfather Domenico, whom everyone called Mimí—appeared on the scene later. He stood next to his wife in his Regia Marina sailor's uniform. The midwife held the newborn up in the rays of fiery light, and how he cried! Don Mimí was immediately bothered by the child's birth and all the good omens that surrounded him. The baby cried constantly, day and night, clearly he wanted everyone to hear him, and all his father could say was, "The *cacacàzz* never shuts up."

It's true, my father admitted: his crying must have been particularly bothersome. Even his very own mother, Nonna Filomena, complained in dialect while she was recovering from childbirth. "Hand me a shoe so I can crush the baby's skull with the heel. He's just been born and I already can't deal with the kid!" But Filomena's rage was the norm; she got angry easily. It wasn't her fault and my father never doubted for a minute that his mother didn't love him. It was the hostility his father felt toward him ever since he was born—he said with great tribulation—that weighed most heavily on him.

As a child, I always felt contradictory feelings for Don Mimí. Even though my father extolled his intelligence and good looks, he also spoke about him with such loathing that even the mere mention of his name scared me. But at the same time I was fascinated by him, he seemed untouchable. On the rare occasions that he came to our house or we went to his, Federí was always pleasant, made a few jokes, bragged a little, but always with delicacy and caution. My grandfather showed no feelings whatsoever. He never even smiled. He was unflappable, and just sat and read, or pretended to read, the newspaper. If he ever said anything at all, it was along the lines of, "You were a shithead then, you're a shithead now."

I was always shocked to hear him say things like that, and I'd quickly glance at my mother. It was strange not to see my father react in his usual way, and kill him right then and there. What's more, Don Mimí always said it right when Federí was talking

about the things that meant the most to him. Things like the bonfires, or the repetition of the lucky number 17 in his date of birth
(January 17, 1917). As soon as Federí started talking about such
things in front of his father, Don Mimí would start to grumble
sarcastically, "Right, the bonfire. Right, the number 17." And
that would make my father moody; the vivid scene of his birth
and those lucky numbers were important matters to him, serious issues, and signs of his great destiny. He relied on them to
justify the obstinacy with which he sought to prove that he was
different, cut from a richer cloth, better animated by the breath
of God, and to this end he wouldn't tolerate anyone doubting or
correcting him.

Who cared if his identity card or some other document
showed a different date of birth? That was the midwife's fault,
he said. Like all the rest of them, she had mixed up apples and
oranges and had registered his birth along with all the other babies she delivered only when it was convenient for her, on the
23rd at the Sezione Mercato, thereby denying him the possibility
of relying on official documents for the date that meant so much
to him: the 17th of '17. "But even so, my birthday is on the 17th,"
he'd point out, in particular when we adults had a hard time
remembering.

Truthfully, we always remembered, but those of us who were
bitter about the way he managed to shape his life by an excep-
tion and not by the rules, resolutely denied him the possibility of
celebrating on the 17th, which we considered not as his birthday, but the day all the lies began. Sometimes we wished him
happy birthday a day before, sometimes after, but never on that
exact date; it was a silent form of resistance. We didn't want to
indulge his interpretation of the facts that took place on Vico dei
Barrettari. I, more than anyone else, made the mistake but I did
it on purpose, even though I always apologized. Oh, how foolish
of me. Of course, I wasn't thinking straight.

Don Mimí, on the other hand, didn't bother with such subtleties.

Whenever he heard Federí talk about the bonfire, or the seventeenth, or any other such nonsense, he'd sneer, look up from his newspaper, and deliver his usual line: "Kid, you were a shithead then and you're a shithead now." Quickly I'd glance first at my father and then my mother. But nothing ever happened. Federí would grow tense, then laugh, sometimes start bickering over something unimportant with his sisters, but never much more than that. The words had a different effect on Rusinè. They made her eyes sparkle.

I can still hear his voice in my head, talking and drawing. What has stayed with me from holding that pose with the demijohn under my arm is the pain of not being able to move and the tone of his voice. It occurs to me now that he was trying to communicate something urgent to me through his stories. He was endowing the moments of his exceptional childhood with a corrective message intended to extinguish the glimmer of hostility, the flash of antipathy, that he may have seen in my eyes. Something akin to, "Pay attention to what I'm saying, Mimí, and don't listen to your mother; don't underestimate me." But maybe it's only the residue of concerns that I had back then. On a thousand other occasions, so many over the years, his detailed anecdotes served only to adjust a life that continually tried to disappoint him.

It was as if he remembered everything since the day he was born. He spoke in detailed terms about events that took place when he was only a year old, in 1918, when he and his parents moved out of Vico dei Barrettari. His father was then a man of twenty-six, tall and slender, with elegant features, and all his teeth, though not for long. He wasn't dissimilar to Jimmy Stewart, but better. He was better proportioned, he said, less lanky, more handsome, without that idiotic gaze that blue-eyed people have.

In terms of his profession, Don Mimí was a turner, and an excellent one. During the Great War he was a sailor on a torpedo boat, then a laborer in a workshop that produced wartime materials. After the war, he was hired by the Ferrovie dello Stato as a first-class turner and sent to the Reggio Calabria trainyard facility.

Federí recalled all the details of the housing facility provided for railroad workers on the outskirts of the city, shacks that had been built after the earthquake in Messina and planted with flowers of all colors. The season? It could've been spring with that sharp as razor sky, or summer, with its steamy and opaque heat. Beyond the field was a brook where, at the age of eighteen months, he went and played every single day, sneaking away from his mother's watchful eye. He toddled across the pebbles and through the mud with precocious confidence: the water was cold, the grass was tall, and there were flies, wasps, frogs, either rabbits or chickens, and definitely cicadas.

Filomena, who was pregnant again and consequently had a hard time moving around, tried to keep up to stop him from running off. As her belly grew, her dress got longer in the back and shorter in the front. She was also twenty-six, and rather high-strung; some people say it was because of the meningitis she had suffered as a child, which left her with a constant whistling in her head, as if a sirocco blew between her ears, while others said it was because of the worries her husband gave her: his passion for cards and gambling, and less for his family. But she attributed all her problems to my father. She said he was a *cacacàzz*, she couldn't control that pain-in-the-ass kid. "F-d-rí! F-d-rí!" she screamed, as if she wanted to stab him with her voice, chasing him through the laundry hanging out to dry in the sun between the shacks, with her hands outstretched, practically falling over her belly in her high-heeled shoes with their pointy toes, every single nerve in her body raging with ferocity.

As soon as she got her hands on him, she'd smack him so hard and so many times that she almost broke his bones, including his skull. Fdrí screamed, wriggled, whined, cried, got away, and ran to hide; it was risky because of the danger of drowning in the brook. "Do you want to drown, Fdrí? Fdrí, do you want to drown?" she'd scream at him in a growing crescendo of anger, hunched over him and walloping him, harder and harder.

My father was only one-and-a-half years old but he remembered it as if it was yesterday; no, he didn't want to drown. He just couldn't sit still, he said. So he ran away from his mother and through the grass that was taller than he was, and went and looked for his future beyond the fence. A future, he quickly came to realize, that had to do with his vision, his breath, and his hands. A mysterious gift, the instinct of art, was nesting there, and it shaped him deeply. That was what led him to the brook, over and over, with the dandelions scattering their seeds on the wind and cabbage whites fluttering around him like a halo.

Fdrí advances. In the distance is the sound of the trainyard and the workers' voices. But the child only wants the cool mud at the water's edge. He stops, digs, and piles some up into a mound, but it's no good, there's not enough. And so he walks further off, the shacks recede behind him. When the clay-rich mud is just right, he can let go, the game begins, he feels a flow of energy run through his body and he dissolves, it's as if he's fainting, his fingertips have eyes, he gasps repeatedly with pleasure.

A worm wriggles by, a snake darts past, the smell of the grass intensifies, the shadows lengthen. There's also a faraway sound: it's Filomena, she's calling his name, and other women soon join the chorus. Fdríí, Fdríí. But the child doesn't hear the way he usually does. His senses have all been transferred to the ductility of the mud. His eyes see, his hands make, and his sense of smell and hearing and taste only absorb the smells and sounds and flavors that are associated with handling the clay, whether it's the salty snot that runs from his nose, or the thick soup of petals and insects that macerate in puddles of water. Everything else has ceased to exist. Time has stopped. There are only his rapid intakes of breath, the wondrous "ah" sounds he makes as the number of his creations next to him on the shore grow.

For hours on end, he toys with the power of forgetting one world in order to build another. He feels as though—he told me practically in a whisper, as if he was revealing a secret that he'd never told anyone before—he has a mass of beings inside him who come out of his fingers on command: a flower, a frog, a snake, a butterfly, his worried mother. Clay creations lined up along the babbling brook. There's even a mud statue of his father, Don Mimí, sitting on the water's edge, the same Domenico, apprentice turner, who comes home from work swearing left and right, up and down, to all the virgins and saints. Where's the kid? Did that little *cacacàzz* disappear again? He's probably drowning at the bottom of some pool of rank water this very minute . . . Filumè, Filumè, he's dead for sure, slimy snails are probably crawling all over him, country mice are probably chewing him up as we speak, spiders are probably weaving their webs over him in the humid air of night. Help us, everyone. Hurry, please.

The men, exhausted workers who've just gotten home, give up their dinner, band together, light their torches, leave their huts, and tramp through the countryside screaming Fdrí, as if my father was a figure from a poem by Giovanni Pascoli set in nighttime Reggio Calabria.

And then the child is startled and he remembers that he is that name, Fdrí is him, his eye and hand and breath, everything that has gone into making his creatures and objects that line the water's edge.

When he recognized the reality hiding in that name, he temporarily abandoned his own, and left his mud-parents on the river's edge, afraid of being punished by his real ones and ran off in fear of the torch-bearing shadows, of the sound of his name, which, hollered by throats who knew nothing about the art he created by the stream, and knew nothing of the importance that one day it would have. It was only the name of a moment in time that was not yet his; it was the name of the son of Don Mimí the sailor and apprentice turner with a passion for cards.

Fdrí ran through the night like the frightened ghost of a child who died in the middle of a game along a river's edge. He tiptoed into his parents' shack and hid in their bedroom, behind the door of the wardrobe. He had to pee, but he squeezed it back so tightly that he broke out in a cold sweat. And still, he didn't move. His heart was like that of a wounded puppy. At a certain point he realized Filomena had come home. She walked down the hallway, her nerves quaking as if being rattled by some evil god, limping, there was the sound of only one of her shoes. She entered the room, opened the wardrobe, and stood—massive, black with anger, and fiery-eyed—above the child, the missing shoe in her hand, high above her head, far above her swollen belly. With a scream, she struck him over and over with the heel, without holding back. The child couldn't hold back either and peed all over himself.

My father later said with a laugh that he didn't harbor any bitterness toward her. He reserved that emotion for his father, the turner, who, following that horribly frightening night, did something of enormous cruelty. To hell with the clay, the child's creations, any joy that the river might have ever given him. Towering above them all, his father made an unappealable decision. He called for the mailman, Simeoni, and entrusted him with his firstborn; he told him to take the child from Reggio Calabria to Naples and deliver him to his mother-in-law, Donna Funzella. Address: Via Casanova, across from the parish church of Santa Maria delle Grazia. "You'll see a large five-story palazzo, Simeò," my father said, imitating his own father's cruel voice. "It was built two hundred years ago to be a monastery, its front door is one whole story high and wide enough for a horse and carriage. Go through the entrance to the large courtyard, which is at least 40 meters long. On either side are two wide stone staircases that lead to the different floors. All the front doors of the apartments in the building look out onto the big central courtyard, all the way up. Donna Funzella, my mother-in-law, lives in a small apartment on the second floor, take the staircase on the right. Bring her this *cacacàzz*."

Door-to-door delivery, like a package, not a person. From one day to the next, Don Mimí expelled him from his natural family and their shack in Reggio Calabria. He didn't care about his son's artistic vocation or his urgency, and he exiled him by entrusting him to Simeoni. I bet my grandfather didn't even interrupt his card game. "Take him tomorrow," he probably said. I pictured the mailman in his uniform as a dour man with a mustache, dragging the child away, then sitting with him in a train compartment as it made its way through the dry and scorched south, surrounded by piles of letters tied with twine and packages sealed with wax, while he, Fdrí, that explosion of consonants, sat bound and gagged, eyes darting this way and that, in a corner.

It was a long journey. Finally, the dirty, red-eyed, snotty-nosed child was handed over to Donna Funzella Pariota, his maternal grandmother, who was originally from Solofra and a good woman, the last of 24 children. Her father, a man named Salvatore Guarino, had been a customs clerk for the Bourbon dynasty. Fdrí's grandmother took him in, cleaned him up, and took care of him. But Fdrí cried for a long time. In 1920 his father was transferred back to Naples and he and Filomena came to live in an apartment in the same building on Via Casanova with their second-born son, Antonio, one floor above Funzella. But they didn't want their firstborn back. They left him downstairs at his grandmother's. They said it was as much to protect the porcelain figurines that Filumena had graciously placed around the house as the life of Antonio: Fdrí's displays of fraternal affection were so violent that the baby, who was horrified by him, screamed "*Gnòppete!*" each time his brother came near, as if he was a Calabrian bogeyman. What torment!

As he told his story, he shook his head bitterly and continued to sketch. No, he said, the problem wasn't Antonio or the porcelain figurines. The problem was a different one entirely. The problem was that Don Mimí had perceived the child's vocation to become something greater, something more. He realized that his son was practically an incarnation of a "plus" sign, and this irritated him. In that + sign, he perceived the cross that he—or anyone close to his son—would have to bear in order to keep up with his childhood antics, that *artéteca* of his, a word of the south used to describe both the arthritic pains of the elderly and squirrely children. So Don Mimí washed his hands of his son and left him with Nonna Funzella, without worrying how the child might suffer the exile from his family or the nostalgia for the mud of Reggio Calabria, that clay-rich sludge which was so perfect for making dolls and effigies.

Gradually, Fdrí surrendered. "But a true need, Mimí," my father instructed me at this point in the story, "never stops making itself felt." The child stopped crying, wiped his nose on his sleeve, and started looking around for other ways he could use his eyes, hands, and breath. He started by drawing with bits of gesso he peeled off the plaster walls (white on black) and then with charcoal gathered from the ashes of the hearth (black on white). He rediscovered, even there in that apartment on Via Casanova, the sensation of sight slipping into his fingertips, his breath growing heavy, sputtering, and snapping into flame the way blackthorn catches fire under a cauldron with a whoosh.

Squiggles and swirls and decorative lines soon connected objects and dreams on nonna Funzella's door, the wall outside the apartment, along the landing, down the stone stairwell. When people walked past, they had to climb over the sailor-turner's son, and would often stop to say "bravo." Those bravos stayed with him, helped sharpen his eye, made his sight keener, his hand more precise. His marks spread across the walls like a creeper. Numbers, too. He copied Arabic numerals from the calendar and learned them on his own, precociously, at the age of two: 1, 2, 3, 1920, 1921, 1922. His hand saw them and he copied them out onto Nonna Funzella's dark door. She was pleased with them, or maybe just happy that something kept the whiny, fussy child busy. Not only did she not erase them, she went and bought him colored chalks and paints; as long as he was good, that he didn't bother anyone, especially not Filomena, mark my words.

But he didn't always know how to control himself. His hand wanted nothing more than to leave signs that went up the stairwell to the third floor, to spread his colors as far as his parents' front door. And when he did manage to sneak inside their house, he'd demolish his mother's porcelain figurines. While I'm sure it got him into a lot of trouble at the time, when my father talks about it, while he's sitting at the easel, he only mentions the joys of childhood, how pleasant it was to explore the world around him, his curiosity, and the mysteries that lay in darkened rooms in summer. "I only wanted to caress them a tiny bit," he says to justify himself.

Apparently he caressed them ferociously: the fear of getting caught mixing with a disregard for other people's belongings that would later become his norm. He ran in, picked up an object, smashed it into a thousand pieces, and ran out. When he managed to get away from his mother and the heel of her shoe and run crying to Funzella, his head pounding, his grandmother would say, "Fdrícchie, don't worry. Filumena's shoe is moving something in your brain. You should be happy, it's why you're so intelligent." Rusinè never quite agreed with her husband's grandmother on this; years later, she modified the woman's interpretation with her own, more pessimistic one. "His mother messed up his brain by hitting him so many times with her shoe. That's how he got so crazy."

My father took his wife's occasional accusations of insanity as a compliment. In his eyes, the craziness attributed to him by common people was actually a sign of genius. "For you I might be nuts," he said in dialect, "but actually I'm a born painter." His childhood provided a solid basis for this argument, where "born" signified that he hadn't learned it from anyone, there was no trace of artistic tendency in his family of origin, and that art had come to him either from nothing or directly from the *padreterno*.

Certainly not from his father. His father, for fuck's sake, only ever humiliated him. "You were always a shithead and you always will be a shithead," he used to say. His parents had never understood him, he said, they always treated him like an odd child, to be kept under close watch. And not just them, to tell the truth. Not even his Nonna Funzella trusted him, and she loved him deeply. According to her, Fdrí had quicksilver running through him; he was mercurial, and it wasn't just a case of *artéteca*. So she sought to limit his range of movement. She barely tolerated having him in the house, and constantly sent him out on the landing where, to keep him quiet, she let him colorfully scribble the numbers, days, months and passing years on her door: 1923, 1924.

When Don Mimí crossed his path, either going upstairs or coming down, he'd merely climb over the child without the least bit of interest. He was concerned only with getting his two packs of Macedonia a day, a stack of newspapers, and a little money for gambling: cards, horses, and dogs. For Don Mimí—my father said bitterly—life was all about the excitement of peeking at his cards, of seeing whether they were good or bad, if he won or lost. Out of love for that thrill, he was always on the hunt for money. Before the fascists started running everything, he used to go and play down at the socialist party headquarters, in Piazza Principe

Umberto. Once, he lost his entire pay there. He got to his feet, calmly said goodbye, and walked out. Then he collapsed, fell down the stairs, and broke his teeth. The accident gave him an even angrier expression than the one he naturally had. He came and went in silence. At the very most, when he noticed his son playing on the landing outside of Funzella's house, he'd say, "One day I'm going to make you clean all that up."

Pfft, clean it up. Funzella loved those numbers, my father said, sighing with heartfelt gratitude. Initially he drew them in white chalk, and he kept getting better and better: 1925, 1926, 1927. Later he drew frames around them in red and orange, and shaded them with yellow, green, blue, and purple, going back to orange through red. This went on until 1931, the year his childhood masterpiece was interrupted.

"It came out so well," he explained to me (but not in 1953, when I was afraid that the demijohn might slip out of my hand because I had lost all sensation from kneeling without moving for so long, but in 1997, when we celebrated his eightieth birthday in a bleak and funereal mood). "That door, Mimí, was Pop Art before Pop Art even existed."

As an elderly man, with all those years behind him, he often expressed regret at not having saved that door. "Today," he'd say in a mix of sarcasm and bitterness, "it would fit right in at the Biennale, next to the works by that shithead"—that shithead! he'd say again for good measure if he saw a hint of irritation in my expression—"of Andy Warhol."

At times, when he mentioned the names of famous artists like Oldenburg or Rothko or anyone else, his swagger would give way to glumness, which made me glum, too. "If only my father had encouraged me," he said. He never complained about Don Mimí's cultural shortcomings, he complained about his overall shortsightedness. But then he'd sneer with revenge and go right back to talking about the early signs of his vocation, of the happy period when he was all but forgotten at Nonna Funzella's, who, in order not to have to deal with him, also let him spend time on the street-facing balcony.

"You can only stay out there a little while," Funzella would say but then would forget about him. What an amazing place the balcony was. My father used to say that he trained his eye on that balcony for at least two years of his life, sometimes trying to squeeze his head in between the bars in order to see better, sometimes sitting on a pile of flowerpots to watch life go by on the street below. He was out there in rain and shine, he was out there constantly, he wanted me to believe.

I was mesmerized. That image of an extended period of explorative solitude, interrupted not even by a change in season, stayed with me. I lost myself in a reverie about a child who'd been forgotten on the balcony, exposed to the wind and elements in both hot and cold temperatures, with the plants next to him either flourishing or dropping their leaves, the soil in terracotta pots freezing over, the nightingale with burnt-out eyes (the work of a cruel Calabrian) singing in his gilded cage, the yellow Christmas melons hanging over the edge and ripening, and the sea breeze, which Fdrí tried to grasp in his hands, continuing to blow, pulling the seasons along, those with perfumes that waft on the air, those that turn your nose red, those that burn your skin, and those that soak you through with their sudden squalls.

The sorbs change color and their flesh sweetens, he prods them with grandfather Angelo Pariota's walking stick, and eats them when they're ripe; or if they're bitter, he spits them onto the fruit and vegetable shop display below that belongs to Maria, who's an expert fryer—her deep skillet positioned over an open flame just a few steps away from the tram stop—and cooks up so many *ciurilli, scagliozzi, pastacresciute,* and *panzerotti* that people call her Maria the *panzarottara.*

Odors blend with colors, colors blend with sounds. Fdrí's eyes take in the perfectly visible labels and signs that advertise

the numbers and prices of products to the public, signs that have
been drawn by skilled craftsmen and tucked into the large cloth
sacks of dried chick peas, favas, and lentils situated in front of
the store belonging to Ferdinando *'o casadduoglio*, who also sells
cheese and real Bitonto oil, which he measures out with a cast-
iron cup: however much you want, one-tenth, two-tenths, whatever you want.

The child sees, smells, and listens. It's 1920 and he's three
years old, no more than that. From the balcony he looks down
and admires the radiant numbers on the price tags—did he learn
how to do the numbers that appeared on that avant-garde door
from these?—and the bluish paper they use to wrap up pasta,
the chrome-yellow swish of handfuls of chick peas, the smoky
scent of lye, potash, and soap for sale in the piazza in either liquid or chunks, created to great acclaim by Mira Lanza.

Fdrí can concentrate for long periods of time, and he uses this
skill when he manages to get his hands on some white butcher's
paper (which is rare, with what meat and salami cost) and from
the balcony on Via Casanova he draws, in charcoal, Maria the
panzarottara, Consiglia the milkmaid with her cow that produces
frothy milk, the priests from Santa Maria delle Grazie parish,
donkeys either passing by or waiting, and even the zeppelin that
appeared in the skies in 1920 or 1921, striking fear into the people on the streets below.

Every so often, when she remembers, Nonna Funzella sticks
her head out on the balcony as if to supervise him and pretends
to be impressed by his drawings. "Well done, Fdrícchie, that's
Titina, isn't it?" she says. "Yes! It's Titina," he replies with pleasure; the real Titina wears a red skirt; he made hers out of a tomato peel. "And that one? That's Sarina isn't it?" Nonna Funzella
asks. Of course it's Sarina. The actual Sarina has golden blond
hair; he managed to create a similar color by using the skin from
a yellow bell pepper, which he stuck to her circle-shaped head.

He lists his miracles to indicate his genius and the incredible life that lies ahead. Even Don Carmeniello the house-painter, father of Don Federico the cop, once happened to see the child's work and said, "Those aren't just little kid splatters." Not just finger painting. Not just doodles or scribbles or crap that falls out of the sky like bird shit onto a clean shirt, onto a blank page, soiling it. Don Carmeniello makes an unsettling pronouncement that day; he wants to be clear with the kid. "Fdrí," he says, "this stuff has the dignity of art." My father goes on to use that expression in his stories, he heard it with his own ears—the dignity of art—and it's followed by the objective comment, "You're an artist!" which, in turn, is followed by a prophetic one: "Yep, you're going to be a real artist one day, Fdrícchie."

Don Carmeniello was not alone in his observations. Even the neighbors upstairs, Donna Graziella and her children, said so when they peered over their balcony and watched the child-artist at work. These were people who knew what hard work was, they cut leather and made patterns for shoemakers from home. The whole family admires him; they encourage Fdrí from one flight up, leaning out over the railing, and hollering with amazement. Donna Graziella, Aldo, Zaccaria, and even Elisa, who's sixteen years old and goes out at night with her brothers and friends to the local cabaret dressed in the latest Charleston style, wearing a silk skirt with fringe that doesn't even reach her knees and her blond hair cut in a pageboy.

They encourage him by giving him the gift of a tin that contains a special kind of glue that they use on leather, together with some strips of shiny paper of various tonalities and colors. "Bravo!" they call out to him in harmony. And the child runs away into his imagination and disappears into his hands, into the charcoal and glue and strips of colored paper. He starts to draw and then carefully tears the shiny paper into strips (no one wants to give him scissors, not even Funzella), trying hard to be precise, and then he tries it again and again with all the tonalities and colors without ever getting tired of that extraordinary game, until he finally obtains, like a god in heaven and on earth, the effect that he really and truly thinks is good.

Only then does he stop. People look down from their balconies and exclaim how marvelous. These are people who are used to struggling, but in those circumstances, when they see what beautiful creations young Fdrí has made, they feel invigorated. He, at feeling their collective consensus, freezes, his arms bent at the elbows, his hands in tight fists, his whole body a painful and happy contraction of muscles.

Relaxing and returning to himself is a slow process, and it leaves him with an irritating sense of disorientation, ill at ease with everyday life, and the need to start over.

Via Casanova is a wide street, a bedlam of both living and dead material that he can use to make his mark. The precocious child trains his eye to notice things quickly: a tram, the sidewalk, the tracks, the streetlight, even the zeppelin. He sees the outline of the city, with its variety of edifices: churches, public housing, the sooty nail factory, the rows of five-story complexes that were built on Corso Garibaldi during the Risanamento phase, the prison of St. Francesco with its inmates standing behind the barred windows, the low-cost Magazzini clothes warehouse, and the dark cavernous building that looked out onto Via Cavalcanti. There are curved and straight lines and perfect circles drawn with the care of Giotto. With his head tipped to one side, he can capture the variety of the world from the balcony as far as the great curve in the distance, Corso Novara, and beyond, all the way to the narrow-gage tracks of the so-called Nola–Baiano line.

People and things. The two-story electrical tram that connects the towns of the province with the city, that zips through the streets, and almost crashes into the balcony. It feels like he can reach out and touch it. The child feels its vibrations, how it lacerates space, how it musses people's hair and sends up gusts of heat from the deep-fryer, smells of cacio cheese and oil from Don

Ferdinando *'o casadduoglio*, flies from Don Angelo *'o chianchiere*, smoke from the kitchens of Don Ferdinando *il cantiniere*.

But when the tram moves off into the distance, things settle back down. The balcony railings stop thrumming, the hot metal sheen of the normal-gage tracks fades, the roadbed reappears with its metal tee beams and side drains, which fill with rain when it pours and then run off into puddles along the sidewalk, which gets trodden by priests, donkeys, and even Consiglia the milkmaid, who pulls her cow with its heavy udders by a rope tied around its neck.

Handsaws scream as workers cut slabs from blocks of marble that glisten white in the distance, just below the public housing building and practically next door to the enormous old factory where steel nails are made. The metal teeth grind through the stone, raising white dust. The blade goes back and forth, turning a fiery red, with a worker periodically cooling it down by spraying water on it, making it sizzle and steam. This goes on until ding! ding!—a jolt runs through Fdrí—the railroad signal for the departure of the Nola–Baiano train sounds, not far from where the stonecutters are working. The signal changes from red to green, and the train sets off. The plume of smoke from the steam engine gets farther and farther away, the black shadow of the little train running along the gorge, which was dug parallel to Strada Vecchia, with its road of beaten earth known as Poggioreale. Trailing behind the locomotive, the train cars whip through the buildings of the city, hurrying after the grey smoke from the engine, gradually turning into a string of dark yarn that gets pulled taut between one road and another, between one alley and another. It runs all the way to the level crossing on Via Casanova, all the way to the tram stop that then leads back out to the provinces, where, at a certain point, it seems to the child that it competes with the electrical tram; and instead it turns brusquely to the right, following the wide curve all the way to Corso Garibaldi.

And finally, there's the gas streetlight. The glass and metal fixture sits just beyond the balcony, right where the railing is missing a post. An inert eye during the day, it comes to life at dusk. Every evening it gets lit by a mustachioed man whom Fdrí assists by reaching perilously through the gap in the railings and opening the little door of the fixture so the lamplighter can fill it with his flame, thereby illuminating the shiny tracks, the Christmas melons, the sorb fruit, the blind nightingale, and the child's own eyes.

And then the reds and blues dart to life, carrying with them the odor of gas. Moths fly about crazily then fall with soft thuds and die. Shadows are born, but not the kind that shift and stretch during the sunlight hours; these remain the same, all night long.

Fdrí observes, imitates, and learns. The joy of his art begins there, on that balcony. Unfortunately, one day Don Mimí suddenly appears, swearing and blaspheming—*Mannaggiamarònn, mannaggiopatatèrn! Cazzoncefàstacriatúraccaffòra?*—and angrily weaves metal wire between each one of the railings. As much as the *cacacàzz* screams and tries to tear and kick it off, the metal fence impedes his path to the light fixture forever.

I made my way back up Corso Garibaldi to Via Casanova. I could not recall a single happy story of my father's where his own father was involved. As a child, I wondered whether fathers were naturally forbidden to spend time with their children when they were happy. Perhaps—I thought—moments of joy are a mother's prerogative, or else grandparents', sometimes maybe an uncle's, but never a father's. Sometimes Don Mimí's role was to step in like Death and deny the child what brought him most joy.

I had a headache from the heat, I was tired, my good mood had vanished. I bumped into people distractedly, brushing up against snippets of conversation: it's too hot, there's going to be an earthquake; somebody was pickpocketed in Piazza Carlo III; maybe it'll rain tomorrow; two ATAN bus drivers were almost killed; the stench by Porta Capuana is unbearable. As I was distractedly walking by, at a certain point I bumped into someone who was so shocked, he jumped. "*Mannaggiamarònn!*" he exclaimed. I apologized numerous times, the man nodded as if to say it's alright, but before walking off he chided me in dialect. "Just watch where you're going."

I had been watching but could only see what was going on in my head: a boy holding a demijohn, kneeling in the middle of a room; a thirty-six-year-old man intent on drawing and talking about himself; a child on a balcony on Via Casanova, the same road I was walking along now. What happened to that big building where Funzella's apartment had been? I couldn't see a trace of it; that road conserved so few signs of the past. No more family-run shops, the artisans were gone. Maybe the time had come to take my father's words at face value. Enough of this back and forth. There was no balcony that stood as a testament to the play of light from the flickering gas streetlamp. I had to entrust Federí's childhood and stories to his adult voice, and let him creatively and scrappily choose the nouns and verbs he wanted to highlight his grand achievements. My father would've been disappointed to hear that I was trying to tell the story by relying on actual places, facts, and dates. "Come, sit down, I'll tell you everything you need to know," he would've said immediately. You want to know where Don Ferdinando *'o casadduoglio*'s was located? You want to know what shop was next door, what their wares smelled like, the customs and habits of the vendors and their customers? You want to hear the story about the carabinieri officers? Did I ever tell you that one? All of it? And then he'd jump right in, adding a wealth of details. One morning, he'd begin, as if it was the first time he was telling the story and not the hundredth, he walked into Don Ferdinando's cantina and saw the bright-colored uniforms of a few carabinieri of gigantic stature. "Those figures, Mimí, had a huge impact on me, even if I was only three years old," he'd say to get me interested. They were one of the most important steps in the formation of his childhood genius. And that's pretty much all that mattered to him.

It was a Sunday in May, 1920. His grandfather, Antonio Parota, the husband of Nonna Funzella, turned to him and said, "Fdrí, you want to come with me to get a liter of Gragnano?" The surprise invitation pleased the child enormously. The sun was warm, the air smelled good, and he held his grandfather's hand. Don Antonio, whom Nonna Funzella sometimes called Briacone for how drunk he got on weekends and festivities, carefully made his way across the street to o' casadduoglio with a Toscano cigar in mouth, grandson in one hand, and empty fiasco of wine in the other. Grandfather and grandson (naturally, joyful moments never have fathers as tutelary deities) walked past the leather tanning warehouse, past the barber shop run by Don Giuvà and his assistant Don Luigino, and finally came to the two entrances that led to the below-street-level cantina, a space that smelled of the barrels of aging wine that lined the walls beyond the tables.

The child and Don Antonio walked in. All it took was a moment's glance, a fraction of a second, and nothing else existed beyond what Fdrí saw on the wall behind the bar where the white wine was kept on tap. Two enormous carabinieri officers. Looking straight at him. The tall, flame-like red feathers on their military caps went all the way up to the ceiling. They both kept their left hands on their sabers, which hung across their chests in white holsters. Their right hands held glasses of wine to their lips. They were stiff, as identical as twins, and each one was outlined in black. In the background, a long row of wine barrels and tables where men sat calmly drinking.

He never forgot those two figures. Whenever my father told the story, even as an old man, he grew emotional. He had seen his fair share of carabinieri from the balcony. He had studied their uniforms at length and compared them with the less elegant ones of the royal guards. But there they stood in front of him in a gigantic format with painted faces, painted mustaches, painted uniforms, painted sabers, painted plumes: proof that other people out there looked at the world and took ownership of it through the eyes in their fingertips, too. For the first time ever, he said with a touch of emotion, he felt that life is beautiful only when it can be painted.

Sure, the person who had painted the mural of the two carabinieri, wine barrels, tables, and drinkers on the large cantina wall—he added with a critical air, when he was an already experienced artist who knew how to judge better than a child could— didn't really know what he was doing. The anonymous painter was just some handyman from the neighborhood, a fellow who got by doing odd jobs like that. Briacone, his grandfather—a man who knew a thing or two about cantinas—explained to him that the mural had not only been done to embellish the wall but to communicate, as was the custom, that in Don Ferdinando's osteria people respected the law, that only non-belligerent people were allowed to drink there, that wine was meant to be consumed in good cheer and that's all.

"You see," he pointed out so that I'd understand the complexity and importance of art. "An artist says so much with his work when he paints, even without realizing it." But then he'd pull a long face and start to point out the painter's ineptitude: the black outline, a wrong use of perspective, a stiffness in the figures, the similarity of the two men. And yet it was evident that the first painted scene he witnessed as a child had a greater effect on him that any real-life one that he had observed from the balcony. He went on and on about it, he even wrote about it 1991, in his notebooks. "From that moment on, the words 'cantina' and 'cantiniere' always made me think of carabinieri officers, not cellars or wine."

In other words, it had such a powerful impression on him that it was hard to say exactly what the consequences were. Now it's meaningless to even try and understand. The point was that, sometime later, Fdrí broke out in pox—but the good pox, well, no pox is ever good, but these were the ones that Nonna Funzella called "the black pox," or at least my father remembers her calling them that, but the actual term was Asian pox, which meant they were exotic, and so closer to mother nature although still a problem—and came down with a dangerously high fever and started to hallucinate. In his delirium, Funzella said later, deeply shaken by her grandson's illness, he saw the two enormous carabinieri standing in front of the barber's shop. Somehow they had come unfastened from the wall of the osteria and made their way out into the street and now they stood staring up at him, their heads bobbing on their necks: two of them, four of them, ten, their eyes, noses, and mouths multiplying and warping as if they were alive, as if they were painted on the expanding and contracting bellows of a concertina.

Via Casanova and its surroundings had a hold on him and made their way into his visions, dreams, and even hallucinations. Fdrí was young, four years old at the most, but growing quickly in both intelligence and sensitivity. He studied his father's behavior. If his father read the paper, the child wanted to sit in exactly the same position and pretend to read. But his father didn't want him around. He was protective of his belongings and didn't want the child to touch his newspapers. So Fdrí would sit off to one side and observe him. Over time, all that observing taught him to read, even when the writing was upside down and backwards.

The inhabitants of the building on Via Casanova were proud to have a child who was not only a precocious artist, but also a reader, in their midst. The turner, however, couldn't for the life of him figure out how to get that pretentious firstborn child out of the way. "That little shit better not touch my newspapers. There'll be trouble if he does," he'd grumble. But Fdrí would touch them anyway, and shouting and threats ensued.

One day, Nonna Funzella, whose nerves had also been worn

thin by the child, came up with a solution. "He's so intelligent we should send him to private school." And even though Donna Filomena was extremely moody, even though she regularly hit the child on the head with her heel, she also intuited that he was gifted, and she managed to convince her husband to send him to a school located in Piazza Carlo III, in the enormous Palazzo Salsi, across the street from the Albergo dei Poveri, the poorhouse.

The school was run by Maestro Umberto Piantieri who, for nine lire a month, agreed to find a place for Fdrí. It was a long walk from Via Casanova to school, and my father recalled every single detail of it. He spoke about it as if the bars of the balcony where he had spent so much of his early years had dissolved and he finally managed to descend into the real world. Funzella—his voice cracking with joy—took him to school each morning. They walked hand in hand, breathing in the scent of the perfume factory, past the cemetery (which his grandmother called the Protestant graveyard), past the Donvito wallpaper factory (which was called the money factory because once there had been a mint there), past the bicycle store that smelled of rubber, and very slowly past the cookie factory so that they could taste the aromas that emanated from it.

When Sant'Alfonso de' Liguori church came into sight, Funzella crossed herself and told Fdrí to do so, too. The child obeyed but he was distracted. What caught his attention were the colored shapes and words on the posters on the walls. He sounded them out as best as he could and associated colors with the letters, without knowing a thing about Rimbaud or his sonnet about vowels.

At first things didn't go too well at school. It was a grim place. The teacher was unkind and not encouraging, my father said. Actually she didn't give a flying fuck that he knew how to do things and she treated him like a bratty child. He cried and didn't want to stay there; he couldn't stand the fact that they didn't acknowledge his gifts. One day an inspector from the Ministry of Education came to check on them, the type of person who's tough on teachers but kind with pupils. The inspector wanted to see what such a young child could do and was surprised to learn that he knew how to draw, paint, read, and write far better than the other children not only in first grade, but even in third. The inspector was amazed and called for Maestro Piantieri. He then ordered the teacher to take especially good care of Fdrí. Piantieri obeyed with pleasure. He scolded the teacher for not pointing out the young pupil's exceptional skills and focused on the child himself, swiftly administering end-of-year examinations and moving him up to second grade.

When my father spoke about Maestro Piantieri, his affection for the man was evident. He described him as patient, watchful, kind, and a great admirer of Fdrí's natural Italian genius. But Piantieri was especially impressed with the speed with which Fdrí could draw and paint anything at all. For example, if he saw a dog on his way to school, as soon as he got to class, he'd dip his pen into the metal inkwell and draw a dog. Or, if he saw some graffiti that showed a bundle of twigs, as soon as he got to class, he'd replicate the fasces perfectly, together with the "long live fascism" slogan that appeared alongside it. Piantieri encouraged him. Bravo, he said.

The most gratifying episode took place one day when, on his way home from school, he noticed some graffiti that showed a repeated series of heads, all of the same person, one after the other, in black on the grey wall. His grandmother, who had gone to pick him up at school, realized that the child was interested. "Do you want to see how they do it? Look," she said.

Not far away a group of teenagers stood with a pail of black paint, a brush, and a perforated zinc plate. They held the plate up to the wall and brushed it with the paint. Then they removed the plate and that person's face remained on the wall. *Cazzo*—my father exclaimed as he told the story—seeing that had a major impact on me.

When he got home, he immediately went and told Don Mimí what he had seen, and then asked his father whose head that was. Don Mimí replied curtly, without the least bit of satisfaction: "A shithead named Musulline." And that's it. The turner was usually a man of few words; for Musulline and his comrades he had even less to say. They were either *schiattamuorti* or *becchini*. Undertakers or gravediggers. That's what they were.

Fdrí was disappointed and couldn't get that black-grey portrait that he'd seen on the wall out of his mind. He couldn't resist, he had to draw it, even if the man was a shithead. But since he couldn't do it at home, afraid that his father would get angry, the next day he drew it at school in his math notebook.

Maestro Piantieri noticed it while he was walking between the desks. He stopped. There was a long and amazed silence. Piantieri congratulated him warmly. "That's beautiful," he said. He wanted Fdrí to give it to him as a gift and he showed it to everyone: colleagues, friends, and relatives, and he even said he would frame it. Apparently, he did—my father happily recalled as an old man—but he didn't keep it for himself. He gave it to the honorable Mussolini when he came to Naples to give a speech in Piazza Plebiscito. Maybe Mussolini even hung it on the wall of his office in Palazzo Venezia.

My father had a stellar career, in other words. From a river bed in Reggio Calabria in 1918 to the portrait of Musulline in 1922, at the tender age of five. What other great things did the future hold for him?

Maestro Piantieri talked to everyone about the child's extraordinary talents. Fdricchiè knew not only how to draw, color, read, and write but he could also hold his own in a conversation about art, showing a precocious critical spirit matched by equally precocious skills.

One day, the story went, Piantieri brought an oil painting to class by an artist named Colizzi that showed, as the title indicated,

Effetti di neve all'alba (Snow at dawn). It was the first oil painting that my father ever saw in what would be a very long life and, then and there, it had a strong and positive impression on him. But after observing the painting carefully, he noticed endless problems with it and started critiquing it and its mistakes, revealing the weaknesses of Colizzi, the painter. Piantieri, who was beside himself with amazement, telephoned Don Mimí right away. "This child must immediately go to art school."

Don Mimí showed up grudgingly. His presence was like a deathly illness to any and all possible gratification or happiness that the child might have felt. The teacher showered the child with praises and listed all his merits to the father: he was the best in arithmetic, he wrote well, he could hold a tune, he had an ear for music, and he had even drawn a beautiful portrait of the honorable Mussolini. Nothing. Don Mimí didn't give a fuck, especially about the last thing. As soon as they got home, he announced his verdict. "Your teacher's a shithead! Does art school put food on the table?" From that moment on, he started to wonder out loud, to a public made up primarily of Filumena, "Is Fdrí better than me?" Before his wife could butt in, he'd answer his own question. "No, he's not. So he can be a worker, too. After all, what's so bad about being a worker?"

At this point, my father, who was sitting at the easel and drawing, would look up and explain. "If someone knows only how to be a worker, Mimí, there's really nothing wrong with it. But if someone has another destiny, if there are all the signs that point to something different, what the hell does 'What's so bad about...' even mean?" It didn't mean a thing. It was just a way for his father to send him off to work at a young age and pocket the money that his firstborn made so that he could squander it on cards or at the dog races.

That's how Don Mimí was. He didn't want to see or hear a thing. He had perfect sight and hearing and was an intelligent man. He could've said, "*Cazzo*, would you look at the son I've gone and created." Instead, my father pointed out with deep suffering that his own father stubbornly insisted on digging his son's grave. He was a monster, a forerunner of all the other monsters that would appear in his future: damn spineless *scurnacchiati* railroad managers, presumptuous nouveau riche, and shithead, idiot painters who stole his important exhibition prizes away from him.

I leaned up against an iron railing that functioned as something of a parapet over a raised mound in the cobblestones. "Is this the Casanova bridge?" I asked a youngish man who was walking briskly by with eyes downcast, mainly to hear the sound of my own voice.

The stranger turned out to be very nice. He said yes, and went on to explain clearly and knowledgeably that behind me, where there was now a ditch, there used to be a canal that would carry run-off rain down to the Arenaccia. The bridge went over it, he said, but bridge is too grand a word for what it was, it was never a real bridge. "How do you know all this?" I asked him. "I studied it at university," he said with a laugh.

I observed old Corso Nóvara, sliced in two by the elevated train, and continued on toward Piazza Nazionale and Via Poggioreale. I meandered up and down and across the streets and piazzas that linked my adolescence with that of my father. For example, he used to say that he met up with his friends in Piazza Nazionale, and decades later, that's where I met up with my friends, too. In reality, though, the only similarity that existed between us was in the words we used, that we met up with friends in those places, and nothing more. What did my adolescence share with his? Studying is, above all, a show of faith in language: whether it's knowing about bridges, knowing how to whine and complain, or about making a mark to describe people and things, it's always a tool for making the center hold. Studying gives a person the illusion of continuity, cause and effect, an event and its consequences, syllogisms. All you really have to do is grab one end of the thread and tug on it to unravel the knot. Something that was never true will soon start to seem it.

My father talked a lot about the importance of school and studying. The urge I feel to study comes from him. In everything he said, in all his chatter, whether aggressive or heartfelt, there was always the seed of regret of not having been able to study enough, which was then quickly followed by a harsh critique of the inept people who taught with neither substance nor imagination. He'd gladly spar with anyone who had gone to high school or university. He wanted to face off with them and prove that he knew more than they, or at least that he knew how to make more out of the little he knew better than anyone who had completed high school or university.

As a young man I didn't quite understand. One day he'd say he had graduated high school, another day that he had not. He was capable of talking about all sorts of subjects, both in theory and practice. To my mother's great chagrin, sometimes he even went out on a limb and said that he had a university degree. This confusing situation was a source of embarrassment for me for years on end: I didn't know how to define him to my friends. Then, gradually, Federí stepped back and, as he got older, preferred to admit that he had neither a high school diploma nor a university degree. But he only did that so that he could inveigh more effectively against his own father.

It was all Don Mimí's fault, he said. When his genius son reached the age of ten, the turner decided to send him off to work in France with a brother of his who had emigrated. But he encountered strong opposition from both Nonna Funzella and Filomena. And since he feared his wife's brand of drama—true manifestations of rage with no limits, because Filumè could be dangerous both to herself and others—he resigned himself temporarily to enrolling his son at the Casanova vocational school: eight hours of classes a day, a taste of factory work to come.

At that point, Federí usually opened a parentheses. "You, however, will go to university. I will not behave with you the way my father did with me. You will be able to become whatever you want: a railroad engineer, whatever. I will not stand in your way." Listening to him, I sensed that I actually would've preferred some kind of opposition. I confusedly intuited that behind his desire for me to become "whatever you want" lay his need for me to do something deeply gratifying for him, such as become a railroad engineer. And so I was trapped by the fear of not meeting his expectations; I ended up envying him his father who obstructed his path at every turn, which then made it easy for him to say, "It was all my father's fault."

But he didn't realize it. The parentheses would close, and he'd go on. "My father wanted me to do grunt work." It was thanks only to Filomena's dramatic tirades, which were witnessed and remembered by the entire building, that he managed to wriggle out of going to work after his apprenticeship. Don Mimí gave in and sent his son to the Alessandro Volta institute to get a degree as a specialized machinist but did everything he could to make his son's school life difficult: he paid his school taxes late, never purchased him the books he needed, and tried to get him to fail or be held back or expelled.

At that point of his life, my father's stories, which were generally so colorful, became muted. Even later on, in the 1990s, and in his notebooks, a veil fell over his blustery stories of artistic precociousness, his lively tales of self-celebration faded, the desire to constantly reinvent himself from head to toe dried up. It was as if for a number of years he kept his genius inside, and, feeling deep humiliation, decided to silence it.

Sure, if the opportunity arose, he wouldn't hold back from talking about the time that he impressed a painter who was copying masterpieces at the Museo di Capodimonte; he spoke of that encounter as if the two of them were Cimabue and Giotto. But he did it joylessly. He preferred talking about his first romantic interludes or his friends when he was a teenager or his boxing or his exceptional skiing skills, which he developed in the railroad militia. All his value as an artist, which had exploded onto the scene as a young child, suddenly grew dormant. Did he continue to draw or paint at the age of twelve, thirteen, fifteen or eighteen? Did he continue to garner praise for his talent? It's hard to say. There was a gap between 1927 and 1935, the year his father won out and forced him to leave the Alessandro Volta institute without receiving a diploma, despite Filomena's wailing and screaming. No art school, no vocational school, no academic degree. That's what Don Mimí did to him.

"You should be grateful to him," Nonna Nannina once interjected. "He let you stay in school until you were eighteen."

I recall the heavy silence that fell after she uttered those words. I was aware that even my mother disapproved of Nonna Nannina voicing her opinion, which she did rarely. It was as if my grandmother were pointing out a discrepancy in his story, as if she was reminding her son-in-law that while Don Mimí surely had his flaws, he had paid for his son's schooling for a dozen years.

Her silence extended like a slow sigh until Nannina herself broke the silence. "Me, I had to send my son Peppino to work." And with that, Federí's jaw dropped in shock. "Are you really comparing Peppino with me? Because your son is a shithead."

The paper on which he sketched, which he held steady with his left hand, lay across a large board that rested on his crossed legs. He sat with great composure, his back to the window. I hear him speaking softly. "At the age of eighteen, Mimí, my father forced me to take an entrance exam for a job on the railroad, and that's how I ended up in that grime and filth, always one step away from death." When he talks about the beginning of his life on the railroad he speaks in a particularly dramatic way. I can't separate the significance of his words from a general sense of physical pain. Maybe it was a blending of different kinds of suffering: that of the young artist forced by his father to work as an electrical repairman with my own, a boy who had been compelled, out of love for that large-scale painting that he'll go on to call *The Drinkers*, to pose as the apprentice, servant to the master builder and overseer, knee bones crushed against the hard floor, the straw of the demijohn digging into the flesh of my arm.

"I had to do inspections and repairs on the electric locomotives," he continued. He was forced to squeeze into narrow, foul places. His overalls were always lurid with rancid grease, his body covered in it. After work there was no way to wash up, there weren't enough tubs or sinks at the depot, all they could do was rub their hands with oil and sand. They could only bathe comfortably on Sundays, when the tubs at the depot were free. And what came out of all that horror? Nothing, not even money. At the end of every month, he'd go to the cashier to sign his chit, the cashier would count out four 100 lire bills and five silver coins, but he didn't even have time to handle the money before his father would swoop down and whisk his treasure away. It was pointless for him to try and ask to keep part of it. The answer was always, "What do you need money for? What do you need?" Just to be sure, though, out of fear that he wouldn't go and tell Donna Filumè, he slipped his son a silver 5 lire coin.

Don Mimí confiscated his first three paychecks and kept the money for himself. He didn't hand over a single lire to Filomena: he told her that new employees were on probation for the first three months and he gambled away the entire amount. First, the man suffocated his artistic vocation. Then, he took away his money. Over the years, he did even more than that. During wartime, Don Mimí even found a way to steal the part of his salary that was destined for Federí's wife, Rusinè. That socialist screwed every one of them.

Days and years of great hardship passed. The electrical repairmen worked on the locomotives in a large area big enough for thirty iron beasts, protected from the elements by a roof and yet exposed on all sides. The engines were dismantled with the assistance of a rotating platform which, when the work was complete, was used to recompose the machines and reconduct them to the trains that needed to depart. Each locomotive engine was positioned above a pit that was as tall as a man. Resting at the bottom of the pit, which was made of cement, stood a ladder with four steps. That was their workplace.

It was hard to balance on the ladder because it was rickety and the ground itself was slippery with oil and grease. They had to hold onto the locomotive wherever they could, so as not to fall. But even worse was when they had to work on the roof of the train. Under the depot roof ran the high-tension wires for the copper pantographs, two for each train engine. The two pantograph arms usually lay flat, each one having its own command cabins, forward and aft. The personnel in charge was able to maneuver them as needed, using four-bar high-pressure compressed air to raise them up until the slides touched the high tension contact wire, and lowering them by releasing the pressure.

Details such as these were precious to my father to explain to me exactly where my grandfather had forced him to work, to show me what a miracle it was that he didn't lose his life there. As a matter of fact—and here he started mumbling—an awful accident took place one rainy afternoon in February 1936. He was hard at work deep inside a locomotive that had been assigned to him. Not far off, a twenty-four-year-old fellow named Barca was working on his own locomotive. Barca was an expert and very confident; he knew how to get things done quickly and never wasted any time. In fact, he only turned off the high tension wire when he had to balance the pantograph, which was done by switching it on and checking how much pressure it required to get into place. If Barca had to change the sliders— which was done when the pantograph arms were lowered—he didn't even switch off the electrical current so as not to waste time. And that's exactly what he did that day, the rain coming down in buckets. At a certain point, my father had to get out of his pit because he needed some special brushes for the dynamo. He headed toward the warehouse. As he walked by Barca, he saw him standing on the roof of the train, two meters up, struggling to remove a pair of pantograph sliders. It was a dark day, the lighting was dim, and the workshop roof was being hammered by pounding rain. My father had to jump over puddles that had formed on the ground. Suddenly a flame lit up the workshop as bright as day. Federí barely had time to turn around to see what happened when a second blaze lit up the sky, followed by a loud snapping sound. The air turned pink and smelled like burnt flesh; it was hard to see what was going on. Long tongues of fire flared up in the space between the two pneumatic actuators on Barca's locomotive.

My father ran toward the train immediately. He saw Barca leaning over the actuators amid gusts of steam and flashes of light, as if the young man was soldering something with an oxyhydrogen flame. Then there was a third flash, blinding, followed by the cracking sound of a whip. The high-tension wire had snapped, it flicked through the air and came into contact with Barca's body.

Federí called for help. A middle-aged worker named Ranauro shouted at him to stay away from the locomotive and then ran to hammer off the lever on the high-tension wire. Barca was already dead when they brought him down. They calculated that he had just finished changing the slider on the pantograph and was about to descend from the roof when he slipped and instinctively reached for the first thing he could: the high-tension wire.

Over the years, a number of people were wounded or killed in the repair depot. I listened to him and imagined that grim place, with its dangerous electrical currents. Once, even my father fell off a locomotive, a drop of two meters. His right hand got bent back all the way up his arm, but luckily someone had been able to yank it back into place.

He told his story without exaggerating. The subject was so worthless to him that he didn't even try and embellish things as usual. When he talked about the dangers his colleagues found themselves in, he never endowed himself with any kind of salvific role, always admitted to being paralyzed with fear, never showed off or said that he was the fastest to respond. In that somber phase of his life, he was never the most agile or strongest, he was never brilliant. The end of his marvelous childhood had been traumatic and debilitating. The real proof of his strength and intelligence—it seemed to him now—was not getting acclimated to the setting or executing memorable tasks, but getting out of there unharmed, holding on tight to the mane of good fortune and galloping out. He needed to get back to the surface and tap back into the good luck that the bonfires at the feast of St. Anthony the Abbot had illuminated in him, rediscover the ecstatic joy he first felt in the brook in Reggio Calabria, forge his way through the crowds of scum and dabblers who always sought to clip his wings, sit at the easel like he was doing, and work on a piece like *The Drinkers* despite the fatigue, the lack of space, the lousy models, his family, Rusinè.

My computer suddenly crashed. I tried turning it off and on again, but nothing happened. The screen stayed white. For a while I just sat there, depressed, looking at the bright rectangle, reading the words Macintosh Powerbook 145B. For months now, I've been pouring my father's words and manners of speech into this machine, one of the few objects in which he was not interested in solidifying his expertise and never used. Not too long ago, I even playfully thought that this contraption is too modern and elegant and sophisticated to contain words like Fdrí, Asiatic pox, Musulline, pantograph sliders, and even that beat-up mandolin. One day this machine is going to break down. And now that it has, I'm terribly upset about it. How can an electronic memory, which is usually so indiscriminately receptive, refuse to "save" Federí and his language?

I took it to a computer technician right away. The man took one look at the laptop, smiled gently, and said, "Nice machine. But once in a while, sir, you need to update your model. Using this is kind of like taking a road trip in an Alfa Romeo Giulietta. You remember the Giulietta?"

What a relief. This time Federí wasn't to blame, not even metaphorically. The guilt was my own and that of my computer, which was now, I learned with some surprise, considered old. I had not entrusted the facts about my father to who knows what kind of modern machine, as I believed I had, but to a tool that precisely because of how quickly technology ages was equivalent to the car driven by Zio Attilio the sausage-maker. I had been working on a computer that was the equivalent of a Giulietta, an automobile that was a symbol of wealth back in Federí and Rusinè's day. Forty years ago, my mother gaily and coquettishly climbed into Zio Attilio's car when he came over to flaunt his wealth, my father always standing to the side and fidgeting with envy, bitter about being an artist and not being able to possess an automobile. What sense did his miraculous childhood and all its signs and portents have—he'd whine, but in his words—if any old guy, a man who sold deli meats, could possess all kinds of luxurious, modern objects? Zio Attilio didn't have his vision, his artist's eye, he wouldn't have been able to see a damn thing from his balcony, not even with a pair of binoculars. And yet, there he was in his shiny, blue-green Giulietta. Federí seethed. I seethed along with him as I stared at the technician. "But I bought this laptop only three or four years ago."

The expert got to work on it. "When did you start using a computer?" he asked, trying to make small talk. "In 1985," I replied. "Are you sure?" he said with a snicker. "Perfectly," I snapped. "Well, I'm sorry to tell you but, in all this time, you haven't learned a thing. It's apparent that this machine has suffered a great deal in your ownership," he said regretfully. He then made a general comment about how too many people don't really understand technology, and so on. Eventually, in some roundabout way he even uttered a cliché along the lines of, "In today's world, when something new comes on the market, it's already obsolete."

Most of his rambling meant nothing to me but I was caught by the expression, "in today's world." What is today's world? Did Federí live in today's world? Is my laptop from today's world? What about me? What measurable span of time makes up today's world? Does it mean "now?" Or does it mean "in the past couple of years?" Or does it allude to your whole life, memories and all, until the day you finally close your eyes—both the inward-looking ones and the ones that gaze out—and today's world comes to an end?

When I went home with my laptop repaired, it occurred to me to try and write using only the *imperfetto* and the *passato prossimo*, the two tenses that I love most because of the way the "now" is never over but, at the very most, stationed nearby, like the shades of the dead in scary stories. For a while I tapped away diligently, hoping that sooner or later the *imperfetto* and *passato prossimo* would definitively take the place of the *passato remoto* and the *presente*, while continuing to grant the future tense its humble role of inducing anxiety, the glimmer of hope. But then I stopped. I went back to using Federí and Rusinè's syntax. All those words, an astounding number of characters that formed a compendium of facts, places, and periods in time. I am in my house—I wrote—I am on Via Casanova, I am in Piazza Nazionale, I am kneeling on one aching knee so that my father can paint a builder's apprentice, I am my father himself and my mother, I am even my grandfather, Don Mimí, the turner, who refuses to acknowledge his son's great talent. I am so many things. And if I press the "delete" key, I said to myself, resorting to the simplistic way I thought about things when I was still an adolescent, I become nothing: nameless, sexless, just a blur on a broken screen.

The thought frightened me. I started typing diligently again. Now I'm in Piazza Nazionale. An inflated condom, identical to the ones the Allied soldiers threw down from the boxes of the Teatro Bellini, bounces down the lurid cobblestone street in the hot wind. From here, and for as long as I believe that I possess a thread that can be unraveled line after line, I will make my way back to the boy kneeling in pain on Via Gemito, and to the father who continues to paint and talk about himself.

When I reached the park in Piazza Nazionale, and while looking around for a fountain to cool off, I suddenly decided to add a stop on my itinerary and phoned the city-hall offices. My father, I said in the same way that I introduced myself to the employee in Positano, was a painter. A good one, well known. Some of his paintings are hanging in Palazzo San Giacomo. Would it be possible to see them?

The operator gave me the number of the person in charge of city-owned cultural property, a certain Dr. Guidi. I called the number. "Is this Dr. Guidi?" I asked. Yes, it was she. I went on to explain to her, too, that my father had dedicated his life to art: he was a painter, yes, quite well known; if it was no trouble, I would really like to see his paintings that hung in the town hall. Dr. Guidi asked me if I was sure that my father's paintings were in Palazzo San Giacomo. No, I said, with my father nothing was ever certain, but I insisted and asked to have a look. "Come tomorrow morning at half past nine and I'll show you around," she graciously replied.

Even though I had a pounding headache, I was satisfied. Suddenly, I experienced what my brothers had suggested I do all along: accept the image that Federí wanted to portray of himself, pay homage to it, and behave as though I was going to see his art in a famous gallery. Yes, I was happy. This way, I thought, I'd be able to draw a straight line between the eighteen-year-old boy who had lost all hope and was resigned to not becoming an artist but a worker, and his many works of art from decades later, works that had escaped from Lavinaio, Via Casanova, from Don Mimí's persecution. I told myself that I'd go to Positano at a later date, when I felt calmer and had clearer intentions.

I walked in the direction of Piazza Carlo III looking for a bus that would take me back to my brother's house. For a while I felt like a good son, freed from the generations of chains of indentured slavery and conflict. Then, ever so gradually, I went back to feeling like I was still holding the pose, kneeling on the floor in the house on Via Gemito. I felt all the pain of having to stay still for an endless amount of time, I experienced both the fascination and abomination that Federí's voice inspired in me as he fabricated details that would prove to me just how talented he was while also shedding light on the infinite wrongs he'd suffered. I imagine Rusinè, too, her head tipped to one side as she looked with puzzlement at how her bedsheet had been transformed into a scene from a construction site. I experienced anew all the dismay I felt back then.

When I got on a crowded bus that headed slowly up Santa Teresa degli Scalzi, I realized that my mood and sentiments had changed yet again. I was already regretting the appointment I made with Dr. Guidi. I should've just slammed the book shut on the story behind *The Drinkers*.

How long did I hold that position that day? Fifteen minutes, half an hour, an eternity? It's hard to say. To be honest, I don't have a clear memory of the passing of time, nor do I feel the need to invent one. I prefer to let my memories amass randomly, the way I have done up until now: the time my father called me over and did a bunch of charcoal sketches of me, the time my mother walked in and announced "Dinner's ready," the time that he finally seemed pleased and we really did go and eat, the time he called for me and told me to take up the position again so that he could transfer the sketch of the boy pouring water onto the canvas.

I remember details, phrases, lighthearted moments, and moments of tension, but not in any chronological order. In my mind I see him drawing and then painting, sitting and then standing, the painting is almost done, the painting is still a sketch, on the right of the canvas is a grey blotch to mark the space where my body will be, directly above the builders' meal, which has already been completed: bread, four tomatoes, and some grapes.

In short, I can't say anything specific. I only know that the position was very uncomfortable, I know the pain. I can't rule out that as he glanced at me, intending to capture a kneecap, a big toe, or an elbow, he stopped to ask, "Everything ok, Mimí?" He may well have encouraged me by saying, "Another little bit and then we're done." He might have even said something like, "In a few minutes we'll stop to eat." But what has stayed in my memory above all is the fatigue of holding the position, a growing sense of inadequacy, and the way he insisted, first earnestly and then with braggadocio, on his successes, his artistic precocity, on the way his father tried so hard to reduce him to being just an ordinary man.

As I tried to stay still, I remember thinking to myself, "What's so bad about being an ordinary man?" And when I had those thoughts, I suddenly felt like an empty shell, as if the admiration my father urged me to have for him left me with a sense of loss. I can't find any other words to describe that feeling. It felt like I had lost something because I had paid too much attention to it, like when you're seduced by something. My fascination with his extreme vitality, a trait of his ever since he was born, devitalized me to the degree that, to this day, I think that I was able to stand as still as a statue for him only because I didn't have the strength to have a childhood, an adolescence, an existence on a par with his.

There I was: apprentice builder suffering the condition of servant to master. As he talked, the pages of his childhood and his titanic struggle with my grandfather turned as if blown by an invisible breeze. Pain running through each muscle, I scrutinized my few years of life for something equally as powerful but found nothing comparable to those hints of his greatness. This led to a feeling of paucity that sunk its teeth into me and stayed with me my whole life.

And then he'd say, "That's enough for now," and interrupt his storytelling. I remember those words perfectly, as if his voice was a cannon shot, the kind they used to use to signal lunch break. Enough for now, he'd say and start to pick up the sheets of paper that were scattered all over the floor, my figure roughly sketched on them.

My limbs felt like they melted with relief. I'd put down the demijohn and stand up straight without even daring to rub my knee, without stretching. And thus would begin his generous praise of my self-discipline, how I never complained. And when we sat down at the table—my grandmother, mother, and brothers all waiting for us, food already served and covered with other plates to keep it warm—he'd start insulting all the other people who had sat for him, especially Zio Matteo and Zio Peppino, who, he recalled, were incapable of sitting still for one single moment. He did it just so that he could turn to my mother and say about me, "But he didn't even move a millimeter." He then went on to praise our race—that was the word he used, race, in the sense of bloodline—and with that he meant his family, the one he descended from, but him above all, as the superior example of it. We, as his offspring, promised even greater things. He used me as an example of someone who had skills that other races, especially those on my mother's side, couldn't even dream of.

That's more or less it. Facts and the desire for facts blend together, like words that were actually spoken and words that were merely desired. I'm not even entirely sure if his excitement and good mood really existed. Occasionally he was happy, and I like to think that his happiness derived from how he managed to resolve the pictorial puzzle of the painting. That made me happy, too. My knee was purple and the arm that had been holding the demijohn ached terribly. I'd rub my wrist theatrically so that my mother and grandmother, and in particular my brothers, would appreciate the full extent of my undertaking. I'd look over at my father, who sat there devouring his food and joking, and I was proud of having helped him just the way he wanted. Things at home were good, finally.

And then? And then, suddenly, the way a door slams in the wind, I'm back in that terrible position I just left, in front of the easel. I'm back kneeling on the floor, holding the empty demijohn. I don't know what happened in between. Maybe something my grandmother said got him angry. Seeing me continually rub my wrist, she'd suddenly pipe up, "Are you hurt?" Right away, I'd stop massaging my wrist out of fear that he'd get angry. But the words had already been uttered and my father's mood had already changed, and he'd say something like: "He's fine, dear mother-in-law, nothing wrong with him at all. Your grandson isn't made of ricotta, not like your son." And then he'd get up halfway through the meal and beckon to me to follow him back into the room where he painted. Harmony was delicate back then and it didn't take much to make it end.

But maybe things happened differently. Maybe there was a long silence, with me wishing I had a net strong enough to catch my grandmother's misspoken words, or my wrist-rubbing, or even the sound of my brother snapping his fingers, because Geppe was always practicing his finger-snapping back then. But since that was impossible, I'd resign myself to waiting to see the shape my father would give the rest of lunch, even though, at moments like that, it was entirely predictable. If something irked him while we were eating, he'd immediately go quiet, purse his lips tightly together, and then eventually break the silence by choosing an interlocutor—me, usually, he liked choosing me—and, just to irritate everyone, he'd start droning on and on, so that by the time the rest of us had reached the fruit, he'd still be on his first course. My mother and grandmother would wait for a bit and then, with utmost discretion, start to clear the table. He'd ignore them and keep talking. My brothers would get up from the table and dawdle about nearby, waiting for me to join them in the hall. But he ignored them and kept talking. We'd sit across from each other, my father and I, dishes and cutlery on his side of the table only, everything else cleared away, while he ate and talked, talked and ate. Lunch became like a guillotine that, because of some strange spell, took forever to fall. The two women stood to one side, wondering if they should start washing the dishes or not. My brothers hovered nearby, uncertain if they should come and sit back down and pretend to listen. I dreamed of being liberated by a flash of light or something. And then Federí suddenly stopped talking and, in reaction to some gesture or slight movement made by my mother, he'd start screaming and yelling and throwing things. He yelled at us all, called us ball-busters, and got up quickly from the table. And that is precisely what happened, I think, on one occasion when, after swearing to the high heavens, cursing all the saints and virgins, he said, "Basta! Enough of this ball-busting! Come on, Mimí! Let's go."

Or maybe it didn't happen that way. Maybe he spent days on end mulling over the shapes of those builders—travelling from home to work and back again—visualizing them in detail inside his adult head and yet very much still that child on the river's edge in Reggio Calabria, the child who scribbled colored numbers all over Nonna Funzella's door, the child who saw everything unfold from the balcony, who saw the two carabinieri.

When his eyes opened inward they saw things more clearly than his outward-looking eyes. He imagined his figures alive, each one occupying its own space at the construction site, the mastiff keeping a vigilant eye over things that took place beyond the canvas, even Zio Matteo looking off in that direction, a slightly bemused expression on his face; Luigi, meanwhile, just sat there, his left hand resting on the bare ground and his right arm, which would eventually reach out with a glass in hand for the water, was not even sketched yet; the water-bearing boy was still in a gestational phase like the two builders who would eventually be situated next to him, but doing what? Who knows. Basically, half the painting still needed to be painted. He wasn't even sure how to use the sketches that he had done; he needed a burst of imagination, energy, and time. And then one day it all came to him. That was the day he said, "You'll make one more small sacrifice for your dad, Mimí, won't you?" and the torture, the immobility, the posing began again.

Of that I am certain: it definitely began again. From the top. And so, here I am, holding the pose in the center of the room, next to the vitrine with its broken glass where the silver is kept, a few inches away from the table. Even if there had been a period of reprieve (and as I remember it now, there wasn't one; I believe I stayed in that position day in and day out for weeks on end), it definitely didn't ease the tension or fatigue. I'm a tightly knotted and taut rope. Time goes by, nausea hits, I feel feverish. I start hallucinating. I imagine that the man sitting at the easel busily painting *The Drinkers* is not my father, but Federí as a child. He's the one who's doing the painting: a three-year-old version of my father is painting his future ten-year-old firstborn son. What difference does it make if the person who is painting me is three or thirty-six? My father always used to say that you either have talent or you don't, and if you do it's because you were born with it. He was born with talent. And that's why I envision him as he appears in a childhood photo, with a large head and chubby cheeks, but with a cigarette between his lips, a paintbrush in his right hand, looking at me, and sighing *ah* as he dabs the canvas with his brush.

I see this and other things. I see the floor has turned to dirt. The setting of the painting has practically spilled over into the room. My knee rests on the earth of the construction site, my bare foot in contact with the white cloth on which lies half a loaf of bread, a plate with four tomatoes, and some grapes—the builders' lunch. But the perspective is different: I now see those things from my position, not from my father's perspective. I see them. I also see Luigi. While my father placed him so that he can see his back and partial profile, I see his face, his dark hair, his low forehead, his cheeks unshaven for days, his hairy chest. The only thing that's missing is his right arm, the one that will hold the glass.

I'm dreaming with my eyes wide open—or maybe they're closed, I'm not sure, but the vision is perfectly clear either way— when something odd takes place. The empty demijohn I'm holding starts to gush water. But the water doesn't spill into a glass, it splashes onto the tomatoes, the plate, it wets the coarse cloth, spatters the grapes, it's soaked up by the earth and the doughy part of the bread. I flinch as I realize something terrible. In my mind's eye, I quickly complete Luigi's arm. I place an imaginary glass in his hand and have him extend it toward the demijohn. I'm overcome with despair and feel like I'm going to die.

My position is all wrong.

The water will forever spill onto the tomatoes, the plate, the cloth. My father placed me in a position where, even if Luigi reaches out as far as possible, I will never be able to pour the water into his glass.

As I write this, I try and put order in my thoughts, I look for reasons, I draw on what I have learned over the years. Back then, however, I felt the urgent need to save Federí, once he discovered his error, from blaming me or my mother, her relatives, everyone in the family.

Emotions crowded my mind. I was paralyzed with panic. I felt bitterly angry because all the energy I had put into being statu-esque had been pointless. I was afraid that he'd be furious for all the time he'd wasted and would scrape away the fresh paint from the canvas with his spatula or knife, curse all of creation, in heaven and on earth. I felt pain for him because ever since he was born, he never actually managed to become the great artist that he said he was. My heart was exploding with a sense of responsi-bility because the destiny of that painting now depended both on my skill as apprentice builder and my filial devotion.

It didn't take much to double check it: the space between Luigi and me was too great. My father would be forced to paint a disproportionately long arm if he wanted the builder's glass to reach the flow of water from the demijohn.

I couldn't think about it without feeling ill. The more I pic-tured just how long that arm would have to be, the more I broke out in a cold sweat. There was no fix for it. I knew how he'd jus-tify his mistake. First, he'd shout at me. "See what you've done? You moved!" Then he'd start moaning and complaining about not having a proper painting studio like other genius painters did. That, in turn, would've made him angry with my mother, who hadn't let him move the rest of the furniture or throw it out, or even burn it, which would've given him all the space he needed to give rise to the idea in his head. Finally, he would've railed against his great misfortune of being a decent man, a fam-ily man, incapable of abandoning us and running off to live in some attic in Paris. It would've been pointless to try and con-vince him differently, to say something like, "Fine, Papà, but you made the mistake, not me, not Mamma, not the rest of the fam-ily." That would've only made him angrier. He would've grown distressed the way only he knew how, full of rancor. He would've said he was misunderstood even by his firstborn son and gone on to enumerate, just to be clear, the thousands of complexi-ties inherent in the painting, both in terms of conception and execution. How could we possibly understand—he'd scream indignantly—the gravity of the problems an artist has to face? Did we have any idea of the mass of thoughts that crowded his brain? Did we have any idea, for fuck's sake, how many thousands of different hypotheses there were: this one, that one, and a third? *Padreterno*, this wasn't like slicing caciocavallo or filling pastries with cream, or anything.

I was always worried, back then, that one day he might say, Mimí, you don't understand me. I always hated it when he took that tone with my mother ("How could you possibly understand me?") and I was scared that one day he'd eventually speak that way to me, too.

Because I did understand him. I forced myself to. I paid attention to his every word and gesture. By the age of ten I already knew a lot about working at an easel. I had seen the birth of a large number of paintings and drawings and oils and watercolors. To my mind, he had two ways of working: either he took a person, thing, or landscape (like my mother, my grandmother, the iron, the countryside and trees that you could see from our window before it became a construction site) and he drew them just as they were and called them "Mamma," "Nonna," "Iron," "Countryside," or else he took, for example, Zio Vincenzino, who was an electrician, and he drew him as he was but added the sea in the background and a bucket with fish and called him "Fisherman."

His large-scale painting *The Drinkers* followed this second route. And yet, as the days and weeks passed, there was the sense that something far more complicated was developing. It wasn't hard to notice; it was enough to walk into the room while he was working. In addition to the usual smell of paint thinner and sweat, in those days the room was also filled with the aura of a labored and joyful excitement, the way a room smells after children have been playing in it for hours. I recognized it as the scent of our childhood games, back when we pretended to be heroes.

I was amazed that he released that fragrance. Could it be that he was playing the same way that we kids did?

I studied the painting carefully. I looked at it so many times, in all phases of its composition, during the day in full natural light, and at night when the kitchen light filtered in and illuminated select areas and left others in the darkness. The construction site in the background was identical to the one outside our window: devastation, a wasteland, the skeleton of a building under construction, fencing, tool sheds. But the workmen's knife that rested on the white table cloth was entirely foreign to those piles of cement and the mixers and the pile drivers. It was associated with a piece of plywood that he used as a palette, it was the knife that my father used to scrape away dried paint. A huge leap, both in terms of use and setting. Even the plate, the tomatoes, the bread. They didn't belong to the builders, they came from our kitchen, straight out of Nonna's domain (the bunch of grapes, no, it wasn't the season for grapes, who knows where he had gotten them). The wooden crate that Zio Matteo sat on as the overseer came from my uncle's fruit and vegetable shop, so yet another place, a space of other voices and sounds, foreign both to the construction site and our home. And Zio Matteo himself—what did he have to do with bricklayers and builders? What did he have in common with Luigi, who sat on the ground shirtless at the center of the painting? Sure, they both sold vegetables, but they didn't know each other, nor did they want to meet each other. Luigi was a street vendor and traveled with his cart in the sun, wind, and rain; Zio Matteo had a shop and sold his produce under a roof, protected from the elements.

And then there was me. I was in fifth grade, studying for my middle school exams. My own father used to say that I, as his son and natural heir of his genius, together with my brothers, would go on to accomplish great things in my life. I didn't see what connection there was between me and the young apprentice builders that I saw toiling away below on the construction site. Actually,

I felt a certain unease for how he decided to use my persona, as if for some vague reason he had decided to brusquely erase all the grace that in other circumstances he insisted on attributing to me.

I felt my unease snake across the painting between the animate beings and inanimate objects, as if each one of us nursed the idea of "I'm not happy, I want to leave." I saw my father sitting for hours on end with his mouth slightly open in front of the painting, sometimes mixing colors, sometimes painting, and I could detect the effort that he was putting into forcing us to blend together, to live together with ease and naturalness, people and places and things that normally didn't mix together, but that stood on their own, without any real points of contact. Was this what made him sweat so much, even if he was sitting still? Was this why, when everything seemed to be going well, he gave off the scent of a child at play?

At some point during that period of anguish—I can't say exactly when, whether it was before or after this particular thought or that sigh or cough or anything like that—I discovered something else. I realized that, sitting next to him, unseen and yet giving him expert advice, was the ghost of Zio Peppino di Firenze.

From all the objects that he bequeathed us came, I believe, whispered words of enchantment that filled my father's head with far too much advice and too many suggestions. It was a persistent hum that I attributed to that relative, the marshal of public safety, with his Tusco-Neapolitan accent. "Do it this way, Federí; no, maybe better that way," the voice said, offering a surplus of physical gestures and expressions, objects, and exceptional colors, all of which confused my father by providing solutions or tips that ultimately weakened his faith in what he had already accomplished.

Today I can't say exactly which suggestions from that Florentine voice or objects he followed for *The Drinkers*. Unquestionably, many aspects of the Neapolitan mastiff made their way there, as I already mentioned, from a book of photos with a bright blue cover. A fifteen-centimeter-tall statuette—a crude piece of art, the head of which we kids later broke while playing ball, and made by an unknown artisan—depicting a seated male figure who looked slightly drunk, also had a relevant role. Then there was the book with the cloth cover dedicated to the great painter, Manet, that my father kept open on a chair next to the easel, so that he could glance at it now and then. "My painting, Mimí, is also an homage to the great painter, Édouard Manet."

I understood exactly what had happened with the mastiff. The photo in the blue book showed a marble image of the dog. My father, perhaps on advice from the ghost of Zio Peppino di Firenze, or perhaps on his own, initially made it vigilant and aggressive, but then he confused it with all the mastiffs he had seen in his life or drawn while exploring the countryside. Finally, after a number of different interpretations and iterations, he decided to transfer it onto the canvas: one more difficult presence to control among so many disparate figures.

It was harder to trace the mutation of the painted gesso statuette. Without a doubt, Federí had extrapolated Zio Matteo's pose from it: sitting, glass in hand. But only the pose. The body was clearly that of our uncle. The influence of the statue could also be seen in the old hat that the figure wore on his head and in his expression. Zio Matteo, sitting there on the canvas in his role as master builder, no longer looked like one of our relatives, but as though he was related to the statue, whom he had bumped into and asked, "May I borrow your hat?"

How much life my father must've seen in that object from Florence, which had originally been chosen by the thick-fingered yet expert hands of Zio Peppino. It certainly inspired the figures who stood to the left of the boy holding the demijohn, to my right, in other words. The two men, also builders, stood staring at the flow of water with an unreasonable amount of curiosity. I really didn't understand what there was to see. Their expressions came out so well that when the painting was done and I examined them closely, I was amazed to see that they looked real, even though he had not used real live models for them. My father must have turned the statue ever so slightly, just enough to change the perspective, and in so doing had extracted more life out of it, and had artfully invented two men without having to deal with or complain about models and how they never stayed still. I studied them: they looked like Siamese twins, like Zio Matteo's distant relatives. Their resemblance made me think about the actual person that the unknown sculptor must have used for inspiration. "Who knows how long ago he died, and yet he's still here," I said to myself. Back then, art seemed to me to be a bizarre, constant migration of ectoplasms.

And finally there was Manet. In the long span of time that my father worked on his painting, the cloth-bound book about Manet was always next to him at the easel, opened to *Le Déjeuner sur l'herbe*. Whenever my father wasn't home and I went in and spied on the canvas, I ended up examining that image. I wondered why he kept it within view, seeing that his painting and the reproduction had nothing in common. Until one day, while I was posing for him, undergoing the torture, I realized that Luigi was not just Luigi. My father had done something strange with his chest. That's right. There was, in Luigi's bare chest, something of the nudity of Manet's woman. *The Drinkers* didn't contain only a photo of a statue of a mastiff that was used to inspire his portrait of a real mastiff. The painting didn't only celebrate a statuette by sharing its attributes and physiognomy, as well as its hat, with a total of three figures in the painting—one painted from life and two invented ones—with the final result that the invented ones seemed to be relatives of the real one. My father's painting also sought to transfer aspects of Manet's *Le Déjeuner sur l'herbe* to a squalid construction site.

Now, as I write about it, I imagine my father with his big forehead and small eyes seeing things we relatives can't see: the grey earth taking the place of a lawn, construction workers sitting in the place of well-dressed bourgeoisie, and gaunt Luigi, stripped naked down to his pants, audaciously stepping in for Manet's opulent, nude woman.

Beyond the apparent silence of the scene and lurking deep within the painting was a tumult of real gestures and fictitious ones, homely shapes and elegant poses. *Le Déjeuner sur l'herbe*, *Los Borrachos*, *The Drinkers*. Statues and statuettes and Zio Matteo. Who knew what else. I even got to the point of wondering in confusion, but not with these exact words, "Is the boy who's pouring water even me? Or does he also derive from some drawing or statuette or small painting or print hidden among all the pieces of art that Zio Peppino di Firenze left us?" I began to think of myself as inhabited by strangers. Reassembled, recreated, wildly distorted. And so I looked around the house when my father wasn't around for sources of the figure of the boy with the demijohn. But I found nothing and eventually stopped looking. I doubt now, at this point, that I'll ever find anything.

One thing is for certain: a mobile carnival of shapes, an effervescence of images spun around that painting for days and weeks on end. They came and went in an unstoppable flow, like bubbles in seltzer water. That's why my father always looks so delirious, it occurred to me. That's why he's so jumpy and yells for no reason. Maybe, while I was sitting for him, even the carabinieri that Federí had seen as a child came around as if on patrol, even if (or maybe because of this) they drank wine while the builders preferred water. I tried not to be shocked by anything. I understood. I understood that a piece of art was a meeting place for a crowd. My father's head was filled with shadows and he had to keep a handle on a thousand different ghosts, all of them situated at the forefront of his brain, in his forehead—"here, Mimí, right here"—without any possibility of being able to keep them in order: men, objects, dogs. He could see them all at once. He could see if they balanced each other out. He had to deduce the right distances and right proportions, what colors they'd have in the light of day, and what color they'd have under electric light. If he wanted, he could just use the light from a light bulb, as if that were daylight, and paint with the shutters closed and the light always on, even if the sun was out. Because, Mimí, because it's so damn difficult. It's been difficult ever since I was child; you never really know what to do: realism, abstraction, tradition, the avant-garde, that shithead Picasso, that cocksucker Léger, what is art anyway, what can you do, really? What can a person who wants to paint in this hellhole really do? He meant us kids, how we screamed and ran up and down the hallway, he meant Nonna, who complained because she couldn't make up the beds at night or take off the sheets in the morning, he meant his job on the railroad, the night shifts, the day shifts; he meant Paolo Ricci, who says do this, and Carlo Barbieri, who says do that. You can't possibly stay on top of everything, you know?

Yes, I knew. I understood what had happened. What had happened was that in that chaos of people and places and things and books and Zio Peppino di Firenze, and presented with all those choices of how to make, invent, reinvent, and remake, my father had made a mistake: he had not calculated the distances well. Now he was forced to paint an arm that was too long, an arm that would look out of proportion.

I decided that I needed to do the one thing that up until that moment I had tried with all my might not to do: move. It seemed to be the only way I could fix that awful situation. I couldn't possibly say to my father: "The position you put me in is wrong. From where I am now, the water will never reach the glass. Maybe you don't realize it from where you are, and I know you have so many things to think about. But from where

I'm kneeling, I can imagine Luigi sitting in front of me, and I assure you that I'm too far away, the water will spill onto the ground, the bread, and the tomatoes. Please, before the damage is irreparable, it's better if I move." No, no. Even if I had found the courage to speak up, which I exclude a priori, he would've been so taken aback by my first few words that he would've just scoffed and, if by chance, he was in a good mood, at the very most he would've said, "Mimí, please. Just trust Papà." Or else he wouldn't have even bothered replying. He would've just looked at me in complete silence as if to say, "Are you the painter here? Are you an artist? No, so stand still and zip it." Consequently, I made a plan to shift my position little by little, in tiny increments, moving so carefully that he'd never even realize I was doing it. I saw no other solution.

It was a long process and, as I recall it now, one of tensest experiences of my whole life. I actually only had to shift my position ever so slightly. My right knee on the floor would act as a pivot. All I had to do was creep my left foot forward so that I could rotate my chest just the right amount and the neck of the demijohn would be in line with the future glass in Luigi's hand. My knee ached, my right leg and foot were asleep, but I began the procedure nonetheless.

Children exist on the cusp of either dreams or nightmares, or at least that's how I did. Back then I was always chasing down feverish thoughts that sought out explanations or details in meaningless facts, that amplified or shrunk space as needed, and that either made time fly by or dilate. Without a doubt, I would've rather died than give up; every day I died numerous times. The millimeters I advanced was like traveling an immense distance, and with my bare feet I was better off than the cat and its seven-league boots. How much time passed? How long did the attempt take? I can't be sure; sometimes, the duration of something depends on the significance that we attribute to our actions. In some ways, I think that I am still rotating, and that I will be for as long as I live, or rather, for as long as I think about it and write about it.

In the meantime, my father talked and talked about his childhood, his teenage years, girls, women, his father, his fellow painters and enemies. I shifted with the smallest movements possible. My big toe and the toes of my left foot gripped the tile floor, the muscles in my leg tensed. My body pivoted imperceptibly on my right knee. The neck of the demijohn left the white cloth and the plate of tomatoes that I had imagined so clearly in order to orient myself, and made its way toward Luigi's glass, another necessary fiction. I was the boy who poured water and I wanted to pour it well, if only to guarantee the success of my father's large-scale painting, which would then translate into peace and harmony for my mother and whole family.

Suddenly Federí stopped talking. A silence fell over the room that sent a chill up my spine and I interrupted my slow rotation. I waited. "Mimí, you're moving," he said curtly. "What's the matter? Are you tired? Do you want to rest?" he added. "You've been so good up until now," he said, trying to encourage me. "We're almost done for the day, just a little bit longer," he promised. And then he started to paint again.

I waited a few moments, then started shifting again. I was drenched in sweat, my toes slipped across the tiles, couldn't get a grip. But I was almost there: the green neck of the demijohn was almost at the height of Luigi's glass. Finally, I was in the right place.

But not for my father. He jumped up with his brush in his hand and cigarette between his lips. He had lost his patience. Why couldn't I stay still for one more minute? *Padreterno*, just one more minute.

He came over, kneeled down, and gruffly shifted my body back to its original position.

My experience as an artist's model ended there. There was no more need for me, not then or ever again. The painting still required a lot of work and my father continued to paint for hours, in all his free time. I came back from school anxious, expecting that from one moment to the next he'd realize his mistake. I imagined seeing him standing silently in front of the painting or in a fury. Even as I climbed the stairs, I seemed to hear him screaming about how impossible it was to work in those conditions, I imagined seeing him standing with his knife in hand, the painting shredded in rage.

But none of that happened and gradually the tension lessened. I forgot my anxiety about that problem, I had my own things to worry about. I periodically noticed the progress of the painting, I saw how I had been reproduced on the canvas, head downcast but all there, still recognizable, knee on the ground, demijohn under my arm. The two Siamese twins stood next to me, side by side, construction workers derived from the gesso statuette, looking at me with amusement, though I'm not sure why. Luigi finally had a right arm, and it was out of proportion as I expected. No matter now long my father painted Luigi's arm, his glass would still never reach the neck of the bottle—it was too high up—and the water flowed into the glass in one long, white stream, like a miniature waterfall.

My mother came in often, either to bring a coffee to Federí or to get something that she needed. She'd stop and look at the painting for a bit in silence. He pretended he didn't notice and continued to paint but he was clearly eager to hear her opinion. If she didn't say anything, he'd ask her opinion without actually asking. "You like it," he'd say affirmatively, and she knew he needed her to say yes.

She always said yes and, if he hadn't acted cruelly to her of late and she was bright-eyed and felt like talking, she'd point out how well this or that had come out. Afterward, my father always seemed to paint with greater passion, and often, as soon as Rusinè left the room, he'd either begin to sing or even whistle

Neapolitan songs and arias. I was disoriented by this: I didn't understand why he, who usually mortified my mother with his cruel
manner and words, derived so much pleasure from her positive
judgement. It was a hard to solve mystery.

Either way, when they were happy I was happy, and especially
when Rusinè said that I had been painted particularly well, that
I really did seem to be holding that demijohn; Federí agreed, I
had come out better than all the others, and that was because
Matteo was a shithead and Luigi was a shithead, too, but I, as his
son, was not.

He never mentioned the last time I sat for him, and how I
had moved. He had generously forgotten it. He went through
a period of unusual kindness and willingness; the end of that
great labor put him in a good mood. One day he was even kind
with Zio Matteo who came to see himself on the canvas. "Federí,
you made me just as I am," he exclaimed, even though to me he
looked more like the gesso statue than his true self. My father
was so pleased that he insisted Zio Matteo stay for lunch and, between the first and second course, he even acknowledged that his
brother-in-law may actually have had a brain capable of understanding. He explained, "I didn't make you just as you are, Zio
Mattè, I made you better. I made you so that you will never die."

He was even patient with Luigi, who came over to the house
a few days after Zio Matteo. Shy and apologizing for being in his
work clothes (an undershirt and baggy pants), the street vendor
was worried about dirtying the house with his presence. But my
father said no, you won't get it dirty, come on in, and he walked
into the room and just stood there, without moving, amazed,
awestruck. Then he peered a little closer to see his hand better, to make sure that all his fingers were there. "Thank you, my
finger really did look like that," he said when he saw that my
father had kept his promise. "No need to thank me," my father
graciously replied.

But the best day of all was that of the final brushstroke. Federí couldn't wait to hear what a qualified person thought of it and so, to celebrate, he invited Armando De Stefano over to the house. De Stefano arrived. My father ushered him into the dining room and while Rusinè and my grandmother kept asking him in all different manners and tones, "Pardon the disarray, can we offer you a coffee?" Federí turned to him and said theatrically, "Voilà, have a look."

It was a truly gratifying moment. Federí recalled—and even wrote about it in his notebooks—that Armando De Stefano first stood there with his mouth agape, then complimented my father, and finally exclaimed, "For heaven's sake, how on earth did you paint such a major piece of art in such a small and dimly lit room?" The only glitch in his visit was that he left without mentioning the show of large-scale works that they were supposed to do together. He didn't even say anything like we have to talk about it, we need to set a date, or anything like that.

My father didn't seem to notice, but my mother did. From that moment forward, not a day passed that she didn't ask him, "Everything alright? So when are you and De Stefano going to have your exhibition?" In any other situation, it might have seemed like a normal question of an artistic nature, and thus legitimate to my father's ears. But even I perceived her real meaning, and whenever I heard her hit that key, I got anxious. What Rusinè was really trying to say, if she had been able to speak her mind without being slapped was, "When are you going to take this painting and all your stuff out of here so that the children can go back to sleeping in beds like good Christians and we can all go back to having a normal home?"

Of course, my father understood perfectly what his wife was driving at when she asked him about the show with De Stefano. And that made him squirm. On good days he'd say something like, "I don't know, Armando hasn't let me know yet." On bad days, he'd say, "Rusinè, quit busting my balls." And then one day he came home in such a foul mood, his face filled with such

delusion, anger, and desperation that we all knew we had to hide
and stay out of his way, and even my mother watched him out of
the corner of her eye, careful not to say the wrong thing.

We were all sitting at lunch when he finally couldn't hold back
any more and started talking about the fire blazing through his
mind. He wasn't angry with us. He was angry with Armando
De Stefano. "That shit-shoveling bastard is a shit-talking shithead," he yelled for the whole neighborhood to hear. De Stefano
had changed his mind. He didn't want to do an exhibition with
my father. That drawing professor *di questo cazzo* was afraid of
looking bad. Instead, he wanted—my father whispered short of
breath—to exhibit his work on his own, to avoid comparisons.
The coward, the hypocrite. If people liked De Stefano and not
him, it was because they were hypocrites. I still didn't know what
a hypocrite or hypocrisy was so I had a hard time understanding
why people would like De Stefano, and I understood even less
when my father screamed, "That shithead calls it good manners,
but it's just hypocrisy!" Now and then he'd add more explicit
phrases. "De Stefano has never had the balls to call a shithead
'Shithead!'" He, on the other hand, had no problem doing it;
he was fearless. If someone was a shithead, he said so straight to
his face, immediately, because that was his nature; he was frank,
loyal, courageous, he didn't know how to fake it; on the contrary,
it was his duty to tell shitheads how things really stood. Just like
Caravaggio. Because even Caravaggio—he screamed, bowled
over by humiliation, by the pain of being wounded by an artist he admired—would say "Shithead!" to another painter if he
was a shithead. De Stefano, meanwhile, being a professor at the
Liceo artistico and a member of the Accademia and a man of elegance, didn't have it in him to be like Caravaggio. Sometimes De
Stefano defended himself. "I'm not a hypocrite, Federí. Unlike
you, I'm not a *chiàveche* overflowing with raw sewage, I'm just a
respectable person."

I listened and suffered. In cases like that, I was in favor of people who created less trouble, and so thought to myself, "I want to become like De Stefano, not like Caravaggio." I couldn't stand the thought of spreading tension around the way my father did. He talked and screamed and sputtered with rage. None of us dared interrupt him, not even my mother who was sitting at his right, a place where it was easy to get slapped. She had turned a greyish color and looked melancholy. Now and then she opened her mouth as if to say something. I held my breath and prayed she wouldn't say, "Now what are we going to do with that painting?" I felt calmer when she didn't speak. Such an endless tide of words gushed forth from her husband's throat, like stormy waves crashing down one after the other, that she couldn't get a word in edgewise. Luckily.

When she finally did manage to talk, she amazed me and my grandmother and my brothers. She had only consolatory words for him. She did not say, "Did you tell De Stefano that you painted it expressly for the exhibition you two were supposed to have?" She did not say, "You've ruined our lives; you, De Stefano, and this obsession of yours of taking on more than you can deal with." No, instead she said that he shouldn't be offended, he was much more talented than De Stefano or anyone else, she had always known it, and now even De Stefano knew it, and everyone else knew it, too. She said exactly what he wanted to hear.

In fact, he immediately came back to life, leapt up from the table with a burst of renewed energy, and ordered us all to come to the dining room. The whole family lined up and stood before *The Drinkers*.

It was a beautiful moment. Here I should mention that the sun never shone directly on the house on Via Gemito. It was always dark and damp. Even on sunny days, only a cold, pale, bluish light filtered into the rooms. And yet on that day, the painting seemed illuminated from within. The flesh of Luigi's hunched-over bare back was blinding, the mastiff looked at us warily, Zio Matteo beamed with the smile of a Greek divinity, the two Siamese brothers chortled mysteriously and tacitly, and

I poured water from the demijohn with no trace whatsoever of the fatigue that it had cost me to hold that position for so long.

What a large-scale masterpiece. It moves me to write about it. I listened as my father explained the colors and the effects of light the way an art critic would. He spoke about tonal values and mass, the perfect eurythmy of the lines (he had collected so many words, all the better to impress his many enemies), the opposing sine waves within which the weight of the builders had been so elegantly positioned. We all paid careful attention, or at least I did. When he looked at me, I nodded to show him that I understood. But it was pointless, he didn't need the support any more. He was so taken by the results of his art and the desire to explain how he had obtained them to someone that I don't think he even saw me there. He only needed to be sure that he wasn't talking to himself.

Everything was going smoothly—it was sufficient that he felt as talented as he was verbosely describing himself to be—when he turned to my mother for one more formal confirmation. That's when Rusinè did something incomprehensible, something that left me breathless. In reply to one of his final questions, something like, "It really is beautiful, isn't it?" she said, yes, it really is beautiful, but then she added, possibly to substantiate her yes and show him that after so many years of being married to an artist she, too, had a critical spirit and an expert eye: "It's just Luigi's arm. It's too long."

I'm not entirely sure what followed. I only remember those words. The rest is dust, fragments of sound, words that have fallen like shavings under the plane of time, and other clichés that basically say, a story is just a story; even if tells the truth, it just uses and abuses the imagination.

My father looked at the painting and then at my mother. He repeated her words to come to terms with it. "Too long? And where exactly do you see that it is too long?"

Rusinè was endearing. She walked joyfully over to the canvas and pointed at Luigi's arm, from his shoulder all the way down to the glass, exclaiming in dialect, "Can't you see? It's long. But it's alright, it's still beautiful."

Federí lost all sense of reason. He started screaming: how was it possible that his wife, a person who hadn't even completed fifth grade and barely knew how to read and write, dared tell him the arm was too long. Long? I'll show you long! The arm was like that for depth. Did Rusinè know what depth was? Did she have any idea of all the calculations and practice sketches and work he had done to achieve that depth? Or did she just think that a person sat down and bam-bam-bam he was a painter? He had put all his learning, thinking, technical skills, and prowess into it, he wasn't just some shithead. Did she know who else used the same effect he had used on Luigi's arm? Michelangelo Buonarroti. In the Sistine Chapel. That's right. Michelangelo had done the exact same thing with Jesus Christ, giving him short legs and a long torso so that it would look to the people from below like his slender body was rising up into the air with strength. So shut up, since she didn't understand a thing. That's all he needed, to have to justify himself to her. Long arm. Stand over there and look. Now where's the long arm?

He had a furious look in his eyes, his mouth was open, he theatrically waved her over to a place in the room where she should stand and observe the painting.

He seemed confident in himself, but actually it wasn't at all clear if he was explaining the reasoning behind his art or, wounded by the sudden awareness of his error, he was clutching at straws to demonstrate, first and foremost to himself, that the mistake wasn't a mistake but an artistic need.

In the meantime, ever so slowly, while her son-in-law was braying, my grandmother turned around and walked out of the room. She did so in the hopes that her daughter would follow her example. But it was pointless, we all knew it: once Rusinè opened her mouth, she tended to keep talking without thinking of the consequences.

As a matter of fact, while Federí was screaming and shouting, she continued to stand and look intensely at the painting as if she couldn't even hear her husband's voice and was only concerned with understanding if she was right or wrong. Finally, she confirmed that yes, there was no doubt, the arm was excessively long. And look, she said, even though Luigi has such a long arm, the glass still won't reach the neck of the demijohn. And this poor child—she pointed at my figure with a hint of irony—is too far off to one side, it would be a miracle if the water landed in the glass. You might as well admit it: everything else is perfect, that's the only mistake you made.

It's hard to say how long it went on. I can't write down every single word that was said, but it was unquestionably a long war of words during which all my father's rage found one outlet only: his wife, who commented on his work as an artist as if she were much more than just a glove-maker, a seamstress, an aspiring shopkeeper, like all her stinking piece-of-shit relatives, as if she herself were a painter who wanted to give him a lesson, with the classic presumptuousness of an incompetent ignoramus. Just shut up, Rusinè, he yelled. De Stefano hadn't critiqued one single thing and now she was critiquing him? Oh fuck it all, fuck the arm, the glass, the water. You see the two figures standing next to Mimí, you see them? Why do you think they're looking at the kid and the water? Why do you think they're laughing? Why do you think they're amused? You don't get it, do you, you're just talking out your ass. Those two are looking at the boy and laughing because they want to see if he'll manage to pour the water into Luigi's glass. You didn't get that, did you, huh? You didn't get it, he screamed; of course the glass has to be down there, far from the mouth of the demijohn, otherwise there's nothing to look at, there's no joke, nothing to laugh about. And now basta, that's enough, I'll be damned if

I'm going to explain anything else; you say one more word and I'll slap you.

His hand was raised to hit her but she had already rushed out of the room with my brothers close behind. I couldn't move, my head was empty from fear, I couldn't command my legs. I stared at the canvas. Is it true that he painted the arm long on purpose? Is it true that the two men are looking at me and laughing to see if I manage to pour the water into Luigi's glass? Was he lying, inventing as he went? Or—and I was struck with this doubt then and still am today—were my mother and I making a mistake and using our mistake to put a stick in his spokes? Were we, for whatever unknowable reason, his main enemies, the principle detractors of his art?

I didn't know what to think; my distress was immense. At this point I didn't know what to make of my presence in the painting anymore. I was bewildered, in shock. What an intense feeling shock is. A thought that consumes itself because of excessive tension. I was confused about why I remained in the room alone with my father, who now stood stock still in front of the painting, his eyes glazed over like a madman, which at that point he was.

Federí stared at Luigi's arm for a long time as if someone else had painted it. It was clear he was returning to his senses. He was starting to feel the torment of being alone and regret for having treated his wife that way, although I wouldn't swear on the latter. When he realized that I was still in the room, he seemed surprised. He made a face that was both angry and considerate. "Do you think the arm looks long, Mimí?" he asked. I energetically shook my head, no.

The story of *The Drinkers* ends there. Or rather, there ends its story within our four walls. Its public story begins in July 1953 but it is a confused one and it shares many similarities with other unhappy stories that my father told throughout his life.

After days and days of quarreling with my mother, but the

normal kind of bickering, not violent arguments, and a consistently bad mood, one day Federí came home with a couple of helpful acquaintances and took the painting away.

It was a memorable occasion. I had gotten used to seeing its rich colors in the background, and without it the room seemed both large and squalid. The women of the house must have had the same impression. My father had barely shut the door behind him and Nonna Nannina was already in the room dusting, sweeping, washing the floor, performing her rites of purification, while my mother dragged the furniture back down the hall and into the room. While waiting for Nannina to finish polishing the floor and scratching away all the dried paint from the tiles wherever possible, she looked in from the doorway to see how she could give the room a fresh touch.

Meanwhile, the painting traveled across Naples, maybe in a truck, or perhaps on a cart. Federí ignored all those kinds of details when he told the story, and got straight to the heart of the matter. His goal in telling it was to underscore the progress that he and his artistic career had made since the exhibition in Rome. While, at that time, he had been obliged to submit his work to a jury and be approved to participate in the show, now he had been asked to take part, as an invited guest, in an important Neapolitan event, the "first ever figurative art fair in the Mezzogiorno," which was set to open in August in the Mostra d'oltremare exhibition hall. "Not accepted," he stressed, "but invited, just like they do with famous artists." There was also a number of important prizes: the 500,000 lire Salvator Rosa prize; the 500,000 lire Regione Autonoma della Sardegna prize; and the 500,000 lire Città di Napoli prize.

He was visibly euphoric. I was happy about all those prizes he could potentially win and for the invitation that he had received. I could visualize the invitation, how it had probably been written with all the formality and flourish that my elementary school teacher expected from us, how it had probably been addressed to Maestro Professore so-and-so, the way my father liked to be called so as not to feel less than the artist-professors at the Liceo artistico and the Accademia. It even said, in black on white, that he could show three pieces of work. But he chose to only show *The Drinkers*, which was worth ten paintings.

A final confirmation of how far he had come and the importance he had acquired, eight long years after the initial exhibition of the rejects, was evident when the fair opened. His painting was hung in the main hall, right in the center of a large wall. My father spent the entire evening looking at it as if for the first time, and he even watched visitors who stopped in front of it, enchanted. He couldn't get his mind around the fact that so much weight had been given to one of his works of art. The main hall, for Chrissakes, and a whole wall. He repeated it over and over to every painter that came within range: "Well, I guess that if they put me here, they must've liked the painting."

But it didn't take him long to realize that the others didn't share his enthusiasm. On the contrary, they tended to cut him off while he was speaking. Some of them couldn't hide their envy, others shot daggers at him, while others just had bitter and curt words for him, like, "Well, where else would they put such a large painting?" In short, it was clear that most people did everything they could to spoil his pleasure.

But then people started saying things to him that sounded allusive and unpleasant. "They treated you better than Spinosa, and he's got an entire room to himself because he's the president of the ACLI union of artists," they said, or else, "Friends in high places certainly do help."

At first my father didn't understand. He thought their comments were an invitation to inveigh against the system of favors and he jumped in with both feet, hurling long tirades against the scheming organized by fags and other wimpy-ass *scurnacchiati* to divide up the prizes, spouting a list of all the wrongs he had suffered both in Rome with the Mancini prize and that rotten,

stinking mess at the Cinema Ideal. But gradually he started to realize that the people who complained about the system of favors
were angry with him, and not with other people. People kept saying how well-connected he was, that he had sold his ass—that's
what those shitheads said, and they meant his wife—just to be
invited to the first figurative art fair in the Mezzogiorno and see
his painting hanging in the main hall. This wounded him deeply.

He later learned that the rumors began at a dinner organized
by a number of other artists to celebrate Carlo Siviero (famous
painter and president of the commission that decided how and
where the works of art should be hung), where they intended to
jockey among themselves for one of the prizes. Apparently, the
guest of honor amazed all the guests by announcing that he—
"Your very own father, Mimí"—would surely go on to become
one of the major exponents of Italian painting in the second half
of the twentieth century. "I'd like to meet this talented painter,"
he went on to say in so many words. "Oh, we don't see him
around much, he works for the railroad, you know," the most
malicious among them commented immediately. "I know he
works for the railroad, but please tell him all the same that he
has enormous talent and that we want to give him the recognition that he is due," Siviero concluded.

This was traumatic news for the guests. My father was told
about the gracious comment and good news by Mele, owner
of the Medea gallery, who had taken part in the dinner. Of
course, my father would've preferred to hear Siviero praise him
personally, but first of all, none of the painters who had organized the celebration had invited him; secondly, even if they
had invited him, he wouldn't have been able to afford the sat-
urnalia in honor of Carlo Siviero; and thirdly, he was working
a shift that night. However, Mele gave him a full report and
even told him that Siviero's comments had soured the mood.
So that's why people were looking at him with such animos-
ity, Federí suddenly understood. That's why there were rumors

that he—he!—had been showed some kind of favor. But by whom, for fuck's sake? By Siviero, whom he didn't even know? By other members of the commission? Superintendent Maioli? Canino, the architect, whom he had never even laid eyes on before? By the painters De Vanna, Di Marino, Rossomando, and by Mennella the sculptor, who'd rather have their balls cut off than see him receive praise? By the communist art critic, Paolo Ricci, who now detested him? By various doctors, engineers, architects, lawyers, and senators who made sure the prizes were given to their friends and clients?

Federí was indignant. The thought that people considered him, the least well-connected artist who had painted on canvas or wood in Italy since the time of Cimabue, a person who asked for favors! Every evening he made his way to the Mostra d'oltremare in a state of high alert, ready to react to any allusion whatsoever.

In fact, when the painter Giuseppe Carrino came up to him in front of *The Drinkers* and jokingly said, "Tell me your little secret, Federí, tell me who pulled some strings for you," he retorted, "You bastard, let's take it outside, I'll tell you my secret and you tell me yours." So they went into the garden to duke it out but Carrino, according to my father, pulled out a switchblade, flicked it open and held it up to Federí's throat, screaming, "Now fess up! Who's your connection?"

It was a horrible moment. Although he had nothing to confess, Carrino kept the switchblade pointed at his throat, just a bit above his Adam's apple. If it hadn't been for Maresciallo Cardona, who was also a painter and had been passing by and managed to step in between the two men and prevent a tragedy, my father's throat would've been slit, my brothers and I would've become fatherless, and Rusinè would've been left a widow.

That pretty much sums up his mood. From that evening on, he avoided going in other rooms of the exhibition, not for fear of Carrino—my father was afraid of nothing and even if he did get scared, he had been trained as a youngster to dominate it, the way European champion Bruno Frattini had taught him—but to avoid seeing certain shitheads that couldn't hide their homicidal desires. You'd think, he used to say as an old man, when he was even jumpier than when he was young, that the art world is full of people who say lovely things to each other about Nature, Mankind, Feelings, Techniques, and Aesthetics, but no, Mimí, it's a world full of goddamn, shit-spewing *chiavechemmèrd*, people who spend more time promoting themselves and screwing over others than talking about art; people whose only objectives in life were money and fucking. Even after he turned eighty, he still suffered deeply at that discovery.

Meanwhile, at the end of September, a few days before the official awards ceremony, Carlo Siviero, the man who championed his work, died. He had been ill for a long time. Everything that Siviero had deliberated as president of the commission with regards to the prizes, my father pointed out, was scratched. The Salvator Rosa prize of 500,000 lire went to Maestro Striccoli. The Sardinian regional prize was given to a Sardinian artist, as the regulations of the prize dictated. And the prize money of 500,000 lire from the coffers of the Comune di Napoli was split between eight artists, one of whom was Raffaele Lippi. Federí didn't get a thing.

When he found out, he walked out of the house with the goal of doing what had become usual for him in those situations: go to the Mostra d'oltremare and crack someone's skull open. He was about to beat up Mele, when the gallery owner offered him the runner-up Città di Positano purchase-prize of 100,000 lire. "Yes or no?" Mele asked. Federí was one step away from saying no and throwing a punch, when, at the thought of having to bring *The Drinkers* back home and having to fight with my mother and grandmother about where to put it, at the thought of maybe even having to destroy it because he had no idea where to put it, he changed his mind and shouted, "Fine! Yes! But

I want the 100,000 immediately, before you give them to some *scurnacchiato*!"

And that—he concluded when he told me the story—is how *The Drinkers* ended up in the town hall in Positano, where it is still hanging to this day; all you have to do is go and see it. "Just think," he added. "The art critic Piero Girace wrote in an article in *Roma* that the composition of the painting was truly complex and even reminiscent of Brangwyn."

I listened and nodded and looked impressed but I had never even heard of Brangwyn.

I didn't end up going to Positano. Maybe I'll go one day, but not for this book, nor to see if *The Drinkers* really is reminiscent of Brangwyn. I lost all desire to explore any further after spending the morning at Palazzo San Giacomo.

In the guard booth I found not one staff member, but three or four, all squeezed into a tiny space. I had to explain what I wanted down to the smallest detail. I wanted to see, I said, some of my father's paintings that were hanging there; I had an appointment with Dr. Guidi. "You want to see the marriage banns?" one of them asked, ruddy in the face. I slowly explained to the group that, no, I didn't want to see the marriage banns but real pictures: oils, pastels, watercolors, even drawings, not words. I finally succeeded and the ruddy employee asked me for some ID. He examined it carefully, looked in an agenda, and told me that there was no pass with my name on it. After some back and forth, he called Dr. Guidi and finally let me in. "Go up to the third floor."

I took the elevator. Dr. Guidi was a genteel and elegant middle-aged woman. "I had entirely forgotten about you. I'll get someone to show you around right away," she said. Then she looked around the office, where in addition to hers, there were three other desks: two occupied by women, one by a man. She chose the man. "Massimo," she said, "can I entrust you with this gentleman? He's looking for some paintings done by his father."

Massimo, a young man with a kind and intelligent expression, seemed happy to have been given the task, and led the way. We walked through grandiose rooms with beautiful carpets, antique furnishings, and gilt-framed paintings on the wall. He stopped in front of every single artwork even if it was clearly from the nineteenth century, and asked me with amused concern, "Is this one of your father's?" No, I would reply. And then he'd lead me in another direction. "Let's go this way," he'd say, adding comments like, "Artists are so lucky. They have such creative and liberating jobs. What could possibly be better than being an artist?"

We peeked into the mayor's office, taking advantage of the fact that he had not yet arrived. No trace of Federí's paintings there, of course. We then headed into the town council meeting room where Massimo gushed over the frames, a painting of a heavy-set woman in a painter's studio, and a depiction of two people kissing. "But they're not by your father," he said sadly but chirpily. He then walked me through a number of offices, proclaiming as he did, "Sorry everyone, but we have to see if there are any of this gentleman's father's paintings in the room."

Doors opened and shut. Eventually my chaperone got weary and said, "Let's go back and see Dr. Guidi; we can call my colleague who keeps the inventory." I looked at him. "There's an inventory?" I asked but I suppose I wasn't that surprised that we hadn't begun with it. Somehow it seemed normal.

We went back to the office and Massimo got on the phone. After a few failed attempts, he nodded at me. "Here we go . . ." I listened as he explained to a friend named Rosaria exactly what he needed. I watched tensely. He noticed it and made a gesture to relax. "The paintings exist," he said. Then he raised two fingers. "Two of them." He then gave more detail, making some notes on a piece of paper at the same time: "One shows an industrial setting and is in Accounting. The other is a nude in pastels and is in Sanitation." He thanked Rosaria, hung up and said smugly, "See? We did it. First we'll go to Sanitation."

We started roaming down the halls again. We left behind the elegant staircases, the wide and clean hallways, the grand halls, the rooms decorated with stucco, gilt, carpets, and tapestries, and turned down narrow hallways, through dark and decrepit rooms painted the colors of third-rate medical clinics.

"Let me do the talking," Massimo suggested. He started opening doors and asking questions without preamble. "Any paintings here?" The replies were usually answered with some alarm— "No," even if there were paintings on the wall, or, "We left it wherever it was, we never touch a thing"—as if the municipal staff was worried less by the question and more about proving that they had no responsibility in the eventual disappearance of what we were looking for. One fellow, sitting at a desk in a room in deep shadow muttered, "Paintings? Never seen any paintings here, only junk." Massimo laughed, amused by the word "junk." He pressed on. "Follow me."

He knocked and we walked into a room the color of rancid grease. On one side of the room, sitting at a large desk under a painting of a marina with an elaborate frame, was a man with a pinkish face, who was visibly bothered by the heat. He must have been some kind of office manager. On the other side of the room, sitting behind a smaller desk, was a brunette lady who looked pleasant. Massimo turned to the man. "We're looking for a pastel painting that shows a nude woman." The man smiled. He recalled the painting. "A lady with an ass this big," he said, opening his hands wide. The woman remembered it too. "She had a towel over her shoulder," she said, "she had just gotten out of the bath." The boss shook his head, he didn't remember the towel; only her ass had impressed him. A short discussion about aesthetics followed. Massimo and the other man started to praise small, well-shaped asses, meaty but not overly fleshy, still firm. The woman, speaking with the tone of someone who had grown accustomed to sexist talk in the workplace, defended larger, softer ones. "The Mediterranean woman," she said, "is beautiful precisely for this reason." To show how well-inclined they were to all examples of the opposite sex, the two men declared that they were also fans of the Mediterranean woman. "Sure, of course, you are," the lady said. "You talk but you don't understand a thing. The beauty of the Mediterranean woman is for connoisseurs, not for the man on the street." The back and forth continued along those lines for a while before returning to the painting. The boss also recalled, among other things, that it had an ugly frame. "And then let's be honest," he added. "The painting didn't look so good in here. So we sent it over to Via San Tommaso d'Aquino. Actually, it was pretty ugly, if I can be honest."

"No, you cannot. My father painted it," I said sharply.

The man hemmed and hawed and said it was definitely because of the frame. "With a better frame," he said to justify himself, "it surely would've made a better impression on me."

We said goodbye and left the room.

Back in the hallway, Massimo looked pleased with how our research had gone. "I did good not to mention at the beginning that the painting was by your father," he said, complimenting himself. "That way people don't censor themselves, they say what they really think. Don't you like to hear the truth?"

I didn't answer him, and just smiled weakly. I was too busy thinking about how my father would have reacted. He would've been glad to get involved in the conversation with the brunette lady, going far beyond Massimo and the boss with sexual allusions. Then he would've punched the man who criticized his work, and wouldn't have let him say one more word. Then he would've whispered threateningly to Massimo: bastards, one and all. I had held back, and only said "No, you cannot." As usual, I was dissatisfied with myself but I realized that my timid manner derived from a reassessment of Federí's own. It was a shame that I had pushed his away from me forever.

"Now," Massimo said, "let's go to Accounting and see if the

other painting is there." While we were making our way down hallways that were just as dusty and decrepit, although significantly more luminous, he explained to me exactly where I needed to go to find the nude pastel: exit the building on Via Imbriani, turn onto Via Verdi, go straight along Via Cercantes, turn left on Via San Tommaso d'Aquino to number 15, and up to the third floor. "Unfortunately, I can't come with you," he said regretfully.

We passed beyond a partition. I immediately saw my father's painting hanging above an empty desk. It was done in dusty tones and showed the view from his studio on Corso Arnaldo Lucci, where we had moved at the end of the 1950s. The painting was dated 1960. Clearly distinguishable were pylons, a crane, train tracks, and on the right, one of the pillars typical of the new station in Piazza Garibaldi. Large swathes of color, from a different period entirely. *The Drinkers* and my childhood were far away.

"Is it that one?" Massimo asked. I nodded. "Beautiful," he remarked with a quick glance, immediately starting to banter with another employee, also just passing through, from which office I don't know, about union issues. "We're eliminating the fourth tier," his interlocutor said. Massimo offered his opinion: It's all CISL's fault. "I'm sorry, because what did CGIL ever do to help?" his colleague said. "You're right," Massimo said, sounding like someone who is looking at the facts objectively, "Sometime CGIL can be very submissive. Are we done here?" he asked, turning to me. The other employee wasn't ready to give up. "You're slaves," he said. I focused on the paltry frame. When Federí didn't have any money, he took four planks, nailed them together, painted them with silver or gold paint and that was the frame. "Are we done here, can we leave now?" Massimo asked again.

Just then a woman in her forties came in, walked over to the empty desk, and asked, "What's going on?" My guide explained everything. The civil servant looked at the painting as if for the first time, then went up close to it, read the signature, and turned

to me emotionally. "Who did you say the painting is by?" I gave
her my father's first and last name. She came up to me, warmly
introduced herself, and hugged me. Her aunt was Zia Lina, the
wife of Zio Peppino, my mother's brother.

I embraced her warmly, as if by standing next to that painting I had suddenly tapped into a deep sentiment of affection
that had to do with Rusinè. "Amazing, it's like something on a
Raffaella Carrà talk show," Massimo said. Later, as we were saying goodbye, she said, "This has been deeply moving for me.
Be sure to go and see the pastel nude in the offices on Via San
Tommaso d'Aquino. Don't forget." I ought to have forgotten everything, erased it all forever, I thought to myself.

I walked out of Palazzo San Giacomo and, bowled over by
the heat and humidity, I made my way up Via Guantai Nuovi
delaying my decision until I stood at the intersection with Via
San Tommaso d'Aquino. At that point, it seemed impossible not
to turn left and walk into number 15.

A man on his way out almost fell on top me while busily talking to a friend. "Giuvà, the workers' struggle doesn't exist anymore. Nothing exists anymore. There's only shit."

I headed up the dark staircase.

I pushed open a door, walked in, roamed through a few rooms.
No one paid me any attention. I walked up to a man around my
age and casually said to him, "I'm looking for a painting by my
father, a nude, done in pastels. They sent me here, from Palazzo
San Giacomo." The man turned out to be helpful. He couldn't
recall the nude but he took me from room to room. "This gentleman is looking for a painting by his father, a nude done in
pastels," he said to the other employees by way of introduction.
They looked at me as if to say, "Lucky guy, doesn't have a thing
to do." A man sitting at a table covered with files and papers
said, "I remember the painting." He then gave us directions how
to find it: go left, go right, see this guy, see that guy.

My escort guided me through the building to a room where

six men sat at a big, long table covered in piles of papers. I looked around but didn't see the painting. "There's supposed to be a drawing of a nude done in pastels in this room," said the man who had brought me there. "We didn't take it. It's over there," one of the men said in an annoyed tone, while eating an orange.

He pointed to a corner where two metal cabinets stood at right angles. There, in that dead space, was the painting of the nude. The figure was depicted from the back, the flesh of her body almost violet, as if she had just stepped out of a sauna, done in large blocks of color in a Fauvist style. That painting was also from 1960. I remembered it perfectly.

The municipal employee who had accompanied me there turned to me. "It's impasto, not pastel," he exclaimed. The others started teasing him. "Impasto, pastel. What the hell do you know about that kind of stuff?" Something of an argument ensured. The employee said that he was actually an expert and a painter, too. The color had clearly been spread with a palette knife. His colleagues continued to mock him and laugh and gesticulate. "Well, would you listen to the artist? You know what you can paint? Paint this!" The man turned to me for verification. "Is it impasto or pastel?" he asked. "It's impasto," I said, thanking him and saying goodbye, I hurried to leave 15 Via San Tommaso d'Aquino.

Once outside, I went and sat down on the curb. A memory of my mother came to me, back when she was in hospital, in the summer of 1965. I was keeping her company one afternoon when she turned to me and said in dialect, "I know I'm going to die." And then she broke into tears. I never forgot the pain I felt when faced with her desperation.

The suffering I experienced that morning while walking from floor to floor through the city offices was no different. The pain had grown gradually and now I was devastated by the sad truth. I was certain I had done the wrong thing and I didn't know how to resolve the situation.

I think that's how I came to the conclusion that I had had enough. I gave up all hope of finding *The Drinkers* and preferred instead to hold onto my father's outrageous stories. For a little bit of time, with a certain amount of pleasure, and in total silence, I indulged in his ferocious and recriminating tone until a woman who looked to be around sixty came up to me. "Do you feel ill?" she asked in a worried voice. "No, I feel amazing, thank you," I said, leaping to my feet and making my toward Piazza Carità.

PART III
THE DANCER

My father died on the morning of November 16, 1998, while being shaved by the hospital barber. I know nothing further about his death, none of us children were present, but I have often thought of that interrupted shave—one cheek smooth, the other stubbly, lather still on his face. He was a man who generally cared little about his appearance. It's impossible to know why, on precisely that day, he asked for a shave.

Three weeks earlier, when I got home from work, I found a message on my answering machine that said he was in a coma at the hospital in Luino. I called Geppe. He always knows what to do. "If he's in a coma, it's pointless to drive there tonight. If he comes out of it, he'll have survived yet again and we can go see him tomorrow."

None of us thought he was close to dying. He had always wanted to live until the year 2000. He could've lived for another two years, maybe even more. His ultimate goal, as already mentioned, due to his love for numbers, was to die in 2017. We all knew that being the stubborn man he was, he'd do everything in his power to live that long. "Papà, you'll die only if someone shoots you," my brother Walter used to say.

He came out of the coma that night. The next morning, I drove up north with my cousin Enzo and his wife. We traveled the length of Italy, not rushing, chatting as we drove through the rain. Enzo is a doctor but his passion is photography. Since he also had an artistic bent, he both appreciated and admired my father's outgoing manner, his struggle, his desire for recognition and success. Enzo talked about him in a reverential tone that I never used for him. I almost felt ashamed. Maybe, I said to myself, my cousin loves him more than I do.

By the time we arrived at the hospital in Luino, my father had already reacquired his capacity for firing off verbose sentences non-stop. When we walked in he was ironically defending himself to an exasperated patient in the bed next to his. "My kind sir, what on earth do you expect? I have just risen from the dead and you want me to be quiet?" This he said despite having needles stuck in all his veins, oxygen tubes coming out of his nose like whiskers, and a tube that ran from his chest to a machine by his bed where a clean red liquid bubbled and frothed.

When he saw us, he looked pleased and tried to pull himself up. He was gaunt and pale, the skin on his forehead and cheekbones pulled taut, no wrinkles. At almost eighty-two years of age, he may well have looked practically the same as he did when he was young.

He embraced and kissed us. My cousin burst into tears and walked out of the room. I sat down on a chair next to the machine with the red liquid.

"The kid got emotional," my father said with a certain amount of satisfaction. He wanted to introduce me to the many enemies he had managed to make in the hospital as if they were his friends. With neither rhyme nor reason, and in a loud voice so that everyone could hear him, he started talking about himself, the prices of his paintings, the time he met Giuseppe Ungaretti. "Guttuso introduced us," he clarified to me and everyone around us. Fifteen minutes in, he had already started to annoy me and I couldn't wait to leave.

He noticed. "I haven't told you how I met Ungaretti, have I?" he asked me quickly, sitting up. I shook my head, no. "Remind me later to tell you," he said. Then he thought about it and took it one step further. "Don't forget the things I tell you. And don't forget about me." I reassured him that I would never forget a thing. He lay back in bed.

He slept for a while, moaning in his sleep. I counted the years that had passed since my mother died: thirty-three. How had he lived those years? What had he done? He left the railroad, traveled, remarried, had another son (Massimo), left Naples, settled in the north, first in Varese and then in Lugano, where—he said—art dealers did their job better and life was more civilized. Although thirty-three years had passed, he never bothered to organize them into one big history or even into a collection of rivers of stories. Both his written and verbal accounts stopped just before my mother died, and he never talked about that. He never had the time nor desire to talk about the second part of his life. When the years start to wear thin, what is remote becomes a story, and what is close at hand becomes merely a disappointment.

He woke up with a start, saw me sitting next to the bed, and said with a pasty mouth, "There was a guardian angel." He then went on to tell me his dream. He had dreamed about a brother of his who had died at a young age, named Enzuccio. Filomena, his mother, had put the child in his care once. The child was small, only two and a half, and he was fourteen when he had to keep an eye on him. But he had gotten distracted and Enzuccio slammed the door on his own fingers. A minor incident, but at that point in his life it felt like the only serious mistake he had made. In his dream he tried to explain it to the child, maybe he wanted to be forgiven. "Where was the guardian angel?" I asked him. He looked at me confusedly. He couldn't recall what the angel had to do with anything.

In the meantime, my other brothers arrived. "How nice you came, you're here even though I'm not dead," my father exclaimed. "When you die we won't bother coming to see you; we're interested in you alive, not dead," Geppe said, trying to be lighthearted. But the joke didn't go over well. "Interesting philosophy," my father said, "but I see things a little differently." He thought he deserved to be remembered forever. He had worked his whole life to last, and it made him uneasy to hear his own child say we're interested in the living, not the dead. He started to explain his thoughts on the subject, but we already knew them, so we interrupted him. To indulge him, we lined up in front of him. We wanted to give him a broader vision of how he had multiplied, and how long he would actually last. He had six children: five boys and one girl, and then there were the grandchildren. He looked at us strangely. He continued to watch us even when we broke into smaller groups, some of us going out to smoke, some to talk, and we left him on his own, a distracted half-smile on his face.

When I went to say goodbye—I had to leave with Enzo—I found him joking with a girl who couldn't have been more than twenty years old. When I approached, the girl walked off, laughing. He watched her walk away with both admiration and desire, which may have only been the fruit of distraction, as if his brain had put his body, with its drip, oxygen cannula, and tubes running out of his chest, between parentheses.

I leaned down and whispered in his ear, "Look at you! I guess that means that you're feeling better." He glanced up at me smugly. "Mimí, up until six months ago, I used to . . ." and then he started in on his sexual prowess.

My father often talked about sex. It was one of his favorite subjects. While mentioning relatively little about women and love, he boasted about his particularly strong appetite, he was proud of his perfectly functioning genitalia, and said that all the men in his family had been red-blooded and virile. He was certain that, as his sons, we would carry on the tradition.

His passion for girls—he often told me in the cheerful tone that the subject aroused in him—revealed itself early on. Even as a little boy, when he started going to Maestro Piantieri's private school, he thought constantly about little girls. He drew them, he chased them, he wanted to kiss them, and whenever possible, he tried to stick his hands down their panties.

Initially his drive was hampered by an ugly, pimply teacher and by the girls themselves. The problem was his appearance, which made it difficult for superficial people to see the substance that was there. The Fdrí of those days, obsessed with his vocation of drawing every single thing and person he saw, was constantly uncombed and ink-stained, which made him look like a dangerous savage. Consequently, the little girls, who were so cute and pretty with their ribbons and braids or curls and heart-shaped mouths, ran away from him when he tried to kiss them or pull up their dresses. "Go away, you're ugly," they said. Even the teacher, who preferred squeaky clean boys, didn't hide her repugnance.

Consequently, when Fdrí decided to write his first love letter to a classmate, Maria, the parish priest's niece, all hell broke loose. He confided in her that he was a great painter and that he wanted to take her with him to Africa, that he wanted to kiss her and pull down her panties. Maria didn't appreciate the letter. She started to cry and showed it to her teacher.

The teacher, a lay sister and member of the parish where Maria's uncle-priest held Mass, read it, went pale, and grew terribly angry. She gave my father ten smacks with the ruler on the palm of his hand, sent him behind the chalkboard to kneel on dried chick peas, and screamed that he was nothing but a trash child of trash parents and ugly to boot. Fdrí was rescued by kind headmaster Piantieri, who came into the classroom by chance, found him kneeling on chick peas, scolded the teacher, and explained the situation to the child. "Fdrí, I know that you are a great painter and that like all artists you are filled with a zest for life, but you're still too young. Forget about Africa, and stop writing those ugly things to Maria," he said gently.

After that, my father was sad for a long time. The teacher forced him to sit at a desk apart from the others, next to the window. He could draw girls if he wanted to, on the condition that he'd never actually touch them. His classmates, clean-cut kids, the children of doctors or lawyers or landowners, never talked to him, not even by mistake. Two members of the aristocracy, the little countesses Nina and Pina Narni, who had been kind with him in the past, echoing the teacher's praise of his drawings by saying, "Oh, how pretty," now kept their eyes straight ahead, like two little statues. In other words, everyone started to treat him with disgust. The days passed and soon he started to think that there was something wrong with him, that he really was ugly.

At home he looked at himself desolately in the mirror. "Why is my mother so pretty, my father so handsome, and I am so ugly?" He also asked himself another question. "Why are the parents of my classmates so ugly and my classmates so good looking?" Sometimes he puzzled over the connection between those questions, intuiting a contradiction, but was unable to find his way out of it. And so he'd start drawing. He drew little girls, both when he was at school and at home. It was the only way for him not to be sad.

One day he just couldn't take it anymore and told his mother, Donna Filumena, everything. He told her that at school the girls refused his hugs and kisses, and called him ugly. "Ugly? You?" Donna Filumena screamed in her dramatic way, the blood immediately rushing to her head. She decided to hurry over to the school and slap those snotty-nosed toilet brushes and pull the teacher's hair. "How dare you call my son ugly! My son? Ugly?" she screamed.

Hearing the sound of her friend's shrill voice, Donna Luisella, the wife of Don Federico the cop, appeared, and in her gentle way she tried to calm her friend. Now Donna Luisella, she was a woman. At the mere mention of her name, an enchanted expression came over my father's face, even later in life. When he spoke about her, it was as if she was an incomparable matrix of all the women in his life, imagined and real. Brunette, large eyes, elegant. She came into his life like a vision, right when he hit the rock bottom of humiliation, his mother screaming that she wanted to run to school and raise hell. But then Donna Luisella stepped in. "Easy does it, Filumè," she whispered calmly in her throaty voice. And while Filumè continued to shriek and holler, Donna Luisella said, "This child is the most beautiful child in that school." She took Fdrí in her arms so that he could smell her to his heart's content; her memorable perfume went on to become the scent of all beautiful women. Gradually, he stopped crying and actually started to feel happy. His mother also calmed down and changed her mind about going to the school and slapping the little girls, dragging his teacher down the hall by the hair, and forcing Piantieri to host a beauty contest to prove to everyone that Fdrí was the most beautiful child there, just like Donna Luisella said.

On an entirely separate occasion, Filumena—now calm—met Maestro Piantieri out on the street and talked to him about all the wrongs that the little girls had done to her son. She told him how they called him ugly and how they didn't let him kiss or hug them, and how he suffered as a result. How was she supposed to convince her son that he was not ugly, and that he didn't have to worry?

Maestro Piantieri consoled her and gave her some advice. "Signora, don't worry. Take Fdrí to Iride cinema in Piazza Garibaldi." They were showing a film, he explained, called *The Kid*. All he had to do was watch it: the child in the movie looked just like Fdrí. And seeing that actors, both old and young, were generally good-looking, if Fdrí looked like that child, then Fdrí was good-looking.

My father went to the Iride that same afternoon, accompanied by an uncle by the name of Zio Giuvannino. When the movie started and the character of the kid appeared on the screen, he was startled. It felt like he was looking in the mirror. "I look just like The Kid," he said with pleasure to his uncle. "You? You're even better looking!" his uncle replied. Donna Luisella said exactly the same thing when he got home later, hugging him tightly to her chest, which was so soft and generous that my father never wanted to let go. "Oh Fdrí, you're far better looking than Jackie Coogan," she said to him.

From that point on, at school, he sat at his desk and looked down his nose at the other boys. "None of you bastards look like The Kid. I do. I'm the best looking boy here," he said to himself. As for the little girls, he just sneered at them. He didn't want to kiss or hug them anymore. He wasn't even interested in putting his hands down their panties. From that moment on, all his thoughts were for Donna Luisella. "Have you ever seen a picture of Claudia Cardinale when she was young?" he asked me as an old man, in the hospital. That was what Donna Luisella looked like. She was an amazing creature of God. "God," he exclaimed with laughter, "is a masterful artist." He had created Donna Luisella with the greatest of care and attention.

Whenever she came over to Filumè's house, my father behaved intolerably. He'd throw himself on the floor and wait for her to step over him. Luisella would see him there and laugh and say, "Fdrí, what are you doing?" Then she'd step over him and he'd sneak a peek at her white undergarments under her dark skirt. He wished he could've touched her with his fingers and prolong that warm scent that wafted over him when she lifted up one foot and slowly lowered it over to the other side. But she didn't stop, she just kept on walking. So he'd jump up and rush over to her and grab her legs, and rub his face against the fabric of her dress. "Filumè, what's gotten into your son? What does he want from me?" she'd say. "Cut it out, Fdrí, leave Donna Luisella alone," his mother would scold him. But when her son continued to hug Luisella's thighs and press his mouth up against her belly, she'd take off her left shoe and thwack him on the head with the heel. "Let go!" she'd scream, but Fdrí would hang on as long as he possibly could. He preferred the risk of having his head bashed in than letting go of that exceptional woman's body.

When, three weeks after my final visit with my father, I made my way back to his bedside and saw him there, emptied of life, rigid, a poorly drawn sketch of what he had been, I thought back to the three-year period from 1957 to 1960 when I carefully plotted to kill him.

As hard as I tried to remember, I never recalled having warm, loving feelings for him. In the years leading up to that particular period, I often hoped that for some reason or another he wouldn't come home. In the years following it, I sought to reduce our interactions to a bare minimum. But during those three years I did nothing but daydream about killing him. I wanted to sink a knife into his chest. At night, before falling asleep, I reveled in imagining his blood on my hands.

After he died, I asked myself explicitly for the first time why I had nurtured that desire for so long. I discovered with surprise that my urge for parricide was motivated less by how he treated my mother than by how he spoke about women and sex overall.

I can't deny that the intolerable climate at home didn't play its part. I recall one Sunday morning, in the spring of 1960, when I got up early and found Rusinè in the kitchen on her own. She was out of sorts. One of her eyes was puffy and purple with broken red veins. "I'll kill him," I said, as convincingly as possible. But the worst had already passed, and even I didn't believe myself. The desire to murder him had blasted a road into me some years earlier and knocked the wind out of me. It was 1957, a year of horrifying awareness. And yet to pinpoint the conventional beginning of my homicidal impulse, I should go back to an afternoon in 1956, or 1955, or even 1954, when I was standing at the kitchen window in the house on Via Gemito. It may have been summer. I was watching a kid scribble something in chalk on the metal shutter of a shop under the porticoes of the building across the street, the one that had just been built. He was surrounded by other kids who were all laughing. The word he was writing was *pucchiacca,* a word that, at the time, sounded to me like sticky fingers, rubbing together, the sound of that inadmissible pleasure of heavy breathing and falling off into emptiness.

The kids ran off and I stood there secretly reading the white letters on the dark shutter, when suddenly I heard my father come up behind me. I turned around and saw him. His hair was uncombed as usual, but he looked amused, he had a devilish look, as if he had had a good day. I started to walk away but he put a hand on my shoulder and held me there, in front of the windowsill. He leaned over and pointed to the porticoes and the graffiti. "I can't see very well from here," he said in dialect. "What does that word say?"

I stared at the columns, stared at the shutter, and read it to myself: *pucchiacca*. But even though I read it in silence, it was no longer furtive, no longer solitary, as it had been up until a few seconds before. The word echoed in my head, it felt like the whole neighborhood could hear it, all of Via Gemito, the building across the street, even the sports field. It had lost all its sense of furtive pleasure and now seemed like a grey, opaque slab. I could only hear the obscenity of it, the shame, it had the nauseating smell of boiling rabbit glue, the kind my father melted over a flame in a tin can.

"Don't you know how to read, Mimí?" he laughed, holding me firmly against the window sill to make sure I didn't wriggle away. Then, behind him, off to one side of the window, I think other people appeared. Maybe Zio Antonio, maybe Peppino, my mother's brother, maybe my older cousins, maybe my brothers, or even my mother. I felt that the public had grown, but in my memory I could only hear his voice. "Read it," he said.

It took me a long time to accept the sound of that word after that day. I'd have to grow up, look up its etymology in a dictionary, understand it in terms of the natural metaphor of plowed earth and gardening, in terms of a bunch of grass at the edge of a puddle of water. *Portulaca* and *pucchia*, a leafy green with a pulpy opening, an ingredient in soups and the name given to tender female genitalia, a source of pleasure and consolation. That's what the word means, and maybe that's how Federí thought of it. It didn't seem like a bad word to him, and I should've played along. Instead I continued to stare at the shutter. All I knew was that what was amusing for my father was humiliating for me. It seemed to me that he was asking me to say something that shouldn't be said. Saying that word out loud seemed cruel and risky to me, it was a way of having him hear the languor that it provoked inside of me, of making it public, of making it a point of derision. I didn't know how to behave, and I felt myself burning with embarrassment.

"Mimí doesn't know how to read," I heard him exclaim with disappointment. He grabbed my shoulder and shook me. "It says *pucchiacca*."

I reflect on the years I spent disturbed by homicidal thoughts and recall the key events that took place: my brother Geppe got sick with nephritis; my mother grew progressively unwell; my father started to paint cityscapes of Paris in the style of Utrillo; we moved house and left Via Gemito forever; I discovered dancing, received my first communion, and fell in love for the first time.

I fell in love with Nunzia, a girl with long, dark hair, skin so smooth that it seemed like wax paper, and a prosperous chest despite her young age. But "I fell in love" doesn't quite cover it. I need a term that describes not the idyllic infatuation of early adolescence, but captures the tempestuous rush of blood, the flowing waves of moods, and the fantasies of pleasure that gushed out of me for her.

I first set eyes on Nunzia during a dance lesson at the house of Zia Maria and Zio Espedito. The year was possibly 1956 but it might have been 1957. Back then, without even realizing it, I was searching for a Nunzia with my entire body, from the roots of my hair to the ends of my toes. Meanwhile, I sought gratification in anything I could find at home. I would wait until my father was out or for my mother to go shopping or deliver clothes to her clients and then I'd riffle through secret hiding places throughout the apartment. I leafed through art books inherited from Zio Peppino di Firenze, hunting for pictures of naked women. I examined my father's drawings, the ones inside folders or on top of the wardrobe in the bedroom, so that I could freely study those female bodies that he had drawn while he was at the Scuola libera del nudo.

I no longer felt the mild childish excitement I once felt, that languid weightlessness that slowly overwhelmed me, page by page. I now felt a frenzy that I detested. I couldn't control it, it controlled me. Each time I'd say to myself this is the last time, but it was never the last time. The drawn or painted images would come back to life, become flesh; if they were profile drawings, they'd turn around and show me their backsides or face me and show me their breasts and spread their legs.

I was consumed with the desire to feel pleasure, a pleasure that always bordered on violence. Sometimes I wanted to rip up the pages of paintings and drawings, driven by confused motivations: I wanted to pull the bodies off the paper, eat them, bite them, lick them, shred them, destroy them forever, as if they were guilty of making me feel this way, subservient to a state of bliss that never allayed me but, on the contrary, asked to be gratified ad infinitum. I felt like a dirty and dangerous animal, blinded, and furious about being blind, unaware of everything, capable of anything. I couldn't shut my eyes at night without feeling the desire to go in deep, break through, drown in pleasure and mutilation and, eventually, experience exhaustion.

One day, while I was looking through the wardrobe in my parents' bedroom, I came across a box. I opened it. Inside were photographs, lots of them, printed on thick, grainy paper, black and white pictures that were starting to yellow. There were photos of naked women, surely a part of the inheritance of Zio Peppino di Firenze; they couldn't have come from anywhere else.

The women in the photographs smiled and showed their most private parts without timidness, without any modesty. I looked at them endlessly. They stepped out of the wardrobe, from in between my mother's clothes that hung on wooden hangers; they themselves had the smell of clothes that have been worn, of shoes, gloves, and hats. Sometimes they sat with their legs crossed and looked up at the ceiling, sometimes they sat with their legs open showing the black stain of their sex, sometimes they offered up their wide bottoms and deep rifts and slits, peering coyly at me over their shoulders as if to say, "What're you waiting for?"

I studied those women for days, months, years. I saw them night and day. I couldn't resist those vivid fantasies. They overpowered me. When Signorina Pagnano came to try on dresses that my mother sewed for her, I watched her walk gracefully by, imagining what was beneath her slip, inside her bra, what came into contact with her underwear, details from bodies that I knew from those photographs. It frustrated me that I was too grown up to run up to her and touch her everywhere the way my father had done when he was young with Donna Luisella. On the other hand it also came as a relief to me. It alarmed me to think that my silent thoughts and hushed experiences were not that far off from my father's uttered ones, from actual experiences he had talked about thousands of times.

At the bottom of the box I also found a group photo, men and women all together. It was smaller, the paper was flimsier, the blacks and whites of the photo were in sharper contrast. I had to squint to be able to see the whites, which were blanched white, and the blacks which were the deepest of black. The people were assembled in complicated positions that allowed each of them to do something to his or her neighbor with their mouth or hands or feet or genitals, while also having something done to them in return. It was one long receiving line. I studied that photo in all its minimal details whenever I had the chance. Every single detail was like a fiery tongue, capable of burning deep inside me. I was filled with mixed emotions, a thousand questions, fantasies. When I put everything back into the box, I felt dazed with pleasure and yet wounded with shame.

Whenever I closed the wardrobe, which I tried to do without it making the slightest creak, I'd catch sight of myself in the long mirror that hung inside the door. My hair was a mess, my eyes were startled. Behind me was their double bed, a folded yellow blanket on one side, a blue one on the other, and an Assumption of Virgin Mary hanging lopsided and frameless on the wall. I always got out of that room as fast as I could.

Going in there was never pleasant. Sometimes, on Sunday mornings, Federí slept in late, and when he woke up, he'd holler for coffee. My grandmother and mother would prepare it and then say to me, "You bring it to him." So I'd carry the cup and saucer down the hall, open the door, and walk into the darkness. There where I had once seen the peacock and his colorful train, I now saw a cluster of naked women standing by the wardrobe in all their poses, which I knew by heart, like cards in a magician's hand. I smelled the heavy odors of night almost as if they were a sign of the presence of those women, or traces of my fantasized paramours. I'd turn on the light and my father would sit up, cough, spit out his smoker's phlegm and have his coffee. He always had a few kind words for me, sometimes he even made a joke, and I couldn't leave because I had to wait for him to drink the coffee so I could bring back the cup. I was exceedingly careful not to look in the direction of the wardrobe. I was worried that he'd realize from the expression on my face that I knew about the photographs. I was scared he'd say something like, "How dare you!" Or, even worse, I was terrified he might say, "Bring them over here, let's look at them together," and then go through them one by one, explaining them in that pedantic way of his: "These are tits, this is an ass, this is an asshole." They were all words that already existed in my head; at the time they were the only ones I knew for those kinds of things.

Even worse were the times the command to bring him coffee came when my mother was still in bed, too. It happened rarely, but now and then it did. On those occasions, my grandmother would hand me the two cups with a furrowed brow. I couldn't dare say, "I don't want to," because I knew that she, for her own unspoken and unwritten rules, never set foot in her son-in-law and daughter's bedroom. At the very most, she would open the door for me. Even while we made our way down the hall, we could hear them chit-chatting the way that couples do, with my mother laughing now and then. My grandmother would halt, lower the handle, push open the door, and retreat, leaving me there on the threshold.

When I walked in, the bedsprings would creak, Rusinè would shuffle about, and then the bedside lamp would be switched on with an explosion of light. But even before the room lit up, my mind made a connection between the bed and the wardrobe, between my parents and the box of photos. It was a fantasy that was both seductive and intolerable, triggered by other, older fantasies from when I was a child, when my parents used to shut themselves in their bedroom. Judging from the sounds I heard, I worried that my father was torturing my mother, poking her with pins, scratching her, and pulling her hair. Now I thought he was forcing her into the same positions that those women were in, but when I heard her laugh, I suspected that she bent to his will with pleasure. And on other occasions, when he yelled at her, hit her, or screamed "Vain!" at her in the middle of the night, and then burnt her hair combs over the fire, I even started to suspect that maybe she wasn't all that different from those women in the wardrobe, and that she got into those positions of her own free will, and actually, that she knew perfectly well that the box of those images sat behind the door with the mirror, and that she even studied them frequently, the same way she studied the models in the lady's fashion magazines or the gestures of the movie actresses or the women painters in the art galleries, so that she could copy them, not just with him but with anyone she pleased.

Basically, it was not a great period. Days passed, things got worse. At a certain point my father started to paint female nudes—he went on to paint them for the rest of his life—but without using models, relying on memory. Women looking in the mirror, women undressing, women after bathing with a towel draped over their shoulders. Their bodies were painted with large swathes of color spread with a palette knife. They were done in violent hues and seemed to me to be a translation of what I felt about the naked female body. In his paintings I saw my own furious desire to hold, bite, penetrate, shake. On the canvases I felt the presence of a frenzy akin to mine, and it was intolerable. I would've preferred to have a father who expressed himself chastely, without certain unmentionable experiences, of pure mind, the way I imagined my friends' parents to be. But in his nudes and their poses, I couldn't help but envision the photos in the wardrobe, as if they had come to life, as if the women had been reincarnated from black and white images into warm, colorful skin tones, not in front of the easel, but in the secrecy of his bedroom: immobile and yet living models. There was a chaotic, messy joy to them, a trace of sudden good humor, something that often bothered me about his moodiness. The way, for example, when he was sitting at the table and my mother passed by to serve him, he'd sometimes pat her on the bottom, or slip his fingers up her skirt, making her step back dramatically, giggling and embarrassed, while Federí would glance over at us kids with a devilish look on his face and raise his hands in the air dramatically and pretend to berate himself: "Dirty man, foul creature, hands off."

I caught a glimpse of the paintings hanging on the wall before he found a way to sell them. I didn't like that just anyone could see into his desires, and my own. It would take years, decades, for me to accept that I had a father who could reveal, without any trace of modesty, through words and paintings that which I would have gladly erased from myself in order not to feel that need. The more he insisted on and proudly exhibited his sexual desires, the more I brandished a haughty impassivity, remaining silent before his allusions, retreating from his displays of power.

He was sixty when, in 1977, I went to visit him in his studio in Lugano, where he was living at the time. I traveled there with the woman I loved, I was happy and felt safe. He welcomed us with his usual squandering of verbal energy. Right away he started talking about himself, his paintings, the money he was earning, his young models. He laughed, he liked showing off and laying it on thick. He hadn't changed at all with the passing years.

At a certain point he said that, if we wouldn't be shocked, he'd happily show us a few things that he was currently working on. He pulled out a number of folders and showed us some pastel drawings that he told us proudly had been commissioned by art dealers. They were images of coitus done in lively colors, practically luminous in their obscenity. I suddenly felt that old, adolescent awkwardness. He made a few jokes, laughed, and we laughed with him. But even so, I discovered that for me it made no difference that years had passed. Just like in the days of Nunzia, I continued to be of the opinion that all his suggestions or advice or comments or illustrations or erotic colors were dirty and that, despite the show of good cheer and banter, they soiled my loving sentiments, my desires.

Even before Nunzia appeared on the scene, my brother fell ill. It started with him repeatedly saying he was cold. But no one paid him any attention. The apartment on Via Gemito was always freezing, even in the summer, but Geppe was a kid who didn't usually complain. "I'm cold," he'd say and go curl up on a chair, his knees up to his chest to keep warm. Always pale. My mother had a lot of work to do. "Go outside and play, so you warm up," she'd suggest. I was too busy with my own secret frenzies and personal turmoil. My father was either at the station or painting. He had no time for anything else.

At a certain point Geppe's eyes started to swell and the skin on his face turned ashen. Rusinè got worried and started in on her struggle to convince her husband to call Dr. Papa. The doctor arrived and looked concerned. It turned out that scarlet fever had caused the nephritis. To heal, he said, he must never catch a chill, in winter or summer.

From that day forward, my brother rarely left the house. He stopped playing and grew sullen. Whatever the temperature, he wore wool undershirts, a boiled wool jacket, long pants, and a hat, always. Our father paced back and forth, swearing and slapping himself out of anger, he blasted his wife's obsession with keeping the windows open and their dangerous drafts, he raged at the *padreterno* for further complicating his already complicated life. And then he sat his son down and did a gloomy portrait of him with results far superior to those of Battistello Caracciolo. He later showed the work at the Galleria San Carlo, when he had his first solo show, but didn't manage to sell it. He was never able to get rid of that painting.

Out of all of us, our mother suffered the illness of her second son the most. She loved Geppe deeply and never hid it, recognizing in him qualities that the rest of us definitely didn't have. Sometimes I thought that she saw in him something of her own relatives: he was more similar to her physically; other times I suspected that she saw only the best aspects of her husband in him, a kind of purification of Federí. The fact is that she favored Geppe. When he was sick, she dedicated herself to him anxiously. Whenever my father yelled something like "The child had scarlet fever and you didn't even notice! What the hell were you thinking about?" at her, she'd cast her eyes down, her lower lip trembled, and she didn't reply, as if she truly felt guilty.

And with that began my mother's campaign for us to move out of our home on Via Gemito. She was fed up with that dark, damp apartment and the fact that we all continually got bronchitis. She tormented my father softly and endlessly until he put in a request for a new apartment. She forced him to substantiate the request with a certificate of illness for my brother as well as other certificates that stated that Toni, Walter (who was only one or two at the time), and I all had bronchial catarrh. "Tell them we're all sick," my mother insisted, because she wasn't feeling so well either. Her teeth ached, she was having troubles with her digestion, she had pains in her stomach, and felt an overall weakness. "If the house wasn't so cold," she said in her defense, pointing at Geppe, "the scarlet fever wouldn't have caused such damage."

And then suddenly she remembered that neither I nor my brother had received our first communion. She had stopped going to church years earlier. My father never went. As for me, I tried going to Mass three or four times, encouraged by several devout friends, but I always got bored. I didn't understand all that standing up and sitting down; I only knew the Ave Maria and Our Father. I used to play games in the parish yard, and once my friends even convinced the priest to allow me to be an altar boy and serve during the Mass with them. They let me hold the bell and said they'd signal to me when to ring it. But then they signaled me at all the wrong times on purpose, I rang the bell for no reason and the priest got angry. When he discovered that I didn't know the first thing about church and that I hadn't even received my first communion, he said some cruel things about my mother and father, and so I quit going to the local church.

But then, because of Geppe's illness, Rusinè went back to religion and started praying, in particular to a martyr saint of Egyptian origin named St. Cyrus, who together with St. John, another martyr saint, had healed all kinds of illnesses at the Gesú Nuovo church and at the church in Piazza San Ciro in the Portici neighborhood. She became very devout. With my brother always looking so dejected, always wearing his woolly hat to protect him from the drafts and damp, she turned to the saint for his powers of healing. And that is how she came to make the vow. She promised St. Cyrus that if Geppe was healed, both he and I would receive our first communion in brown tunics just like the one the saint wore. And that is how our period of catechism began.

My father never expressed his views outright on the vow. I deduced, therefore, that he was not contrary to it. Even if he hated the church and all the priests and those grey monks with their flaccid dicks and the black nuns with their dried up pussies, he himself often turned to the *padreterno* and saints, either to insult them or ask them for urgent help in times of need. That's just the way he was: churches made him sad, the importance that priests and popes gave themselves made him angry, and above all, he reminded us that he wasn't the type of person to get down on his knees for anything or anyone. In terms of religious events, he only enjoyed the festivities that took place on the city streets and in his old neighborhoods: the one in Piedigrotta, the one in Borgo Sant'Antonio Abate, and the one for the Madonna delle Grazie that they celebrated right on Via Casanova, where he grew up.

That one was a real spectacle. From Nonna Funzella's balcony, Fdrí saw everything unfold and, even in his final years of life, could recall all the details. The workers arrived early in the morning to unload the bright blue wooden posts, and positioned them along the road. They worked hard under the direction of the master supervisor of the festivities, a boss who was always dissatisfied, and about whom the builders whispered as they slaved away, groaning in pain and sweating. Come over here, you *figliezòccola, canteremmèrd, mannaggiopatatèrn* sonofabitch, and tell it to my face for fuck's sake, and I'll teach you a thing or two about how to do this shitwork, and other such comments that the child listened to attentively, learning to see compatibility in a mix of blasphemy, obscenity, the three graces, the Virgin Mary, and all that flashy color. The sun shone down on the tin-capped posts, the flags fluttered, the ornamental wooden banners were strung between the pairs of posts, the glass ampoules of oil were lit when it grew dark, illuminating shapes and figures in a grand and festive celebration for the Virgin, saints, and the eyes.

My father enjoyed talking about those festivities. Although they already had electricity for lights—he said—they continued to light candles on Via Casanova for some time. There was a transition phase when the ampoules of oil and wicks from gaslit streetlights shone alongside those powered by electrical voltage, creating a grand archway of light: oil, gas, and electricity, each landscape with its own tonality and sheen. Fdrí looked and learned: when the kind of light changes, so do colors, and so do shadows.

Then the celebration ended, but not for him. He had been so impressed by it that he tried to reproduce it at home by making colorful flags and even trying to light small lanterns that he fabricated with oil and rags; once he almost burned down the house and received a sound punishment: Filumena's shoe heel to his head.

But he didn't mind. He continued to create his own personal celebrations at Funzella's house. When he was only six and his brother Antonio was four, he created colorful altars by affixing triangles of colored tissue paper to pieces of string with soap, he placed saint figures and Virgin Mary figurines inside empty matchboxes to create tabernacles, and then he invited all the little girls in the building to come and take part in a procession. The little girls joined eagerly. They said Mass, sang hymns, and carried the Madonna and saints around the house. And then, in the midst of the celebrations, Fdrí and Antonio would pull down their pants, get on all fours, and call out to the girls: "We're Consiglia the milkmaid's cows!" and pretend their little penises were udders and needed to be milked. Sometimes the little girls ran off, but other times they agreed and gave the boys a tug.

My father talked and I sat and listened, but not willingly. I myself had few sexual memories from childhood, more wishes than actual experiences. I never liked thinking back to when I was thirteen and fourteen. But he'd encourage me and look at me devilishly and say, "I bet you did stuff like that too with Signora Mirusio's daughter, you filthy, dirty boy." I retreated, he advanced. He resurrected other stories: the time, for example, that his brother Antonio had presided over his marriage to a little girl nicknamed la bella Rosina. And then he'd start in on that story.

How many Roses there had been in his life, it was destiny, it had to be: Rusinè, Rose Fleury, that little Rosina whom he had married at the age of six. They had said a Mass and even had a wedding party. Later, he and la bella Rosina took advantage of the fact that the adults were busy canning tomato sauce and hid under Nonna Funzella's bed. Fdrí immediately stuck his hands down the little girl's panties, which wasn't easy because she was wearing long underwear. She did her best to try and help him: she made his willy grow into a small hard dick, and he liked that a lot. She touched it and rubbed it and then said to him in dialect, "Fdrí, put it inside me." Fdrí wanted nothing more, but the space between floor and the walnut bed frame made it complicated for him to move around and take off his pants. Also, there was the noise of the adults with their jars of tomatoes in the background, and Antonio was looking for them and calling their names. At one point, the little girl got fed up. "Let's go to my house, the bed is higher up off the ground, it'll be better there," she said.

Fdrí agreed without thinking twice. The two of them wriggled out from under Donna Filumena's bed and cautiously, without being seen by the adults, went up to the fifth floor and snuck into the house of Don Ciccillo the housepainter, Rosina's father. They immediately slid under the double bed. The girl tried to take off her long underwear but it turned out to be connected to an undershirt with suspenders and was a complex task, my father explained. She tried a number of times, sitting up to unfasten the suspenders but bumping her head on the slats of the bed. Don Ciccillo came running to see what the hell was going on. My father snuck out and ran down the stairs with Don Ciccillo close behind, screaming, "*Chiavechemmèrd*, you filthy boy." My father managed to dodge Donna Luisella's husband, Don Federico the cop, and ran into his parents' house and hid under their bed.

The story ended with Don Mimí grabbing Federí by the arm, Don Federico the cop hitting him with a coachman's whip, and Don Ciccillo the housepainter jabbing him with a rod. "Don Mimí beat me to a pulp right under Donna Luisella's eyes," my father commented with a melancholy smile. "Be careful if you have daughters, kid," he'd sometimes add for good measure. "They get ruined easily."

Occasionally he went on to tell me what became of la bella Rosina. Her father and brothers beat her up so roughly that her bruises showed for weeks. Time passed, and she grew into a flirtatious young woman. She did just about anything to seduce anyone, my father said disapprovingly. And then, at the age of eighteen, she killed herself by jumping out the window of her fifth floor apartment.

The priest who prepared my brother Geppe and me for our first communion talked to us at length about carnal sin without ever really giving us any explicit information. He was especially worried about me, as I was almost fourteen years old. He pulled on my peach-fuzz whiskers, pointed to the dark, curly hair on my legs (I still wore short pants), and laughed. "Ciuccione," he called me, which was like saying "retard." "What dark circles you have under your eyes," he'd say. Other times he'd poke my skinny chest, grab one of my nipples, and said, "Why, shame on you! It's as hard as a *tarallo*."

I was a little confused. In terms of sins, my father always said that he was open-minded. He could gloss over all of them except for one: desiring another man's woman. Even though he always enjoyed joking and laughing about sex, stories of adultery disturbed him. Or rather, he was disturbed by stories where a legitimately married woman let herself be courted to the point of betraying her husband. He'd listen for a while, then start to inveigh against the adulterer. "That's not a woman, that's a spittoon," he'd say with disgust.

I listened carefully and absorbed the metaphor with revulsion. From what he said, it was clear that the spitters were perfectly fine people; when you needed to spit, you had to spit somewhere. The problem, as I understood it—for years and years—wasn't the need to spit, which is natural, but the vocation of women such as la bella Rosina to behave like spittoons. My father warned me: "Be sure to find a decent girl." I nodded yes, I promised I'd be careful, but in the meantime all I thought about was finding a girl, any girl, even one who'd welcome my spit.

I lived in a web of contradictions, tension, and alarm. Once, for example, when I was about twelve years old, a kid my age came over to play. After giving Rusinè an admiring look up and down, he asked me if I thought she'd ever blow him, give him *'nu bucchino*. I tried to kill him with the tip of an umbrella that we had been filing down to make a sharp arrow. Obviously, I didn't succeed, but I never let him set foot in my house again. And I continued to dream of murdering him for months on end. I knew that was what I was supposed to do. I also knew that the kid was lucky he didn't say it in front of my father. While I had merely attempted to kill him, my father would've smashed his head against the wall, paying no mind to his young age.

On the other hand, my father's inflexibility made me sad. While I desired nothing more than being able to spit into a girl's sex, I was unhappy about reducing her to a state of being that would induce me, my father, and others to say, "That woman is nothing more than a spittoon." I also detested having thoughts about the opposite sex that were no different from those of my classmate who came over to play. I had no idea what to do. Caught between the catechism of the priest who warned us against all impure acts or fornication, and my father, who encouraged me to do both things whenever possible but with a heavy-handed contempt for the girls or women who might indulge me, I grew up like a caged and frightened beast.

One Saturday we all went to my mother's relatives' house for a celebration, I don't recall what kind exactly. Usually, on festive days like that, we ate all sorts of delicious things and I played with Zio Espedito and Zia Maria's kids and Zio Attilio and Zia Carmela's kids, for whom I invented all sorts of tall tales. I'd tell stories and they'd listen captively for hours. But on this particular occasion, something different happened. My girl cousins had a friend with them, Nunzia, an olive-skinned girl with black hair and pitch-black eyes. I had seen her around but never paid much attention to her. But that day, when I looked at her I felt my cheeks and forehead and ears blazing. I cautiously tried to capture her attention with my storytelling, but didn't succeed; she got bored right away and wanted us all to dance. There was no music but that didn't stop her. She danced and sang, first on her own, then with my other cousins, teaching them the steps. I wound up sitting in a corner, forgotten by everyone, just watching.

She danced so well, with light and graceful movements. She taught them the polka and showed them all the steps, for both the man's part and the lady's. Her small feet flitted across the floor, she hopped elegantly, her skirt twirled around her and revealed her knees, her chest swelled with joy. "Come and be the gentleman," she said at one point to me in dialect. I replied that I didn't know how to dance and, scared she'd insist, I ran out of the room. I thought I was going to faint at her slightest touch.

Later, I learned as much as I could about Nunzia. She was in eighth grade but wasn't very good at school. She was constantly reading gossip magazines like *Sogno* and *Grand Hotel*. She preferred to wear dark clothes because she thought she was chubby and wanted to look more slender. She knew how to dance well because her father's brother was an expert dancer and had taught everyone how to dance.

I met that uncle of hers not long after. He was slight and wiry and I recall him as being elderly, but in truth he couldn't have been more than forty. He always wore a tight-fitting brown vest. He had a blonde, carefully trimmed mustache and a crown of reddish hair around his balding head. Extremely gracious in his manners, he bowed to kiss the hands of the ladies, something my mother enjoyed greatly, as did her aunts, and even my grandmother. He had three children, all younger than me, and a quiet wife whom we hardly ever saw. I don't believe he had a job, but in the past he had traveled through Germany, France, and Belgium selling something or other. Now he lived off what he had earned.

I don't know his name, but everyone called him *'o ballerino*, the dancer. Not me, though. I always considered him Nunzia's uncle, and when I had to mention him, I always referred to him as "Nunzia's uncle." I think I did it purely to multiply the opportunities of saying "Nunzia." It made me emotional: Nunzia, Nunzia, Nunzia. Everything that had to do with her was an occasion to talk about her, Nunzia. She inspired only good things, and was a subject that was treated with great care. That's why I liked everything about her uncle, the dancer: his courteous ways, elegant manners, and his willingness to teach his dance techniques.

He was an excellent teacher, and it didn't take long before he taught all my relatives, old and young, how to dance the polka, the mazurka, and the polka-mazurka. He even tried teaching me one afternoon, when my cousins dragged me over to his house. I only went because I hoped to see Nunzia. She wasn't there, but the dancer was. He was always home. "Do you know how to do the Viennese waltz?" he asked me. I didn't even know how to do the normal waltz, I confessed awkwardly, which led to a great deal of teasing from my cousins. But Nunzia's uncle was kind, and he started by explaining to me that you have to spin constantly. "The waltz is the dance with the most spin turns in it," he said, starting casually to pirouette around the room. And then he explained: it has two beats and six movements. He grabbed me and started to hum a little music, showing me the steps. It was pointless, I didn't learn a thing. He didn't say anything, but I discovered that I was hopeless at dancing. "You're as stiff as a salami," my cousins laughed.

If it had been for me, I would've spent all my free time with Nunzia's uncle. But my father didn't like him much and it bothered him if I talked about him with enthusiasm. The feeling was mutual, I believe. When the two men met, they immediately stared each other up and down. Federí let him know that he was an artist of great merit, well known in both Italy and abroad. He mentioned that his work had been shown in Florida and Paris, that he had met Guttuso when he was in Rome and they had become fast friends, and he even said a few words in French and English to show that he was not a nobody but a man of the world. The dancer picked up where he left off and started chatting in French, English, and German, talking about places abroad that he had seen, customs that he had assimilated, things that had happened to him. After a while, the dancer was holding court, not my father. And even worse, Zio Attilio and Zio Espedito both encouraged the dancer to talk.

Federí's face clouded over. And it was not, I believe, because that man gave himself all sorts of airs and pretended to know everything about everything—that presumptuous piece of shit, he later defined him—but because he had been so discourteous that he had not even stopped to marvel at my father's artistic renown. Actually he had even minimized his prestigious status. "You're a painter and I'm a dancer; we're both artists, we're the same, you and me."

The same? "*Chistènnuddiestrúnz?*" Even though the dancer had a wife and kids, Federí said that he had to be a fag, just like all men who like to dance. "Even fags can get married and have children," he explained to me when he suspected that I didn't believe him. "Just look at how he moves, that little vest of his, his narrow shoulders, that wispy moustache, no real hair on that ass of a face."

He repeated those things several times, a little bit here, a little bit there. At first I was bothered by it in the usual way, just like whenever he demeaned people. But then, suddenly, I felt a deep impulse of hatred, the first that I recall with total clarity, and not because I liked the dancer so much but because he was Nunzia's uncle and it seemed to me that my father's belittling of the uncle might end up sullying her.

From that moment forward, I started to feel afraid that one day my father would fight the dancer and that, as was his custom, he'd either spit on him or piss in his face or whip his ass. There'd be a fight, I told myself, but I wouldn't stand around watching. I'd jump into the fray in defense of Nunzia's uncle.

Was he so adamantly against the dancer because he himself didn't know how to dance? It's hard to say. Acquiring certain information about Federí was not always an easy task. Out of contempt for Nunzia's uncle, he'd often say, "That bastard is a scummy *chiavica* of a dancer, I can dance better than him." But he always said that he was the best at everything: whether it was an art, craft, or science. And even if someone challenged him, it still wasn't easy to judge. He'd sigh in exasperation and start talking about his adventures in an exaggerated, grotesque manner, as if he didn't need to prove it, so disgusted was he by his adversary.

He often said, for example, that once he had been a brilliant skier, and for years his old, pre-war skis stood in our house. We kids grew up admiring a photograph of him on the snow: young, around twenty, dressed like an athlete, in a classic downhill position. But did he really know how to ski? We never actually had any proof that he did, nor did he ever show any passion for the sport, not even a passing interest. The only thing he told us, in his usual and casually flamboyant way, was that one day in 1937, while doing his job as a locomotive repairman, a marshal from the railroad militia, Don Mimí Tavolozza, showed up at work. The marshal explained that the general command office of the militia wanted to put together a team of capable skiers so they could compete in the mountains in Italy and across Europe. "Who here knows how to ski?" he asked the young railmen present. My father, seeing a chance to get out from underneath the grime of the locomotive engines, raised his hand. "I know how to ski!" he shouted, even though he had only seen snow once, at the top of Vesuvius. Taking his word for it, the railroad gave him a leave from work and he was recruited by the militia and sent to Roccaraso for training. The cohort leader, commander Astorri from Campobasso, realized immediately that Federí didn't even know how to strap on a pair of skis. But by then, he had already grown fond of the fellow: he always paid for drinks and had even done some watercolors of the mountains, woods, and zampogna-players, which he gave away, and often to Astorri. So the cohort leader just glowered at him and made sure he learned everything there was to know about skiing. Federí trained hard and became an ace. He took part in lots of races and competitions, and when he made his way down the famous "Roma" ski-jump, people thought he was the strongest and most courageous athlete, and he was desired by all the girls.

Dancing was the same. He never had time to really learn; it was a hobby that didn't attract him. But once, when he was off skiing with the militia in San Candido, Federí met a beautiful girl. It was bitterly cold and he was staying in a large barracks with the eight other team members, where they were served meals by young women who worked on the Austrian border, stunning beauties all, with the most beautiful one named Friedel Gruber. When Federí saw her, he was awestruck. He flirted with her, they had a drink together, take me dancing, she urged him. He resisted at first but then agreed. Once they were in the dance hall, Federí asked Friedel to teach him the steps and he learned them instantly; they danced the polka, mazurka, quadrille, and cotillion. But especially effective, he said, lowering his voice so that my mother couldn't hear him, was the tango, with all that slow rubbing-up against each other. It didn't take long before all they wanted to do was hug and kiss and squeeze and love each other. "That," he explained to me, "is the real purpose of dancing." It wasn't to put on airs and act like a pansy, but to be able to get your hands on a woman's body.

At a certain point in time, there was a dance party at the dancer's home every Saturday. Initially, when we still lived on Via Gemito, my family and I rarely took part: their house was far away, and to get there we had to cross the entire city. But when the railroad accepted my father's application and we were assigned a new apartment in a recently constructed building (sixth floor, four bedrooms, a living room, a large kitchen, a bathtub, and even a bidet), everything changed. The new house was only a few steps away from the station, inside the freight-yard fence, on Corso Arnaldo Lucci. From there it took only ten minutes to get to the dancer's house. To top it off, he lived only a hundred meters away from Rusinè's relatives and their shops.

We started going every other Saturday to see Zio Attilio, Zio Espedito, Zia Maria, and Zia Carmela. But we never stayed long at their houses. After exchanging a few words, all of us—uncles, aunts, cousins, my mother, grandmother, brothers, and my father, albeit unwillingly—would set out for Nunzia's uncle's house to watch people dance and see how joyful life could be.

I, of course, used the time to observe Nunzia more than anything else. It must have been because of these dance parties that

I don't recall a single thing about our move from Via Gemito to Corso Arnaldo Lucci. It was such a momentous event for my whole family and yet I have no recollection of it, not before, during, or after. This morning I tried to put the following facts in order: a) Geppe got well; b) we received our first communion in our St. Cyrus tunics; c) we went to a dance party at the dancer's house. But I honestly couldn't recall if any of these things happened when we were still living on Via Gemito or when we were already in the house on Corso Lucci, next to the station.

It wasn't an insignificant difference. They're far apart, both in terms of the city of Naples and sentimentally speaking. Via Gemito belongs to me; for better or worse it is the street of my youth. Corso Arnaldo Lucci, on the other hand, seemed like a street that was suited to my father: noisy, crowded, dangerous. The decrepit buildings, the sound of traffic and trains, the constant flow of ugly people, and not a single tree.

This impression stayed with me for years. I rediscover it intact when, taken by my desire to search for *The Drinkers*, I go and see, among many other places in Naples, Corso Arnaldo Lucci. I walk past the monument dedicated to Garibaldi, past the deadbeats and people waiting for trains. I look up and down the long piazza, full of cars and pedestrians, cut off at one end by the undulating roof of the station like the steel blade of a saw, towered over by the parallelepipeds of skyscrapers and empty strips of sky. I follow the sidewalk to the Hotel Terminus, all the way to the gate that leads to the tracks of the Circumvesuviana, and further, all the way to the Hotel D'Anna. The area feels both chaotic and festive; there's the smell of pizza, fried dough, *panzerotti*, and vermicelli with clams; there's a lot of trafficking going on, both of legal and illegal merchandise; it's a stage set for all the languages of the southern hemisphere, for all colors of skin, for all kinds of music, and song; there's the call and response of ancient voices and contemporary ones. In front of me, on the left, is the building where I lived for almost a decade, until Rusinè died. It looks unchanged: grey with green shutters, trains passing on one side, cars on the other. I discover the area that was once the train yard—which my father walked across each day to go to work, and which we crossed, too, heeding his words, "If they stop you, the secret codeword is 'On duty'"—has become a large parking lot. Everything else is as unstable as it always was, as though it had all come tumbling downhill and crashed into a crowded space where it was being jostled about by pushy, belligerent people. This was a clear sign that nothing—not my familiarity with the streets, not my old fascination with trains, not my escapades into empty cars on dead-end tracks, none of my nocturnal ramblings with other kids—had managed to erase my sense of alienation.

Corso Arnaldo Lucci is both disorienting and a little frightening. It's true that it was my mother who wanted to move, but I refuse to accept that she wanted to move there. Federí dragged us to the new apartment angrily and with no further explanation. It was just a few steps away from his much-hated job on the railroad and not far from the places of his youth, adolescence and early adulthood: surrounded by the noises of Lavinaio, Forcella, and Duchesca; close to Corso Garibaldi, where he learned to box, and the Teatro Apollo, where he knocked out the shoe shiner's front teeth; and a short distance from Via Casanova, Piazza Nazionale, and Via Zara.

"Come with me," he ordered us and Via Gemito promptly disappeared. I forgot about it for years. Now we live in this strange place. It feels colder, more exposed, the wind whistles the same way it does in a movie about mountain climbers in a storm. We wander around the rooms in sweaters, scarves, and knickerbockers, with woolly caps on our heads, especially Geppe, who can't risk catching cold. At night, we kids continue to sleep with our grandmother in one room, but in big beds. I toss and turn in the dark with my confused thoughts and desires. Even though the house has vast, empty areas, we're still crowded, there's no privacy. My mother conceded herself an endlessly large living room, a place where she can pretend to be an elegant lady playing hostess to who knows what kinds of guests. My father has a room all for himself which we soon learn to call "the studio." No great surprises lie within it: when he's not working on the railroad, he's there, sitting at his easel. He paints and paints and paints, more exasperated than ever.

He's putting on weight, his eyes have lost their feverish look, all that's left is the rage. He has started to paint landscapes of Paris. He'll do it for years, he'll paint kilometers and kilometers of views of Paris à la Utrillo, infinite canvases, from now until his wife dies in 1965. In the evening, after the paintings have dried, he rolls them up and takes them to the person who commissioned them, who pays him promptly. My father can't handle it anymore, he wants to make money. He wants a car; his wife's relatives just bought an Alfa Romeo 1100, the Giulietta. He also wants to travel to Paris, but not Utrillo's Paris, he's sick of that. He wants to go to today's Paris and sell his art there, his own work, not the views of Paris, which he refers to as his "commercial work." He feels that his future lies abroad. He continues to talk about himself, maybe even more insistently than before, as a man with a great destiny ahead of him, just you wait and see. Everything passes, he says. The worst will pass, the best is yet to come. And yet his ambitions have weakened. Now, if he's not painting Utrillo's Paris, he travels around, takes part in exhibitions, and joins extemporaneous painting competitions where, he says, he always wins first or second place, a gold or silver medal, and endless cups. It's like a sport. But paintings like the two fishermen, which he showed in Rome, or one like *The Drinkers* with the boy pouring the water, he will never do again. Or maybe he does, but I just don't realize it.

I'm too distracted. I can only think about the photographs of the naked women in the wardrobe, about Nunzia, about the

Saturday dance parties. For a while I even start to think about becoming a dancer, too. When we receive a visit from a young man named Palummiéll, a distant relative of my father's who used to sell fish at Porta Capuana but wants to learn how to draw, it even seems possible. Palummiéll spends hours on end in my father's studio, even while Federí is at work. He starts off with great enthusiasm and draws all sorts of objects in charcoal. Then my father tells him that he's crap and the enthusiasm fades. At the end of his stay, he doesn't even want to draw anymore, he just talks. That's how I find out that he knows how to dance. I don't, I confess to him. So he decides to teach me the steps to the tango, waltz, and polka, all while my father is out of the house.

I remember trying really hard to follow his lessons. Palummiéll was the man, and I was the woman, and then we'd switch roles. You're awful, he'd say with a laugh, and I knew it but I still wanted to learn the steps to at least one dance. I told him all about the Saturday-evening dance parties. "Do you think I can invite a girl to dance now?" I asked him. "How can you possibly ask a girl to dance if you don't feel the music?" he said with a laugh and then went on. "You clearly don't feel the music. You just want to feel up a girl." It was true. I denied it energetically but it was true. I took one step this way, and one step that way in the fervent hopes that one Saturday evening I'd muster up the courage to approach her and say, "Nunzia, would you care to dance?"

I always wished that my father would stay at home painting rather than torture us with his presence at the dance parties. First he'd sigh heavily, then he'd grumble, and then with an expression of deep suffering, he'd decide to come with us to Rusinè's relatives' houses. "Why should I even come?" he'd say and go on to complain about all the precious time that we made him waste. What annoyed him in particular was my mother's constant desire to see her family. The more she said, "Hurry up, it's getting late," the longer he sat at his easel, sometimes applying final brushstrokes, sometimes not even painting, just scratching his palette with his knife and brooding.

Meanwhile, Rusinè got carefully dressed, choosing the most fashionable outfit from the ones that she had sewn for herself. Since that was the only legitimate social occasion that she was permitted, she went to great care with her presentation: she'd tweeze her eyebrows perfectly, apply a layer of Nivea cream to her face, and put on her lipstick, making funny faces at herself in the mirror. While she was busy doing all these things, every so often she'd call out, "Federí, we're ready. Are you ready, too?"

This made me tremble with fear because I knew that my father was always just one step away from breaking into a fury, and the pressure she put on him could easily make him explode. I could still smell the odor of the hair combs that he had burnt one June night, maybe a year earlier, after his solo show at the Galleria San Carlo. "Vain!" he had screamed insultingly at her deep into the night. I was worried that he'd start again, from one moment to the next, but with even greater and more desperate violence. I felt like curling up in a corner and covering my ears with my hands before it even happened.

But my father generally contained himself. "I was born ready," he'd say, continuing to sit at the easel, his hair unbrushed and wearing his paint-splattered work pants. By that, he meant that if it took his wife two hours to get ready, he was faster, he'd be ready in a minute, he could keep sitting there thinking or painting without her constantly busting his balls. This went on until my mother appeared in the door, her hair perfectly coiffed, my grandmother dressed to the nines, and us kids too. "See? Now we have to stand around waiting for you," she'd say impatiently. And only then would he stand up, drop his trousers, run to the bedroom in his underwear, drag a comb across his head, slip on a pair of more decent but still shabby trousers, throw on on a threadbare jacket, and exclaim, "See? One minute, not a second more."

The whole way there, down Via Taddeo da Sessa, he continued to scowl and dwell on his own things. Then, once we got to the relatives' house or Zio Espedito's bar, he suddenly lit up and became cheerful. He talked to everybody, laughed, and told amusing stories. He was about forty years old at the time and was inclined to make vulgar comments and tell lewd stories. I watched him, hoping he'd stay at the bar, that he wouldn't come to the dance party, that he wouldn't do anything that would make Nunzia notice him. But what I feared most back then was that, due to carelessness on my part, he would intuit the secret desires that she inspired in me and make them public, laughing about them with Zio Espedito, Zio Attilio, Zio Matteo, and my older cousins, who considered him a master in all things related to sex.

The idea horrified me. I knew how men spoke among themselves about girls. Once, a cousin's friend took me aside and told me all the things he and his girlfriend did in the darkest corners of the neighborhood, in the park on Via Taddeo da Sessa and behind the parked trucks on Corso Novara. I was shocked by his language: he spoke in dialect, with words that were coarse, crude, imaginative, that sounded like sex itself. He talked about how he jizzed everywhere, and especially in her hands and between her legs, how it dripped down like cement when you're laying bricks, and then you spread it around with your trowel, and other liquids get mixed in, from her mouth, her ass, her pussy, her cunt, that moist ditch the boy sucked on so he could taste all its juices, with a chocolate candy in his mouth in the winter, or lemon juice in the summer, it's like when you see live oysters for sale on Via Caracciolo and your mouth starts to water and you say, "Mmm, let me get some of those oysters."

I couldn't stand the thought of my father standing in a corner with my cousins and their friends talking about Nunzia that way, snickering. I mused over ways of killing him. But at the same time, those images (the melted piece of chocolate, the lemon juice) had already taken root in my mind and I couldn't get rid

of them. I submitted to them at all hours of the day, letting myself go with growing ardor and fantasizing about her body, and
yet I was worried that, like when you're watching a movie at the
cinema, images of her would be visible in my pupils and make
for a repugnant spectacle.

The dancer was truly a perfect dancer. Each time he danced
with Nunzia, I stood there watching with bated breath. Their
combined skills created such an amazing display that all the other
dancers felt second-rate in comparison and eventually gave up
and leaned back against the wall to make as much room as possible for their superb exhibition. Enraptured spectators formed
a circle around the uncle and niece, who danced as if the music
came directly from their bodies and not from the record player.

Their performances brought tears to my eyes. The dancer,
whether inventing tango steps, windmilling through a waltz, or
hopping lightly to a polka, always had an expression of ecstatic
concentration on his smooth face. The more he danced, the paler
he became, but at the same time, the light in his eyes grew ever
more radiant, and his ears turned so red that just looking at them
made my ears turn red, too. Gradually I started to identify with
him. My whole body tingled as if I, myself, had the ability to
follow the music with the necessary skills, as if I could actually
dance with Nunzia.

And there she was: to my eyes, beautiful, with her black hair,
fair skin, and bright cheeks. She darted through the room as if
she were a ray of light, visible only to the descendants of visionar-
ies, like those on my father's side. The only sign of effort were the
beads of perspiration that collected on her upper lip, which her
uncle courteously wiped away with his handkerchief when the
music stopped, when we all applauded with enthusiasm.

A couple such as they had never been seen in our neighborhood before: she, so petite, almost a child, with her black dress
and white socks; he, tall, bald, with deep wrinkles at the corners

of his mouth and his eyes, slender, always wearing his vest. But the tempo of the music erased his baldness and wrinkles, and made her appear taller, more mature. The rhythm made me feel as though I had grown up, too: in my long pants and vest, I would be able to guide Nunzia in the same gentle but firm way that her uncle did.

And so one Saturday, consumed by that fantasy, as soon as a tango came on, I went up to her while she was chatting with her uncle, even though she was rosy and perspiring. "Would you care to dance?" I asked her. "You need more meat on those bones," she said with a hearty laugh. Her words wounded me so deeply that all strength drained out of me; I could neither walk away or say a thing. I stood in front of her, dazed and frozen, I couldn't feel my hands or feet. Luckily, the dancer stepped in to save me. "The tango is too difficult for you. But don't worry, later we can all dance the quadrille." I shook myself out of it. "Thank you, yes," I said. While he and Nunzia started in on the first movements of a memorable tango, I glanced around the room for my father. I was worried he might have witnessed the scene. If he had, he would've unleashed all the insults he could possibly think of on the girl who'd turned me down, and all the rage and fury he could dig up for her uncle, who hadn't forced her to dance with me, as he ought to have done. How dare someone say, "You need more meat on those bones," or any such humiliating phrase to his firstborn son. Offending me was like offending him, or worse. "Slut," he would've said. Luckily, he was distracted: he was busy whispering something into Zia Assunta's ear, and Zia Assunta, who was red in the face owing to her high blood pressure, was laughing. Luckily. I stood in a corner and waited for the quadrille.

The quadrille arrived. This was the dancer's true specialty: no one knew how to direct it as well as he. He called us all forward one by one: children, teens, young adults, adults, even my grandmother. Then he chose his lady, Nunzia, and in a mix of

Neapolitan and some other mysterious language he called out clearly, "Ladies and gents, gather 'round."

The couples formed a circle at the edges of the room. Rusinè tried to draw her husband into it, but he didn't want to dance. He wasn't that type of man, he grumbled, wouldn't let himself be manipulated like some puppet at the hands of that ballerino. "Dance with Mimí," he said to her, and went off into a corner to sketch in peace and quiet on the back of some railroad forms that he carried around in his pocket for such occasions.

My mother took me by the hand. "Let's dance, you and me," she said gleefully. The dancer lowered the arm of the gramophone onto the record—the boisterous music of a quadrille—and called out in that foreign language that only he and perhaps my father knew: "*Promenàd!*"

It was the language of the quadrille. We heard it at all the parties, I adored it, just hearing it made me feel better. Lined up and paired off, we took turns sashaying around the room: children whooped with excitement, we older kids were tense and carefully followed the unmistakable and yet indecipherable orders called out by the dancer, the adults smiled their gap-toothed grins, my grandmother twisted around stiffly, making Zia Assunta laugh and cry out, "Nanní, now don't pee on yourself!"

At the end of the first sequence, the dancer halted, raised his hand above his bald head, and rotated it in a circular gesture, calling out, "*Muliné dedàm!*" All the women rushed to the center of the circle: the little girls contended for space between the ladies' heavy dresses, the teenage girls imagined they were ladies and danced coyly, adult women like my mother behaved even more childishly than the children themselves.

I tried not to lose sight of Rusinè. With all the passing Saturdays, I had acquired a certain familiarity with the quadrille and I knew that in a matter of moments I would have to offer her my arm and have her do the *tur demangòsce*, a sashay around the room from left to right. But then something happened that left me breathless. The dancer surprised me by nimbly coming over to me and ordered me softly to "*Sciangè dedàm!*" and switched places with me, so that I was left standing alongside Nunzia. Then, as expected, he called out "*Tur demangòsce*" and under my father's horrified stare, he spun my mother around the room, all the other couples following suit.

Nunzia was annoyed. "Just shut up and give me your hand!" she whispered to me in dialect, I offered it to her—it was the first time that I actually touched her—and we traveled the length of the yellowing wall, under the feeble electric light. "Don't forget you have to bow after," she said curtly while I moved tensely through the sequence, struggling to keep the sensation of falling reined in.

I remembered to bow in the nick of time. In the meantime, surrounded by the general hullabaloo, the dancer called out a new sequence: more music, more laughter, "*Promenàd!*" and then "*Muliné devcavaliérs!*" And then "*Promenàd!*" again. We windmilled and promenaded with gusto, while my father continued to draw, growing sulkier by the minute.

That quadrille, it seems to me, provided me with what was possibly the best few moments in an otherwise awful period of my life, one that, thankfully, has passed forever. I write about it, then pause to look up the sequences and terms in dance manuals to refresh my memory. But then I put them all aside and no longer feel the need. I remember the music, the dancer's voice, and even his image, perfectly, and that is enough. I can see Nunzia's uncle before me as I write: skinny, pale, red-eared, hardly even touching my mother's hand but guiding her ably through the promenade. My grandmother is unsteady on her feet, flops down in a chair, starts to laugh and never stops, while her sisters continue to promenade with their gentlemen (Zio Espedito, Zio Attilio, Zio Matteo). "Everything alright, Nanni?" they call out to her, but they're not worried. "Look at Nannina laughing! When she starts, she never stops." As for me, I can't believe what's happening to me. I'm doing the quadrille with Nunzia. That's all that matters. And I am exceedingly careful not to make a single mistake.

"*Dossaddòs!*" the dancer calls out. I follow his steps exactly. I move forward with everyone, I walk back with everyone, I move forward again, I circle with the other gentlemen. I am entirely aware that the dancer did something for me which I will be eternally grateful, and it doesn't matter a bit, right now, that my father hates him, that he's raging inside because that stranger is dancing with Rusinè. I do the *tur demàns* with Nunzia the same way he is doing it with my mother. When he calls out, "*Scevò debuà decavaliers,*" I realize what it means to be happy, to feel music in your blood, to be on fire, to dance with Nunzia.

Then the dancer claps his hands. "*Sciangé dedàm!*" I leave Nunzia's side as dictated by the command, stroll past my mother, who is ahead of me, past Zia Carmela, Zia Assunta, my cousins, and all the little girls, one after the other. I can't wait to be back with Nunzia. But it's not as easy as all that. There's mayhem, it's exhausting, the music speeds up, the dancer is already calling the next sequence: "*Scevò debua dedàm!*" and I feel like I'm losing her, I've lost her, we're all back in a circle, the dancer has taken her back as his partner and they knit their fingers together, raise up their arms and form an archway. Dejected, I sidle up to my mother again. "*Lespònts!*" the dancer orders, and the couples pass under the bridge he and Nunzia have created with their arms. Everyone is having a grand time. I smell a wave of perfume and sweat, my mother and I are about to pass under the arch.

My father is fed up with drawing. He jumps up, grabs his wife, and calls out "*Lespònts!*" while diving under the archway with Rusinè and brutally ramming aside the dancer with his shoulder. The dance goes on, there's laughing and hollering. I find myself partnered with an eight-year-old girl; when I go under the bridge, I breathe in Nunzia's scent. The dancer, meanwhile, twists like a toreador around himself, bravely slipping under his own right arm, a dance move of great complexity. He quickly tries to unravel himself in time to call out new commands. But my father gets there first: "*Escargò!*" he calls out in a strong foreign accent. Suddenly, all of us, the dancer and Nunzia included, are following him as he leads us in a spiraling move like the whorls on a snail shell. He leaps about erratically, scrambling around with furious good cheer. Everything fades.

That's how the quadrille comes to an end, although I'm not entirely sure now if all those sequences took place that very night; maybe at a certain point the music stopped, maybe it was necessary to crank up the gramophone again. Fragments of various quadrilles fill my head, but it doesn't really matter: what happened one Saturday may have happened on other Saturdays, and something that never seemed like it could have happened, may have actually happened.

I choose to follow that afternoon's events not with an actual argument between my parents but more of an *appiccico*, a word in dialect that means something along the lines of a tussle but which also has a puzzling secondary meaning of being sticky, like glue. In fact, when we say "*Ci siamo appiccicati*," it can mean both we had an argument and we forcefully made out, as if hatred is not all that different from love: in both cases you want to get close to the body of the other, open it up, sink into it.

There had to have been an argument or *appiccico* after that quadrille. Whenever Rusinè seemed especially happy about some kind of interaction with unfamiliar men, my father felt he had to correct her ways to the tune of slaps.

During that Saturday-evening party, she and the dancer had been hand in hand; her sweat had mixed with his sweat. I'm certain that Federí made her pay for it: he was constantly in a state of alarm, especially when it had to do with his wife. He vilified her, beat her, told her in no uncertain terms that she was lucky to be with him, that she was not up to his exceptional level. And yet, at the same time, he was always scared she'd choose someone else, and he kept a close eye on her.

One of the many times that I riffled through his things (maybe a year earlier, or was it two?), amidst his drawings I came across one of those railroad forms that he scribbled on, with a story written on the back. It was in the third person and about a railroader named Franco, who was an excellent husband and good employee. Franco had casually discovered that his wife was betraying him. First he cried in great despair; then, once he figured out who his rival was (it turned out to be his best friend, a colleague), he killed the man by throwing him off a bridge and under a passing train. Then he went home to kill his wife.

As I took in every single word written in his decisive hand, I couldn't help but think, "He's the railroader and the wife is my mother." I didn't know what to do about it, I struggled with the thought that Rusinè had betrayed him and, if she hadn't yet, that one day she would, and that he would kill her. I still have that piece of paper somewhere. He gave it to me years later. "Your father," he said to me, "could have even been a writer." I accepted the gift from him without telling him what I really thought of it, that it was a sign of his anxiety, written proof of what lurked in his mind.

He wanted me to think about things exactly like he did. As a child, I was always afraid that my mother would somehow offend him. It made me constantly anxious because I knew it could happen from one moment to the next. I felt alarmed when she smiled or glanced in any given direction. Federí's opinion about all forms of contact between men and women had gotten wedged so deeply in my head that I couldn't get it out. Physical contact— he said—is never innocent, even when a person's intentions are. It all starts with an apparently meaningless gesture—he went on to explain to me, even as an old man, laughing—and then you end up fucking. Mimí, people really don't think about anything else, they just want to screw, any place, any time, with anyone. That's how men are, and women are even worse. That's why he didn't trust her, that's why he never trusted her. When, for example, he screamed "Vain!" at his wife on that June night after his exhibition at the San Carlo gallery, even if I didn't know exactly what the word meant, I knew what my father was trying to say and I made every effort not to listen to him. That word foreshadowed what my mother's sociable nature might lead to, it embodied her skill of making herself look pretty, her desire to please, to feel admired. That's why I withdrew in fear and horror and didn't even look up the word in the dictionary. With every hurtful sound, I curled up into an even tighter ball.

Lose contact, become impervious, choke back feelings, feel no pain. And that's why I retain only a faded memory of the *appiccico* that followed the quadrille. That's why I can describe—and not even that well, as I already mentioned—only two definite episodes when Federí beat up Rusinè in the course of their twenty-three-year marriage. I imagine she tried to defend herself from his accusations of having wanted to pair up with the dancer by saying something like, "Well, what was I supposed to do? Say no? Dance the quadrille with my husband and son only?" I also imagine that I curled up in some corner and covered my ears with my hands in order not to hear. I must have thought if I can't hear their voices, they don't exist.

But my father's voice was invasive. After that Saturday evening and with no clear motivation, Federí started to talk more frequently about sex. He directed his discourse at me, as if the time had come for him to pass on to me his propensities and fantasies and the benefits of his experience.

There was no shortage of opportunities for him to engage in these complicit conversations. To begin with, there were several weddings. My cousins, my mother's cousins, and relatives of people that my parents were connected to as godparents got married. The happy couples always asked my parents to participate as *compari di fazzoletto*, handkerchief godparents, a role I didn't quite understand, and which Federí and Rusinè each had their own way of interpreting. For example, according to my mother, it would seem that they had been asked to provide everything that had to do with the couple's needs for linens: sheets, blankets, the wedding dress, travel clothes, and consequently even handkerchiefs for the bride. My father, meanwhile, made the handkerchief the focus of his participation, and always talked about it in allusive tones, laughing and winking at me as if I got the joke.

My father took an active part in his role. When the betrothed couple came over to the house and he was at home, he never left them alone. He'd get up from his easel and greet them warmly and then entertain them, whispering in the groom's ear and making the fellow chuckle, whispering in the bride's ear and making her smile demurely and turn bright red or else give a hearty, raunchy laugh. The self-proclaimed "handkerchief" was deeply amused by his own role, they seemed flattered by his attention, and I just smiled to show that I understood. But clearly I didn't understand. And then my father would start to invent little ditties (demented, silly, a little vulgar, he did it often, for me and my brothers, my mother and my grandmother) like: "In bed you need a hankie / to clean your hanky-panky," and so forth. My mother would always interrupt him in dialect. "Cut it out," she'd say, and then whisk away the bride.

I always played along but I never had as much fun as everyone else seemed to be having. I didn't understand why so many people wanted him to be their handkerchief godfather. Maybe because he was now first-class station master and head of operations, and so having him as a godparent was prestigious. Maybe they wanted him because he told everyone that he was a famous painter throughout Italy and abroad, and the couples' parents and the couples believed him. They were happy to have such an important godfather. Maybe, on a more basic level, they appreciated having my mother as godmother, and if they wanted her they had to accept him, too. In my head, I excluded the fact that they chose him for his pleasant and amusing ways or because he was full of vitality. I simply could not perceive this side of him. I looked at the bride and independently of whether she was pretty or ugly, chubby or skinny, cheerful or sad, all I could imagine was the groom stickily sticking it to her: hands, tongue, everything. I was devoured by those thoughts, couldn't free myself of them. I felt both the pleasure and the guilt of carnal sin, an expression I had learned in catechism that had spread like a shiny, scarlet stain, that gave meaning to my father's puns, that helped me understand why my mother was so annoyed with him, and which fostered a hostility in me toward the notion of handkerchief godparents, all these weddings, and the obsession of relatives near and far to involve my parents in their plans and parties.

Sometimes it got to the point that the couples even had their wedding parties at our house, in the living room of the apartment on Corso Arnaldo Lucci. Occasionally, if the newlyweds were poor and lived out in the provinces (somewhere like Casavatore or Afragòla) they stayed at our house for their honeymoon. When, in the morning after the wedding, the couple eventually tiptoed out of my parents' bedroom, which they had been granted with a fussy show of hospitality, my father always quizzed the bride. "So, how did the groom behave? Up to expectations?" The bride, depending on what type of woman she was, either answered shyly or with the freedom of a now-married woman who no longer had to fake modesty. In both cases, Federí made up amusing sexual metaphors and teased the young couple until they confessed their bedroom antics. There were wild peals of laughter, guffawing, lots of ribbing, and back-slapping. I recall one time in particular. "Did you break her in good, *cumparié*?" my father said to the newly married man, a red-haired fellow and traveling salesman by trade. "What a struggle, *cumpà*, what a struggle," he said, muttering over and over and shaking his head, his bride unable to contain her nervous giggle.

On one occasion, Nunzia came to a wedding party at my house. One of my mother's no-longer-young cousins had gotten married to a traffic cop who had a Clark Gable mustache. It was chaos: the big living room was filled with sunlight, the floor was sticky with spilled food and drink. There was definitely a small orchestra to bring life to the party, but I know for a fact that Nunzia didn't dance. Everybody else danced, adults and children, but not her. Maybe because they were all lousy dancers. Even the groom, although he behaved like he knew how to dance the tango and waltz, wasn't up to Nunzia's level. Accustomed to dancing with her uncle, Nunzia was not easy to satisfy. But Nunzia's uncle wasn't there; my father detested him and the man never set foot in our house.

But Nunzia didn't play with the other girls, either. She considered them too babyish. Instead, she opted to run around with us boys and, in particular, had fun with a couple of my friends to whom I had hinted that between her and me there might be, or maybe already was, something special.

We all played together for a long time. She ran down the hall laughing and screaming, and we followed her. She fled like Ariosto's Angelica through the rooms, around the loggia. My friends and I chased her like paladins through the wilderness, but Nunzia was swift and had quick reflexes. She slammed doors, jumped up onto beds, ran into the kitchen and knocked things over. Sometimes I got close to her but I never reached out and grabbed her, I was afraid of touching her arm, grazing her breasts, feeling her live and kicking between my hands. I knew my desire so well that I slowed down my pace on purpose, I couldn't risk it. Consequently, I got shoved to the back by my friends, and one in particular who was two years older than me, a boy who didn't hold back the way I did. He rushed up to her, grabbed her forcefully, pushed her back against a wall, and pressed himself against her. Sometimes they even fell to the ground or onto the bed and wrestled fiercely. She screamed with the thrill of it, and so did he. Afterward, she got back up and started running again. The chase went on.

Eventually I quit playing. I leaned up against a doorway, annoyed and angry with myself. It occurred to me that I should step in and say, basta, that's enough games, and pull my friend off her, even if he was bigger, and punch him, remind him that I had seen Nunzia first, that I had even told him about her, that it wasn't fair he was interfering or touching her like that. But I stayed quiet, and not because I was afraid of him. I thought she might yell at me. "Mind your own business, it's catch me if you can, and clearly you can't."

The wedding party continued, one agonizing moment after the next. When Nunzia went home, I was glad. I didn't even say good-bye to my friends. I decided I never wanted to see them again. I threw myself down on the soiled sofa and out of a corner of my eye watched my grandmother, her sisters, and mother clean up. I was a wreck, and the smell of wine and food only added to my malaise.

Before I went to bed, the house gleaming again and everyone gone, my father suddenly came up to me. Without any preamble, he said in a disappointed tone, "Mimí, you don't have to ask girls for their permission, you just have to grab them." He would go on to use that expression on several other occasions when he thought I was being timid with girls. "Just grab her!" he'd say in dialect and laugh. Clearly, he wanted to tell me exactly where I should grab her. But he didn't need to. I knew perfectly well that I should push Nunzia's bra out of the way and grab her tits, grab her between the legs. But the thought that my father was going to suggest what I should do in his bitter and disappointed tone was intolerable to me. I was afraid he was going to refer to Nunzia explicitly. I felt the blood pounding in my temples. "He'd better not say her name," I snarled to myself.

Back then, Federí even started neglecting his painting in order to focus on me. When we still lived in the apartment on Via

Gemito, I used to study in a tiny, windowless room that led to the toilet. He'd walk in on his way to the john, and then on his way out he'd stop and stand in front of me. "Lots of schoolwork?" he'd ask. I tended to cut our conversations short, worried about him wanting to get involved in my work. But he didn't notice. He'd pull up a chair and sit down next to me. "Let's see what you're doing," he'd say seriously.

He wanted me to believe that he knew everything: Italian, Latin, history, geography. He invented long phrases with difficult terms that he forced me to use in my essays, dictating them to me word for word; he took pride in his ability to translate into and from Latin; most of all, he enjoyed working on my math homework. He puzzled over geometry or algebra problems while chain-smoking. My books and notebooks became impregnated with the smell of his cigarette tobacco. I sat next to him in silence. He tried to find answers using the most complicated methods, filling pages and pages with numbers and getting so wrapped up in the problems that he'd end up forgetting all about me and the other subjects that I had to study, and focus on a single problem for hours, keeping me nailed to the spot. "Do you understand what I'm doing here?" he'd say. "Now I'll show you how to find the answer."

Often, the answers in the book—at the bottom of the page, in brackets, or printed on pages tinted pale green—were entirely different from his. So he'd start over, but I had to hurry back to school after lunch for an extended day; it felt like I was wasting time, and yet I couldn't exactly say, "Alright, Papà, that's enough now, I have lots of other homework to do." He would inevitably get angry and be disappointed with me. Here he was, wasting his precious time, neglecting his painting out of his love for learning, with all the regrets he had for not being able to study, hoping to recoup something. So I waited, and when he asked me if I agreed with him, I'd always say yes, that looked right. Then he'd sigh in frustration. "The answer in the book is wrong, Mimí. There must be a printing error." Or else he'd say the author was a shithead, don't ever let anyone try and persuade you, always think with your own head; clearly, this idiot doesn't know how to do math.

The whole thing was deeply depressing. I knew exactly what he'd say next. "When you go to school, tell the teacher that the answer in the book is wrong." I knew that I would never, ever do that. I also knew that there was no need. Invariably I'd see that the majority of my classmates came up with an answer that was identical to the one in the book, and when I came home, I'd be forced to lie about it. I always lied in situations like that. "You were right, Papà, the answer in the book was wrong and yours was correct." He'd only be happy if I told him that.

And so that's usually what I said when I got home. And then a smug expression would come over his face. "Never let anyone try and influence you, kid. Always trust only in yourself," he'd say proudly between one brushstroke and the next. "*Memento audere semper.*" And he'd continue, "Fortune favors the bold," he'd explain for my benefit. And, then, somehow or another he'd manage to use that to remind me about girls. "With women, it's not respect that counts: what counts is getting your hands on them and grabbing them." He himself had always followed that rule, he explained to me. And I should follow it, too. Good blood doesn't lie, he said. It was a question of race; our race was always good at handling women.

All his stories on the subject were great triumphs. There was the time when, standing outside Apetino bar with lots of other keen young men, he had managed to seduce a beautiful girl that all the boys in the Ferrovie neighborhood were crazy about with a single exchange of glances. Then there was the time in his life, when he was still a teenager, that he regularly went to Pensione Rondinella, a bordello on the corner of Vico Segente Maggiore and the Chiaia Steps, where the prostitutes liked him so much that they'd touch him for free, pants zipped and unzipped. Then there was the time when he was skiing with the militia in San

Candido, and he took Friedel Gruber back to the dorm; everything went smoothly until she got up to leave at dawn and tripped over some skis leaning against the wall and woke everyone up, including Astorri, the cohort leader. There was also the time that he snuck off under the porticoes of Campo Ascarelli with a young prostitute, confident that a friend of his was footing the bill, but when his friend disappeared and he didn't have a cent, the girl started screaming, "You lousy, stinking bastard! Thief! Help me, oh God, help me."

He had a tall pile of stories to tell, and they were full of tits and round, firm asses. Now I think he told them to me for educational purposes. He wanted me to learn how to behave with women. Instead, without realizing it, he obtained the opposite effect. Every time he hinted at stories like that, I got annoyed. Not a single one of his sex-based stories made me think, "Hmm, I could do that." No, on the contrary, my reaction was almost always the opposite: Damn, I would never do that.

I didn't like his stories. I didn't like the language he used. And I especially didn't like how often he mentioned the idea of destiny. The majority of all the women he ever met, especially the true beauties, was thanks to divine intervention. Free will, he said, was utter nonsense. You turn right instead of left. If you go right, you meet Enza; if you go left, you don't meet anyone. To impress me, he'd quote Pelagius the monk, cite St. Augustine, and always conclude that the Omnipotent is the only true arbiter of all things.

At the time, I was preparing for my deferred first communion and was being pulled in opposing directions. I was equally troubled by the problem of God and that of sex; God seemed squeaky clean and sex filthy. I hated how passionately he relied on both free will and the Omnipotent to explain how things lined up for him to have an affair, squeeze some tits, grab some ass.

"It was destiny that I met your mother," he said solemnly. He explained how, on that day in 1938, as on any other day, the chances of them meeting were infinite, like sparks shooting this way and that. Amidst all that chaos, he might not have even noticed Rusinè. He could've bent down to tie his shoe when she walked by. He could've been distracted by the sight of a mouse running along the tracks. He could've been engaged in conversation with his colleagues at the switching yard. Basically, the chance of seeing her from the bridge where he was standing when she walked by—beautiful, in her bell-shaped skirt and bolero jacket—were slim to none. But he saw her. It was written in the stars, Mimí. Destiny.

I tried to see Nunzia on other occasions, not just at the dance parties. I lied in wait for her like a hunter across the street from her school, but either she went straight to the metro together with her friends or, even worse, stood around laughing and flirting with the older boys. I always hoped she'd see me standing across from the entrance to the school and call out to me. "Hey, it's you! What are you doing here? Want to walk me home?" But she noticed me only once and quickly looked the other way.

I also spent a lot of time trying to draw her portrait. Since the intoxication of my passion for her had led me to believe that she resembled Silvana Mangano, I cut a photo of the actress out of a magazine, stuck it to the window, placed a piece of white paper over it, and traced the outline of her face in pencil.

I can't be sure how long that undertaking took me: days, weeks even, trying to line up my idea of Nunzia with the photo of Silvana Mangano, constantly redoing parts, erasing, refinishing, and shading. Dedicating my time to the drawing gave me a pleasurable warmth inside, but I was scared my father would find out and, since the similarity to Nunzia grew ever more pronounced, that he would recognize her.

Once, in fact, he surprised me while I was working on it. "Mimí, I think one artist in the family is more than enough," he said ironically. Then he examined my drawing and asked me who it was. Silvana Mangano, I said. He shook his head critically, leaned down, and with a few erasures here and pencil marks there he redid the drawing. "Now it looks like Silvana Mangano," he said with satisfaction. When he walked off, I looked at the drawing. It was a perfect portrait of Nunzia.

I kept that drawing for a long time. I actually carried it around in my pocket for months on end and often showed it to my classmates, saying, this is my girlfriend. I even got into the habit of praying on it. "Virgin Mary, I beg you, let me run into her tomorrow." I did this even while I walked down the street. "God, I beseech you, let Nunzia be around the corner; let her be walking out of the park." When my prayers weren't answered, I felt anger and embarrassment. I knew I was thinking like my father: I expected God to step in and help me bump into Nunzia, I was mixing her up with the virgins and saints. And if I went on to justify myself by saying something like, "But she's worthy of God's attentions, she's not a spittoon," I'd end up hating myself for having thought that. I wanted to think and speak with my words alone: I couldn't stand my father's words anymore, I didn't even want to have to negate them. It felt like they interfered with any and all intensity or depth I might feel.

If I continued to put up with him—I told myself with a boy's conceited rage—it was only because he was a good artist. I looked at the drawing, which was by then consumed and tattered at the folds. He had done a Silvana Mangano with Nunzia's exact expression, the very one I saw on her face one Sunday when I went to her parish church hoping to bump into her. That Mass wasn't boring. Actually, I wished it would never end. She stood on the ladies' side of the church with a blue veil over her head; sometimes she sang. At just the right moment, she got up from her pew and went to kneel at the altar, waiting for the priest to give her the sacrament.

That was when I started thinking intensely about religious terms: divine providence, the holy spirit, immaculate conception, communion, grace. It was as if they were glued to a smooth surface and I kept trying to peel them off with my nails. I spent hours and hours working at it.

At a certain point, I remember being struck by the expression "the Good Lord." It actually became something of an obsession. I noticed it everywhere: in textbooks, my teachers said it, some of my classmates' mothers—the devout ones—used it. They kept saying things like the Good Lord wanted this to happen, the Good Lord wanted that to happen. I started to wonder why people used that adjective: wasn't it enough to call him Lord? I started thinking that the Good Lord was named that to distinguish him from the Bad Lord, his twin brother, who was always present and extremely active but less talked about, like a relative stained by some unmentionable sin.

I quickly excluded the devil from the equation. The devil was like the friend who played the part of the bad guy for as long as our games lasted. The Bad Lord was something else entirely. He actually scared me and, for a while, I blamed him for all the devastating things that happened in our family: my father's anger, Geppe's illness, and my mother's decision to have me receive my first communion dressed in a monk's brown tunic.

The Good Lord, I calculated, would never let my father torture my mother, or let him talk about women in that way. The Good Lord would have never let my brother fall ill in order to get Rusinè to pray to St. Cyrus. The Good Lord, I concluded, would never let her come up with the idea that, to thank the martyr saint for healing him, she could dress up Geppe and me—who had nothing to do with any of it—like the monk.

No, evidently there was a Bad Lord who, out of pure evil, created situations that were simply intolerable, a Lord that acted through my father's rage, my mother's fatigue, and against the Good Lord, who was too weak to react and could only pout and say, "Fine, if you really want to ruin this boy's first communion, go right ahead."

I was discouraged. What good was a god like that to anyone? Why even pray to him? Why side with his army of intermediaries, all those virgins and saints? I didn't know how to get out of the muddle. Tangled up in my late-childhood Zoroastrianism, one day I'd erase the Good Lord for his ineptness; the next day I'd erase the Bad Lord merely because, with everything going from bad to worse the way it was, he seemed superfluous. The following day I erased them both, seeing that my father was all I needed.

The date of my first communion was growing closer. My mother talked about it often, while Federí, who usually had a comment for everything, stayed silent on the topic. I wondered why he didn't stand up for us and say something like, I'll be damned if my children receive their first communion dressed as St. Cyrus. He certainly could have done so if he had wanted to. He did it when Rusinè said, "Mimí doesn't ever go to Mass on Sunday," while we were sitting at the table. He got angry and told her to butt out. "Mimí can do whatever he wants. If he wants to go to church, he can. If he doesn't want to, he doesn't have to," he said.

He also revealed that he had absolutely no fear of God whatsoever. Every time his bright and shiny destiny seemed as though it was fading, he raged against God directly, swore and blasphemed, grabbed him by the collar, and got just as angry with him as he did when he started a fist fight with any other shitty bastard, whether it was down at the station or in the art world, at a local, national, or international level, people who bent over backwards to make his life more unpleasant than it already was. When he was especially pissed off, he railed in dialect and paced up and down the house, spewing his theories about how God first illuded you and then deluded you, like a shithead playing at cat and mouse. "The worst idea that God ever had," he once said darkly, "was giving us the awareness of our own death. Not even the sickest mind of the worst Camorra mobster could come up with such an evil idea."

Death and finality were horrifying to him. He was afraid of chance. Sometimes, after dinner, with the dishes still on the table, he compared his palm and lifeline with that of Rusinè. "Mine is really long," he said happily, "And so is yours. We're going to live until the year 2000." It comforted him to think that everything was written on the palm of his hand. To the year 2000, but maybe even 2017. "You too, Rusinè," he'd say. But Rusinè would shake her head, no. Her skin was jaundiced, she didn't feel well at all. She lived her days as if life was slipping away from her. "Look," she said, "my lifeline breaks halfway up." It made Federí nervous to hear her talk like that. He'd take her hand, examine it carefully, and came to his own conclusion. "That's a minor interruption. Probably just a cold. The line starts up again. Look, yours is actually even longer than mine." He'd pause for a second and then issued a warning. "If I die before you, don't you dare even think about getting remarried."

The thought made him furious. Rusinè had to remain faithful even if he died. To be entirely certain of it, he'd say, "Kids, if I die, you have to make sure your mother doesn't get remarried." Rusinè would laugh. "Fine, but then if I die, you can't get remarried either," she'd say. But he always had a reply at the ready. He was always eager to make a joke. "No, I'm a man. I have my needs. Married or unmarried, every so often I need to dunk my cookie." He'd smile coyly. "An artist always needs to dunk their cookie." Then, looking at all of us, but especially at me, he'd say, "Kids, your father has always enjoyed dunking his cookie and will continue to dunk his cookie for as long as he lives." At this point we were supposed to smile in amusement at his joke.

And yet there was little to be amused at. I already knew that his furious and amusing fusion of God, death, and sex suppressed a difficult knot that was hard even for him to untangle. And that is why he remained silent when my mother made her vow to

St. Cyrus. "I know something exists," he used to say when the two of us would be left alone at the table. He seemed desperate. He talked about nothingness, emptiness, the infinite, and other complex ideas. He reveled in asking himself fundamental questions, and then sinking down into the depths and elaborating a reply. He did it when he was young and even more as an elderly man, always with philosophical and scientific overtones. Depending on the situation and ongoing events, he talked about the big bang, matter and anti-matter, saturated forces and energy masses, pressure transfer, eternity. He went to great efforts to formulate opinions on these topics. He casually cited Plato, Aristotle, Bacon, Kant, Darwin, and Einstein. But then, and especially when I haughtily declared myself an atheist and materialist, or even more moderately just a non-believer, he'd frown, look me straight in the eyes, and exclaim, "Mimí, I really do believe that after death there must be something." And then he'd add emphatically, "But I don't believe in an anthropomorphic god. I believe in the Original Force, the Ultimate Essence, the Decisive Ending." I nodded and indulged him, especially when he was deathly ill. "That's good, Papà."

I wasn't surprised by his admission of faith. I thought of how many times we kids had watched in terror as he leapt from blasphemy to prayer with the same ungovernable generosity of emotions and sentiment. If something offended him or frightened him or made him feel trapped, first he broke into a rage and then he screamed in desperation, "*Padreterno*, mother Mary, *caggiafà*? What should I do?"

When, messy-haired and unkempt, he looked towards the heavens and repeated the same question over and over, he was the apotheosis of all the ancient cultures of the Mediterranean. *Caggiafà?* He had experienced a number of miracle stories that had the reply to that question of *caggiafà?* at their crux. For example, he often spoke of what happened to his mother, Filomena, as the prototype of all miraculous events. Filomena suffered from meningitis as a child and had been saved by a miracle. She was two years old when she came down with the illness, and her mother Funzella had to run find the doctor, leaving the child alone in her bassinet. No luck, the doctor was nowhere to be found, so she ran home in desperation. As soon as she walked in, she heard a celestial voice singing a lullaby; she ran into the room where she had left Filumè. No one was there, or no one visible anyway. And yet the bassinet was rocking back and forth, and Filumè was awake, smiling and laughing. The fever had passed.

Whenever my father told that story, he shook his head in awe. Even if he never went to church, he believed in divine intervention. "There's no question that miracles happen," he said. Indeed, the most shocking story about the power of prayer, and one that he told often, happened to him at some point between 1958 and 1959. He had just purchased—do you remember, Mimí?—a Fiat Cinquecento on an installment plan, but he wasn't entirely pleased with it. It was practical but it didn't measure up to the powerful cars that Rusinè's relatives drove; the payments were bleeding him dry; he had even been forced to take in Zia Nenella, Zio Peppino di Firenze's widow, to add a little something extra to his salary and the cash he made from commercial paintings. Basically, it was hell. He had to contend with four sons, his mother-in-law Nannina, Zia Nenella, his job on the railroad, his own artwork, those Parisian street scenes that paid for food, and Rusinè's nervous breakdowns, which were becoming ever more difficult to tolerate.

His wife was not doing well: she had palpitations and was often short of breath. He even had to deal with that situation. On advice of Dr. Papa (famous for his, "Women are only happy when they're pregnant, that's the way the *padreterno* made them" cure), Federí had to help his wife get better by getting her pregnant yet again. And so Rusinè found herself expecting for the fifth time, and this time her belly was all the way out to here.

Seeing that her work at home as a seamstress no longer brought in much money and that it was impossible for her to sit idly by, which only made her feel worse, she decided to try and go into business on her own again.

The idea was a second-rate imitation of the dream she and the Slavic woman had originally shared: this time she would open a haberdashery-stationery store with her brother Peppino and his wife, Lina, two people she always adored, and whom I adored, too. They were affectionate and kind, a solid couple with a home that, unlike ours, was always clean and tidy. He was a practical and sensible Alfa Romeo factory worker and she was a housewife. She had gone to secondary school, knew Greek and Latin, and always looked put together. I constantly wished that I could've gone and lived with them. The more I adored and admired them, the more my father spoke ill of them. At that point in time, my instinct of reacting to his sentiments with exactly the opposite feeling was stronger than me. Secretly I was very much in favor of my mother going into business with Zio Peppino and Zia Lina.

The plan was for the haberdashery-stationery store to be located in an empty storeroom below our relatives' home. It was made up of two separate rooms, a few steps below street level. At the end of 1958, my mother and Zia Lina worked hard to dignify the place. They procured an old counter and some equally old shelves. They went to the wholesaler in Piazza Mercato to buy some essentials and, while waiting for their sales license to be issued, they started to test out the shop's potential. They imagined a booming business, people coming and going, buying pens, buttons, hair clips, with clients growing attached to the store thanks to the shopkeepers' affability and warmth.

But according to Federí, things didn't go quite as planned. As usual, he said that the burden of the undertaking fell squarely on his shoulders, but instead of getting to the heart of the story, he digressed and went into great detail about how his wife had

always complicated his life and how his brother-in-law continued to bleed him dry. The list was endless: I had to come up with
the cash so they could start off the business, and that came out of
what I earned from my commercial paintings; I wasted gasoline
accompanying your pregnant mother to and from Piazza Mercato
and had to deal with the chaos of wholesale warehouses; I had to
wait in line with her at the municipal offices to petition for her
license; no one listened to me when I said, "Your relatives all sell
things like salami and provolone, cassata and *sfogliatelle*, things
that you eat, things that people spend money on. You two, meanwhile, choose to sell pens, pencils, buttons—things that people
don't eat, that people spend little or nothing on. How on earth
do you expect us to get rich from this?"

But his wife didn't listen. She even wanted to expand the business, and start selling school textbooks; she said they could make
good money from selling schoolbooks. Good money *di questo
cazzo*, he said in reply. He couldn't stand it anymore. He had to
get up at six in the morning, take his wife to the basement-shop,
rush to his shift on the railroad, rush to paint his paintings à la
Utrillo, rush to pick up Rusinè at eight o'clock in the evening. It
was a pointless waste of energy, all time stolen from his real artistic activities. No, he simply couldn't deal with it anymore. He
deserved another woman, someone who would stay by his side,
someone who understood him completely.

Things went on like that until one stormy night, complete
with thunder and lightning, Rusinè went into labor. It had been
incredibly challenging for Federí to find a midwife in time.
Actually, at each one of their births, he had gone to even greater
efforts than the mother had herself with labor. He went out in a
hurricane, drove around in his Cinquecento, and ran enormous
risks and dangers. He finally found a midwife, Signora D'Eva,
and brought her back to Rusinè just in time to happily welcome
his only daughter to the world, a baby of enormous beauty, whom
they immediately baptized Filomena.

And finally, we get to the miracle at the heart of the story. As usual, Rusinè soon recovered her strength after childbirth and went back to rushing around here and there. She had to take care of the newborn, and she and her husband—who constantly grumbled about her failing business activities—had a commitment with her in-laws for shifts in the shop. She used to get up early, prepare the baby, whose name had been shortened to Nuccia, and bring her with her either in the car, accompanied by Federí, or by public transportation to her job at the haberdashery-stationery store. She had a thousand worries: she had things to do in the shop and to feed the baby, who was subjected to all sorts of trials. One Sunday morning, even though it was January and bitterly cold outside, my father decided to spend the day with his friend and fellow painter, Cardone, and go paint outdoors, in the forest of Capodimonte. Before leaving, he gave everyone a kiss, as was his habit, and even Nuccia, who was asleep in her bassinet. As he did, he realized that the baby's skin tone was slightly violet and her nose was cold. "Are you sure the baby is alright?" he asked. "She's fine, she just has a little cold," Rusinè replied. And so my father walked out of the house.

He was driving toward the forest with Cardone in the passenger seat when, tortured by the memory of his daughter's skin tone and her cold nose, he decided to tell his painter friend about it. Cardone's brother-in-law was a pediatrician and maybe his friend knew a thing or two about newborns. "This morning my daughter's skin had a purplish hue," he said. Cardone was startled. His brother-in-law had indeed transmitted some medical understanding to him. "Stop the car," Cardone exclaimed, "Go straight home. Your daughter has capillary bronchitis with no fever. If you don't hurry, it could be fatal."

My father went pale, left Cardone by the side of the road, and ran to find a phone. He called Dr. Papa and described his daughter's condition to him. The doctor agreed with Cardone's diagnosis. "The baby definitely has capillary bronchitis," he said, and ordered Federí to get his hands on an oxygen tank while he rushed to the apartment to verify the diagnosis.

Heart in mouth, Federí drove from one end of the city to the other, his foot on the accelerator, pushing the Cinquecento to go as fast as it could, but nothing doing: none of the pharmacies had any oxygen tanks. Finally he managed to snag a small one in gleaming nickel out near Pianura. He rushed home, ran up the stairs two at a time, found Rusinè wailing in desperation, and Dr. Papa waiting anxiously. Nuccia was deathly ill. She had turned blue and was having a hard time breathing. The doctor hooked up the oxygen and then took his leave. "We're in the hands of God now," he said.

For the next seven days the baby hovered between life and death. When my father told the story, he put great emphasis on just how dramatic that week was. I recall little, but I can imagine the extent of Rusinè desperation, how he dumped an inordinate amount of blame on her that would've crushed people even stronger than she: all that time she had wasted in the basement shop just to indulge her in-laws, how the baby was exposed to cold and damp, the deathly illness her actions had caused, the money they had thrown away and wasted, if the child dies I'll kill you and all your stinking piece-of-shit relatives. That's what I imagine happened. Federí, however, talked about himself as if he was shattered, annihilated with grief. During those seven days, he said, he didn't eat or sleep, he watched over his daughter in her mother's arms, who rocked her like the Grieving Virgin Mary or other such images. When Sunday came, the seventh day, he gave in to exhaustion and dozed off. Rusinè elbowed him at five o'clock in the morning. She was too exhausted to cry. "The little one is dying," she said in dialect.

Nuccia was still breathing but with great difficulty; she had a death rattle. My father turned to my mother with sudden courtesy. "Excuse me for a moment," he said and hurried out of the room, opened the front door of the apartment, and ran down the steps, his screaming voice ricocheting in the stairwell. "*Padreterno*, why do you want to take my baby girl from me? I believe in you! Don't do this to me. Take me instead, I'm forty-two years old, I've lived long enough," and other such dramatic things, more or less all in the same tone. Since no one replied, he grew even angrier, and when he got out on the street, the noisy Corso Arnaldo Lucci, he started hurling profanities at every saint in heaven for how they were treating his daughter. It was only when his mother-in-law, Nonna Nannina, ran after him to stop him from doing something stupid, when she grabbed his arm and yelled, "Shut up! Now!" did he break into tears. Finally, deeply upset, he came back inside and went into the bedroom and sat down next to Rusinè.

In the meantime, Nuccia's wheezing had grown even more agonizing. But then, as if she realized that her father had come back into the room, she opened her eyes and stared at him for a long while before abruptly vomiting a blob of blackish mucus. Her breathing then went back to normal and she smiled at him.

My father was beside himself with joy: the miracles of his life were many but, for as long as he lived, that one felt to him like the greatest. Immediately afterward, though, he broke the truce he had stipulated with his wife. He forbade her from ever going back to the basement shop, he screamed at her that her place was at home with her only daughter, he complained about how much money, sweat from his brow, and fruit of his labors had been wasted in that shitty enterprise, and he forced her to dissolve the business with her in-laws. At that point, even Peppino and Lina gave up on the idea of the haberdashery-stationery store, and chose instead to open a branch of Papoff's laundry, thanks to which, according to my father, they made heaps of money, but unfortunately not for him and Rusinè! While Federí conveniently believed in good fortune and miracles when they pertained to him, he got terribly angry when even the slightest breeze of wellbeing wafted over other people. Actually, anything good that others experienced was a direct slight by the *padre-terno* against him.

The idea that God didn't exist hit me when Dr. Papa officially declared that my brother Geppe was healed. "He's fine now," he said, "but he will have to be careful." When my mother heard the news, she lit up with joy and believed that it was all because St. Cyrus had listened to her prayers and extended his grace to her. She rushed off to buy the brown sackcloth for our tunics, took out her measuring tape, held it up to Geppe and me, and sewed up our robes, tying a white cord around our waists. Dressed like that, she said to us with emotion in her voice, we'd receive our first communion in only a few days, in June.

I looked in the mirror. The tunic barely reached my knees. My hairy legs and skinny ankles were visible to all. I burst out crying in embarrassment. It was the last time I ever cried. "No," I thought, "God definitely does not exist."

Then June came, the month of first communions. Rusinè wore a lovely party dress, and even a hat with a veil. My father cleaned up the bare minimum, as if to say, I'm ready for a party. My grandmother put on her one dark dress for all special occasions: weddings, funerals, and baptisms. My younger brothers, Toni and Walter, were bathed and groomed, their hair combed and neatly parted on the left. My brother Geppe and I put on our tunics and some monkish-looking sandals and were dragged out of the house as if to the stake.

It didn't even occur to me to rebel. In that particular situation, I think I relied on the idea of destiny that had been transmitted to me by my father. I ignored the neighbors' amused looks, my friends' taunting, the curiosity of passers-by, and all the jokes from my cousins, aunts, and uncles, who rushed to the church to see us.

The piazza in front of the church looked particularly vast to me that day, and I remember it as being dirty white and damp grey, porous, like a sponge that swallowed you up. Other children, all younger and shorter than me, make their way toward the church portal with their parents. The little girls are dressed like brides and the boys are wearing pearl-colored suits and blindingly white shirts. It's swelteringly hot and the sultry summer wind is debilitating.

The air in the church is hard to breathe and smells like burnt wax: I'm holding a candle in my hands. Everything looks golden, there's gold everywhere, even the altar, the arches, the cupola. I don't see St. Cyrus straight away but I do recall a massive Christ on the cross. Then my mother points out the saintly healer to me. I notice that he's wearing a much longer tunic than mine. I don't know why Rusinè made mine so short. She's kneeling nearby, praying. I look at her with hostility. I think bitterly that she could've easily offered herself to St. Cyrus; she could've dressed up as a nun, crawled prostrate into the church or made her way toward the altar, licking the floor. That definitely would've impressed the saint and I would've been saved my cousins' deriding looks.

They're all there: old and young. I peer at them out of the corner of my eye. They make funny faces, put their hands on their hips, and sway back and forth like women. That's when I realize that I don't even look like a monk to them. I look like a woman, my tunic looks like a girl's dress. It feels like someone has sliced me open from my throat to my bellybutton. Until now no one had said anything explicit. And it won't end here: after the Mass, we'll all go to Zia Maria or Zia Carmela or Zia Assunta's house to celebrate. There will be a lunch just like at any other important family event, there will be a party, and I'll have to take part in it dressed like this, with only underwear on beneath my tunic, vulnerable to the worst imaginable jokes. And dancing. That's something else I've avoided thinking about until now. I no longer want communion with the body of the son of God. There will be dancing. Nunzia will be there. She'll see me.

I feel absolutely no debt of gratitude for Jesus Christ and don't see why I should. Nunzia is going to see me dressed in this tunic.

I glance around in desperation. One wall is heavily decorated with silver ex-voto. The images look like butchered pieces of human bodies: legs, arms, half a head, necks, mouths. But the image I recall most clearly is a decoration inlaid in a marble balustrade: a black pincer and a white hammer. Suffering and torture.

The year after my father's death, I went to visit the church of Gesú Nuovo. There was hardly any trace of St. Cyrus left. I noticed that a new saint now held the place of honor: St. Giuseppe Moscati, a doctor to the poor, who died in 1927 and was canonized in 1987. There were bright, clean spaces in the church dedicated to him and a statue in bronze, I think it was, and even a website had been created in his name. A fair number of devout followers had gathered nearby. There were shiny ex-voto and other bits of nostalgia from his generous earthly existence hanging on the walls, and even an incendiary bomb that fell on the church in 1943 but didn't explode. It occurred to me that perhaps people consider younger saints to be better equipped to deal with the ills of our modern world.

I looked around and for a little while I wasn't even sure if that was the church where I had received first communion. When I found the chapel with the statue of St. Cyrus, the massive crucifix, the ark-shaped reliquary box, and the corridor that led to the sacristy decorated with the tarnished silver ex-voto, it didn't have the effect that I expected and imagined it would. Maybe this wasn't the right church. Maybe I received my first communion in the church in Portici.

I turned to an elderly man (maybe a sacristan?) who told me he had been serving in that church since the mid-1950s. I told him about my first communion and asked about St. Cyrus and the ex-votos. "I remember an entire wall of them," I confided in him. I also wondered out loud if Moscati hadn't usurped some of the space from John and Cyrus, the two Egyptian martyr saints. No, no, no, he replied emphatically. St. Giuseppe Moscati had many followers even in the 1950s; actually, people prayed to him as early as the 1930s and 1940s. Sure, since they canonized him, since he was given his own statue and chapels, the number of devotees had grown. But St. Cyrus, the sacristan reassured me, is always St. Cyrus; every Thursday they pray to him and no one would ever dream of scaling him back. His statue is still where it always was, and the ex-votos, too. Only the arrangement is slightly different. Any other questions? All clear now? The elderly man sighed impatiently and walked off toward the sacristy.

I wandered here and there, looking around, annoyed by my utter lack of memories. Finally I sat down in a pew and stared long and hard at St. Cyrus, the crucifix, and the reliquary-ark while a stream of devotees walked by, kissing their fingertips and caressing it with gratitude. Had I received my first communion here or not?

I felt inclined to say yes only when I noticed the inlaid pincer and hammer on the marble balustrade. At that point I clearly saw my mother deep in prayer, elegantly dressed, her pronounced cheek bones, her eyes moist with emotion under her half-veil, giving off an impression of joy mixed with suffering that I distend over her gaunt body each time I think of her. I also imagined that after we swallowed our wafer, once the service was over, she took Geppe and me by hand and out into the piazza. As on countless other occasions, I tried to write about that what followed, this time in a small notebook while sitting in the pew.

I left the church—I wrote—but not with my mother. I stuck to my father's side because that seemed like the only place I was safe, where none of my cousins would risk teasing me. Throughout the entire car ride to my uncle and aunt's house, I was silent, apprehensive. I tried not to think about what awaited me, fully aware that things happen even if you don't think about them. Once we arrived at Zia Maria's house or Zia Carmela's house we almost certainly ate and drank. Federí made a toast to say more or less explicitly that his children were better than everyone else's, that they were excellent students, and thank God they would go on to become important men like their father. God and destiny. I wondered if they were the same thing or if they bickered among themselves: my ideas were all tangled up. Laughing and joking, Federí then went on to talk poorly about all the other children, how they weren't born to study or get good grades like his children were, and would go on to slice salami or provolone or make pastries or work in a factory like the Alfa Romeo factory or Ilva steelworks. I didn't know where to look. I knew perfectly well that, dressed like that, the situation was hopeless. While my father talked, the other kids looked at me, snickering. They couldn't wait to crucify me.

Lunch was almost over. Those celebratory lunches were endless: they began at two o'clock and we were still at the table at five o'clock in the afternoon. In the meantime, friends of our uncles and aunts had started arriving, friends of friends, acquaintances, everyone bringing their children.

Each time the door opened and someone walked in, I jumped. Each time someone came up to Geppe and me and said, "Oh what darling little *munaciélli*," I looked straight ahead of me, held my breath, and knew that the worst was yet to come. Soon Nunzia would arrive.

But instead, the dancer walked in with his wife and their children. The children started to run around the house while his wife stood quietly in a corner and the dancer kissed all the lady's hands. He kissed my mother's hand with a particular flourish.

I sat up in alarm. I knew exactly what my father was thinking when he saw the man bow, when he saw the dancer's lips graze the back of Rusinè's hand. Even Rusinè knew what he was thinking. In fact, I saw her suddenly stiffen. She didn't laugh or smile. She quickly pulled her hand away and turned to make a comment to Zia Carmela. I suspected that she and Federí had come to an agreement after the quadrille, a secret pact along the lines of if you want to continue going to your relative's parties, don't encourage the dancer. Or maybe there was no need for a pact. Maybe Rusinè had already learned her lesson. She shouldn't let anyone kiss her hand.

When would she have learned it? Maybe on the night of Federí's solo show at the Galleria San Carlo. At one point an elegantly dressed middle-aged man came up to her; I no longer remember his name, but it stayed in my mind for years, it had been spoken in my presence, I had heard it with my own ears. The man introduced himself to Rusinè, bowed, and kissed her hand. Maybe it was the first time someone kissed her hand because— and I have a crystal clear memory of this—she burst out laughing as if she had been tickled. At the time, my father had been discussing art with Chiancone the painter, or maybe Cucurra, or maybe someone else entirely. Either way, he turned around, frowned, and glared at his wife as if to say, "Watch out or I'm going to come over there and smack you so hard . . ." But Rusinè didn't notice. So the man went on to tell her that he was a poet, and he ended up never leaving her side the whole evening, chatting away, a real lady's man. At one point he said he was sad that he didn't have his most recent book of poems with him, that he would've gladly given it to her, complete with a dedication. But the day after—he promised—he would come to her house personally and bring it to her; where did she live? "On Via Gemito, number 64," my mother said in a worldly manner. And so, the following day, the hand-kisser came and brought her the book. He arrived while Federí was at work, but Don Ciro the porter stopped him. "Who did you say you were?" he asked, going on to add, "I'm sorry but no one goes up when the man of the house isn't home." As a result, the poet was forced to leave the book complete with its dedication with the porter and didn't have the pleasures of handing it to my mother. When Federí came home from work, Don Ciro gave him the slim volume. "A man who said he's a poet brought it," he informed Federí. A man? With silver hair? An unctuous fellow, your typical hand-kissing bastard? Yes, yes, yes.

How deceptive memory is, each single memory the first phase of a lie. This episode, which represents an important moment in the unending *appiccico* between my parents, somehow, while I was sitting in a pew in the church of Gesú Nuovo, snuck its way into my memories of that night in June when Federí burned Rusinè's haircombs, screaming, "Vain!" At first it was just an unpleasant event without any real outcome, without any unpleasant consequences. But then, sitting there in the pew, it seemed that the man's initiative—hand-delivering a book of poems to Rusinè, a woman who had never even read a poem in her life—was the real cause behind the screaming and beating. I couldn't decide—and I still can't today, while I continue to try and put order in these observations and even invent connections—if my mother was beaten to a pulp immediately that night, even though that man hadn't brought her the book yet, or if the beating happened the night after, following the poet's visit to the building, after Don Ciro told my father, anger exploding through his head and chest.

The fact remains—I continued to scribble furiously in my notebook—that when the dancer kissed Rusinè's hand at my first communion party, I already knew what my father thought of the gesture. A man who kisses a lady's hand had to be *'nu franfellíc*, an ingratiating sap who thought he could screw over another man by fucking his wife. And so I immediately felt a sense of apprehension come over me, in addition to the disconsolate feeling I already had. It was depressing. "Now this. More *appíccichi*. More beatings. God really does not exist."

And then Nunzia walked in.

When lunch was finally over, Geppe ran off to play with all

the other kids. He didn't seem worried about his outfit in the slightest. They pulled up his tunic and he pushed them away, he ran down the hall, he was chased by kids, and he chased them back. He and all the other kids helped the dancer move furniture out of the way to make room for dancing.

I, meanwhile, stayed seated in my chair between my mother and father. I tried to look serious and thoughtful and when someone called to me or waved me over to come and play, I shook my head and laughed in embarrassment. "I'm fine where I am," I replied. But honestly, I didn't trust them. I felt safer sitting between my parents. I hoped that people would forget about my tunic. Nunzia, meanwhile, had merely looked over in disgust. Now she was busy moving chairs. She didn't even sneer at me.

The dancing began and I stayed right where I was. Not even my mother got up from her seat. Usually she went and chatted with her aunts, her sister-in-law, anyone. But now she just sat next to me in silence, tapping her foot to the rhythm of the music. She was dressed like a real lady and was even wearing lipstick, but she didn't seem happy. She watched everyone dancing but without amusement, as if she were forcing herself to act statuesque in order not to make any mistakes. Whenever anyone came over and asked her, "Would you care to dance?" she'd reply, "I don't really feel like it." When the dancer made his way over and invited her to dance, she replied without the least hint of coyness, "No, thank you."

After a while, my father got up and wandered around the room, talking to people. He laughed, teased all the uncles, called them padrone, chief, boss, maestro. "How's business, *padrò?*" he asked Zio Attilio. "Fine," Zio Attilio replied courteously, a man of few words. What else could he say? He knew perfectly well that, coming from my father, the word "*padrone*" was something of an insult. It was as if Federí was saying: you think you're such a hotshot because you own a shop, you made a little money for yourself, and you own an automobile, but in truth you're just a stinking piece of shit. You own a deli. You own a car. So what? My father thought that he was the only true maestro present: he was a master of form, a master who could recreate things exactly as he wanted. It wasn't just a question of money, he was perfectly clear about that. To call yourself a maestro, boss, or *padrone*, you needed far superior qualities, and the uncles saw those qualities in him, they recognized them in him without argument, in silence, simply by not opposing him. And somehow this put him on edge. He walked around the room looking for someone to engage with, someone with character, someone who could offer a rejoinder to his jokes, someone willing to dialogue with him so that he could show off how intelligent he was. Nothing doing. After a bit, he returned to his chair, bored, and sat down next to me. "Go and dance, Mimí. Don't be shy now."

I had more than enough problems already: my tunic, God, and my incapability, despite my recent first communion with the body of Our Lord Jesus Christ, of keeping my eyes off Nunzia's generous breasts as they jiggled up and down while she did the polka and mazurka. But what I feared most of all was a cruel prank known as *salatura* or *salasso* that boys used to do to each other, and maybe still do. Basically, it involved jumping the victim, knocking him down, immobilizing him, and stripping off his pants and underpants. Even my father knew what it was. When he was in his first year as an apprentice at Casanova vocational school—he once told me—there was a kid in his class who had been held back a year. His name was Servillo. He was big and strong, had brown hair, and already had facial hair. He was the son of a racketeer from Acerra and acted like he was important, constantly knuckle-rubbing the younger kids on the head. Naturally, Federí, who hated being knuckle-rubbed, rebelled and planned a vendetta. He got together a group of kids who were also fed up with being knuckle-rubbed, and one day after classes were over, they followed Servillo out of school. He also made sure that two other kids, Raiola and Pardo, got outside of the school building before they did, and stood on the sidewalk pretending to be in a fight. When class was over, Servillo made his way down the stairs that led into the street, where Pardo and Raiola appeared in front of him, while the other conspirators stood behind him. When Servillo shouted at the two boys to let him by, the boys behind him shoved him hard, Raiola got down on all fours and made him trip, and that young Camorra mobster from Acerra flew into the street, arms open wide, face in the dirt. Federí quickly ordered the heaviest of them to sit on his back and legs, to keep him from moving. Then he let every single one of the kids knuckle-rub Servillo. When he saw that the kid's face was bloody and confused from the thrashing, he called out, "*Salasso!*" Servillo squirmed this way and that, he screamed and begged, but my father was adamant. They yanked down his trousers, pulled his underwear down to his ankles, and left him there naked, in the dirt. People walked by, looked at him, and laughed. Servillo was so humiliated that he stopped knuckle-rubbing kids and, whenever he saw Federí, he'd look the other way.

While the prank might have been common back in Federí's day, I, dressed in that tunic, without proper pants, and exposed like a girl, felt particularly vulnerable. I was a bundle of nerves; every part of my body was tense. While I try and recollect the order of things now, back then it was as if a pair of giant hands were crumbling together an assortment of different objects, both tender matter and things with rigid bark, mixing the detritus together. I could still smell the scent of wax from the church candles and taste the flavor of the wafer. But I could also see Nunzia's breasts jiggling in her bra, feel my father poking me in the ribs with his finger, and muttering, "Go on and dance." I felt the possibility of shame, of ending up stripped in a corner, the cruel scrutiny of my aggressors as they peered at my miserable sex. All these feelings were inseparable, there was no hierarchy. It was a terrible age: Nunzia, God, desire, sin, my disparaged nudity, the voice of my father, my mother.

Rusinè sat there without saying a thing. She felt forced to behave differently than the way she truly was: that was the impression I had then and that has stayed with me. She was a forced woman. Induced to sadness. I realized what was happening, I felt it confusedly through the melee of the interconnected harassment. It was clear that my father didn't want her to enjoy herself because he was scared that her fun would not be honest. And so she resigned herself and tried not to give him any reason to think that she, like all women, was dishonest. The poet, for example, who had come to bring her a gift of his book; the dancer who had kissed her hand—all were potential risks. So she sat as still as a statue, she didn't dance, she didn't even smile. I remember a lot of parties being like that back then. Or at least, that's how I perceived them. All kinds of tensions got confused together: mine, my father's, my suspicions and fantasies. Even Rusinè—I used to say to myself—is susceptible. Maybe that's why she doesn't dare dance, and especially not with the dancer. Everything felt unstable, I felt queasy, the earth trembled underfoot. Thoughts came to me even without wanting to think them.

In the meantime, Federí didn't utter a single word to her. He decided to focus solely on me. His kindness toward me made him seem like an entirely different man that watched, forbade, or threatened Rusinè. He seemed like a pleasant father, a boy's best friend. I saw him look slyly at Nunzia and then at me. "Go on and dance, Mimí," he said. "Don't be shy. Your dad was never shy."

It was around that time that I got my hands on a switchblade. Actually that's not the right word for it, but that was how I referred to it back then with childish exaggeration. It was nothing more than a jackknife. It belonged to a classmate who kept it in his pencil case. I asked him to lend it to me once and then never returned it. "Give me back my knife," he said. "I still need it," I said. "I'll give it back to you soon." Eventually I think he forgot about it.

I don't know if I got the weapon before or after the first communion party. All I remember is holding it tightly in my hand, in my pocket, the blade always open. I walk fast, my head down, the blade extended. That's the feeling that has stayed with me. Everything else has a name, it's a person or a thing, words connect disparate facts, my imagination is measurable in heartbeats. The truth—today I feel I can write, but today is overcast, dark, heavy clouds pass overheard, the trunk of the larch tree is wet with rain, I see it exhaling its steamy plant-breath—is the aftermath of an explosion, words spoken urgently to fill the void, followed by the slow work of paving, of compacting the various detritus with careful syntax, ultimately useful for declaring: "I exist, I have my life and my own story."

And so I go on. I go back to feeling my grip on the knife, deep in my pocket. But I'm not holding it now, during my first communion party. That will happen later. The tunic doesn't have pockets. But the hostility is there, and it spreads like an illness that can't be stopped, a plague in my glands. I feel my father's fingers jabbing me in the back again, I hear his voice. "Go on and dance." Even though he's careful not to name her, I know that he's urging me to dance with Nunzia. He does it with insistent but affectionate warmth.

Nunzia meanwhile dances only with her uncle, never stopping to rest. They're doing a Viennese waltz. While all the other couples look like bumbling drunks randomly kicking up their legs, she—in her black dress, with her dark hair and fair skin—and he—slim-hipped and wearing his tight vest, his ears bright red—form an elegant and harmonious couple, and hop with composure, first on the right foot, then on the left. What a gracious couple they are.

When the waltz comes to an end, my father forces me to my feet. He waves to the dancer. "Old people should be with old people, and kids with kids," he yells. I wish I could magically disappear: I perceive that not only is Nunzia unhappy about it, but that there's something wrong about Federí's intrusion into my business, in his jostling on my behalf. It's incongruous. On the one hand, he impedes Rusinè from dancing with the dancer because he is repulsed at the mere thought of that man touching his wife, and on the other hand he acts in such a way that he persuades Nunzia's uncle to allow me to dance with his niece. As everyone knows, it all has to start somewhere, that's why people dance after all, so reach out and grab her, Mimí, and so on and so forth.

I'm incredibly tense. I intuit the substance behind Federí's gestures and words, and it fills me with both a fiery rage and debilitates me. The substance is his belief that Nunzia doesn't need protecting, but that she exists just so I can reach out and grab her. This offends me because it offends her. I can't stand him guessing my objectives, pushing me to take action, creating an occasion for me to do so. And yet, I also know that it is true: I have no other thought in my head than that which Federí is trying to encourage. And so, if on the one hand I am on fire with anger at the thought of him intervening and using one of his foul words to define Nunzia, on the other hand I hope that the dancer doesn't see what my father is up to and agrees with him about "Old people with old people, kids with kids" and says, "You're right, Don Federí, let Nunzia and the kid dance together." It all has to start somewhere, and so on and so forth.

Nunzia's uncle smiles. He wipes the sweat from his forehead and gently pushes me toward his niece. "Go ahead, you two, and dance. That way I can rest." Then he starts chatting amiably with Federí. He actually seems like a reasonable, discreet man. How I wish my father were more like him. In the meantime, someone puts on another record, and adults and children crowd the floor, yelling happily. I start dancing with Nunzia, but I don't know what the dance is. The music isn't loud enough, I can't hear it well, I don't notice anything except the touch of her hand, her skirt brushing up against my nude calves.

Slowly I start to hear snickering. My cousins and friends are laughing. It's because of the way I'm dressed, I think to myself, and unquestionably it is that, but it's also, I suddenly realize, because we have reversed the roles. Nunzia is dancing the man's part, and I am dancing the lady's. "We made a mistake, I'm supposed to be the man," I say, trying to courteously get out of her grip and lead her through the steps. But she stops me, she holds my hand firmly and squeezes my waist tightly. "If you want to dance with me, I'll be the man," she says.

I don't know what to do. Maybe I should walk away and leave her in the middle of the room. I stumble. I'm not a good dancer, not as a man and even less so as a woman. I keep stumbling, I'm too embarrassed, both because of my tunic and with her in the role of the man. Eventually, I walk off, and go hide in a corner. I look to see if my father has realized what happened. No, he's still chatting with the dancer. I slither along the wall and leave the room.

I feel an intolerable sense of inadequacy come over me, a feeling that will return to me time and again through adolescence. I suffer the way a fourteen-year-old suffers when the image that others have of him does not correspond to the image he has of himself. The suffering grows and turns into a desire for self-destruction. I know that my cousins will come and prank me sooner or later, with *salatura* or *salasso* or whatever it's called, and I don't do a thing to seek safety. I almost hope it happens. I want to punch someone and be punched. Naturally, I'll be at the losing end, they'll jump me, nail me down, lift up my tunic, pull down my underwear. They'll call out to Nunzia. "Come see, Nunzia! Come see his little willy." But I'm not going to bother looking for a safe harbor anymore. No, I just want to drown in the darkest expectations.

And then they arrive, a group of boys. "You're girly even when you dance," they say. I look around for an object to defend myself with but I see nothing. I take off one of my sandals, wave it at them, but they laugh at the sight of me in one sandal, in that tunic, the white cord around my waist. Then one of them yells the command. "*Salasso!*" and dives in to grab me. I beat him back repeatedly with the sandal. "Leave him alone," one of them says. "He's about to cry and then our godfather is going to get angry."

Their godfather is Federí, who is both respected and feared. At the mere thought of him, they sigh in resignation, yell a few obscenities, and slink off. I feel a hatred in my chest that's even greater than if they had humiliated me. My eyes sting, my heart is pounding in my ears. After a while, I go back into the room where everyone is dancing. It's chaos. They're dancing a cotillion, there's the polka, the waltz, the galop. Naturally, it's being directed by the dancer, who says funny things while calling out the sequences loud and clear, making everyone laugh. Even my father has joined in the fray with his usual exaggerated moves, calling out, "*Galop!*" My mother sits in her seat and looks on in amusement while everyone else has fun.

I go and sit down next to her, pulling my St. Cyrus tunic down over my knees as far as it will go. Next to her, I feel calmer. I reflect on something I will think about often in the future. It occurs to me that if I'm sitting there in silence, in this tunic, putting up with the music, the whooping and hollering, all this dancing, it is purely out of love for her. I am obedient, patient, and silent. I know full well that Rusinè is already suffering enough as it is, and I do not want to make it worse for her, I do not want to make a mistake that will make her suffer any more than she already is. It occurs to me that if she were to die, it would just be so much easier. There would be no one to hold me back. I could run away from home, join the navy as a deckhand, or the circus as a stable-boy, play the harmonica, and finally learn some new kinds of music.

For a long time I reflected on the fact that if Rusinè fell ill in 1953, she actually started to die after joyless evenings like my first communion party or the night her hair combs were burnt. I believed she suffered in agony for years and, for a long time, I carried—I still carry—the regret that I didn't realize it, that I had trained myself not to realize it.

In the months that followed, I lost all my interest in religious terminology. I resolved my problem with God by receiving communion one morning without going to confession first. Seeing that the *padreterno*, as my father continued to call him, didn't smite me with lightning, I deduced that his existence was just an ancient lie and I moved on. Instead, I concentrated on words related to common life. I became convinced that within words lies true suffering, and so I started to observe them carefully, filter them, slow down my perception of them. I trained myself to hear them as if at a distance, so that I could reduce my reaction to them to a bare minimum. In order for the filters that surrounded my each and every nerve to grow thick and strong, I learned to walk through life slowly, to move carefully through space, to live in distraction, in a state of rapture.

My father often looked over and asked with curiosity, "What are you thinking about, Mimí?" He always hoped that I would offer up some notion that would contrast with his own. Ad infinitum. "Nothing, Papà," I always said, and it was the truth. I wasn't thinking about anything. I was doing whatever it took to empty my brain, to chase away the words and beliefs that Federí had instilled in me over the years.

His words were the ones that had gotten stuck in my brain, they were the ones I tried hardest to erase. It was the obdurate task of a teenager. "If I manage to empty my brain," I thought to myself, "I won't be his prisoner anymore, I won't suffer anymore, I'll become invincible." Since I was certain that words represented the root of all torture, I tried both not to hear them (wouldn't it have been better not to have heard "Vain!" that night in June?) and to scratch them definitively away from the surface of the things they represented. I imagined a tree without "tree," a cloud without "cloud," a father without "father," a mother without "mother." I wanted to fade away until I was nothing more than an intimate sigh, a moan, a *gemito* of pleasure.

I actually managed to obtain decent results over the years. The sense of distraction that I applied to things transformed into indifference. My imperviousness to what was going on at home became a dominant character trait. I focused on courtesy, duty, and impassivity, shaping them into a screen behind which I hid my obsession with losing contact with my father and, consequently, my entire family.

And that is how I lost Rusinè. She was there, under my eyes, but I couldn't see her, nor did I want to see her. And then there was the fact that she was ever quieter, ever less present in the life of us boys. She went out little, she said, because the street gave her palpitations and made her feel dizzy. Her malaise grew more intense: despite Dr. Papa's suggested cure of the conception and birth of Nuccia, she had an even stronger breakdown. Each time she stuck her nose out of the house, it felt like she was choking, she couldn't breathe, had nausea, and was forced to stop at the first bar along the way to have a glass of mineral water with lemon and bicarbonate of soda. But she was fine, she insisted, she was a strong woman, she felt perfectly well.

At that point in time she still didn't show her age. Actually, she looked five or even ten years younger than she really was. She didn't have a single grey hair in her brown locks. Her Saracen skin was taut, she had no wrinkles. She sewed fashionable dresses for herself with affordable fabric and, whenever she had the chance, she'd dress up the way a child dresses up as an adult. "You gussy yourself up too much," my father grumbled, bothered by her efforts, but she never stopped focusing on her appearance, and continued to gussy herself up as much as she wanted.

Federí generally reacted sarcastically to her obsession with elegance. Over the years he developed a different notion of beauty, and it did not coincide with Rusinè's. For him, being beautiful meant an aggregation of positive qualities that he had observed in certain wives of businessmen who were also admirers of his work: good looks, professionally styled hair, demur behavior, a use of proper Italian, a smile, but not laughter. Women so well brought up they didn't even seem like they came from Naples. Beautiful city, but hell, the stink of shit from the sewers completely erased his desire to make and create.

Around the time they had a telephone installed in the house— a black device that looked like a giant beetle had been nailed to the wall in the hallway of our apartment on Corso Arnaldo Lucci—he started to nag his wife about the inadequacy of her accent. Sometimes he said it playfully, but sometimes he berated her. He'd hold the phone up to his ear. "*Pronto*," he'd say. "You have to say '*pronto*,' not just *pront'*!" He'd repeat his *pronto* clearly, elegantly, standing in a composed manner next to the device, articulating all the letters in the word. Then he'd mimic her *pront'*, shouting rambunctiously and gesticulating wildly with his hands, or making faces, the letter T suspended over the abyss of vulgarity.

How we answered the telephone was very important to him. Anybody might call: a gallerist, a professor of art, a painter, an amateur, and he didn't want to make a bad first impression. "I know how to fit into any setting whatsoever, and you don't," he said to Rusinè. Then he'd go on to show her, passing from humiliating her in a furious tone to expressing kindness, showing her how he could do all the accents from central and northern Italy. Most of all he enjoyed speaking and acting Tuscan. "Tuscan is the real Italian," he said, and then he'd turn to me and smugly and self-contentedly say in a Florentine accent, you speak so well because I created you in Florence, at Zio Peppino and Zia Nenella's house.

I couldn't stand it. And I couldn't stand him. It frightened me more to hear him speaking in that charming way, his mouth contorting to articulate that proper accent, than when he screamed in his usual working-class dialect. Although his unhappiness was audible in both, it seemed that his bitterness grew even more dangerous when he forced it into those genteel forms of his acquired dialect. So many words, and yet the resentment spilled over nonetheless, spilled over even when he turned to English, French, German, all the languages he knew fluently, he said. Foreign languages could open doors for him and allow him to exchange ideas with other artists from all the civilized nations of the world. He wished he could travel to Sweden, Norway, Denmark, Finland, Canada, and the United States. Long-legged blondes with slender thighs. He'd suddenly laugh heartily, amused by all the things he could do with foreign women. When he acted that way, my mother looked at him out of the corner of her eye, and pursed her lips as if to say, "You'd better watch yourself!" To which he'd reply by waving to the four of us boys with an over-the-top paternal gesture. "I'm thinking of them, Rusinè, not of me," he'd say, nodding and winking at us and letting us know: your father, kids, is always on the lookout.

I laughed, but there was really nothing funny about it. Zio Peppino di Firenze was probably right, years earlier, when he said that I didn't know how to have fun. As a kid, I was always sulky. I laughed and smiled but on the inside I nurtured only unkind sentiments. Always on the lookout: what an annoying allusion. It seemed even worse than the beatings he gave Rusinè. I laughed and smiled as if my face was not my own. Even my eyes and ears felt like they had lost all sensation. I didn't listen, I didn't see: it was all part of my strategy to anesthetize myself forever, at least if everything went according to plan.

Rusinè meanwhile saw and heard everything and this made me feel hostile toward her, too. I didn't want her to just accept his words and playful insinuations, as she had always done, in order to keep the peace at home. Since she seemed better than him, it made me angry that she didn't react. I was aware of her seductive beauty. When relatives and acquaintances saw her, they always exclaimed, "Lucky you to still have your youth and beauty." I wanted her to muster up courage from the consensus that surrounded her and say something terrible and definitive to her husband. It's hard to accept that the illness was already enlarging her spleen and eating away at her liver.

In March 1965, my grandmother died. Once, I remember, around the time of my first communion, I walked in on her in the kitchen. She was ably chopping parsley on a cutting board with a big knife, her thoughts elsewhere. "Promise me that when you die, if the otherworld exists, you'll let me know," I begged her. She, the person who had taught me my prayers as a child and the one person who had always taken it upon herself to worry about our faith when we were small, surprised me with her reply. "I already know that it doesn't exist. Basically, I'll become like this chopped parsley," she said in dialect. I looked down at the parsley and then went back to begging her until she agreed, amused. The years passed. First, the left side of her body was paralyzed, and then, one cold afternoon, she was suddenly struck with the final blow. I raised up all the protective shields that I had prepared. I allowed myself to be wounded only by the blood that ran from her nose and her icy cold forehead—an object—that I kissed, as was the custom. She did not tell me a single thing from beyond the grave. I therefore deduced that she had seen clearly: she was chopped parsley. To this day I am disgusted by that herb, how its greenish life-blood drained out of it beneath her swiftly moving blade.

What surprised me was the immensity of my father's grief. Their relationship had always been tense. Nannina never forgave Federí for his vulgar language, for the way he tortured her daughter, and for his doubting that her son Peppino was more handsome and better-mannered. "Peppino's a selfish bastard," he said to her practically every other day, reproaching her more or less explicitly that when he tied the knot with Rusinè he had also married her, since her son had dumped her, pure and simple. "In addition to being far more intelligent, I'm also more handsome than your son," he'd point out. "You were always ugly," she'd reply, and they'd go on squabbling, she'd laugh and turn bright red, and he'd get annoyed. But when she died, he truthfully grew sullen and sad; Federí hated all contact with death. But as soon as Nannina was buried, he started criticizing Peppino for being born stingy and for contributing little or nothing to the funeral expenses.

As for Rusinè, she mourned the death of her mother in a way that, accustomed as we were to her restrained behavior, surprised us all. She cried for days and nights on end, without stopping. Not long after, her skin turned ashen. Her eyes, stomach, hands, and ankles all swelled up and became puffy. No one could calm her, it was as if her whole body refused to accept the grief. The weeks passed and the well of tears dried up. But Rusinè never went back to looking the way she used to. Actually, she grew even more puffy, especially her belly. She also started coughing. It was not a deep cough, but a nagging, persistent hack which she herself, accustomed to Dr. Papa's diagnoses, defined as nervous. "I have a nervous cough," she learned to say.

None of us worried about it terribly. It was enough that she had stopped crying. Only her aunts, who came over to the house once in a while, mentioned it. "You're pregnant again, Rusinè," they'd say. "If only," she'd exclaim, shaking her head. My grandmother's sisters insisted. "Are you sure you're not pregnant? If you're not pregnant, then there's something else inside there. You'd better call the doctor." But my mother just shrugged. "It will pass," she said and then explained how it was better to wait it out than do battle with Federí, who was always busy with his painting and so forth. She knew how he was about things like that anyway. "You just want Dr. Papa to see you naked," he'd say.

As a result of waiting for the illness to pass, three months went by, June arrived. Slowly, day by day, the ten years that my mother had carefully kept at a distance came crashing down over her, with some extra ones that she didn't deserve at all. Overnight, she went from looking thirty to middle-aged. None of her skirts fit her any more, her legs grew thick, her eyes turned yellow. It was this last transformation that led her to exasperation. One day, while her husband was painting, she went up to him. "I need to see a specialist, I don't think Dr. Papa is enough."

In those years, even more than the preceding ones, Federí saw his wife as one of the biggest ball-busters that the *padreterno* could have sent his way. He never had time for his own painting, he was overwhelmed by the Parisian street scenes, and he had to go to work on the railroad. Hoping to make even more money, he had enrolled Geppe's help, who showed an inclination for painting. My brother came home from school and before he even finished lunch, he'd be sitting at the easel, laying the foundation for the Utrillos, while my father was still at the station. For hours on end, he painted wet cobblestones, people out strolling, skies heavy with rain, famous squares. He worked ceaselessly, without even making time for his homework for the following day. When Federí came home, exhausted from his job on the railroad, he didn't even say good evening and went straight away to his easel. He gave a few masterful brushstrokes to conclude what Geppe had started and would either pick up the strands of an argument with his wife where they had left off, or start a new one, as if for company. His wife simply didn't understand that the career of a great artist was going up in smoke. His wife couldn't even begin to comprehend the composition problems that haunted him. His wife lacked all sensitivity for the truly important questions in life: the art world was changing. Some shithead artist by the name of Manzoni had exhibited both his breath and his shit in Milan, and there were other assholes out there, like Burri, Fontana, and

Vedova, who didn't even know how to hold a brush but thought they were better than everyone. Rusinè listened to him rant for as long as she could. She didn't say a word. Then she ran into his studio and yelled at him. "So, who's forcing you to do the street scenes of Paris? Me? You're the one who wants to do them!" Or else she'd say bitterly, "Can't you see that Geppe is exhausted? Can't you see that he's neglecting his schoolwork?" Or else she'd complain, "I don't feel so well, there's something heavy inside me. I just don't know what it is." Comments like that were a green light for Federí to begin screaming: this life of shit, quit busting my balls, basta, I'm done, I'm leaving, I'm going to Paris, going to Finland. This went on for years and years. I can add no details or color, I wouldn't know where to find them. By then, I had blinded myself, I was deaf to all words, I had thrown away my pocketknife, I had grown up. I was on my own path and focused on avoiding being drawn in to my parents' troubles at home. Sometimes I went out early in the day and only came back at two o'clock the following morning. "Who gives a fuck," I thought.

And then one day, my mother decided that she couldn't go on any longer; she walked into my father's studio and demanded a doctor, and one that wouldn't say, "Women are only happy when they're pregnant." She'd had enough babies, miscarriages, stillbirths. Basta. This swelling, she murmured, is something else.

There was a pause. It lasted seconds, days. My father tried to make light of it, inventing little ditties and reassuring her, saying things like, "You look fantastic, I've never seen you look so good." She broke down crying, said it wasn't true, that she didn't feel well at all. After some hesitation, old Dr. Papa was called, with all the usual tension that accompanied an emergency doctor's visit: the silences, the embarrassment, the concern they were throwing away their money.

Dr. Papa was thorough. He frowned and said that Rusinè should see a liver specialist immediately. He said it with such gravity that Federí himself went pale and started to despair.

"Mother of God, what's going on? What did I do wrong? What am I being punished for?" The doctor calmed him down and gave him the name of a professor of medicine, an important head physician who would definitely know what to do.

An appointment was scheduled and my parents went to see the expert. Of course my father clarified immediately that he was a famous painter and he talked about his paintings and how much they were worth on the market, promising to give the doctor one. In the meantime, the physician examined my mother—it took only a matter of minutes—and said she needed to be admitted to the Ospedale Gesú e Maria for a series of tests. Rusinè went home in a state of distraction. She quickly filled a valise with some of her things and went to be "admitted," as they say.

Thirty-four years after my mother's death, and one year after that of my father, I decided to go back and revisit the hospital. I set out climbing the Tarsia steps the same way I often did in the summer of 1965. Every so often I stopped to catch my breath and turned around to look at the sea and sky. There was the smell of garbage decomposing in the sun, a smell that I continue to associate with illness. The city, its heavy police presence making it seem so clean and pure along Via Caraccioli, Via Partenope, all the way to Piazza Plebiscito—with Vesuvius resting on the surface of the water, people out walking or jogging despite the heat, the sea staring back at all the mammoth buildings constructed on spec, a few fishermen slicing the air with their lines, kids playing hooky from school, stray cats wandering around the whitish embankment blocks—went back to showing its true colors when I turned down Via Toledo and crossed Pignasecca market, with its stands of fruit, live fish, hot pizzas, and fresh bread; the vendors hawking their wares in their seductive dialect, interrupted only by the deafening sirens of ambulances headed to Ospedale Pellegrini. This is a city of disconnects, where life is good if you're strong enough to push and shove (as the saying goes, "Watch out or I'll send you to Pellegrini"), but difficult for newborns, the elderly, disabled, and ill, where silence is available only to those who have money for double-glazed windows, where new shops appear like psychedelic wounds in ancient buildings with peeling paint, where music from every corner of the globe as well as local tremolo tunes are all played at the highest volume for the tumultuous crowds and the slowly roving clusters of drifters.

I continued up to Via Cotugno, to the piazza where the Gesú e Maria hospital was located. As I went, step after step, I definitively pushed away the boulder from the anguish of that period, I felt all the malaise that Naples brings me, the panic attacks that come over me right after I realize that I love it, that I miss it, that I want to move back here. "What illnesses do they treat in this hospital?" I asked a lady who was buying some fruit, but only because I felt like talking. "Infectious diseases," she replied, revealing that she shared my desire for conversation. "My father was here in 1972," she went on to say, "They thought he had hepatitis. He ended up not having it but it was a miracle he didn't get it while he was there." Federí said almost the same thing a few days after my mother was admitted. He came home furious, saying that Gesú e Maria was a bordello, that men walked freely over to the women's ward, and that women walked over to the men's ward, that the patients pissed in the halls in order to avoid the swamp of shit and blood that covered the floor of the bathrooms, that the level of hygiene was so bad that, if they didn't find a solution immediately, Rusinè, who was as healthy as a horse, would end up getting seriously ill.

He looked depressed, pale, and had dark puffy circles under his eyes. He was convinced that some jealous person had cast an evil eye on him and augured that he waste all his money on doctors and medicine. But who gives a fuck, he exclaimed: he wouldn't leave his wife in that open ward one minute longer. And, as usual, he went over the top. He turned the house upside down, pulled out all the money that he had hidden in books, under floor tiles, in crates full of various trappings, on top of the wardrobe in his bedroom. All the money he had earned by painting Parisian street scenes. He counted it all up and made arrangements for Rusinè to have a private room. "Isn't that better?" he asked in order to hear her pleased reply.

At that point he began scheming how to take off as much time as possible from work on the railroad. And, even more surprising, he stopped painting: no Parisian street scenes, none of his own art, nothing. He spent all his free time with his wife, even sleeping by her side. Of course he was far from serene: he talked and talked and talked. He talked to the other patients, to the nurses, to the orderlies. He dumped even more words than he usually used onto that fragile and unsteady world. Whenever he saw a doctor or head physician, he'd give them drawings, watercolors, tempera, oil paintings, always reminding them that those were valuable objects, worth not tens but hundreds of thousands of lire, all work that was destined to increase in value.

When he felt a little glum, he lay down on the bed next to Rusinè and either read detective novels (he adored detective novels) or sketched in a graph-paper notebook. Sometimes he drew his wife, even though she waved him away. I recall only one of those drawings: her face is puffy, her gaze is empty. There was nothing of how she tried to appear to us, convinced she would heal, careful about not seeming depressed, often even acting cheerful. He knew how to catch the desperation in her face, it was as if he had drawn her when her thoughts were elsewhere, when she no longer had any control over her gaze, her expression.

I never liked that drawing of her. It had the effect of erasing from my memory all the efforts she went to in order to believe in the possibility of healing: her friendships with other patients, the way she made the hospital room seem like a vacation resort, how she welcomed doctors as if they were paying her a courtesy visit. My father's pen managed to catch her abandonment to the illness, her awareness that there was a flaw in life.

That was a phrase she had often used while working as a seamstress: there was a flaw. She had used it when clients came to see her on Via Gemito to try on the dresses she made for them. "It's falling strangely here," Signorina Pagnano would say, looking at herself in the bedroom mirror and she, with pins between her lips, would tug the fabric this way and that, try and fix it, but was always forced to give up. "Yes, there's a flaw," she'd admit sadly. Then she'd accompany Signorina Pagnano out, come back into the kitchen of the house on Via Gemito, throw the outfit on the table, and begin to unstitch it, explaining why to her mother and her two apprentices, one blonde and the other brunette. "There's a flaw at the shoulder," she'd say, her face taking on the same expression as in the drawing. Not being able to talk to her about it, over the years I reflected that she must have thought about death like a seamstress. Dying was a flaw. There was a flaw in the human body, as if the body were a robe that doesn't fit right, a metaphor used even by the Greeks. Tight across the belly. A spleen that weighed three kilos. An atrophying liver. Intraperitoneal leakage.

The entire city started to seem flawed to me, and at some point between July and August I considered leaving it as fast as I could. I got around by foot, I didn't want to spend money on transportation, I had none to spare. Depending on how the day played out, my reference points were either Pizza Mazzini or Piazza Dante. I'd either run or walk swiftly to the hospital. When I got to the entrance to the Ospedale Clinico, I always felt a sense of repulsion come over me. I didn't like the yellowish color of the façade, the peeling paint around the doorway. I counted the steps: first two and then eleven. The inner courtyard garden was crowded, like a jungle, full of exotic plants, maybe because they cured tropical illnesses there. The hallways were grimy with dirt, lined with handrails on either side, and the whitish ceilings were high and vaulted.

When I walked in, I'd always find my mother in bed. From

the open window came the sound of drilling, metal on lava stone, works in progress. Hello, hi, ciao, and then we didn't know what else to say to each other, but it was never embarrassing: we had the warmth of familiarity. Only once did she whisper, "I know I'm going to die," and then break into tears. The rest of her comments were things like, "Take this dish home, remember to ask Zia Nenella to wash my robe, keep an eye on your father, don't let him act crazy."

One day she had swollen legs and a big belly, the next day they gave her a medicine that caused her to expel all the fluids, which gave her the illusion that she was better. One afternoon she fell asleep, and I fell asleep next to her. Suddenly I woke up to see her sitting on the edge of the bed, her eyes bright, gesturing animatedly. She was trying to put on her slipper but heel first. She tried over and over. "Don't worry, I know I'm doing it wrong," she said with a laugh. But she didn't know a thing, she didn't know where she was or the time of day, she couldn't do everyday gestures. I helped her put on her slippers and, as soon as she stood up, she started pacing back and forth in the room, wringing her hands. She spoke in a flurry, angry about a new medicine they had given her the night before. "It was bad for me, I know it," she kept saying.

Some days she showed great faith in the doctors, especially in one young and particularly conscientious doctor who took care of her with absolute dedication; on other days, when she had a relapse after a period of improvement, she despaired. When that happened, the doctors scolded her. "Signora, you have to work with us," they said. But it was unfair of them to say that because she worked hard with them, she let them do almost anything to her without saying a thing. At one point they even mentioned an operation that might resolve the whole problem, but it was only performed in England. For a while, that's all she and Federí talked about. It almost seemed like they were planning a holiday. He practiced his English on her. "We'll go to Trafalgar Square," he'd say. But then nothing came of it. The spleen needs to be taken out in time, or so I read in an old medical book which I found one July morning in the library. Once cirrhosis has set in, it's too late.

In early October, despite her jaundiced skin tone, Rusinè's shape went back to normal. They released her from the hospital. The first thing she did was get carefully dressed and go thank St. Cyrus for healing her. We all went with her; we might even have gone to the church in Portici, where I was bitterly reminded of my first communion dressed as a monk. I watched her as she prayed, so elegant, even after the experience of being ill. That's when I realized that the vow she made in exchange for Geppe, which also covered me, was actually her own sacrifice of the festive occasion. By dressing us in those tunics, she deprived herself of the pleasure of creating clothes for us for that special event. Moments such as those, when she could freely design and sew beautiful outfits for either us or her, were rare and deeply precious to her. This, I realized, reflecting on it at length over the years, was the sacrifice she made in exchange for Geppe's good health.

After she prayed, we went home. She found it terribly messy and immediately started cleaning each of the rooms, from top to bottom. She prepared a festive lunch of pheasant, an exotic dish, cooked in a Tuscan style to please my father. Later that afternoon she felt ill and had to lie down. The young doctor from Gesú e Maria rushed over and stuck her full of needles; she was already covered in bruises from all the injections. The doctor sat her up in bed and tried to get her to drink a yellow liquid. "That's right, signora, there you go, now come sit a tiny bit closer," he said. Suddenly, she looked at him as if she had suddenly woken up and, to prove that she wanted to work with him and save herself, she slid quickly all the way across the mattress, to the foot of the bed. "Is that good? Did I do good?" she asked in dialect.

She fell into a coma. Relatives rushed over. Federí cried and wailed in desperation, but no one paid him any attention. Most people thought, and some even said as much, "You could have been more careful." Eventually, he sat down on the bed next to his dying wife and grabbed her hand. "Rusinè, are you sure you love me?" he asked her. "If you've always loved me, squeeze my finger," he said over and over.

She couldn't see or hear a thing, but Federí, with his usual stubborn manner didn't give up, he wanted to believe that she could still hear his voice. Later he said that not only did she squeeze his finger, but she also smiled at him, to soothe him. I was there—I tried several times to write about it, first with disdain for how pathetic it was, then with moving melancholy, then with tenderness, always trying to erase the growing sense of aggravation I felt—and in the months that ensued, until he forgot about it, he often asked me for confirmation. "She squeezed my finger, didn't she?" Yes, I always nodded. Yes.

My mother died on October 8 without ever regaining consciousness.

Federí reacted to her death in his usual blustery manner. To begin with, he severed all connections with Rusinè's relatives, who stopped being polite from one day to the next and, now that their sister or niece was dead, had no intention of tolerating his insults and offenses any further. From his end, and in no uncertain terms, Federí told Rusinè's aunts, who had helped us survive on a day-to-day basis during Rusinè's hospitalization and even tried to help us afterward, that they were major ballbusters, they had *cacato il cazzo*—and here any number of foul obscenities in dialect could be added—and that, in short, gone were the days when they could screw him out of any money he had worked hard to earn so they could buy cars or apartments for themselves and their shit-shoveling husbands. Evidently, he realized that they accused him of neglecting his wife and consequently he erased them all from his life. When he was an elderly man he even cut them out of family photos.

After that, he proceeded to rage against his own relatives. First he turned to them for help—he still had two young children and needed to move forward—but soon they were arguing. It must've felt to him as though he'd been flung back into his awful childhood and adolescence. He went back to feeling neglected and unaccepted; it was as if they refused to see him the way that he saw himself, just like when he was a child, he yelled. He felt belittled, fettered, exploited, swindled. In other words, it ended badly with his family, too, even though he had always been generous with his compliments, even though he always said they were intelligent and sensitive, even though he had lavished attention on them, which was clearly a waste of his precious energies.

Every argument and fight he had, it should be mentioned, fortified him. Actually, in the months following her death, he frequently asked the young doctor who took care of Rusinè to perform checkups on him, to ascertain if he had any problems with his liver, and he forced all of us to do the same; he was in perfect shape, his blood boiled through him normally, he wanted to get back to his work. We were all in good health, and yet we got into the habit of swilling a tablespoon of Amaro Medicinale Giuliani after every meal to protect us against possible liver disease. We were each on our own path. We left the house in total chaos every morning and halfheartedly straightened up at night. Naturally, our father didn't do a thing except, as he said, make money for the family. Not long after, despite the perpetual mess, he went back to painting, he started meeting up with critics and painters again, and he returned to obsessing about his destiny as he perceived it. And in no time, it seemed natural to him that we got by thanks to help from Geppe, Toni, and even from Walter, who had the revolting task of going through our horribly filthy clothes and sticking them in the washing machine. As for me, I had trained myself well.

I didn't care about anything or anyone, I had been oblivious since long before Rusinè's death.

Only in the evening, before sitting down at the easel for a good part of the night in that desolate apartment on Corso Arnaldo Lucci, Federí grew somewhat melancholic. His wife was everywhere—behind the doors, in shadowy corners, inside the wardrobe—and with his usual wanton verbosity he looked for a way to soothe her, help her find a definitive resting spot in his associations and references and general considerations. He pondered her in his head and exorcised her by talking non-stop. He wanted to minimize her dying to a more general idea of death, to a feeling that he had always had. He dug into his remotest memories. "When I was young, dying meant losing," he said. Losing in the sense of defeat. And then he'd talk about Don Carmine, the father of Don Federico the cop who was married to Donna Luisella. Don Carmine had been a soldier in World War I and, to explain the battles he had survived to Federí, he'd take a big sheet of paper and draw a mountain range and the positions of the cannons on them. Then he'd stick his finger in his mouth, and make a popping noise to represent the exploding cannon shots. With each explosion, he made an x on the piece of paper, representing the dead soldiers and the destroyed cannons. "The Austrians are here, the Italians are here," he'd say. And then he'd count up the crosses, and whoever had the most lost the battle.

Dying, losing. "I always thought of dying like losing," he'd say. And in the meantime, he'd start to recall his first experiences with death. There was Don Carmine, for example, who suddenly vanished. He poisoned himself, no one knew why, by drinking water into which he had dissolved the phosphorus on Swedish matches. That's what Fdrí, little Fdrí, had heard the adults say anyway. A little poison every day. Federí dipped into the dregs of his childhood with a bottle of wine at his side, finding hidden links between disparate facts, and inventing them when he couldn't find any.

At a certain point he found his way: he began to reflect on the tragic reoccurrence of the name Rosa in his life both as a man and an artist. First, there was the beautiful Rosina, who had thrown herself off the fifth floor because of a broken heart. Then there was Rose Fleury, who, following his departure from Menton, had died in some obscure way. And then there was the first funeral of his life, an indelible memory, when a fifteen-year-old girl, who lived on the same landing as Nonna Funzella, died. She was a pretty and much-loved girl; her funeral was like a party. During the wake, they served hot chocolate in porcelain cups and biscuits on a silver tray. Then they handed out sugared almond confetti, and even threw them off the balconies when the white funeral carriage came down Via Casanova. A band accompanied the cortege and played "Palummella, zomp'e vola." Federí could still hear that music in his head, and even wrote about the funeral in his memoirs. Naturally, the girl was named Rusinèlla.

The recurrence of that name, he explained, was a sign of his predestination for widowhood. A sign, just like the dates of his birth, like the blazing lanterns from the feast of St. Anthony. But at this point, I wasn't listening anymore, at the very most I pretended to listen. I was getting ready to move out, to get married by year's end despite my young age, to write my own personal history, which I felt I had every right to without the least bit of guilt. Only many years later did I start to pay a bit of attention to him again; evidently I had to make my own mistakes first.

I left home and, with great relief, left his new collection of stories behind. These were stories of rebirth, as if the death of Rusinè hadn't been the end of his wife's life, but rather a turning point in his own. There were new adventures, travels, love stories, and of course painting. "The Sublime Force," he used to say when he was an elderly man, nearing eighty, "wrote my life story page after page, moment by moment, through ups and downs, and shall even direct the moment when I will return unto the shadows whence I came." His tone and language became more

aulic when he broached the subject of his mortality. He reasoned
in terms of cycles, darkness, and light. It was perfectly clear that
he wanted nothing to do with the shades but, if he was forced to
descend into their midst, he counted on the fact that, thanks to a
stratagem inherent in the Limitless Energy of the Universe, he'd
soon come back into the light and continue to paint.

Even when Rusinè was still alive, he had become a follower
of Roma, a newspaper published by shipping magnate Achille
Lauro, and read by monarchists and fascists. In fact, he often
met with Piero Girace, the art critic for the daily. He saw this
as an advancement of his career: Girace wrote articles and published books, he had friends who debated and discussed important topics, he talked to me about them. Keenly aware of my
condition as a graphomaniac, Federí filled up my own silences
with his overflowing cascade of words, managing on more than
one occasion and thanks to his connections, to have a few of
my pieces published. "You have to let people hear your voice,"
he'd say emphatically. He was so angry about the ugly turn that
the art world had taken that he tried to enroll me in his campaign. "Mimí, we have to write something about those bastards,"
he'd say, slapping the back of his hand against the pages of the
Mattino, whose articles made him both ferociously angry and
worried. The worst of the critics and artists were, in his opinion,
the ones who hid their idiocies behind complicated words. What
the fuck is tachism? What the hell is informalism, action painting,
and nuclear art? Those colorful blobs of shit are nothing more
than paint slapped on the canvas, like cement by a builder. And
collage? Now even collage is considered art? He did collages
when he was three years old, on Funzella's balcony! He painted
with materials that he found lying around the house. Life is what
you see in front of you, not all that babble about fluidity *di questo
cazzo*, or pulsations *di questo cazzo*, or the space of spatiality shit.
He sighed. He got depressed. He wondered out loud, "What's
going to last? All this crap or something like *The Drinkers*?" and I

had to reply, *The Drinkers*. In the meantime he blended together incommensurate readings, he generated rage and multiplied his fury by drawing on various sources. For example, he read things by Filiberto Menna and exclaimed sarcastically, "Hell's bells, now how about that?" Or he sneered and muttered: unformed form, deformed form, informed form, forming the forms. Or he looked desolately at all art work that wasn't figurative and exclaimed, "I knew how to make shit like this back when I was a kid playing by the river in Reggio Calabria!" But unfortunately for me, he went on to add, I never had anyone like Filiberto Menna to write inanities about my inanities. That's just how art is today, he whined, like the Cat and the Fox: the Cat draws a line and the Fox says this line is rich in pulsating flow and subjective self-reflection.

He laughed bitterly but also struggled to understand. He spent entire nights trying to understand. Or else he wandered around the city with Girace. I saw him fall head over heels for anyone who said they liked his painting. He coupled up with or buddied around with or mingled with people and then broke off with them in a matter of days. At one point, he wound up in a movement called *Tradition and Reality*, which had been founded by the art critic of *Roma*. But soon there was bad blood: the movement, he said, was just a bunch of shitheads. What else could he do? Exhibition, competitions. He listed the names of people on the juries and compared it with the people who won the prizes. "Here's how it works: I award you or a friend of yours today, and you award me or a friend of mine tomorrow." He came to his grand conclusion: "If you're out of the circle, you're screwed."

We saw each other every so often, from the late 1960s to the late 1970s, but we never agreed on anything. He presented his ideas to me about everything—they didn't seem like his, more like ideas he had assimilated during the fascist period—and I merely replied, no. If he came to my house and crossed paths with some of my politically minded friends, he was thrilled, and would go to great lengths to win them over with his speeches about his militant period and the consequent letdowns. "What a fascinating man your father is," they even said sometimes. "When did he leave the PCI? After the events in Hungary?" they'd ask. I couldn't even say for sure that he had been a member of the PCI and so I'd just mumble, "I think so."

Usually, though, Federí had to settle for me as his only in-terlocutor. He got angry, then went back to being earnest, then flared up again, then apologized. He simply could not get his head around our divergent political and cultural outlooks. Once, before leaving, he turned to me and whispered, "Get out while you can, Mimí; you have no idea what's going to happen in Italy." I replied that I knew perfectly well. I was an adult but I still dreamed like a child. I imagined that soon we'd take to the streets: my father on one side, me on the other; him, all tradition and reality and me, avant-garde and revolution. It seemed like the perfect grand finale for our history and all its muted conflicts.

That finale never came to pass, however. Even the old ten-sions faded. In the 1980s and 1990s, he started to say that we had always been in perfect agreement: right or left, it's all the same shit, only the left read more books and was more intelligent. He held onto that position until his death. About everything else, he continued to complain. "What the hell is art after Fontana and Manzoni?" he asked. And since I never replied, he answered his own question, counting on his fingers. "Art is: idiotic govern-ment ministers, pandering undersecretaries, faggot art critics, and bisexual gallery owners. The great artist is no longer neces-sary; all it takes is some shithead to smear paint on a canvas." But meanwhile, he continued to paint: illustrations of his philosophi-cal beliefs à la Hausmann; horses and jockeys with a new kind of dynamism, galloping toward the finish line; a Leda with a swan between her legs; a Danae receiving not a shower of gold but a stream of piss from the wreck of a spaceship; detailed images of the Apocalypse. "Hey, what do you think of this?" he'd ask when I went to visit him. "Nice," I'd reply. "Nice, not nice, who gives a fuck," he'd say proudly. "The main thing is that I kept on painting." And then suddenly he'd cheer up. "I was always a free man," he'd say proudly. "I burped in everyone's faces."

But he was terribly pleased when, all of a sudden, from the depths of his past in Naples, his participation in the Gruppo Sud resurfaced. It was the second half of 1947, he said. Via dei Mille, at the house of Mario Cortiello, the painter. That's where Gruppo Sud and the magazine *Sud* was born. "I wasn't at the meeting," he said bitterly. It was all the railroad's fault: he was on a night shift, it always happened like that when important events took place. Everyone else was there (Ricci, De Stefano, Raffaelle Lippi) but not him. However, he did take part in a few Gruppo Sud exhibitions. And one of them, the final show, which took place at the Galleria Blu di Prussia in 1948, had even left an indelible trace in one of his artworks, a work of perfect—"Perfect, I tell you, Mimí!"—composition. It was a painting on canvas entitled, to no great surprise, *Mostra del Gruppo Sud al Blu di Prussia*. He must have forgotten entirely about the painting because he never mentioned it in his stories. But then, in 1991, an exhibition was organized in Naples to celebrate the Gruppo Sud, and that painting of his was shown together with works by other artists from those days; that's when *Mostra del Gruppo Sud al Blu di Prussia* became important to him. He went on to talk about it often and with great satisfaction, turning to the image in the catalog to help him remember. "I chose to represent," he explained, "Raffaello Causi talking to De Stefano, Carlo Barbieri contemplating a work of art by Renato De Fusco, Paolo Ricci in the center with his red kerchief and defensive walking stick, and Raffaelle Lippi sitting in a corner next to the entrance of the gallery, looking at two of his paintings: a building in ruins and the portrait of Anna Maria Ortese." Fuck, he exclaimed, what a piece of work: none of those painters could have ever created something like that, much less think of it. Lippi, for example. For fuck's sake. Old Lippi only painted ruins and dead cats. And that portrait of Anna Maria Ortese. She was a good-looking woman and yet Lippi managed to deform her face. What more was there to say? "But it's not important," he'd say. Time had passed, he was talking just for the sake of talking, without acrimony. Lippi was a decent painter, De Stefano was decent, everyone was decent. He doled out praise, felt satisfied, said he was no longer angry with any of them. All the envy and jealousy and cruelty they had shown him was all a fog now. Or almost. Even though he tried hard to speak in the tone of a detached sage, the waves of anger surged up now and then. "That time, for example, at the Salvator Rosa," he recalled. He had shown some of his paintings of Finnish landscapes there, at the most important Neapolitan gallery. Good stuff, done after Rusinè's death, when he traveled to Finland to paint and revel in the beautiful Finnish women. Unfortunately, Nazzaro the painter, thinking that Federí wasn't within listening distance, said cruelly to someone, "Would you look at Federí! What a blowhard: he just wants to show everyone that he went to Finland." Can you believe it? Without even considering for a second that he might be less than a meter away, inside a small closet, and that he could hear everything. "Just to show you what kinds of things I had to put up with," he pointed out bitterly. He wanted to run out and punch Nazzaro in the face. "But I didn't," he said gently and slowly. "First of all because I was busy banging a beautiful young painter in the closet; and secondly, because it's all water under the bridge, Mimí, you need to let bygones be bygones. Who is Nazzaro, now? A shadow, just like all the rest of them."

He scowled with hatred and went back to leafing through the massive catalog of the Gruppo Sud exhibition. He rapped the page where his work appeared. "I suppose I'm part of art history now, kid. I guess it was destiny," he said energetically and

446 · DOMENICO STARNONE

yet without conviction. Yes, Papà, I replied while asking myself, what destiny? He did it all on his own, with words and deeds, thanks to his obsession with his talent, thanks to his stubbornness, because of his unshakeable desire to persist. He went to efforts that left me agape, like a child, like the time I saw the peacock next to the vanity table, or when he called on me to pretend to pour water from a demijohn, or even back in the days of Nunzia when I used to think, "I hate my father," and could never shake that thought, could never reshape it into some reassuring proportion that would have calmed me down.

Was it three months or a year after the first communion party? Or was it two days? Or was it one week? I accept the dates my father offers up, whether true or invented; I don't trust my own. And so, once more I am obliged to write "at a certain point" or "some amount of time later" or "in those days."

In those days I used to get up early in the morning, earlier than usual, and run to the metro station because I knew exactly what time the train passed that Nunzia took to go to school. This was another kind of rendezvous that I created for myself without telling her. I wanted to see her behind the glass, rap on it with my knuckles, and say hello before running off to school myself. With my hair still messy, lost in my thoughts and the crowd of commuters, all I hoped for was someone to shove me or insult me so that I could pull out my knife and stab them.

For a while I managed to see her every day and say hello. Once she even opened the window and said, "Aren't you going to school?" In order to seem tough, I said no. The train pulled out and I didn't see her for a few days. Then I heard the rumor. They had put the dancer in prison. Nunzia's father had reported him for abuse of a minor. The dance parties were over.

A fiery feeling in my stomach and chest was snuffed out, but I didn't react. From everything that I heard, I remember only one comment. I believe it was something that Zia Nenella said to

Rusinè in dialect. "Apparently, the girl was always bright red in the face when she came out of her uncle's house." Now that I'm writing about it, I imagine Nunzia's face, her dark hair and fair skin, I see her turn bright red; I even see the beads of sweat on her upper lip as she walks out of the building where her uncle used to live. I chased away everything else: words, people's faces, actual facts, using the technique that I was perfecting at the time.

For days on end, I continued to have one, single fear: that my father would say something about that scandalous turn of events. I was scared that at lunch or dinner he'd look meaningfully at my mother and say something like, "See, I told you, didn't I?" He would never have stopped there, he would've reminded us in detail what he had always said, that the dancer was a piece-of-shit bastard, and that you could see straight away that his niece was going to grow up to be a spittoon of a woman. Then he would have commended himself for his painterly gaze, how he could see clearer than others, beyond appearances. That's exactly why he hadn't wanted his wife to dance with that bastard.

I ate with my head bowed, heart in my throat. I felt his eyes on me. Now he's going to say something, I thought. I didn't want to hear his voice, I couldn't accept him boasting about being right. I knew that if he managed to hook me and lead me down the slippery slope of his words, I would have to accept them, that there was no way out. The dancer, Nunzia. I was wounded, but I struggled to find reasons. I didn't know what they would be and I was worried about what my mother's relatives were saying. I didn't want them to chuckle and laugh vulgarly, I just wanted them to sigh, as if to say, oh, the things people do. I wanted to sigh along with them. I felt too exposed, I risked feeling hatred and repulsion, and sighing seemed the best way out. My father's way would be odious to me. I felt that one single word from Federí about the situation would reinforce all the words he had said in the past, and consequently his actions, his suspicions, and doubts about Rusinè, even about the shadowy threat of that poet who

had come to Via Gemito with his book. I could hear him screaming at my mother that June night, I could smell the smoke from
the burning hair combs. Words reinforce other words. You work
hard to erase one, others arrive. I didn't know how to handle it.
I wanted to eliminate "my father" from my father in order not
to hear him anymore, to consider him merely as a sentient being,
perceive of him as some kind of reptile, and, in so doing, protect my feelings and that contemptible story about Nunzia. But
sometimes it seemed meaningless: there were too many words,
he kept speaking, others kept talking, I couldn't scrape away the
film of meaning forever. All I could do was clench the knife in my
pocket. Words, I feared, would come anyway. Language wants to
be spoken. I could only kill and accept the verbs that would follow: those that were thought, those that were uttered, and those
that were unspeakable.

That's how I lived. In a state of confusion. One day I was
ready to explode, howling wildly and crying, and the next day
I was shut inside the silence of detailed and complex strategies.
Until one day—I might have been sitting in a room in the apartment on Corso Arnaldo Lucci, staring into space, or on the sixth
floor balcony that looked down on the noisy street below—my
father, seeing me distracted, asked me with light irony, "What
are you thinking about, Mimí?"

I was startled. I had the feeling that the moment had arrived.
I grabbed the knife in my pocket. He was going to start in with
Nunzia, a spittoon, the dancer, that sonofabitch piece of shit, I
hope he dies. But, instead, he said something else. "Everything
passes, kid," he said gently. I liked those words. They were unexpected and, on that particular occasion, they soothed me. Of
course, what he meant by them, according to his way of looking at things was that everything passes, and it will all get better
than what it once was. One door closes, and a bigger one opens.
Instead, I took his "Everything passes" the way I needed it at
that time. Everything passes; nothing begins anew. Nothing with

me in the role of firstborn, that is. For my wellbeing and for his own.

After my father died, I thought of him much more than when he was alive. Sometimes I thought about looking for all his paintings. Then I scaled back that project to finding only the ones that I remembered well and that had been meaningful to me. Other times I thought about clarifying his relationship with my mother, and the language that he used to talk about women in general. And still other times, I felt that old hatred from adolescence come roaring to life inside my chest: my throat would constrict, I wanted to list every single thing he had yelled, the things he boasted about, his acts of violence.

When I closed my eyes, I saw him the way he was laid out in the viewing room at the hospital in Luino, unnaturally dressed as if for a party in a dark suit and white shirt, his face waxen, his mustache droopy, his closed mouth downturned above his chin like a rainbow deprived of color. Like a Turk, I thought. The kind that arrived on the shores of Chiaia five centuries ago on ships crowded with warriors in the middle of the night, women running and screaming, some barefoot, others naked. He had nothing of the northern princes that he imagined were his forefathers. No, he was the descendant of oriental pirates, a bold corsair who had recently died, the pride of the Mediterranean, artfully sculpted, the single fold of skin in his neck carved with great precision.

Then that image faded and the one of the man I knew returned to me. Sometimes, while I was reading or watching the TV, I'd suddenly see him and Rusinè looking out of a hotel window in Venice. He'd just won the Positano prize for his famous work, *The Drinkers*. Intending to celebrate the good news—or maybe to pay me back for posing for him and modeling the figure of the boy who poured water?—he gave me the gift of a watch that had a cowboy on its face and a pistol as a second hand. What's more, he brought me with him on a trip to Venice—him, my mother, and me—happily squandering the money, giving in to all pleasures, the sea, that city on the water, a newspaper stand.

I saw the newspaper stand better than anything else. I stood there, without moving, studying the covers of the comics when suddenly, the hotel window opened, and Rusinè appeared and waved to me. Then he, his arm around her shoulder, looked out and shouted down at me in a Venetian accent, "Don't move, you hear?" Our agreement was that I had to stay and look at the comics and figurines until they told me that I could come back up. Then they both waved goodbye, Federí said something amusing in Rusinè's ear, and the window closed, leaving me alone in the little square. When it reopened, time had passed. He was now old and I was getting old, too. "Remember Venice?" he asked me in a confidential tone. "Remember how your mother and I sent you to look at the comic books?" Of course I remembered. And then he'd look at me with a malicious glint in his eyes. "Mimí, I was always on the lookout."

Images and images pile up, but my favorites are the ones that come back to me suddenly, never before resurrected. Moments that, if Federí and Rusinè were alive and if I could relay them to them, they'd both have puzzled looks on their faces as if those weren't really scenes from their lives. Unimportant moments, bathed in a happy light that colors them without giving them actual colors, like in dreams. The time, for example, when Federí comes back from work with a sunburnt face. "Did you go to work or did you spend the day at the beach?" my mother asks him with a laugh. "Beach? What beach, Rusinè?" he replies, also laughing. He swears that he was at the railroad station the whole day and only during his break did he spend a little bit of time painting in the sunshine. But she doesn't believe him. She wants to see if his shoulders are burnt, too. "Show me," she says and grabs his arm, puts her arm around his neck and pulls him close, yanks open his shirt to look.

I can see them now. It's one of their games. We kids aren't part of it but we enjoy it anyway. Federí pretends to flee, my mother chases after him. "You went to the beach! I know it, you went for a swim!" she cries out. "What're you talking about? Look!" he says and pulls off his shirt, but it's hard to tell if his shoulders are red from the sun or just pink from all her grabbing and pulling. "Let me see if you taste salty," Rusinè says in dialect, holding onto him tightly because he wants to run off again. She licks his arm and then his shoulder. "See? You're salty," she shouts triumphantly. At this point Federí licks his arm too, puzzled. "I'm not salty," he says. I stand in a corner and watch. My mother notices me and for a moment is flustered. "Come over here and tell me if he's salty," she says. But my father, who stands behind her, looks at me and shakes his head complicitly; don't do it. He wants me to think that he has something to hide, even if it's completely clear that he's telling the truth, he really did only paint at the station. Nothing doing, that's just how he is. More than the truth, he enjoys telling lies; he wants to make us believe with allusive glances that he spent the day at the beach, and in the company of someone special. Above all, he wants me to believe that. But in the meantime, while Rusinè licks him again, his chest, his neck, and even his face, I close my eyes, and I don't remember how it ends.